The Apparition Trail

by

Lisa Smedman

First Edition

Tesseract Books

National Library of Canada Cataloguing in Publication

Smedman, Lisa
    The apparition trail / by Lisa Smedman. -- 1st ed.

ISBN 1-894063-22-8

    I. Title.

PS8587.M485A76 2004   C813'.54   C2004-902210-5

Cover Design: James Beveridge

Tesseract Books and Hades Publications, Inc. acknowledge the
ongoing support of the Canada Council for the Arts and the Alberta
Fondation for the Arts for our publishing programme.

The Apparition Trail is a work of fiction

Tesseract Books
An imprint of Hades Publications Inc.
P.O. Box 1714, Calgary, Alberta, T2P 2L7, Canada
Printed in Canada

Chapter I

*A premonition—The Commissioner's curious summons—My first
ride on an air bicycle—A terrible storm—Superintendent Steele's
unusual request—An unsettling dream—Chief Piapot's
defiance—The sergeant's bluster—Our strange ride back—
Death on the sand—My first assignment*

I awoke with a start, my heart pounding, certain that I'd heard
someone shout my name. Yet all was silent in the darkened
barracks. Outside in the night, I heard an owl hoot softly,
followed by measured footsteps on the boardwalk that
surrounded the parade square: the constable on night picquet
making his rounds. His footsteps passed the barracks door,
then faded into the night as he walked in the direction of the
stables.

Despite this reassurance that all was well, I had an overwhelming sense that ill fortune was about to befall me. The
dream I'd just awakened from had been troubling. In it, I'd
spotted a carrier pigeon winging its way to me with a message
clutched in its feet. A moment later the pigeon was joined by a
second, larger bird, and then these two became an entire flock—
so many birds that they darkened the sky like a thundercloud.
As the flock drew nearer, so too did a sense of dread. The birds
were coming for me, calling for me, clawing at me....

I threw off my blanket, which had suddenly become op-
pressively hot and heavy, and swung my bare feet to the floor.
The straw-filled palliasse sagged under me as I fumbled about
on the table beside my bed. At last I found the box of Lucifers I
had been searching for. Striking one, I lit a candle. Its pale
yellow light revealed the sleeping forms of the other policemen in
the barracks. Their slow, steady breathing should have further
reassured me, but I could not shake my sense of dread. I knew
in my heart that some doom lay just beyond the horizon, and
would rise with the sun that day.

I consulted my pocket watch. Assuming that it told the time
correctly, it was three a.m.— three hours before the morning

reveille. Knowing I would never get back to sleep, I scooped up my pipe and my pouch of Imperial Mixture and crept quietly outside the barracks.

I screwed the pipe together, tamped tobacco into the bowl, and lit it with a match. Taking several quick puffs, I coaxed it into a cheerful glow, then savoured a long, slow draw. As I exhaled, I looked up at the full moon, which was just setting in the western sky. I marvelled at how different it looked, these days. Nearly seven years had passed since the comet had struck it, and the moon's "dark side" was now almost fully turned toward the Earth. Gone was the familiar face of the man in the moon, with its wide, smooth patches of white. It had been replaced by a much more rugged surface—a face as pockmarked as that of an Indian with smallpox.

Although the smoke steadied me somewhat, I was still restless, still gripped by a sense of approaching calamity. I needed something to busy my hands. I knocked out the last of my tobacco and returned to the barracks, then collected up my dress uniform and kit bag. Although the sky to the east was already lightening, I needed more illumination to see by than this false dawn afforded. I walked over to the orderly room, which was brightly illuminated by that wonder of our age: electric lighting.

The detachment to which I had been assigned—Moose Jaw— was one of the first to have been fitted with electrical lights. The blown glass bulbs with their glowing filaments had first been displayed just three years ago, at the Paris Exhibition of 1881, by American inventor Thomas Edison. His invention had been eclipsed, however, by an even more miraculous device that was exhibited for the first time that same year: the perpetual motion machine.

One of these devices sat in the corner of the orderly room, behind a protective metal screen. It stood as tall as a man, and looked like a four-armed windmill, mounted on a wrought-iron tripod. Rods and hinges clattered and squeaked as the hollow brass arms spun round, driven by piston weights inside the arms that alternately fell and were drawn back with each revolution. A coil that crackled with electrical energy was mounted at the back of the device; thick black wires conducted the current from this generator to the pendulous glass light bulbs. They had also been strung up in the inspector's office, the officers' mess, and the guardrooms.

The orderly room was currently unoccupied; the constable on picquet duty would stop in only at the end of the night, when it came time to write out his report. I laid my kit bag and uniform on the table that stood under the single electric bulb and pulled up a wooden chair. As I did so, I thought I heard the perpetual motion machine make an odd whining noise, but it may just have been the scuff of the chair across the wooden floor. I fancied that the machine had sped up a little, and the bulb overhead seemed a bit brighter, but I told myself it was only my imagination. Forcing my eyes away from it, I pulled out my brushes and polish, then set to work.

I burnished the brass buttons on the front of my red serge jacket, polished my boots until they gleamed, and whitened my helmet and gauntlets with claypipe until they were as bright as new snow. I even took a brush to my spurs, cleaning every speck of dirt from them. When this was done, I oiled and cleaned my Enfield, then spun the revolver's cylinder and pulled the trigger several times, watching the hammer rise and fall and ensuring myself that the gun was functioning properly.

Only when everything was in perfect order did I begin to relax. Even so, the sense that something momentous and terrible was going to happen that day did not entirely ease. My nerves must have been wound up more tightly than I'd thought, for when the constable on picquet duty barged into the room, I jumped from my seat. The chair fell over backwards, striking the screen that protected the perpetual motion machine.

The constable, a sandy-haired, weedy lad by the name of Fraser, scooped the chair from the floor and set it upright. He was new enough to the force that he snapped a salute at me, despite the fact that I was out of uniform and in my bare feet. I nodded, and started gathering up my kit to let him use the table, but he stopped me with a hand on my arm. Outside, I heard a trumpet sound reveille.

"I was just going to come and wake you, Corporal Grayburn," Fraser said. His voice dropped to a conspiratorial whisper. "There's a telegram, addressed to the Inspector. It concerns you."

"Oh?" My mouth was suddenly dry. I worked up some spit and tried to swallow, but without much success.

The constable reached into one of the pockets of his jacket and pulled out a folded piece of paper. "This telegram was received at the CPR station just a few minutes ago," he said, holding it up where I could see it. His narrow fingers were curved in a manner that reminded me for some reason of a pigeon's foot. I suddenly felt loath to take the piece of paper they held.

"It's from headquarters," he added. "And it's marked urgent."

Snatching the telegram from his hand, I unfolded it and read. The message it bore—addressed to my commanding officer— was a summons from North-West Mounted Police headquarters in Regina, from no less a personage than Commissioner Acheson Irvine himself. I was to report to headquarters with all due haste. So urgently was my presence required that headquarters was sending one of the new air bicycles to whisk me across the forty miles that separated Moose Jaw and Regina. The air bicycle was expected to arrive at my detachment around noon.

"What does it mean?" I wondered aloud, although I already knew what the answer must be. I could think of only one reason for the urgent summons: the force must have discovered my secret. If so, I faced a minimum of six months' hard labour followed by a dishonourable discharge. All protestations of my exemplary service over the past five years would be in vain.

Normally, the discovery that a false statement had been made upon recruitment would have been dealt with at the divisional level; my commanding officer would have been the one to handle the charges. But in my case, I'd pushed the deception further than a mere lie or two. And now that I was discovered, it seemed that my case could be dealt with only by the Commissioner himself.

Constable Fraser shrugged and plucked the telegram out of my hand, carefully folding it up again. "I don't know what it means. It doesn't specifically say that you're up on charges, but...."

His gaze fell on my brightly polished boots and pipeclayed helmet, and his eyes widened. This time, his whisper was even softer. "By God—you *knew* you'd be summoned to headquarters today, didn't you?"

"I had no idea—not even an inkling," I said hurriedly, lying about my premonition. I didn't want the men talking any more than they already were. "I was unable to sleep and needed something to occupy my mind. Nothing more."

As I scooped up my uniform and kit bag, I heard the perpetual motion machine begin to whine, as if it were under some sort of strain. The constable stepped back, giving me plenty of room to pass, and I moved toward the door. Suddenly, the light bulb overhead flared white. As both of us looked up in alarm, the delicate globe broke and a rain of glass shards fell down onto the floor at my feet. The perpetual motion machine continued to clatter, but the room was suddenly much darker, lit only by the reddish rays of the rising sun.

I opened my mouth to say something, then thought better of it. I decided instead to slip out before the perpetual motion machine went completely awry. Fretting about how I'd explain myself to the Commissioner in Regina, I hurried back to the barracks.

◁—▷

I turned out with the other men to groom and feed the horses, then sat down to my breakfast of coffee, cold beef and bread. I didn't think that Fraser had told anyone else about the telegram and its summons, but the eyes of the other men were on me nevertheless. Our quartermaster had already stomped through the mess hall, lathered into a fury by the sudden and catastrophic failure of all four of the electric bulbs, and one of the constables who had seen me departing the orderly room that morning quickly put two and two together and realized that I was the cause. An uncomfortable silence fell over the mess hall, and suddenly I wasn't hungry any more. The beef sat in my stomach like a cold ball of lead, and when the sergeant returned to deliver the telegram that Fraser had shown me earlier that morning, the stomach ache that had been plaguing me for the past few days returned full force.

Now that I knew—officially—about the summons to Regina, I pushed my breakfast aside. I immediately repaired to the barracks, using as my excuse the need to give my dress uniform a going over. When I was satisfied that it was absolutely spotless, I put it on and conducted a final inspection in the mirror. Everything appeared in order: scarlet Norfolk jacket, heavy blue riding breeches with a gold stripe down each pant leg, service belt with Enfield revolver holstered and snapped in place, high brown boots with steel spurs, white leather gauntlets and helmet.

I was excused from fatigue duty that day, and so I spent the rest of the morning pacing the boardwalk in front of the barracks, waiting for the air bicycle to arrive. The summer sky was a clear blue, marred only by a few dark clouds on the eastern horizon. By noon the air was hot and dry. There wasn't a breath of wind, and spit dried before it hit the sun-baked ground.

At last I spotted the air bicycle in the eastern sky. I watched it warily as it descended. It looked like an ordinary bicycle, but with two seats and two pairs of handlebars, suspended from a large, inflated sausage of a balloon. The operator sat on the foremost seat, intent upon flying the craft. His feet rested on pegs, instead of bicycle pedals, since the motive power for the air bicycle came not from a man's muscles but from a perpetual motion device.

I have always been fascinated by mechanical workings, despite the strange effect I seem to have upon them. I prayed that the perpetual motion device that powered the air bicycle would be an exception to the rule—that my premonition of danger this morning wasn't because it was destined to malfunction in mid-flight.

The device looked sturdy enough: a large, hollow disc of metal, affixed to the frame of the air bicycle by a complicated system of gears and chains in the spot where an ordinary bicycle's larger wheel would be. I had seen diagrams of similar devices, so I knew that the wheel was filled with steel balls that tilted and fell, propelling it in a circle. The wheel was perfectly counterbalanced so that its rotation went on indefinitely, once it had been set in motion. The balls inside it made a clattering noise, like beads rattling against the sides of a tin cup.

Jutting out from the bicycle on either side were sails that flapped like wings, and at the front and rear were lightweight propellers, made of sheets of duck cloth that had been stretched over metal frames. The air bicycle's operator—a member of the Mounted Police who was wearing balloonist's goggles under his pillbox cap—adjusted the flapping of the sails by means of hand cranks, causing the air bicycle to descend. He meanwhile alternated the motive force between the fore and aft propeller by means of a large lever, nudging the air bicycle forward and back to bring the craft to a landing.

I watched the air bicycle's descent, which was somehow graceful and ungainly at the same time. My father would have been fascinated by such a mechanism. I wondered—had he lived to see perpetual motion become a reality—whether he would have denied its existence, just as he had denied everything else that he deemed "impossible" or "mere coincidence."

Shouting at a constable, who was puffing on a pipe, to stay clear, the operator set the air bicycle down with a thump on its four small landing wheels in the middle of the parade square. The propellers stopped turning as he threw the lever into neutral but the wings continued to flap, raising a cloud of dust. He obviously was under strict orders not to tarry in Moose Jaw, but to bring me to Regina posthaste.

A handful of men ventured forth from the shade of the barracks to view the machine at close range. They stood around like boys admiring a grand new toy, casting the occasional envious glance in my direction. I, however, was more concerned with the dust that was settling upon my uniform. After taking such care to make myself as presentable as possible, I was covered head to toe in the stuff.

The operator lifted his smoked-glass goggles from his eyes and shouted over the creaking of the air bicycle's wings at the group of constables. He smacked dusty lips. "Is there any cold water to be had?"

"I'll fetch you a cup," one of the constables said, and hurried inside.

I hoped that they remembered to serve him the boiled water. The springs around Moose Jaw had turned miasmic, of late, and several of the men were down with typho-malaria. The last thing I needed was an operator who was suffering from fever and dysentery. He looked fairly robust, though, with broad shoulders and wide, wind-burned cheeks. Despite the distance he'd just traveled his eyes were bright under his thick dark hair.

"Are you Corporal Marmaduke Grayburn?" he asked as I approached.

"I am."

He jerked a gloved thumb at the seat behind him. "Then climb aboard the *Raven*."

I glanced up and saw the name of the air bicycle painted in neat yellow letters on the side of the balloon. I shuddered at the thought of being borne aloft by a bird of such ill omen, but settled onto the seat, hearing it creak beneath my weight, and gripped the handlebars in preparation for our ascent.

While there were some in the North-West Mounted Police who said the air bicycle would eventually replace the horse, I wasn't so sure. It was an extremely ungainly craft, difficult to master, and subject to the whims of the wind. The air bicycle was also expensive; thus far, they had been used only by officers deployed on important police business—and by a corporal responding to an urgent summons from his Commissioner.

My premonition of impending calamity grew as I settled into the seat; I had to steel myself as I waited for the operator to drink his water and ready his craft for the skies. The feeling wasn't quite as urgent or as clear, however, as the premonition I'd had back in November of 1879, just a few months after joining the police.

On that fateful day, I'd been working at the horse camp upriver from Fort Walsh, and had forgotten an axe a mile or so up the trail. When I considered returning for it, I felt an absolute dread that froze me to the spot. It came to me with fantastic clarity that, were I to ride up that trail, I would die.

My friend George Johnston laughed at my foolishness, and rode back himself to fetch the axe, ignoring my pleas for him to remain in camp.

He never came back.

The next day, a search party found George's body lying in the brush and snow at the bottom of a coulee. He'd been shot in the back. The search party started to follow some horse tracks that crossed George's trail—unshod hooves, which meant Indian ponies—but a chinook came up suddenly and melted the snow, obliterating the trail. Even the remarkable Jerry Potts, a half-breed scout who could track a fly across a pane of glass, couldn't find any trace of the hoof prints after that.

We later learned that a Blood Indian by the name of Star Child had boasted of committing the crime, but when he was brought to trial two years later, the jury acquitted him. Their final verdict: George Johnston was murdered by person or persons unknown, thought to be Indian.

But for my premonition, it would have been myself—and not poor George—who had the dubious distinction of being the first North-West Mounted Police constable to be murdered in the course of his duties.

My feeling of dread as I sat on the air bicycle was less precise, but equally gloomy. I had the distinct sense that disaster awaited me in Regina, but no clear warning of the form it might take. No matter what lay ahead, however, I could not refuse the Commissioner's summons.

The operator slid his goggles back down over his eyes, and glanced over his shoulder at me. "Hang on tight!" he said with a grin. "And make sure the chin strap of your helmet is loose."

As I obeyed this strange instruction, he engaged the crank that reversed the angle of the wings, sending us lurching into the air. My stomach descended into my bowels even as a sudden pressure filled my ears. I worked my jaw to clear it, opening my mouth wide in a forced yawn to pop them.

Within a few minutes we'd reached a dizzying height of more than two hundred feet above the ground. The barracks roofs were laid out below us, and the knot of men who had gathered on the parade square were blots of red, waving the smaller spots of brown that were their Stetsons. I am not normally afraid of high places, but as the operator threw the lever that engaged the rear propeller, sending the air bicycle forward, I gulped and gripped the handlebars more tightly. Moose Jaw slid away below.

The feeling that something awful was about to happen intensified as we winged our way east toward Regina, following the thin black ribbon of the CPR tracks and the telegraph line. For the first while I ignored it, concentrating on the magnificent view of the prairie, but after an hour or so, the feeling was joined by an all-too-familiar ache in my stomach. I wished I'd brought my bottle of Lydia Pinkham's Painkiller along, then decided the patent medicine would be impractical to me up here in the air, where I needed both hands to hold tightly to the handlebars.

As the air bicycle flew east, the pain in my stomach grew. My eyes teared as terrible cramps gripped my intestines, and my legs became so weak that one of my feet slipped off the footrest.

The air bicycle shifted slightly and the operator glanced back at me in alarm, but I gave him a nod that I hoped was reassuring. Then I went back to my suffering.

I supposed that I was suffering from a bout of typho-malaria. If it was dysentery from the miasmic water, I was in trouble. We were nearly three hundred feet in the air now, and still rising. My ears popped a second time. I shut my eyes and clung on grimly.

"We're caught in an updraft," the operator said a short time later. "And it looks as though there's bad weather ahead. The ride could get a little bumpy."

I opened my eyes and saw that the sky was dark with thunderheads. So absorbed had I been in my own misery that I'd failed to notice the change in the weather. I'd assumed that the air felt hotter and stickier due to my debilitated condition, but now I saw a sky that churned as violently as my stomach.

In the distance ahead of us, I could see the familiar red roofs of the Regina headquarters, its buildings laid out in an open rectangle around a parade square and flag pole. A mile or so down the railway track, a cluster of frame houses surrounded the station, together with the slate-coloured rooftop of the Pacific Hotel and the tiny cottage where the corporal and constable who met the trains were quartered. Nearby were the heaps and heaps of sun-bleached buffalo bones that had given the town its original Indian name: *Wascana*—Pile of Bones. They were awaiting shipment to the east, where they would be ground as fertilizer. Farther out was a scattering of canvas tents, erected by the town's newest inhabitants.

The town lay no more than a few minutes away from us now, but the air bicycle was shaking violently. The right wing dipped, and then the left, as the operator fought to bring it back to trim. Gusts of wind caught at the propellers, forcing them alternately into a blurred spin or slowing them to a chuffing crawl. One instant we plummeted down toward the prairie so fast the balloon above us creaked under the strain, bending like a sausage in a pan; the next we soared up to the heavens on an updraft.

"Can we make it?" I asked, fixing my eye upon Regina, which seemed hopelessly distant from us now.

"I hope so!" the operator gritted. "I've never seen a storm as bad as this one. It blew up so fast that I couldn't–"

A fork of lightning leaped from cloud to ground just ahead of the balloon. So close was it that the thunderclap was almost instantaneous. It roared over us like a train engine, vibrating the frame of the air bicycle and setting my very teeth to chattering. For a moment, I thought the balloon above me had ruptured explosively, but when I looked up it was intact.

That was when I realized what the balloon was filled with: hydrogen.

"Can you set us down?" I urged.

The operator shook his head. "It would be worse if I did," he shouted back over the wind. "The prairie here is as flat as a billiard table. The balloon would be the highest point on it; the lightning would certainly strike it. We'll just have to stay aloft and pray that a bolt doesn't hit us."

I nodded mutely and swallowed my fear. It settled in next to the ache in my stomach.

Another bolt of lightning split the air next to us and, with a booming rumble, the heavens opened up. Fat drops of rain splattered on the top of the balloon overhead. We remained dry for a moment or two, and then rain rolled down the sides of the balloon, dripping onto our heads.

Regina was getting closer, but so were the lightning flashes. The next one momentarily blinded me, and the thunderclap nearly knocked me from my seat.

When I could see again, I noticed a curious thing. The clouds were darkest and thickest directly over Regina. And there were two lighter circles—holes in the cloud—that looked distinctly like eyes. The hair at the back of my neck prickled as I fancied that they were looking straight at me.

Then they blinked.

My mouth fell open in wonder as the cloud took on an ever more distinctive pattern. I could see it clearly now: the roundish head in which the eyes were placed, the curved beak, the widespread wings. In that moment, I recognized the creature as the one that had figured so prominently in the stories told by Mary Smoke, the elderly Cree woman who'd done our cleaning at Fort Walsh—stories she'd told me as I sat with her in the evenings over a pipe of Old Chum tobacco.

Thunderbird.

It was all nonsense, of course: Indian superstition and balderdash. That was a storm cloud over Regina, not some fantastical monster. But as I saw lightning crackle from those eyes and felt the baleful glare of Thunderbird upon me, I at last understood the premonitory dream that had awakened me early that morning. A fate far worse than dishonourable discharge awaited me in the skies over Regina. When that black, evil bird caught me, I would die.

I found that I had to turn my head to watch Thunderbird, and that prompted a realization: the operator was turning the air bicycle about. At the same time, he shouted an explanation: "We've no choice. We can't put down in Regina in this weather. We'll have to run before the storm."

I nodded, but my attention was still fixed on the shifting clouds that now were behind us. Mighty wings flapped as Thunderbird ceased hovering over Regina and set out in pursuit. Whatever the thing was—storm or monster—it was fast. I could see that it would catch us—and when it did, it would buffet our air bicycle until it was torn apart.

There was nothing I could do except prepare to meet my maker. Or was there? Frantically, I thought back to the stories I'd been told by Mary Smoke. There was one about Thunderbird that came to mind now. The great storm maker might be the most powerful of creatures, but he had been laid low by one that was smaller and more cunning—by a small black bird that had tricked Thunderbird into losing his eyesight. As a result, there was one animal Thunderbird feared: the raven.

I glanced up at the lettering on the side of the balloon. It was a crazy, desperate idea, based on superstition rather than science, but it was the only one I had.

"We'll be torn to pieces if we try to outrun the storm," I shouted at the operator over the drumming of the rain on the balloon overhead. "But if you turn us about, there's a way we might get through. Turn the air bicycle quickly, so that it points directly at the largest thunderhead. It's our only chance!"

"You're mad!" the operator shouted back. "If we do that, we could wind up caught in an updraft that will force us into the upper reaches of the atmosphere. If we climb to a point where the air pressure is too low, the bag will burst!"

A fresh wave of pain gripped my stomach as another lightning bolt streaked out from Thunderbird's eye toward the ground. Knowing that it was do or die, I released one of my hands from the handlebars and fumbled open the flap of my holster. The rain made everything slippery, and I nearly dropped my revolver as I pulled it out. I tapped the butt against the operator's shoulder to get his attention, then raised the gun until the barrel was touching the balloon overhead.

Thunderbird was almost upon us.

"Turn us now! Point the air bicycle at the thunderhead or I'll explode the balloon with a shot from my revolver!" I screamed.

I had no such intention. But the wild look in my eye must have convinced the operator. Furious, his lips set in a thin white line, he turned the air bicycle about.

The boiling clouds that were Thunderbird bore down on us. Closer... closer... beak open wide and a look of doom in its eye. Just as the beak was about to snap shut on us, the front of the *Raven* pointed directly at the monster.

Instead of rising, the air balloon slipped violently to one side as Thunderbird dodged out of the way. Like a kite with its string cut we hurtled sideways, rushing toward the ground at an angle. I held on with the one hand that remained on the handlebars, lowering my revolver at the same time. In front of me, the operator fought with the controls.

When the ground below stopped rushing up at us and we came level again, Thunderbird was gone. There was no more lightning, and no thunder—just ordinary clouds in the sky. The rain slackened off to a mere drizzle, and after a minute or two it was gone. The sun broke through the clouds, shining down on Regina. I looked down and saw the Mounted Police headquarters bathed in yellow light, and nearly wept with relief as I re-holstered my revolver.

We landed in the parade square, wheels sinking into foot-deep mud. I alighted from the passenger seat, still trembling, and caught the operator's eye. He'd pushed up his goggles, and his face was ashen.

"About drawing my revolver," I said. "I'm sorry about that, but I–"

He wasn't listening. "Did you see it?" he asked in a hoarse whisper. "That... creature?"

I nodded grimly, then glanced up at a perfectly normal looking sky.

"No one will believe it," the operator added.

"I know," I said. I touched him on the shoulder. "We'd best keep this to ourselves, eh?"

He nodded. "How did you know what to do?"

I shrugged. "Just a hunch." Then I strode away through the boot-sucking mud.

◄ — ►

By the time I reached the Commissioner's office, the heat had returned full force and my sodden uniform was steaming. The collar of the jacket, normally stiff against my neck, was damp and drooping and my high brown boots were caked with the thick gooey mud that prairie dwellers call gumbo. I'd gotten the worst of it off by using the scraper outside the door, but my boots had left red smears all the way down the hallway carpet.

A constable showed me into the empty office, and once inside I stood nervously waiting, wishing my uniform was more presentable. The knot in my stomach was tightening and twisting—I was almost tempted to pull up my shirt and see if the scar from my operation had opened up again, after all these years. The typho-malaria made me feel as dizzy and light headed as I had when the doctor had administered the ether. Yet I didn't dare sit down in any of the hard-backed oak chairs scattered about the room. I intended to make a good show of it, to be standing properly at attention when the Commissioner entered the room.

Using the glass front of the wall clock as a mirror, I adjusted my helmet so it sat square on my head. My reddish hair has an unruly curl to it, especially when it is wet. But at least my face was clean below my pale blue eyes. I'd never grown a beard or moustache, despite the fact that regulations permitted it—not after the hilarity that greeted my one feeble attempt to grow whiskers, four years ago. You would think that, at twenty-seven years of age, I would be able to produce a fine crop of whiskers like the ones my father had, but such was not the case.

The harrowing storm we had just passed through had left me shaken, and I yearned for a calming smoke of my pipe. Yet now that I was within the walls of headquarters, Thunderbird seemed nothing more than a bad dream. Perhaps the pain of my stomach—only now abating to a tolerable level—had caused me to hallucinate. In any case, I had other things to worry about now: the reason for the Commissioner's summons.

The wall clock ticked off the seconds to my impending doom— a little faster, now that I was standing near it. The merciless eyes of Queen Victoria bored down at me from a painting that hung on the wall beside the Union Jack, as if chastising me for mucking up the clock's mechanism. Then the door opened.

I snapped to attention, then blinked in surprise when Superintendent Sam Steele entered the room. I'd gotten to know Steele back in the spring of 1879 when I first joined the force; he was the Inspector that accompanied myself and the other new recruits on the long journey from Ottawa to Winnipeg, via Dakota Territory. Steele was fair-haired and every bit as slim as I; he had impressed me with his knowledge of the West, his riding skills and his tireless endurance. He was one of the "old originals" who had signed up when the force was first created in 1873, and had risen rapidly through the ranks since then.

Just thirty-four years old, Steele had neatly parted hair and a trim moustache that curved up at either side of his mouth. He strode into the room, one hand clutching the Stetson that was the unofficial headgear of the mounted police. He stared at me with a look of such penetrating intensity that my hands began to tremble. In that instant, I was certain that he, too, had learned my secret. I clenched my fists until the leather of my white dress gauntlets creaked, and I willed my hands to stay still.

Commissioner Irvine followed Steele into the room. He stared at me with a curious, measuring look. He wore his reddish beard neatly trimmed, and had a thick moustache that completely covered both upper and lower lip. His face was narrow and rectangular, and his nose long. There was a worried look in his keen grey eyes.

The Commissioner seated himself behind the table as Steele closed the door. I waited for someone to speak, every nerve at attention. At last, the Superintendent cleared his throat.

"At your ease, Corporal," Steele said.

I moved my left foot a fraction apart from the right, and slid my hands behind my back. Trying to disguise the tension in my shoulders, I grasped one hand tightly in the other.

The Commissioner laid a dun-coloured folder on the desk and sat forward in his chair. "Do you know why you've been called to headquarters, Corporal Grayburn?" he asked.

"No sir," I said. Then, realizing that my voice had been somewhat hoarse, I cleared my throat and added in a louder tone: "I do not."

It was a lie, of course. Another falsehood, laid upon the rest.

The truth was that Marmaduke Grayburn, the name I had answered to for the past five years, was not my own. The real Marmaduke Grayburn was still in Ontario, living under another name. He was an old friend of mine—one who had known me long enough to trust my strange "hunches" and premonitions. When I'd told him that death would swiftly find him in the North-West Territories, were he to travel west with the other new police recruits, he'd readily believed me, and asked with a pale countenance what he should do. That was when I suggested that I go in his place.

Swapping places with Marmaduke had been more than an act of mere altruism. It seemed my one and only chance to escape the dreariness of working in the tobacco shop, and of marrying a woman I didn't love. It was also a chance to prove my moral fibre, by meeting head-on the rigours of life on the frontier.

Marmaduke at first declined my offer, but was at last persuaded by my gift of the one hundred and sixty-three dollars I'd withdrawn from my savings account. He handed his uniform to me—fortunately it fit well and required no tailoring—and I mustered with the other recruits for the trip west, to pursue a life of adventure under an assumed identity. I was the only man among them who had bypassed the North-West Mounted Police medical exam.

The Commissioner pulled several sheets of paper from the folder and smoothed them with his hand. Peeping out from under them was a photograph. I had a wild thought that these papers might include the letter of character and other documents that the real Marmaduke Grayburn had provided upon his enlistment. But then I saw my own handwriting upon the uppermost page.

"Your summons to Regina was due to this report, made by yourself on–." The Commissioner paused to glance at the date in the upper left-hand corner. "On June 1, 1883."

I felt a slight frown crease my brow. I wondered how the events of more than a year ago might be relevant to the matter at hand. I'd been stationed at the detachment of Maple Creek in 1883, at what was then the end of the CPR line. The railway navvies were working hard that summer, laying better than four miles of track a day as they pushed toward the Rockies....

"The Piapot incident," Steele prompted. His callused, suntanned hands gripped the brim of his Stetson. "And your premonitory dream."

The Commissioner shot Steele a look, and the Superintendent fell silent under the sudden glare in his grey eyes. When they turned back to me, the Commissioner's eyes held that same measuring look I'd seen earlier.

"Sir?" I asked.

I knew exactly what Steele was referring to, but I still couldn't see the connection between my strange experience of a year ago and my impending discharge. I avoided Steele's eyes and concentrated instead on the mechanical brass clock shaped like a shaggy buffalo on the Commissioner's desk. As it softly chimed the hour, the tiny perpetual-motion device inside it caused it to rear up and kick its hind legs. One of the hinges inside it was squeaking a little, and there was on tarnish the buffalo's horns and hooves; like me, it needed a good polish. These deficiencies would have driven my father to distraction, for he always insisted that machinery be well oiled and gleaming.

"Superintendent Steele wants to form a special division within the force," the Commissioner said, in a tone of voice that was carefully non-committal. "It would be a hand-picked troop made up of constables drawn from our existing divisions, and special constables recruited from the civilian population. Each man must fulfill the peculiar qualifications that Steele has set out—qualifications that he believes you possess."

This left me completely at a loss. "Sir, I... I don't...."

The Commissioner held up a hand and I fell silent. His eyes bored into me as if I were a man charged with a crime and he the judge who would decide my fate. Then he glanced down at the paper on the table in front of him. "Your report of the incident suggests that you weren't surprised by the death of Sergeant Wilde. In it, you state that you had a premonition of his death."

"It was just a dream, sir," I sputtered.

It was a lie, of course. The dreams that contain premonitions of the future are always especially vivid for me, and every detail

remains etched in my memory for years thereafter. Yet was I to
recite these details now? If I did, they would think me some
kind of fanciful lunatic.

"It was wrong of me to make mention of my dream in the
report," I said. "It wasn't very professional. I–"

"You never did fully explain the circumstances of the
Sergeant's death," the Commissioner continued.

The blood ran cold in my veins. For a brief moment, I thought
the Commissioner might harbour a suspicion that I was
somehow responsible. For all I knew, I might be. I had no ready
explanation as to why the Sergeant had died and I had lived.

Except for the dream....

"I want you to tell us every detail of what happened that day,"
Steele said in a steadying voice. "The things you didn't put in
your official report. And put your mind at ease, Corporal: you
aren't the first man I've heard a fantastic story from. There have
been many incidents, of late, that defy explanation. There's
something strange afoot on the prairie—something that's been
growing this past year. That's why I'm forming Q Division."

"Q Division?" I echoed.

"Q—for query," said the Commissioner. Then he glanced
sidelong at Steele. "The request has not been approved yet. Nor
will the new division be given official approval until I'm
convinced of its necessity."

I stared from one officer to the other, a growing sense of relief
dawning upon me. They hadn't found out my secret, after all.
I'd been called to Regina on an entirely different matter. Yet if I
told them my tale, I was likely to wind up in a lunatic asylum.
I chewed my lip, uncertain how to proceed.

"Go on, man," Steele prompted me. "Tell us the whole story,
from the very beginning."

◄—►

I'd been sleeping heavily on the night that I had the strange
dream. I'd been on picquet duty the previous three nights, and
had been at the point of exhaustion when my last round of duty
finally ended. With heartfelt relief, I'd crawled into my bed at
three o'clock in the morning, too tired to remove my
undergarments, which, after three days of near-continuous
wear, could have used a wash.

The dream had started ordinarily enough, but soon
developed the clarity and minutiae of detail that were the
hallmarks of a premonitory dream. In it, I'd been standing
outside a cave, from the interior of which came the insistent
barking of a dog. It growled at me in the voice of the Sergeant,
ordering me to crawl inside the cave.

I did so, and felt something round beneath my hand, as cold and slimy as a rain-slick cobblestone. I looked down only to discover, to my horror, that I was crawling across human bones, some of which still had wet, greyish chunks of flesh attached.

I realized then, in that peculiar clarity that comes upon one sometimes in dreams, that the dog was ordering me to my doom. I tried to back away but couldn't—the bones moved under my hands and knees like shifting sand, and I only managed to turn myself about in a circle.

My wild scrambles somehow brought me closer to the rear of the cave, to the spot where the dog stood. It was a massive hound, larger than any I'd ever seen. I'd been wrong about it being alive—it was dead. The eyes were glazed and its fur matted, and fleas leaped away from the cooling corpse.

Fear filled me then. I was trapped in a cave filled with dead things and I no longer knew in what direction the exit lay. I only knew one thing: if I didn't get out, I would die. Heart pounding, I scrambled about on all fours, trying and failing to find an escape.

Then my right hand slipped on one of the skulls, momentarily covering its empty eye sockets. In that instant, everything went dark, as if it were my own eyes that had been covered. At first I was as terrified as a babe in the night, but then I had a childish thought: if I can't see the skulls and the dog, they can't see me....

That was when Sergeant Wilde threw a splash of cold water on me. I awoke with a start to see him glaring down at me, my blanket tangled about me.

"On your feet, Corporal," he growled, waving a piece of paper above my blinking eyes. "The Indians are causing trouble again. We've got orders to roust those copper-skinned heathens."

I wiped away the water that was dribbling down my cheek and sat up, disengaging the blankets. My flannel undershirt was sopping wet, and I was annoyed at having been awakened so soon from my first opportunity to sleep. By the faint light coming in through the cracks in the barracks wall, I could see that dawn was breaking.

"Why me?" I grumbled, looking around at the occupants of the four other bunks, all of them blissfully snoring. "Why not one of the others?"

"Corporal Grayburn!" he barked. "I'll have none of your guff. Another remark like that and you'll be up on charges."

I quickly buttoned my lip. Discipline is strict in the North-West Mounted Police; a single angry remark to a superior bears a five-dollar fine. I didn't want to risk a whole week's pay, especially on Wilde, who wouldn't recognize a proper insult when he heard one.

Wilde was a fierce, hot-tempered man. He stood more than six feet tall, with broad shoulders and a thick black moustache. When he sat, he had a lazy air about him, like a dog taking the sun, but he could bark out orders like no other sergeant. More than one of our men had taken "French leave," deserting the force rather than face any more of Wilde's insults.

Wilde marched, rather than walked, everywhere he went; it was a wonder his thudding footsteps hadn't awakened everyone in the barracks. He looked down at me, hands on hips, a slight smirk twitching his moustache. I realized that he'd chosen me because I'd gotten so little sleep in the past few days. He'd enjoy seeing me yawn and droop in the saddle.

It was no secret that Wilde didn't like me. He was a bad card player and a sore loser, while I, in contrast, was a natural at poker. I win not because I have the stoic countenance of the Indian, or because I am particularly adept at the game, but because I'm lucky. The very cards I'm seeking for my hand come to me, as if by magic.

The other men were good-natured about losing their wages to me, although they refused to let me play with them again. Wilde, however, was convinced that I was a cheater, and took an intense dislike to me.

"We ride at six o'clock," he told me. "I expect you to be ready." Then he turned and strode out of the barracks.

A blanket-covered form on one of the nearby beds stirred, and a sleepy voice called out. "What is it, Marmaduke? Reveille?"

"It's nothing," I whispered. "Go back to sleep."

I fumbled for the pocket watch I keep beside my bed and consulted it. Assuming the time on it was correct—every watch I touch runs either too fast or too slow, which was one of the reasons why I hadn't become a watch maker like my father—I had less than twenty minutes to prepare. I rose from my bed, pulled on breeches, jacket, socks and boots, then stumbled over to the stove and stoked it with kindling. Then I hurried outside to the creek for a pail of water to boil for tea.

I looked up from the gurgling stream at the sun, which was just rising over the hills. It hung huge over the horizon, mottled with a peculiar reddish hue. The Indians call this rare phenomenon a "painted sun" and say it is an omen of ill fortune. I shivered as I thought of this, although at the time I attributed my tremors to the fact that my hands were immersed in cold water. Then I rose with the dripping bucket and hurried back to the bunkhouse, turning my back on the celestial warning.

Breakfast was the same as it always was at Maple Creek: a biscuit hard as rock, hot black tea to soak it in, and a few slivers of dried apple, as withered as the face of a crone. There was no time to fry up bacon; I had barely time to pack my saddlebags with spare stockings, shirt, horse brush, currycomb, and mess kit. I buckled on my spurs and strapped on my cartridge belt and revolver, all the while chewing on the granite-like bread and slurping mouthfuls of hot tea.

I ran a hand over my lips, wiping away the crumbs. Thankfully I didn't need a shave. I ran a comb through my hair, put on the pillbox hat that the sergeant always demanded we wear on duty, despite the fact that he himself wore a Stetson, and adjusted it to the regulation angle of two fingers' width above the right eye. Then I packed the comb away with a razor, shaving brush, sponge, and soap in my holdall and stuffed it into my saddlebags. The Sergeant had neglected to inform me where we were riding to or how long we'd be away, and I'd been too somnambulate to inquire. For all I knew, we'd be on the trail for days. I added a change of undergarments to the bag, then carefully packed my pipe in its velvet-lined leather case. The pipe was a fine bulldog briar with a twisted stem of English amber and a cool-smoking rubber mouthpiece. Here in the North-West Territories, it was difficult to find the fine tobacco that I had developed a taste for during my three years of working in the tobacconist's shop in Ottawa. The best I could do was a tin of Hudson's Bay Imperial Mixture, which I added to the rest of my kit.

I rushed out to the stables and saddled up Buck, the bronco I'd been assigned upon my posting to the Maple Creek detachment two months prior. He was a good steady horse, bred on the prairie and accustomed to its extremes. He wasn't much to look at: just a solid dun colour throughout, and not overly swift. But he was a solid trooper, nonetheless, and devoted to his duties as an NWMP mount. He'd been stolen shortly after my arrival by Indian braves, but he'd returned to the stables all on his own two days later, with an Indian's handprint in ochre paint on his rump as a souvenir of his adventures. I could only assume that he'd bucked the thief right off his back, then ventured home again.

That was when I'd changed his name to Buck, a colloquial term for an Indian warrior—and a damn fine pun, as far as I was concerned.

Buck didn't look any happier at our early departure than I did. He puffed out his stomach as I cinched the saddle tight, but a knee to the stomach put *paid* to that trick. I slid my Winchester into the saddle's carry case, fastened my saddlebags in place, and mounted up.

As I trotted out of the stable, Wilde cast a baleful eye on me and snapped the face of his pocket watch shut. He didn't say a word to me, but instead just turned his horse, a high-tempered black, toward the trail that led to the west. He whistled for his dogs—a pair of fierce hounds that followed him everywhere—but they refused to follow him. Instead they hunkered down with their bellies to the ground, growling their refusal.

Wilde addressed the dogs in a disgusted tone: "What, afraid of the wild Indians are you? Damn cowards." He wheeled his horse around and spurred it forward. I had to spur my own horse to catch up with him. Buck snorted his displeasure, but picked up his pace. Still a little shaken by my dream, I was glad we'd left the dogs behind. They reminded me of the dead hound in my dream.

"Where are we headed?" I asked.

"To the head of the railway line," Wilde said. "Chief Piapot and his band have placed their tepees in the way of the construction crews. We're to give him official notice to move on."

We hadn't far to go, then: no more than a morning's ride. We trotted through the thickly forested hills, following the railway tracks. The freshly laid steel reflected the rays of the morning sun, twin slashes of red across the ground.

As we rode, I mused upon what was to be done. The band of Cree that Piapot commanded had been assigned a reservation, but insisted, instead, on continuing to wander about the prairie. What an irony that, out of all this trackless wilderness, they had chosen a campsite directly in the way of the CPR line!

As if hearing my thoughts, the Sergeant interrupted the silence.

"They chose that camping spot deliberately, you know," he said. "We've been having no end of trouble with those savages. First it was tomahawks, wedged in the spaces where the rails met, and then it was a tree trunk across the line. It's only by the grace of God there hasn't been a derailment, and lives lost. It's time we put an end to Piapot's mischief."

I nodded because the Sergeant seemed to expect it, but kept my own counsel. It wasn't that I disagreed with Wilde: the acts of vandalism he'd listed were against the law and demanded a response. It was just that I wanted to see the right men punished for the crime. All sorts of Indians passed through the Cypress Hills: Cree, Assinaboine, Blood, Blackfoot, and Peigan. It could have been braves from any one of these bands that had committed the mischief. The North-West Mounted Police weren't like the American cavalry to the south, pouncing upon any red man who happened to be in the vicinity of a crime. We were a police force, and we relied upon investigation, rather than brute force, to help us find and punish the right culprit.

I glanced sidelong at the Sergeant as we rode, and revised that last thought. Some of us believed in conducting an investigation more thoroughly than others.

The sun was warm on our backs by the time we reached the end of the line. I knew we were getting close when I saw a train engine and four flatbed cars, piled high with steel rails, just ahead on the track. The engine was powered by one of the new magnetic perpetual motion devices: in the place where a coal car would normally be was a flatcar on which was mounted an upright beam of wood like a ship's mast. A gigantic magnet, suspended from the mast on a wire, swung slowly back and forth, causing a curved steel beam below it to rock, and thus to power pistons below it. When engaged by gears, the pistons drove the wheels. The steady metallic ticking noise the device produced was a far cry from the steam trains of my youth, with their billowing clouds of smoke and chuffing engines. It had the added advantage over a steam train of not emitting burning embers that set the dry prairie grass on fire.

I expected to hear the pounding of sledgehammers and the rasp of saws cutting wood as we drew closer, but the work site was still. Instead of the sounds of men going industriously about their labour we heard the beating of an Indian drum.

The railway navvies—a crew of blond, burly Swedes—stood in a huddled group, drawing on pipes and talking in nervous voices while their foreman cast dark glances at a circle of a dozen tepees that had been erected on the railway's right of way. The edge of one of the tepees—a rude shelter of buffalo hide painted with crimson figures that seemed half man and half beast—was only a few inches away from where the unfinished tracks stopped, blocking the line completely. The drumming came from inside it.

The Sergeant and I reined our horses to a halt and stared at the wild scene before us. Piapot's braves—several dozen of them—were all mounted on their ponies, rifles in hand. Many had daubed their faces with paint, and several were wearing their eagle-feather bonnets and painted war shirts. They rode back and forth across the prairie, every now and again swooping toward the halted train. Each time they did, the navvies stepped back a pace or two as the Indians got uncomfortably close.

Upon spotting our red coats, one of the warriors let out a whoop. Several fired their rifles in the air, and the smell of gunpowder drifted toward us. I winced slightly, but kept my composure. The Indians loathe a coward.

I didn't see any women or children in the Cree camp. I could only assume they were inside their tepees.

The foreman of the railway gang was a short, wiry Englishman who wore a red flannel shirt with sleeves rolled up and a cloth cap pushed back to expose his high forehead. He mopped his brow with a handkerchief and shouted at us over the din of whoops and rifle shots.

"We've been having a bit of trouble with the Indians these past two days," he said with typical English understatement as a bullet from one of the brave's rifles zinged off the steel side of the train engine. Inside it, the engineer and mechanic ducked.

The navvies fell back into the dubious shelter of the railway cars, and the foreman glanced back over his shoulder, his Adam's apple bobbing nervously. "I'm hoping you can settle the Indians down and get them to move on."

"We'll settle things, sure enough," Sergeant Wilde grumbled, looking over the head of the foreman at the paint-daubed warriors. Then he leaned over to open his saddlebag, and pulled a piece of paper from it—the same one he'd waved at me that morning. He straightened in his saddle, and held the paper out in front of him.

"Chief Piapot!" he shouted. "I have here a written order for you and your band to quit this location. You are to take the northward trail to your reserve at once."

The Indians had halted their whooping to listen to the Sergeant, but it was difficult to ascertain whether they understood him. As he lowered the paper, a group of them charged us, waving their rifles in the air. The foreman scuttled away, and I tightened my grip on Buck's reins. I glanced at the Sergeant, wondering if I should draw my Winchester. He gave a slight shake of the head.

The braves thundered toward us, drawing their horses to a halt only at the last possible moment. One of their ponies nudged against the Sergeant's horse, causing it to take a step back and toss its head. Others crowded in close to Buck, who stood his ground bravely. The Indians waved their rifles at us and jeered in their own tongue, no doubt shouting insults.

Sergeant Wilde was unmoved by the display. He pulled his watch from his pocket and consulted it.

"You have one-quarter of an hour to pack up your tepees and go," he ordered. "If by the end of that time you haven't complied, we shall force you to move on."

The Sergeant glanced meaningfully at me—and at my Winchester. By now the railway navvies were nowhere to be seen; they were beating a hasty retreat down the tracks, followed by the train engineer and mechanic, who had abandoned their engine. Part of me wished I could join them. I didn't relish the odds: two mounted police against an entire band of Cree.

The warriors continued to shout and prod at us, trying to goad us into making the first hostile move. I was thankful not to smell liquor on their breath; whiskey whips the Indians into a fury. For once I was glad that the North-West Territories had been declared dry.

There was one tepee that stood at the centre of the circle of tents. In front of it sat Chief Piapot, wearing a trailing war bonnet and smoking a long-stemmed pipe from which a single eagle feather hung. Every now and then he would raise the pipe: first to his left, then in front of him, then to his right, and then over his head. After he had repeated this performance four times, he took one last draw on the pipe and knocked it out. Rising to his feet, he began walking toward us. I hoped he was going to call off his braves and parlay with us.

Piapot had wide cheekbones, a long hawklike nose, and a square jaw. He wore his hair loose over his shoulders, and had a kerchief knotted about his neck. He stared at me with small eyes set close together, and in them I saw a thoughtful look, almost one of recognition, although I had not met the man before.

Sergeant Wilde snapped the cover of his pocket watch shut. "Time's up!" he shouted. Then he slipped his watch back in his pocket and handed me the reins of his horse.

"What are you doing?" I asked in dismay as he dismounted.

"I'm going to teach these heathens a lesson."

Shouldering his way through the mounted braves, Wilde walked in a determined line toward the central tepee. I saw a confused look cross the chief's face as the Sergeant strode past him. The chief paused—then shouted in alarm as he saw what Wilde was up to.

With a swift kick, the Sergeant knocked over the tepee's key pole. The buffalo-skin shelter creaked to one side—then crashed to the ground. Something struggled beneath the collapse of wooden poles and heavy hides, and then three women and two children burst out of the tangle. The eldest of the women shouted at Wilde and shook a fist at him while the other two clutched their children to their breasts and scurried away.

The Cree braves were as stunned by the Sergeant's performance as I was. They watched, mouths open, as he stomped from tepee to tepee, kicking each one over in turn.

"Get!" he shouted at the women and children who emerged from each one. Wilde waved his hands in the air like a farmer shooing geese. "Go on! Get out of here. Go on back to your reserve!"

The Indians closest to me were muttering darkly. The Sergeant's horse, whose reins I still held, sensed the tension in the air and pawed with one hoof at the ground, its eyes and nostrils wide. I eased my right hand in the direction of my Winchester, getting ready for the worst.

Sergeant Wilde shouted at the Indian braves who had leapt from their ponies to cluster in front of the last of the tepees in an effort to prevent him from kicking it over. The tepee was the one with the painted animals: the one that stood just at the end of the tracks. Wilde, the very image of a snarling dog, barked an order at me, but I could not hear him over the din. I expect he was ordering me to charge forward, or shoot—or something—anything that would scatter the braves and let him complete the job he'd begun. Inside the tepee, a drum continued to throb.

I looked askance at the angry warriors who stood in front of the tepee. More than one had his weapon pointed at Wilde's chest. I started to caution him: "Sergeant, I don't think that's such a good–"

The drumming suddenly stopped. A second later, the flap of the tepee flew open. Out strode a peculiar looking figure: a brave with his face painted a solid yellow, wearing a lynx-skin cap with five large eagle plumes descending from it. He looked about forty years of age and moved with the lean, lithe grace of the cat whose ears now decorated his bonnet. His eyes were small and hard, two shiny black flints in a face twisted with hatred, and his long dark hair had a curl to it that is not often found among the Indian race. In one hand he held an iron-bladed tomahawk, in the other, a slender stick with a single black feather attached to it. He strode toward the Sergeant, and the braves parted to give him way.

The Sergeant, to give him credit, stood his ground, arms folded over the breast of his scarlet jacket, his countenance set in a stern expression. Only the quiver of his moustache revealed the depths of the emotion he was feeling.

"I order you to move on," he told the brave in a dangerously low grumble. "You are encamped on Canadian Pacific Railway property. If you fail to move on we will arrest–"

In that instant, the yellow-faced warrior let out an unearthly howl. Leaping forward, he struck the Sergeant—but not with the tomahawk. Instead he hit Wilde in the chest with the narrow wand, which slapped only lightly against the breast of the Sergeant's Norfolk jacket without even enough force to disturb any of his brass buttons. Then the warrior turned, the feathers on his lynx-skin bonnet fluttering, and walked disdainfully away.

The Sergeant paused a moment, his eyebrows puckering in a confused frown. Then he snorted, and strode between the braves before they could again close ranks. With one swift kick of his foot, Wilde kicked the key pole of the last tepee to the ground.

The Indians gave him several dark looks, but now their chief was speaking. I couldn't understand Piapot's words, but his gestures were plain enough. His arms were raised, one palm forward in a calming gesture. He spoke in a steady voice, pointing the stem of his pipe at this tepee and that. The warriors grumbled for a moment or two, and one let out a whoop of protest, but when the yellow-painted brave lent his voice to the chief's, they fell silent. The women came scurrying back to their collapsed tepees and began pulling their property out of them and packing it away.

Sergeant Wilde strode back to where I still sat, mounted on Buck, and swung back into his saddle.

"There," he muttered to himself. "We showed them who's boss. These aren't heathen lands any more. They know now that if they try that trick again, they'll have the mounted police to contend with."

"Yes, Sergeant," I murmured. But I couldn't help but wonder if Wilde had indeed cowed them. As the women packed the camp's belongings onto travois, the braves gathered around the warrior in the lynx cap, listening to him speak. One or two turned to look at us, and when they did so, the expressions on their faces were anything but contrite. They seemed almost smug—as if they'd won this confrontation, rather than lost it.

"Go fetch the foreman and his crew, and tell them it's safe to commence laying track again," Wilde said.

"Yes, Sergeant," I said briskly. I wheeled Buck around, glad to be out from under the glittering gaze of the Cree braves.

I had assumed that the matter of Chief Piapot had been settled. But as we rode back to the Maple Creek detachment my sense of unease only worsened. Sergeant Wilde said we were taking a shortcut back to the detachment, which seemed to me to be a misguided decision. We turned north, leaving the railway line increasingly far behind—yet Maple Creek lay due east.

When I pointed this out to the Sergeant, he cast me an evil look. "I know where I'm going," he said curtly.

The Sergeant appeared confident on the surface, but I could hear a slight hesitation in his voice. Even his horse looked nervous. The big black kept swivelling its ears and snorting, eyes wide.

I tried to engage the Sergeant in friendly conversation, hoping to eventually suggest that we turn to the east. I couldn't very well refuse to follow his lead, or strike out on my own. Arguing with a superior warrants a ten-dollar fine—and disobeying orders is an even more serious offence.

"Those were a few tense moments back at Piapot's camp, weren't they?" I asked, trying to instil in my voice a jovial camaraderie. "I thought you were done for when that yellow-faced brave charged at you with the tomahawk. It was fortunate that he chose to strike you with his coup stick, instead."

The Sergeant snorted. "He lost his nerve, I expect. He knew he'd be stretching a rope if he killed a police officer. The very sight of a scarlet jacket cows them."

I was so surprised at the Sergeant's lack of understanding that I blurted out: "That brave wasn't the slightest bit afraid of you. He was counting coup."

Too late, I realized my mistake—and my poor choice of words. I had inadvertently implied that the Sergeant didn't cut a very formidable figure, when I'd meant to say that the Indian had been unafraid of anything, even a mounted police officer. I tried to explain that Indian braves only bothered to count coup against formidable foes, but Wilde gave me a withering look. "I'll thank you to keep your opinions to yourself, Corporal."

I bit back the rest of my explanation. I could see that further conversation would only do more harm than good. I turned my attention instead to the ground, trying to puzzle out the "shortcut" the Sergeant had insisted on taking. There was a faint trail along the ground: a drag mark like that left by a travois. We seemed to be following it.

We had ridden far from the railway line by now, into an area of rolling, barren hills. The ground was sandy here; sprays of loose soil kicked up every time the horses took a step. A chill breeze began to blow, with just enough force to send the hairs on my arms shivering erect. I thought I heard a voice whispering on the wind; I turned in the saddle, but could see no one.

The light became weaker, as if a cloud had come across the sun. I looked up at the sky and saw that it had turned a leaden grey. The sun was a pale, watery-yellow disc behind the clouds, and the landscape through which we rode seemed likewise drained of colour. The few bushes that dotted the sandy hills were a dull grey-green, and the ground itself appeared flat yellow.

The Sergeant's horse proceeded skittishly, tossing its head as if it wanted to bolt. Wilde kept it in check only by sharp tugs on the reins. Buck gave a short whinny of fear, then fell quiet, his tail tucked tight against his rear.

The wind began to produce ever more curious noises. The thudding of Buck's hooves sounded like the chopping of an axe blade against wood, and at one point I thought I heard the barking of a dog. I could swear that I heard a woman's voice, and the laughter of children, and the crackled chatter of old men. I couldn't make out any of the words but the speech had a slow cadence, as if the language spoken were an Indian dialect. If it weren't for the fact that we were completely alone in this desolate place, I would have sworn we'd ridden into an Indian encampment.

I was just about to ask the Sergeant whether his senses were registering the same impressions when I saw the pipe lying on the trail. I recognized it at once: a tobacco-stained French briar whose mouthpiece bore the teeth marks of long and frequent use. It had belonged to Mary Smoke, the aged Cree woman formerly employed at Fort Walsh to clean the barracks. She'd had a penchant for smoking, and one fateful day her primitive impulses got the better of her. She was caught stealing tobacco from the men.

Because I'd grown friendly toward her, over our many long chats, I'd tried to intervene on her behalf, explaining that she used the tobacco smoke to comfort her aching teeth, one of which was abscessed. The men, however, were too furious to listen. They would hear none of my pleas for mercy, and instead had charged Mary Smoke with theft and locked her in a cell.

When they'd opened it the next morning, she was stone cold dead.

I suspect it was a combination of her panic at being caught and her advanced age that killed Mary Smoke. The Indians have a morbid fear of the hangman's noose, and it is possible that Mary Smoke, incapable of realizing that her theft was a petty crime that would result in only a fine, had died of fright.

Her children came the next day and disposed of her body according to their own practices. Rather than burying their dead, the Cree lash them on platforms in trees, wrapping the body in a buffalo hide together with the earthly possessions that the departed soul had held most dear in life.

Had someone robbed Mary Smoke's bier, stealing her battered pipe and later losing it in this desolate place?

Buck had stopped dead in his tracks in the same instant that I'd spotted Mary Smoke's briar, but the Sergeant's horse continued to move skittishly forward. One of its hoofs landed square on the pipe. I heard a loud snap as the stem broke, then saw it lying in pieces as the hoof lifted from it.

As I stared at the broken pipe, transfixed, I thought I heard the aged crone's voice: "Heya, *samogoniss*," it said, using the Cree word for mounted police. "Gotta smoke?"

Something moved, just at the edge of my vision: a human figure, huddled in a blanket or robe. Startled, I twisted in my saddle, and thought I saw Mary Smoke. But as I looked at the figure full on, I saw that it was no more than a large boulder that had roughly the shape of a squatting figure.

I allowed myself a nervous laugh and turned to the Sergeant to ask whether he'd imagined a figure there, too. Just as I looked in his direction a violent shudder passed through his horse. Then a shriek of utter terror erupted from its lips. The black horse reared up, lashing out with both forefeet at the empty air in front of it.

Sergeant Wilde swore a violent oath and drew his revolver as a figure suddenly stepped in front of his panicked horse. No boulder this! It was an Indian brave in a feather bonnet, his entire body painted with ghostly white war paint.

Buck whinnied in fear, and was proving difficult to control, but the Sergeant's horse was far worse. Terrified at the Indian's sudden appearance, seemingly from out of thin air, it bucked wildly, causing the sergeant to nearly fall from his saddle. Clinging to the pommel with one hand, Wilde drew his revolver and fired a shot at the Indian brave. The bullet missed, and kicked up a tuft in the sandy soil behind the Indian.

The brave gave an unearthly wail and hurled a stone-bladed knife at the Sergeant's chest. I could not see whether it struck the Sergeant, for my own mount shied violently to the side, but I did see Wilde's horse kick violently, tossing him into the air. The Sergeant landed heavily on the ground, his revolver bouncing out of his hand. His horse, at last free of its rider, bucked once or twice more, then turned and bolted to the south, reins fluttering over its back.

When I got Buck turned around again, I looked wildly about for the Indian who had thrown the knife, but he had disappeared. There was no one present in those lonely hills save the Sergeant and myself. Wilde rose, spitting sand from his lips, and scooped his revolver off the ground.

"Damn that horse!" he spluttered, then swept his Stetson from his head and threw it angrily down on the sand. He shoved his still-smoking revolver back into the holster at his hip.

Now that the Sergeant's temper had cooled, I expected him to set off to the south in pursuit of his wayward mount, or to order me to ride after it, but instead he turned once again to the north. "Come on," he said in a voice that was devoid of the passion that had enflamed it a moment ago. "We've got to press on." Without another word, he began trudging across the sand on foot.

My mouth dropped open in surprise. "Without your horse?" I asked. I looked around at the desolate hills that surrounded us. The light had dimmed, as if dusk were approaching, and the breeze held a chill that cut right through the cloth of my Norfolk jacket, yet I was certain that it must still be the middle of the day. I shivered, and clenched Buck's reins more tightly. The bronco's eyes were wide, and shivers coursed down his shoulders.

"Sergeant, I don't think that's wise," I said cautiously.

Wilde ignored my protest. "We have to follow the trail," he said without looking back at me.

"But why?" I sputtered. "Where does it lead? We dispersed Chief Piapot's band, as ordered. Shouldn't we return to the detachment and make a report?"

I still sat on Buck, who had remained rooted to the spot after the Sergeant's horse bolted. Wilde halted, then slowly turned. His lips were twisted into a grimace that reminded me of the face of a frozen Indian corpse I'd found along the trail one winter, and his face had gone strangely grey. His eyes held a look of pure malevolence. His right hand settled upon the handle of his revolver.

"We follow the trail," he growled. "That's an order."

"Yes, Sergeant," I hastily replied, despite the fact that every fibre of my being screamed in protest. Even so, I spurred Buck forward. After a second tremendous shudder, he plodded reluctantly ahead, following the Sergeant.

Things became confused after that. The breeze that had been blowing died away, but a strange chill lingered in the air. I was certain now that I saw tepees and the moving figures of Indians, horses, and their dogs all around us—but whenever I looked at them square on, these apparitions would disappear. I chewed my lip, casting about desperately for something I could say to dissuade the Sergeant from this madness, but could think of nothing. Where were we headed? What strange and secret orders was the Sergeant following?

It seemed to me that, although we steadily headed north, we were traveling in a circle. The travois line we had been following soon was overlaid with our own hoof and foot prints.

I was just about to point out to the Sergeant this indisputable evidence that we were lost when I noticed a peculiar thing about his boot prints. Wilde is a large man, and leaves a heavy print in the sand. Although the hues of the landscape all around me had faded to a dusky grey, one colour stood out vividly: red. The Sergeant's footprints were scarlet with blood. The Indian's stone-bladed knife must have struck home, after all.

I didn't need to rein Buck to a halt. He stopped of his own accord, forelegs stiff, and nostrils quivering. Then he let out a low whicker of fear, barely audible in the oppressive stillness. In that same instant, the Sergeant sighed and slumped to the ground in a loose-boned heap.

A sudden realization chilled me to my very core. I knew in that instant that I had been following a dead man: the dog I had seen in my dreams. I also knew that I was hopelessly lost. I thought I heard the ghostly laughter of savage voices, and the beat of a drum, but it was only my own heart, pounding in my ears.

A sense of dizziness caused me to sway in the saddle as the drumbeat increased in tempo. I heard a ringing in my ears and instinctively knew that death was hovering near.

I am not a religious person, and so I did not pray. I cannot say what it was that saw me through that awful moment when I thought my heart would stop. I can only suppose it was the dream, for the feelings I was experiencing now were exactly the emotions I had felt on realizing that I was trapped in the cave with the dead dog. All the while, laughter filled my ears: the evil laughter of the dead.

I raised a hand to my head, pressing it against my temple in an effort to make the dizziness stop. As the fingers of my hand covered one eye, I closed the other eye.

Silence. The drumbeat and voices stopped.

I started, and nearly tore my hand away, but some instinct of self-preservation caused me to keep my eyes screwed tightly shut. I moved my palm fully over both eyes, like a child playing at hide and seek. Then I applied my spurs—lightly—to Buck's flanks.

The horse took a step forward.

Again the spurs, and again another step by my unwilling mount. I let the reins go slack, giving Buck his head. At last, under my prodding, he began to walk.

I don't know how long I rode like that, with one hand over my eyes and the other on the pommel of my saddle. It might have been five minutes; it might have been five hours. I only know that Buck eventually came to a halt and no end of urging or spurring would prompt him forward. Once more I felt the heat of the sun on my back.

Cautiously, I opened my fingers a crack and peered out through it. I can only describe my stupefaction at the scene that lay before me. Just ahead of where Buck had drawn to a halt, Sergeant Wilde and his horse lay still on the ground. The Sergeant's revolver was in his hand, and a gory bullet hole in the animal's neck was leaking blood. The Sergeant's foot was tangled in one stirrup. His leg was bent, but did not appear to be broken.

Perhaps most curious of all, we were right beside the railway tracks—still within the Cypress Hills. I recognized the area as being only a mile or two away from the detachment. We hadn't journeyed north at all.

I slid from my saddle and walked to where the Sergeant lay. His Stetson lay by his side, but his clothes were otherwise undisturbed. When I searched his body, I found no mark on him, save for a faint black smudge on his left breast when I opened his jacket to listen for a heartbeat. I heard none.

I turned back to Buck, and noticed that his head was drooping. Despite the fact that he had been traveling at a walk, his sides were lathered. I stroked him on the cheek, telling him what a good horse he'd been to bring me home again. It was a sentimental gesture, but heartfelt in that moment.

For my part, I felt drained and ill, as if I had not slept in several nights—which, of course, was precisely the case.

"Are you up for one last push for home?" I asked Buck.

I fancied that he nodded. With all due haste, I rode for the Maple Creek detachment, to report the Sergeant's untimely death.

They put the cause of death down to failure of the heart, which is what I put in my report. That explanation appealed to the rational side of me, even though the Sergeant was a hale and hearty man. I needed some explanation for what I had seen, some way to make sense of my strange experience. I decided later that all I had seen and heard had been mere hallucination, provoked by a lack of sleep. Which was the reason, I suppose, why I mentioned my dream in the report in the first place: to make the state I was in known, and to explain why I wasn't able to minister to the Sergeant.

In my report, I put down the only sensible explanation: that the Sergeant's ill-tempered horse had bucked, throwing him from the saddle. With his foot caught in the stirrup and his brains about to be dashed in by pounding hooves, the Sergeant had done the only thing he could to save himself: shoot his mount. And then, in all of the excitement of the moment, his weakened heart had stopped.

Of course, there was one thing that was never fully explained—something that has made me wonder, all of this time, if my strange dream didn't in fact contain a grain of truth. When they removed the Sergeant's clothing to prepare him for burial, the constables who were ministering to him were interrupted by Wilde's two dogs, which tried to seize their master's clothing. In the resulting tug-of-war, the constables noticed a peculiar thing.

We had ridden to Piapot's camp along the railway line, across terrain that was thickly forested, and had presumably proceeded back to Maple Creek the same way. The weird landscape I had seen—the rolling, barren hills, and sandy ground—could have been nothing more than an illusion.

Yet both of the Sergeant's boots contained a trickle of sand.

—

When I finished my tale, Superintendent Steele and the Commissioner were silent. Steele nodded at me, a pleased look on his face. The Commissioner picked up the reports and photographs, tapped them against the table to straighten the pile, then slid them back in the folder. As he closed the flap, I noticed it was marked with big block letters in red: CONFIDENTIAL.

I stood uneasily in front of the table, trying to ignore the uncomfortable dampness of my uniform, which was still wet from the rainstorm. Had they believed me?

Steele was the first to break the silence. He turned to the Commissioner. "The brave with the painted face and lynx-skin war bonnet was Wandering Spirit. He's a Cree—a member of Big Bear's band. A war chief, and purportedly one with paranormal powers."

The Commissioner nodded slowly, but seemed reluctant to continue in that vein. "Big Bear," he mused. "Is that the pock-marked little troublemaker who refused to sign Treaty Number Six and tried to discourage the other Cree from signing?"

"The very same man, Commissioner," Steele answered. "And now Big Bear is stirring up trouble and discontent once again. For the past few years he's been traveling from one band to another, trying to get the Indians to set aside their differences and unite in a grand council. He had no success whatsoever, until recently. Over the course of this past year, the various Cree bands have joined together, and Big Bear has even made inroads among the tribes of the Blackfoot Confederacy—tribes who are sworn enemies of the Cree. Something's tipped the balance in his favour, so that even his traditional enemies are willing to bury the tomahawk and join his campaign against the settlement of the North-West. And that something is magic."

"Magic?" I couldn't help but blurt.

"I've been collecting reports of strange occurrences for some time," Steele said. "Events that cannot be explained by any known means. The first such incident to come to my attention was the sudden overflowing of the Old Man River in the spring of 1881, and the resulting destruction of Fort Macleod when the banks on which the palisade walls were built were undercut. Six constables and one officer were drowned in that flood, and yet upriver and down, the waters of the Old Man River remained within their normal course. With the exception of the immediate vicinity of Fort Macleod, the river did not rise."

"I heard about the drownings," I said. "And the rebuilding of the new fort, well away from the river. But I thought it was a natural flood." Even as I spoke those words, however, I thought of the strange thunderstorm that had greeted my arrival in Regina, and shivered. I glanced out the window, but saw only clear blue sky.

"The flood wasn't any more natural than the rest of the incidents I've investigated—or that storm that greeted your arrival," Steele said grimly.

The Commissioner nodded. "That was odd, wasn't it? I've never seen a storm come up so fast—or disappear so suddenly."

"Quite so, Commissioner," Steele said. Then he gestured at the folder on the desk. "It's all in there."

Steele summarized his evidence: "Indian agent Tom Quinn, whose body was found on the prairie near Fort Pitt earlier this year, was purportedly killed by a wild animal—probably a lynx, judging by tracks near the body. Yet the attack was unusual in the extreme, in that it was focused exclusively on one part of the body. The cat clawed its way into Quinn's chest and tore out his heart—which it then presumably ate, since the organ was never found. Quinn appears to have offered no resistance: there were no defensive wounds on his arms, and no claw or bite marks anywhere else on his body."

Steele gave a faint shudder, then took a breath and continued. "Equally inexplicable was the strange illness that afflicted the settlement of Swift Current last fall, temporarily rendering blind more than two dozen of its residents. The first cases were in the days immediately following a storm that dropped hailstones bearing an uncanny resemblance to eyeballs on the town.

"Finally, there was the Peigan woman in Fort Qu'appelle who gave birth just over a year ago to a stillborn child. Acting Hospital Steward Holmes, who delivered the infant, noted the peculiar coloration of its skin and hair, and swore upon a Bible that the child had been dead at birth and that its corpse rested for an entire day upon a bed without exhibiting any signs of life. Yet six months later, while ministering to the same family, he noticed an infant with Indian features, pale skin, and blonde hair. The mother told him a medicine woman used magic to bring her child back to life, the day after its unfortunate birth."

The Commissioner listened silently as Steele concluded his list. By the unflinching look in his eye, I could guess that he'd heard Steele spin these fantastic tales before.

"I never heard of any of this," I said. "Except for the news of Quinn's death—and that the animal's attack was unusual, and may have been an attempt by a man to disguise his handiwork. Quinn wasn't much loved by the Cree; I assumed one of Big Bear's warriors had killed him."

"Mark my words," Steele said. "It was an animal that killed Quinn—but not any animal that we've encountered before."

"The full details of each of these occurrences were collected by Superintendent Steele over the past year," the Commissioner added. "The uncanny nature of the incidents was hinted at in the official reports from the constables involved, but they were simply too fantastic to be given credence."

"You've seen evidence of the paranormal at work yourself, Corporal," Steele continued, fixing me with a serious look. "You and Sergeant Wilde both—although the poor Sergeant didn't live to tell the tale. That fantastic landscape you rode through was the Big Sands: the Indian version of purgatory and land of the dead. Wandering Spirit used his magic to send you there."

A chill ran through my body as I thought back upon the instances Steele had cited, particularly the woman who claimed her child had been raised from the dead. If such magic were possible, could a fatal injury or disease also be cured—be made to vanish without trace? If this so-called Indian "medicine woman" truly had magic at her command, anything might be possible.

For a wild moment, I wondered if I were dreaming. My hands were still clasped behind my back in the at-ease position. I squeezed one hand with the other until my fingers hurt. No, I was clearly still awake.

The Commissioner looked directly at Steele. "You believe in the paranormal, don't you?" he asked.

Steele gripped his Stetson tightly, then gave a brisk nod. "As much as I do in science."

"I don't know if I do," the Commissioner said.

Steele clenched his jaw.

The Commissioner's mouth twisted into a slight smile under his moustache. "But after hearing this man's report, I'm ready to reconsider the reports you've assembled for me—especially after seeing that most unusual storm today, first-hand. I'm prepared to consider your request with an open mind. If the Indians really do have paranormal powers that they can use with fatal effect, we need a police force capable of stopping them. Q Division is officially approved."

Steele let out a whoop and smacked his Stetson against his thigh. His grin was as wide as the prairie. "Thank you, sir," he said, then gave a brisk salute. He tucked the Stetson under one arm and strode toward the door.

"Come along, Corporal," he told me. "Q Division has its first case—the complexity of which has proved too baffling for the limited wits of Inspector Dickens—and I want you to investigate it. I'm sending you to Fort Pitt, and thence to the Victoria Mission, on the North Saskatchewan River."

"What am I to investigate?" I asked.

"The disappearance of Reverend John McDougall and his family—and of the Manitou Stone."

❧ — ❧

Chapter II

Inspector Dickens leaned toward me, cupping a hand behind his
ear. "What was that, Corporal Graystone?" he said, in a thick
British accent.

"Grayburn," I corrected, raising my voice a little louder. I'd
forgotten that the Inspector was hard of hearing. "I was hoping
you could tell me more about the Manitou Stone.
Superintendent Steele thinks it's connected with the
disappearance of the McDougalls."

We were seated at the table that served as Inspector Dickens's
desk in his office at Fort Pitt. Messy stacks of papers covered the
table, and on top of them sat an opened tin of Crosse &
Blackwell's Yarmouth bloaters. The smoked fish smelled slightly
off; I guessed it was due to the heat. Beside the tin stood what
looked like a bottle of spirits. Dickens uncorked the bottle and
held up a glass.

"Brandy?" he asked.

I shook my head, declining it. Outside the window, which had
its shutters open, I could hear the *whush-whush* of the perpetual
motion machine that worked the bellows of the nearby
blacksmith's shop. I wondered how the smith could possibly
stand to work his forge in this heat.

"No thank you, sir," I said, as he moved to fill the glass despite
my headshake. "I only drink while I'm off duty."

Dickens winked. "I only drink when I'm *on* duty." He poured a
liberal dose into the glass, and set the bottle on the table in front
of him.

I stared at him a moment, reflecting on the great disparities
between Inspector Francis Dickens, who commanded this lonely
outpost on the North Saskatchewan River, and the dashing

Superintendent Sam Steele. The only thing they had in common was the Mounted Police uniform. Where Steele was athletic and trim, with a clean-shaven chin, Dickens was short, pudgy, and balding, with a long beard that did little to hide his weak chin. His nose and cheeks were veined with red from too-frequent tippling, which he somehow maintained despite the fact that the sale of intoxicating liquors was prohibited in the North-West Territories—a prohibition the Mounted Police were sworn to uphold, although it was as unpopular with them as it was with the settlers.

Dickens was completely unfit to be an officer, but he had friends in Ottawa who had helped him to purchase his commission. I had heard that no less a personage than Lord Dufferin, the Governor General of Canada, was a friend of the family—which was hardly surprising, given that the Inspector was the son of the famed novelist Charles Dickens.

I lifted my haversack onto my knees. Dickens, taking a drink of his brandy, watched as I rummaged for the folder that Superintendent Steele had given me. I hoped he wouldn't see the bottle of Pinkham's at the bottom of the haversack and mistake it for spirits. I didn't want him demanding a drink from it, then draining it dry.

"You're not going to ask me to sign one of my father's novels, are you?" Dickens asked.

I shook my head, and he emitted a brandy-sweet sigh of relief.

"Everyone is always asking me to do that," he added. "Do you know that Chief Sitting Bull himself once called me into his camp by dead of night to autograph a copy of *Oliver Twist*? This was, of course, after he'd skipped across the 'medicine line' into Canada following the battle of Little Bighorn."

"Is that so?"

My scepticism must have been reflected in my voice. Dickens frowned. "It wasn't even a proper edition. Just a cheap American copy."

I nodded in what I hoped was a sympathetic manner, and pulled the photograph I'd been searching for out of the folder. The brownish-black photograph was mounted on card stock and embellished with the photographer's name in gold script. It was part of a series of views of the North-West Territories, taken a few years ago, which included scenic images of the North Saskatchewan River and Victoria Mission. The small church had been founded in 1863 by John McDougall's father, George, a Methodist missionary who came west with his family to minister to the Blackfoot Indians. After the elder McDougall froze to death in 1876 in a blizzard while hunting near Calgary, his son John had taken over the mission. Now Reverend John McDougall, his wife, and their six children had disappeared.

The mission occupied the background of the photograph: a two-story whitewashed log building, set in a clearing on the riverbank. The photographer had focused on a large boulder with a distinctive rectangular shape that stood in the front yard of the mission. John McDougall was shown standing beside this waist-high stone, hands on his hips, his dark wavy hair combed back from his forehead. A full beard hid the set of his lips, but there was a defiant look in his eye. His expression matched what little of his writings I had read: McDougall had railed against the Indians' "barbarism, shiftlessness, and demon-worship," and had vowed to use the gospel to wash away "centuries of ignorance."

Above the mission, the clouds had conspired to mirror McDougall's expression: dark patches within the white vapour looked like scowling eyes, and the bottom of the cloud was like a jutting chin. Other patches of shadow gave this "face" the distinctive high, wide cheekbones and long nose of an Indian.

Before my summons to Regina two weeks ago, I would have regarded the cloud formation as an amusing coincidence. Now, I couldn't help but wonder if the face in the clouds was as real as the thunderbird that had nearly put paid to the air bicycle.

"The Manitou Stone," I said, tapping my finger on the rectangular boulder in the photograph. "According to Corporal Cowan's report, it disappeared from the mission yard around the same time that the McDougalls vanished. Can you tell me more about it?"

Dickens drained his brandy and refilled his glass. "Only what's commonly known," he said. "It was a big, bluish-grey stone, sacred to the Indians, that used to be situated beside the Battle River. They would ride from all over on their ponies to the hill it rested upon, to leave offerings of pemmican and tobacco. Even mortal enemies—Blackfoot and Cree together—would venerate it side by side."

Dickens took another drink, then continued. "In 1868 George McDougall decided that he could convince the Indians that his Christian god was stronger than their creator god. He used a block and tackle to lift the stone onto a cart, then hauled it more than a hundred miles to the mission."

"And were the Indians convinced?" I asked, even though I could guess the answer. I'd had dealings with both the Blackfoot and Cree over my years of Mounted Police service—I'd even picked up a smattering of their languages—and knew them to be fierce warriors, not easily cowed. It was a wonder that the McDougalls— father and son both—hadn't been killed in the process.

Dickens's answer surprised me. "The Indians were terrified. According to their legends, if the stone were ever moved, disease, famine, and war would follow—and they did. Four years later, in the spring of 1870, thousands of Indians died of smallpox. That summer, the Cree took advantage of the epidemic and attacked the Blackfoot along Belly River. The Blackfoot won the battle, but it was a bloody business: nearly three hundred Indians died."

Dickens paused to refill his glass. "Our scout, Jerry Potts, can tell you all about the battle, if you like. He fought on the Blackfoot side—that was back before he came to work for the Mounted Police. On the Cree side, the only tribe that managed to avoid casualties was that of Chief Piapot—and then only because Piapot made them turn for home, after he had a bad dream."

My head came up like a dog on the scent. "Was it a prophetic dream?" I asked.

Dickens shrugged. "Piapot thought so. He told his braves he'd dreamed of a buffalo with iron horns, goring and trampling his people. One hundred braves refused to take part in the battle, and followed him out of the war camp."

I sat and thought about that one. Piapot was the same chief whose braves had put up the show of resistance at the end of the CPR tracks last year, at the time of my own prophetic dream and Sergeant Wilde's death. If Dickens's story was to be believed, then Piapot, like me, had dreamed of his own impending doom in the form of an animal. I wondered if the strange look that Piapot had given me that day by the CPR tracks had been the look of a man with prophetic powers, recognizing those powers in another.

The gurgle of brandy into Inspector Dickens's glass pulled me back to the present. He must have noticed my pained expression, for he repeated his offer of brandy. This time, I took it, putting out of my mind the fact that drinking on duty was cause for a nine-dollar fine. The brandy was surprisingly good.

"The winter of 1872 brought the third calamity that the medicine men had predicted," Dickens continued. "That winter was a hard one, colder than any in living memory, and the buffalo were becoming scarce. Hundreds of Indians that had survived the smallpox epidemic now starved to death."

Dickens leaned back in his chair; the story had obviously come to a close. He gave me a conspiratorial wink. "It's a grand story, eh? Certainly worthy of anything my father might write, but it's pure fantasy. In my opinion, there is only one possible explanation for the disappearance of the stone and the McDougalls: the Indians finally worked up the gumption to retrieve their precious rock and kidnapped the reverend when he tried to prevent them from dragging it away on a travois."

"A travois wouldn't have been sturdy enough," I said, glancing at the photograph. "The stone looks heavy; it would have been difficult to move. The Indians would have needed a wagon or cart. Were any missing from the McDougall home?"

Dickens shook his head.

"What about the McDougall family?" I continued. "Corporal Cowan's report indicated that there was evidence of a violent struggle inside the McDougall home, and that there were several confused hoof prints outside the mission. He asked that Jerry Potts be sent up to trail the kidnappers. But his report doesn't give any details beyond that. It only indicates that Potts was unable to follow the trail."

I was hesitant to accuse Jerry Potts of shirking his duties. He was a man that my own commanding officer praised highly: Superintendent Steele said he had never met Jerry Potts's equal when it came to tracking and wilderness skills. But Potts was half Blood Indian and his bloodthirsty, superstitious nature suggested that his sentiments leaned more toward his mother's side of the family than toward his father's Scottish side.

"I can't believe that Potts lost the trail," I added. "I only know of one other time that it happened, and he had a damn fine excuse: a chinook that melted the snow, completely obliterating Star Child's tracks. Following the pony tracks of a war party should have been a simple matter for Potts, especially if their horses were dragging a travois laden with a heavy stone. Are you certain he didn't see any tracks?"

Dickens blinked. Despite the volume of brandy he'd drunk, he still had his wits about him. His eyes weren't bleary—they were frightened.

"P-P-Potts did find tracks," Dickens said. "B-B-But they weren't those of horses."

He suddenly seemed more interested in watching the last drops fall from the brandy bottle into his glass than in my investigation. His stutter—well known and ridiculed throughout the Mounted Police—was an indication that something was making him nervous. I wanted to find out what it was.

"What kind of tracks?" I asked.

"Buffalo—and l-l-l-."

I frowned waiting for Dickens to get the word out.

"And l-l-lynx."

"That wasn't in Cowan's report."

"N-N-No," Dickens said. He stared down at his brandy glass, rocking it back and forth and leaving sticky trails on the papers its base rested upon. The tips of his fingers had gone white, so tightly did he grip it.

A connection suddenly occurred to me. "Have there been any reports from Victoria Mission of a large cat acting in a peculiar manner? A lynx is suspected to have caused the death of Tom Quinn."

I heard a loud cracking noise. Jerking his hand away from the brandy glass, which had broken in his hand, Dickens rubbed at a spot of blood that beaded on his finger. He looked terrified now, his shoulders hunched and his lips trembling. His eyes pleaded with me. There was something he wanted to tell me, but he wanted it to be because I asked: because I forced him to tell.

"Inspector," I said in a firm voice. "Tell me about the lynx tracks."

The words came out in a rush—or as much of a rush as Dickens's stutter would permit.

"They were all around the house. P-P-Potts f-f-followed them to the river, but then they d-d-disappeared—just like the b-b-buffalo tracks."

"Into the river? Did they resume on the other side?"

Dickens shook his head.

"They just stopped?"

Dickens nodded.

"Did anyone at Victoria Mission see or hear anything peculiar on the day the McDougalls disappeared?"

Dickens shook his head.

"Were there any Indians seen in the vicinity?"

"J-j-just one," Dickens said. He toyed with a piece of broken glass for a long moment before continuing. "There's a shaman among the Indians. A Cree of B-B-Big Bear's band, by the name of Wandering Spirit. Corporal Cowan f-f-found him skulking around the Victoria Mission, and b-b-brought him back here for questioning. Wandering Spirit refused to speak, except to me. When I was alone with him, he said if I d-d-didn't release him, I'd wind up like Quinn. D-d-d-d-"

"Dead?"

Dickens nodded rapidly.

I sat for a moment in silence, amazed at the coincidence. Wandering Spirit was the same Indian who had worked his magic on Sergeant Wilde, sending him into the Big Sands. Dickens had every reason to be frightened of the man, but I was angry that he'd let Wandering Spirit slip through his fingers.

"So you released him?" I asked scornfully. "You let your only suspect go?"

Dickens winced, and began fumbling with the buttons on the front of his jacket. "I had no ch-ch-choice. Not after he d-d-did...." His hands pulled the jacket open and lifted his shirt, exposing his chest. "This!"

I stared, incredulous. On the left side of Dickens's soft, hairless chest, just above the nipple, was a pattern of puncture marks, each surrounded by a patch of angry red inflammation. The marks were exactly what one would expect to see if a large cat had sunk the tips of its claws into human flesh.

"How...."

Dickens let his shirt fall. "I d-d-don't know," he whispered. "Wandering Spirit just made a g-g-gesture with his hand, and the next thing I knew I felt a terrible p-p-pain in my chest. It hurt so badly I thought I was going to d-d-d-"

This time, I waited until he said the word himself.

"To d-d-die," he finally managed. "Right there on the spot."

Belatedly, I realized that I should have been taking notes. Steele had asked for a full and complete report on everything connected with the case, impressing upon me that no detail, no matter how trivial it might seem, should be left out.

An Inspector nearly killed by paranormal forces was hardly a trivial detail.

"How long ago did this happen?" I asked, rummaging in my haversack for a report book and pencil.

"Nearly four weeks ago," Dickens answered.

I stared at the strange wound. It was as vivid and red as if it had been made only yesterday.

Now that he'd gotten the worst of it out, Dickens's stutter was settling down again. "The McDougalls were reported missing on July 2nd," he said. "Corporal Cowan was sent to investigate, and returned to the f-f-fort with Wandering Spirit on July 10th."

Something occurred to me. I pulled a copy of Cowan's report from my haversack and leafed through it. "The corporal's report wasn't telegraphed to headquarters until the 16th of July. Wandering Spirit was long gone by then, presumably."

Dickens nodded, his eyes on his buttons as he refastened them.

"Are you certain that Wandering Spirit didn't conceal a weapon on his person and use it against you?"

"Wandering Spirit was searched," Dickens said. "He had no weapon, and his wrists were shackled together."

My next question was a difficult one, considering the fact that Dickens was an officer, and thus my superior. I reminded myself that his drinking was no secret. "When you questioned Wandering Spirit, were you sober?"

Dickens bristled, but his answer was direct. "I may have had a d-d-drink that d-d-day, but I know what I saw. Wandering Spirit just... gestured. I have no explanation for what happened."

I did, but I kept it to myself. There's a word in the Cree language: *atayohkanak*. It means "spirit power"—we'd use the word *magic* in its place. Wandering Spirit had used magic to intimidate Dickens into releasing him: there was no other explanation for the puncture marks on Dickens's chest. The Inspector was an incompetent officer who liked his brandy, but he had keen self-preservation instincts and was accustomed to strong drink. He'd have to have been staggering and blind drunk before he'd mistake the swing of a weapon for a simple hand gesture. Dickens might be as much of a storyteller as his illustrious father, but I didn't think he had the imagination to concoct a tale like the one I'd just heard.

I tucked the photo of the Manitou Stone and my copy of Corporal Cowan's report back into my haversack. I wanted to question Wandering Spirit myself. I knew where to begin my search: Big Bear's band often camped near Poundmaker's reserve, which was no more than fifty miles down river, near Battleford. Yet if Wandering Spirit really did have the power to wound with a mere gesture—or kill, as I suspected had been the case with Tom Quinn—I'd have to be cautious. I decided I'd gather all the information I could before visiting the Cree encampment.

"I know the trail is probably cold," I told Dickens, "but I'd like to see Victoria Mission for myself before questioning Wandering Spirit. What transportation can your detachment arrange?"

Dickens's look of relief, now that the matter of Wandering Spirit was in someone else's hands, was palpable. "There's the riverboat *North West*. It's due to stop at Fort Pitt tomorrow on its way upriver to–"

A ghastly wailing sound interrupted whatever Dickens had been about to say. So discordant was the noise that wafted in through the open window that it took a moment for me to recognize it as the pipes of an organ in full throat. Whoever was playing it was either completely untutored or halt of limb.

"Who or what is that?" I shouted over the din, which seemed to be coming from an adjoining building.

Dickens had cupped his hand behind his ear again. His frown indicated that he hadn't heard me clearly, but he guessed my question.

"It's probably one of Factor McLean's brats," he shouted back. "Too bad I hadn't gotten one of them to play the blasted thing while Wandering Spirit was in custody: the pipe organ terrifies the Indians."

He grinned at his own joke, but his eye was on the empty brandy bottle. I could see that he still had fearful memories of his encounter with Wandering Spirit and was looking for some liquid courage, even though the Cree shaman was probably nowhere near Fort Pitt.

I just hoped that my own mettle wouldn't be found wanting when it came time to question Wandering Spirit about the disappearance of the McDougall family.

◄—►

I embarked upon the riverboat *S. S. North West*, which sailed from Fort Pitt the next day. The riverboat was long and low, with a flat hull that drew only eighteen inches of water, and the vessel had an open lower deck that used to be stacked high with cordwood back when the boat was steam-powered. Above this first deck was an enclosed passenger deck with a long, narrow saloon and cabins, encircled by a railed promenade where travelers could take the air. The third deck, known as the "hurricane deck" was a flat expanse that was open to the elements, punctuated only by a small pilothouse. Twin smokestacks still pointed toward the heavens near the bow of the vessel, even though the steam engine that had once powered the *North West* was no longer in use. Engine and boilers had been removed and replaced by a gigantic perpetual motion device, housed on the lowermost deck near the huge paddlewheel at the stern of the vessel.

Once my belongings were safely stowed, I walked to the rear of the boat for a closer look—but not too close, lest my presence jinx the mechanism. The perpetual motion device, in this case, was of Swiss manufacture: a buoyancy motor. A series of huge, air-filled balls, connected by slim metal links, bubbled up through a water-filled chamber that from the outside looked like a gigantic brass boiler. The device transferred its energy by means of a series of cogs of ever-increasing size, culminating in the gears that drove the paddlewheel. The machine wasn't any use when the water froze—but that didn't matter since the *North West* ended its season each September, as soon as ice began to form in the river.

The trip upriver to Victoria Mission, one hundred and forty-four miles in all, took three full days, due to the delays caused whenever the ship ran aground on a sandbar. I kept to myself during the voyage—as much as my scarlet uniform would allow—but even so I faced a barrage of questions about where I was going and why, and what the Mounties had learned about the disappearance of the McDougall family. Everyone had a theory, each more ludicrous than the last: that the McDougalls and their six children had all gotten into a single canoe and drowned after it tipped in mid-river; that Indians had carried away the family and cannibalized the men and made slaves of the women; that the reverend had gone mad, murdered his wife and children, buried them in shallow graves, and then killed himself. I was tempted to tell these gossips the truth—that Indian magic had spirited the McDougalls away—just to see the expressions on their faces, but kept my lips buttoned.

Instead, I told the passengers and crew members of the *North West* that I was en route to a new posting at Fort Saskatchewan, and that I had been asked by my new commanding officer to stop in at the mission on the way, to see if any evidence had been overlooked. That would explain why I was disembarking at Victoria Mission, yet not place undue emphasis upon the visit.

The two previous times I'd travelled by riverboat in the course of my duties, I'd been quartered on the open lower deck, but Q Division, it seemed, had deeper pockets than the rest of the force: Steele had authorized a private cabin, which went for the princely sum of five dollars. I spent much of the voyage inside it, luxuriating in its comfort and passing the time by reading old editions of *Canadian Illustrated News* and listening to the piano tinkling in the saloon, just outside my door. In the evenings our captain, Jimmy Sheets, would descend from his pilothouse and serenade the passengers with his magnificent baritone.

I also found in my cabin a hymnbook that a previous passenger had left behind. Glancing inside the cover, I found it was inscribed with the words "Frederick Baldwin." I wondered if it had been lost or left behind deliberately, for the solace and edification of the next passenger. I shrugged and set it aside.

The few times that I did venture out onto the promenade that encircled the cabins on the second deck, a curious event repeated itself. More than once as I leaned against the rail, staring at the tree-dotted banks of the river and enjoying a pipe, I would imagine that someone was calling my name. When I turned, it was always to find the same pair of dark, brooding eyes staring at me. Then the gentleman they belonged to would tip his hat, as if in apology, and move on.

The first time this happened I ignored it, thinking it merely a flight of fancy. I was standing near the stern on the first day of our journey, and the sloshing of the perpetual motion tank and the rumbling and squeaking of the gears and cogs it drove produced a cacophony that could have given rise to any number of imagined sounds.

The second time, I intended to ask the fellow his name, but was distracted when the *North West* ran aground on yet another sand bar. I was jostled by the sudden stop and nearly lost my footing. By the time I regained my balance, the stranger was gone.

These groundings were an all-too-frequent occurrence. It didn't seem to matter that a man was stationed on the bow of the riverboat, constantly measuring the depth of water with a pole;

so silt-laden and unpredictable in its depth was the river that
the ship grounded several times each day. When this happened,
two beams—much like the ones used in lifting heavy cargoes—
had their ends lowered into the water on either side of the vessel.
The paddlewheel would churn up great clouds of silt, forcing the
vessel forward and causing it to rise on these spars like a lame
man on crutches. Having gained a few feet, the boat would then
heave down again, and the process would be repeated.

The third time I imagined a voice silently calling me and
noticed the same fellow staring at me intently, I made a careful
study of the man. He was a handsome fellow in his twenties,
wearing a black derby hat, a button cutaway suit, and stylish
pants cut from diagonal-patterned worsted. He carried an
umbrella with a silver handle, which he used like a cane as he
strolled the decks, and he wore his beard below the chin, with
cheeks clean-shaven except where the beard joined the
moustache on his lip. His black hair glistened with Brilliantine,
and his eyes were a brown so dark it bordered on black. He
smelled of German cologne.

I strode up to the fellow and demanded his name and
business. He introduced himself as Arthur Chambers, and
seemed surprised that I had not heard of him. It seemed he was
a famous lecturer, although he was vague on his area of
expertise, saying only that he lectured on "energy." I decided
that he must be both wealthy and arrogant—two factors that I
have often found go hand in glove. I made up my mind to dislike
him, then and there. Yet something compelled me to engage him
in conversation.

Chambers spoke with a gentleman's accent, and was
obviously from England. But despite his strange habit of
startling me, and despite his obvious displeasure at my not
recognizing his name, our conversation was civil enough. It was
limited to the pleasantries that strangers typically exchange:
complaints about the heat, observations on how odd the moon
was looking these days, and platitudes about the scenery that
passed by on either side. When it came down to it, I could find
nothing suspicious about him, save for his seeming fascination
with me.

After that, although Chambers kept a discreet distance, he
continued to stare intently at me whenever our paths crossed—
which was frequently, on a boat of that size. Although he
remained silent, he seemed to be speaking volumes with his
eyes.

Such constant attention made me uncomfortable, and by the
third day of our voyage I made up my mind to confront
Chambers about it. Yet it was he who approached me that

evening, asking if I liked to play cards. Partially out of politeness, but more out of curiosity about this irritating fellow, I agreed to join him in a game.

As is often the case when cards are suggested, the game of choice was poker. We chose a table in the saloon, beneath the tinkling chandelier. We were soon joined by a soft-spoken farmer from the Red River Settlement who only parted his lips to puff on a white clay pipe, indicating silently with his fingers how many cards he wanted. His breath had a sour smell, and the few times he opened his mouth I could see that one of his teeth had turned black. Also joining us was the Metis steward of the riverboat. The latter fellow, who had the rather pretentious name Xavier de Mont-Ferron, had a boisterous, jovial nature.

We played several hands, and as I settled into the game, my usual lucky streak emerged.

"*Mon dieu!*" the steward exclaimed when I won for the fourth time in as many hands of cards. "You must 'av a lucky 'orseshoe in your pocket, *monsieur.*"

"Nothing so crude as that, I'll wager," Chambers said, his dark eyes studying me intently. "I'd wager that a power other than mere luck is at work here."

Suddenly uncomfortable, I slid a finger under my collar to loosen it.

The steward frowned in puzzlement, and the farmer ignored the exchange, silently concentrating on the cards he was shuffling. I was just working up the nerve to ask Chambers what he meant by his remark when a voice drawled from behind my left shoulder: "Y'all mind if I join the game?"

I turned and saw an American with weathered cheeks and a patchy, straw-coloured beard. He wore canvas trousers, a grey cotton shirt that laced up the front, and beaded, ankle-high moccasins. He smelled like a man who had been on the trail for many weeks. A short-barrelled pocket revolver was holstered butt-forward on his left hip, and on his right hip was a sheath containing a knife with an antler handle. I'd noticed him on the lower deck when I boarded in Fort Pitt; he hadn't taken a cabin, and was sleeping with the half-breeds down below. Given his weapons—and his squint-eyed, challenging stare—I was loath to have him join our poker game. But Chambers waved to an empty chair and invited him to sit down.

"I don't think I've made your acquaintance, sir," Chambers said with a polite smile, half rising from his chair. "Might I inquire as to your name and where you are from?"

The American pulled his chair up to the table, then reached inside his shirt for a metal flask. Grabbing one of the glasses on the table, he poured the residue of cold tea it held onto the floor, then refilled the glass with amber liquid, measuring the amount by holding his four fingers against the glass and stopping when the liquid was level with the uppermost finger. Judging by the smell, it was whiskey.

He screwed the lid back on his flask and shoved it back into the folds of his odorous shirt. That done, he stared at me, as if challenging me to uphold the law that prohibited possession of alcohol without a permit. I met his eye with a level stare, and he at last answered the Englishman's question.

"Four Finger Pete's my name, and I come from here and there—most lately, Fort Garry. I'll play until my drink is done, then quit the game, win or lose." His look suggested that he intended to win—and that we'd better like it when he did.

I'd met men like him before, and had even been forced to draw my revolver on them a time or two. I considered myself a match for this Four Finger Pete. Yet Steele had instructed me not to draw any attention to myself while on this case. I had to satisfy myself with giving the uncouth fellow a glare, and leave it at that.

We played six more hands of poker, three of which I won. As coins and twenty-five-cent shinplaster bills piled up in front of me I saw a spark of anger ignite in Four Finger Pete's eye. I deliberately lost the next hand, not wanting to provoke a confrontation with the American gunslinger. Shaking my head as if bewildered by my change of luck, I secretly sighed in relief as Four Finger Pete scooped up the pot, which had grown to a substantial eight dollars and fifty cents. I could see by his confident attitude that he was used to winning, and guessed that he was a professional gambler. I'd have loved to have taken him down a notch or two—something that would have been easy, given my luck at cards—but Steele's admonition to remain inconspicuous kept ringing through my thoughts.

Chambers was the next to deal. He picked up the cards I had thrown away in that last hand: two queens—and the cards that had been in my hand: a queen, a six, two threes and an ace—and glanced at them as he slid them into the deck.

"Quite a pity, Corporal Grayburn," he said, clucking his tongue. "If only you'd known that lady luck was coming your way, things might have gone quite differently." His long-lashed eyes blinked innocently, but I had caught the inflection in his voice. Somehow he had recognized my talent for intuitively knowing which cards to toss away, and he'd guessed that I'd deliberately ignored it on that last hand.

Chambers dealt a fresh hand. The farmer stared at his cards from under the brim of his slouch hat, took a deep draw on his pipe and let out a stream of pungent smoke that smelled like Fon du Lac Cut Plug, then held up a tobacco-stained forefinger for one card. Xavier, after a quick wave at the chief engineer to indicate that he would return to his duties presently, shrugged and drew four new cards. Four Finger Pete studied the farmer's eyes closely, watched Xavier as he reordered the cards in his hand, gave me a sidelong glance, then asked for two cards. His overall expression did not change as he was dealt them, but I saw a small tic at the corner of his scruffy moustache that might have been a smile.

I was about to toss away the jack, queen and king of hearts that were in my hand—in direct defiance of my strong hunch that they were the cards to keep—but just at that moment an Indian woman entered the saloon from the door nearest the stairway that led to the lower deck. I recognized her by the ochre-painted leggings and American blanket she wore as a Peigan. The hood of her blanket was thrown back, revealing lustrous black hair that hung in two braids, into one of which was tied a bedraggled white feather. She had high cheekbones and long-lashed eyes and was quite beautiful—or would have been, I noted as she drew closer, but for the pockmarks that marred her skin. Given the degree to which the disease had ravaged her features, I judged she was lucky to have survived her brush with smallpox. I was struck by her damaged beauty, and captivated by the shine in her hair. She reminded me—albeit only superficially—of an Indian woman who had for a time haunted my dreams, causing me at least upon one occasion to wake up with a palpitating heart. I found myself feeling a pang of guilt, but at the same time was strangely aroused. I found my eyes lingering on this Indian woman. I kept imagining touching her braid, her cheek, her breast....

Feeling myself begin to blush, I deliberately turned my thoughts away from these dream memories. I continued to watch the Indian woman approach out of the corner of my eye, however. I had the distinct impression that she and I were not strangers to one another, even though I was certain we had never met before. I was struck with the peculiar notion that our paths would cross again in the future. But the feeling was gone in a twinkling, and before I could ponder it further the woman approached Four Finger Pete from behind and laid a hesitant hand on his sleeve.

The gambler whirled in his chair like a man challenged to a duel, closing up the cards in his rough hands. "What you doin' up on this deck?" he barked. "I thought I told you to stay below."

The woman cringed and glanced down at her moccasins. I noted that one of her pretty eyes had a slight smudge of yellow around it, probably an old bruise. "Child has fever," she said in a voice as soft as a whisper. She gave the briefest possible glance at the pile of winnings that sat in front of Four Finger Pete. "Medicine at Victoria Mission. When boat stop there, we go–"

The crack of Four Finger Pete's hand across her face rocked the woman's head to the side. I was halfway out of my seat, a protest on my lips, when the woman caught my eye and shook her head, her eyes wide and frightened. I could see that it would go badly for her later if I provoked her husband's anger further. Much as I would have loved to give the fellow a taste of his own medicine, I forced myself to refrain from raining blows upon him.

With narrowed eyes, the gambler gave the woman a look of pure venom. "I told you never to interrupt me when I'm gamblin'," he growled. "Now git off down below, unless you want me to toss in your worthless hide to sweeten up the pot."

The woman's hands clenched, then she turned and hurried away. Feeling my face flush, I leaned across the table in a threatening manner. "You brute," I growled. "If you strike her again, I'll arrest you and clap you into manacles. Then I'll see how well you can sw–"

I felt Chambers's hand on my arm, and suddenly realized that not only were the others at our table staring at me, but so was everyone else in the saloon. One or two were backing carefully away as Four Finger Pete's right hand drifted down toward his left hip, where his revolver was holstered.

The gambler's eyes were dangerously narrow. "I paid that squaw's father two good ponies and a rifle. She's mine, bought and paid for. I do with her as I like."

Anger boiled inside me like a thunderhead, and only with the greatest difficulty did I keep it in check. I reminded myself that I myself was no saint—I'd broken the heart of a decent woman when I broke off my engagement to Mildred Hughes, five years ago, to join the North-West Mounted Police. She'd no other fault but to be too plain for my tastes, and yet I'd shattered her dreams of marriage and broken her heart.

I reminded myself that there were many other men equally as vile as Four Finger Pete. I'd seen cruel things done to Indian women during my time in the North-West Territories, especially by the traders who smuggle whisky into the country, and who would force a woman—or even a young girl—to debase herself for the stuff. Even the honest traders would casually abandon their Indian wives when they return east, leaving these poor women to struggle on alone to feed the brood of children the traders have sired.

Many of the Indian tribes treated their women no better: among the Blood Indians, a woman who had sexual relations outside of wedlock could, according to Indian custom, be disfigured by her husband. I'd seen one poor wretch who suffered this fate: a once-pretty woman with a gaping hole where her nose had been hacked off by a knife. Despite my urgings, she had refused to give evidence against the man who had so disfigured her. I'd taken the law into my own hands then, and dispensed justice with my own two fists—but that was in the past. I was working for Q Division now. And Steele was a man I didn't want to disappoint.

Chambers tugged at my sleeve. "Please, Corporal, do sit down," he said in a falsely cheerful voice. "There's no harm in a man chastising his wife, and we've yet to finish our poker hand. How many cards would you like?"

I shook off his hand, angry that Chambers had taken the side of the American lout, then forced myself to take my seat. I did my best to swallow my emotion, and felt a familiar clench of pain in my stomach. Still glaring at Four Finger Pete, who had at last relaxed and moved his hand back to the table, I threw down my discards.

"Two," I gritted.

Chambers dealt me two cards, then drew one card himself. Not caring who saw it, I reached into my pocket and drew out my bottle of painkiller. Taking a hefty swig, I winced as it burned its way down. The stuff was nineteen per cent alcohol— very nearly a match for the whisky in Four Finger Pete's glass. As it hit my stomach it burned for a moment, but then I derived some relief from it. I noticed that Chambers glanced thoughtfully at the bottle, then studied my face intently. I hoped he was trying to guess what cards I held, and not what malaise plagued me.

The steward opened with a fifty-cent bid, and the farmer matched it, as did Four Finger Pete. I spread open my cards to look at them, then covered my reaction to what I saw by coughing as if the patent medicine had caught in my throat. Then I carefully arranged my features as if I were hiding a severe disappointment.

"Five dollars," I said when it was my turn, bidding an outrageous sum. It was just the sort of bid a novice gambler would make when the only avenue open to him is to bluff.

Chambers shrugged and met my bid. The steward uttered an exclamation in French and threw down his hand. "Ees too rich for me," he said.

The farmer studied his cards carefully, then without a word folded his hand and laid it on the table. He leaned back to watch the rest of us, puffing on his pipe.

Four Finger Pete glanced sidelong at me, and a light came into his eyes. "I'll see that bet," he said, tossing five dollars onto the table.

Chambers also remained in the game. "I'll raise you a dollar," he said. Four Finger Pete met the dollar and raised the pot two dollars more.

I took another swig of the painkiller, easily swallowing the by-now-familiar mix of camphor, myrrh, and spruce oil, then met the other players' bets and raised them another dollar. Chambers quickly followed, once again adding a one-dollar raise to keep the bidding going, as did Four Finger Pete. When I increased my "bluff" by another two dollars, and then by another four, both kept pace. Only when I upped it by another five dollars did Chambers drop out.

Four Finger Pete laid a five-dollar bill on the table. "Call," he said with a smirk. He laid down four nines and a two.

Slowly, all the while ready to lunge at the gambler and grab his hand if he tried to draw his weapon, I lay down my cards: the ten, jack, queen, king, and ace of hearts.

The eyes of the farmer widened. He slid his chair away from the table, putting distance between himself and Four Finger Pete. The steward leaped to his feet and hurried out of the saloon, muttering about needing to tend to his duties.

For a moment, there was frozen silence. Four Finger Pete and I stared at each other, each waiting for the other to blink, while Chambers sat with a bemused expression, as if he'd expected this all along.

"Damn you!" Four Finger Pete shouted at last. His hand swept down—but not for his gun. Instead he picked up his glass and drained the whisky in it in one gulp. He slammed the empty glass back down on the table.

"My whisky's done, and so am I," he gritted. Without another word he scraped back his chair, rose to his feet, and stalked away.

I scooped up my winnings, and smiled in satisfaction. I'd given the gambler his come-uppance. But the smile froze on my lips when I realized that Four Finger Pete might take his anger at losing out on his wife.

"Well done," Chambers congratulated me. "Of course, winning comes easily to a man with powers like your own."

"Excuse me?" I asked, wadding the money into my pocket. I kept my ear cocked, listening for anything that sounded like a man's voice raised in anger.

Chambers pushed the poker cards aside, then slid a hand inside his cutaway suit. I stiffened, wondering if he had a pistol concealed under it, but instead he drew from his pocket something that was wrapped in a black silk handkerchief. He unwrapped it to reveal a fresh deck of cards, then spread the cards face up across the table with a sweep of his hand. The deck bore the usual numeric denominations and suits, but the face cards portrayed a wild mix of characters: I saw renderings of what looked like a priest, a Hindu fakir, a Red Indian in buffalo-horn cap, and an Egyptian priestess, among other things. When Chambers gathered the cards together and began shuffling them, I saw that the reverse of each card was a solid black.

"During the poker game, you exhibited evidence of psychical powers," he said as he shuffled. "These are faculties that extend beyond the normal range of human perception. I'd like to propose a guessing game to test those powers."

I was still annoyed at Chambers for not acting the gentleman and helping to defend the Indian woman when Four Finger Pete struck her, and I was still listening for sounds of an argument on the deck below, yet I was intrigued by his proposal. All of my life, I had experienced strange hunches, premonitions and spates of luck. Could these abilities actually be measured? If so, I could imagine my father rolling over in his grave—just so he wouldn't have to look at the proof.

Chambers might be nothing more than a charlatan—a fortune-teller who used these odd cards to gull people into thinking that he could predict the future—but if he did have the ability to measure my abilities, I wanted him to do so.

I decided to agree to Chambers's test. "How does it work?" I asked.

"Quite simply," Chambers said, laying the cards face down in a neat stack on the table. He tapped a finger against the top card. "When I turn over this card, what suit do you suppose it will it be?"

I hazarded a guess: "Hearts?"

Chambers picked up the card and glanced at it. A slight downward motion of his moustache as his lips pressed together told me my first attempt was a failure. He laid the card on the table beside the deck. "Again," he said briskly.

I took another guess: "Spades?"

The second card went down upon the first. "Again," he ordered.

The farmer still sat at the table with us. Intrigued, he leaned forward, sucking on his pipe, sending pungent wafts of smoke over the table. He was more intent upon the guessing game than I was; part of my attention was still focused on listening for the sounds of a disturbance on the deck below.

Chambers saw that my attention had wandered, and prodded me.

"The ten of diamonds?" I said with a shrug, forgetting that I had merely to guess the suit.

"That was excellent," he said encouragingly. "You were correct on both the suit, and the number. Let us continue in that vein— if you guess either the suit or number correctly, we'll count it as a success."

I didn't think he was supposed to be offering me any indication, and had a feeling that these new rules were giving me an increased chance of guessing something correctly. I was mildly irritated at this idea, and at Chambers's tone of voice: it was almost as if he were encouraging a child. I had known since my childhood that some sort of "sixth sense" resided within me, and now I wanted to know its extent without stacking the deck— and without my efforts being coddled.

I guessed at three more cards, following Chambers's urgings to concentrate long and hard before each answer, but then I had to stop and take another dose of my patent medicine as pain wracked my stomach. The discomfort made me decide to speed up the game. When Chambers laid his finger upon the next card, I guessed immediately: "The queen of diamonds: the card that shows the Negress wearing a turban."

That startled me. I hadn't directly observed a card of that sort when Chambers spread out the deck a few moments ago, yet I could picture the black-faced woman clearly in my mind.

I heard the faint snap of card against table as Chambers laid it down and I shook my head to clear it. "Again," Chambers said, a slight note of excitement in his voice.

We proceeded in that manner through all fifty-two cards. When we were done, two piles of cards lay upon the table. They were about even in height.

"I didn't do very well, did I?" I said.

"Quite the contrary," Chambers said. "You guessed correctly on twenty-eight cards. Better than I would expect." He scooped the cards up and began shuffling them.

"Better than you would expect, perhaps," I said, adopting a tone my father might have used. "But not conclusive evidence. Twenty-eight correct answers out of fifty-two cards are only to be expected, when either suit or numerical value will suffice. It's no more than random chance."

Chambers inclined his head and gave me a quizzical look. "Let's test another possibility," he said. "Your ability to receive thought transferences."

By now, our guessing game had drawn a crowd of curious passengers. I glanced around at them uneasily, made even more uncomfortable by the ache in my stomach. I was under strict orders from Superintendent Steele to draw no undue attention to my investigations, and had instructions not to discuss with civilians any evidence I found of the paranormal. The last thing

Steele wanted the new division to be burdened with was a barrage of curiosity seekers and sensationalists. I hoped there wasn't a journalist in the crowd.

"Could we retire to a more private place, Mr. Chambers?" I asked.

Chambers shook his head. His eyes held a mischievous twinkle. "I'd like to test you under these conditions," he said. "I have found that discomfort—whether it's caused by physical pain or the emotional turmoil of having observers present—can have a pronounced effect on the results."

The crowd of passengers had grown to about a dozen, supplemented by the return of the steward and two other riverboat men. I felt a bead of nervous sweat trickle down my side under my scarlet jacket, and wished I had made the journey in plain clothes. I was doing what I'd been explicitly ordered not to do: expressing overt interest in the supernatural. Yet I couldn't help myself.

Chambers lifted a card and glanced at it, then pressed it face-first against his forehead with a theatrical flourish. With his free hand, he reached across the table and grabbed my wrist. So startled was I, that I was unable to protest. The touch of his bare fingers, moist with sweat, made me feel even more ill at ease than I had in the Commissioner's office.

"What card am I holding?" he asked, his dark eyes blazing with the intensity of concentration.

I swallowed, my Adam's apple bobbing uncomfortably against my stiff collar. "The ace of spades?" I ventured tentatively, after several moments.

Chambers's hand squeezed my wrist, and he smiled. Then he laid the card facedown on the table and drew another. Several people crowded around behind him, trying to peer at the card.

This time, I guessed more quickly, eager to end the test and return to the solitude of my cabin. "The eight of hearts," I said.

He placed the card on top of the first.

"Again," he prompted, raising another card to his forehead.

"The four of diamonds."

My flesh began to tingle under his fingers.

"Again," he said.

"The seven of diamonds."

So far, Chambers had placed every card in the same pile. Either my guesses were all wide of the mark or—even more frightening—I was guessing every card correctly. My nerves buzzing, I continued guessing as quickly as Chambers could raise the cards to his forehead. Although each card was presented to me with its black side facing me, I had a curious double vision that showed me its face slightly above and to the left, as if in a prairie mirage. A curious tickling feeling centred itself upon my forehead, just between and above my eyes. The crowd of onlookers that surrounded me, and the saloon walls behind them, took on a translucent appearance.

At long last, two piles of cards had replaced the original stack. One pile was large, the other quite small. Chambers counted them silently, then announced the final tally: "Forty-four correct in either suit or number, and eight incorrect. An excellent score of eighty-four per cent, well above the statistical average."

I pushed my pillbox hat back from my forehead and mopped my brow. "That's astounding," I said. Then my policeman's instincts took over. Despite the evidence I had seen with my own eyes, and Steele's assertions that paranormal powers did exist, a part of me—albeit an ever-diminishing part—remained as sceptical as my father. I added, for the benefit of our observers: "But not so surprising when you consider the fact that no one saw the cards except Mr. Chambers himself."

Chambers shot me a challenge with dark eyes. Silently, he handed me the larger stack of cards, face up. I rifled through them, and found to my amazement that, from what I could remember, they were in the very order I had described.

"Would you care to be tested a second time?" Chambers asked. "With independent verification by Monsieur Mont-Ferron, perhaps?"

He half turned to the steward, who drew back in alarm, one hand making the sign of the cross. But others in the crowd pressed toward the table.

"I'll do it!" one cried.

"No, test me!"

"He must be a spiritualist," another whispered to a friend. "Next thing you know, the table will be knocking and tilting and ectoplasm will ooze from his ear!"

I leaned toward Chambers and indicated his cabin with a glance. "Let's continue this conversation in a more private place," I hissed.

Chambers nodded, and carefully re-wrapped his cards. "Agreed," he said. Rising from the table and picking up his silver-handled umbrella, he indicated the ordinary deck of poker cards that still lay on the table. "The guessing game is merely a parlour amusement that anyone can play," he told the curious onlookers. "You are welcome to use my poker deck to test each other."

We retired from the table, leaving the crowd of passengers to amuse themselves. As we walked to Chambers's cabin, the optimist and the sceptic were at war within my breast. I wanted the results to be true—oh, how I wanted magic to be real, and psychical powers and perhaps even miracles to be within my grasp. I tucked the bottle of painkiller back into my pocket, and stepped inside Chambers's cabin as he held the door open for me.

I had expected the small room to be filled with the trappings of the occult: crystal balls, tambourines and trumpets, beeswax candles, or even a human skull. But it was as ordinary in appearance as my own—although it did contain more luggage. Chambers was well appointed when he traveled. I noted two large steamer trunks and three valises, in addition to two hatboxes: they must have tallied well in excess of the hundred pounds luggage permitted each passenger. A shaving case, pocket mirror and clothes brushes were neatly laid out on a shelf near the narrow cot that served as a bed. The room smelled of Brilliantine; an open jar of the stuff sat on the counter.

Chambers placed his kerchief-wrapped cards inside one of the smaller bags, then pulled something from the valise. He turned and presented me with a calling card. Printed on it, in small, neat letters, were his name and that of an organization: the Society for Psychical Research. The card was otherwise unadorned, and its reverse was blank.

"I've not heard of your organization before," I said to Chambers.

"That does not surprise me," he said with a smile. "Our society was formed just two years ago, in Cambridge, and our journal, while highly regarded, is not widely circulated in the Dominion— it's no wonder you are ignorant of it. Very few of our members have traveled to Canada, and I am the first to visit the North-West Territories."

"And what does your society do?" I asked. "Other than play 'parlour games' with cards, that is."

"We investigate the paranormal in all of its myriad forms, in a scientific manner, without prejudice or presupposition," said Chambers, as if reciting the society's mandate by rote. "Our members study mesmeric trance, apparitions, faith healing, spiritualistic phenomena, thought transference, automatic writing, communication with the dead, perceptions beyond the sensory organs, and premonitory warnings."

I glanced sharply at him, to see if he'd meant to imply anything by the last item on the list. I was starting to wonder whether this gentleman had heard about Q Division, and about my premonitory dreams and hunches. But his eyes were innocent of ingenuity. I yearned to ask him if he knew whether it was actually possible to heal by faith alone, but was already wary at the degree of attention he'd paid to my use of a painkiller. I didn't want any word of it to reach my superiors.

"You listed a number of topics that the society studies," I said. "Are there any among them that you yourself have special knowledge of?"

Chambers stroked his beard and gave me a coy expression. His eyes lingered momentarily on the bulge in my jacket pocket where the bottle of painkiller rested. "I know very little about faith healing, if that's what you're asking."

I quickly changed my angle of approach. "You mentioned something you called 'thought transference.' What is that?"

He took a deep breath, like a lecturer about to speak. Even though we were both standing, and both about the same height, I felt as if I were seated in an auditorium and looking up at him.

"Thought transference is the ability of one human being to communicate with another, by means of thought alone," Chambers said. "Whenever I travel, I amuse myself by testing the psychical abilities of the people I meet. I choose an individual at random and attempt to contact that person via thought transference. All human beings are capable of it, to a limited degree: simply focus your attention on someone long enough, and eventually he will sense it and turn his head. The more quickly and frequently a person responds, the greater his potential psychical ability. Later, when you were guessing at cards, I was using thought transference to send you the correct answers."

"How does it work?"

Chambers's eyes gleamed as he warmed to his subject. "Human beings exist both on the material plane and on the astral plane. You and I may have been silent as we sat at the card table, here in the physical world, but on the astral plane I was speaking the name and suit of the card—and you were listening."

"The astral plane?" I asked, confused. I'd not heard the term before.

Chambers rummaged in one of his bags. When he found what he was looking for—a slim pamphlet whose cover bore the name of the Society for Psychical Research—he passed it to me with a flourish. "This will tell you all about it."

I glanced down and saw that the pamphlet bore a mysterious title: "The Unseen World." It had been authored by Chambers himself—an etching of Chamber's face, bearing a scholarly expression, had been printed at the bottom of the pamphlet, under his name.

I'd grasped enough of what he'd said—even without reading the pamphlet—to spot an inconsistency. "Thought transference doesn't explain how I was able to predict the cards during the first round of guessing," I said. "The cards remained face down; you never looked at them until after I'd made my guess."

"You are quite correct," Chambers said, with the look of a teacher who is pleased that his student has asked the very question he was looking for. "You were instead using your astral body to look into the future and observe an event that had not yet occurred—the turning of a card—just as you did during the poker game. It's the hallmark of a true sensitive."

I frowned, not understanding the reference.

"People with psychical abilities," he continued, "are called 'sensitives' because they have heightened senses that extend into the astral plane. Because the astral body is not fettered in time and space as the physical body is, 'sensitives' can use their astral bodies to glimpse the future. Unfortunately, they most often do this in a random and uncontrolled manner: typically, while the physical body sleeps. And because these premonitions are jumbled together with the detritus of dreams, their warnings and signs are often misunderstood—and unheeded."

I listened to Chambers with rapt attention, the pamphlet he'd given me clutched tightly in my hand. In the space of a few short minutes, he'd explained a mystery that had consumed me all of my life: the source of my strange premonitions that guided me away from trouble—premonitions that saved my life on at least one occasion. I had spent my childhood enduring my father's dismissals of my hunches as mere "coincidence" and my mother's outright fear of them, and during my adulthood had tried my best to hide my oddity. Now, in the space of a few short days I had not only had my premonitions accepted at face value by my superiors in the North-West Mounted Police, but had also met a man who provided a scientific explanation for them. My sense of relief was overwhelming. I found myself telling Chambers a story I hadn't spoken of in years.

"The premonitions began when I was just ten years old," I said. "I can remember the first one very vividly. I had a dream in which my grandfather came to me, and told me that he had died in a carriage accident. He was so sad—not at his own death, but at the fact that his favourite mare had broken her leg and had to be shot.

"When my mother found me crying on the stairs and asked what was wrong, she told me it was just a bad dream and sent me back to bed. But when the telegram came from London two days later, with details of the death that matched what I had told her that evening, she was seized by fits of trembling. She was convinced that my dreams were the Devil's work, and begged my father to call the minister to pray with me. My father, who regarded religion in much the same light as he did premonitions, told her that she was being foolish and gave a dozen different reasons why my dream could be nothing more than coincidence.

"To appease my mother, I started attending church. I had hoped to convince her the Devil did not reside inside me, after all. Despite this effort, my mother never embraced me with quite the same affection that she had before. It was almost as if she expected me to predict her own death at any moment. She continued to look at me as fearfully as if I had become a ghost—not just seen one in my dreams.

"In the end, sneaking out of the house on Sundays to avoid my father's scorn for my newfound 'religious convictions' proved tiresome, and so I gave up on church. I didn't want to risk losing my father's affections as well."

Chambers nodded thoughtfully. "It is interesting that you should use the term ghost," he noted. "I would use the words 'astral body' instead. The astral body is immortal, and lingers on after death; it's what we see when we observe a 'ghost,' and thus astral body is the correct term to use. But do go on."

I wasn't really listening to Chambers. My thoughts had turned to something else entirely.

"I also foresaw my father's death, six years ago," I said quietly. "He didn't believe me that time, either."

I paused then, not yet trusting Chambers enough to tell him the rest of the story. The premonitory dream—of an enormous clock that suddenly stopped ticking and refused to start again, no matter how furiously I turned its key—had repeated itself every night for a week, causing me to awaken in a cold sweat. That same week, the pocket watch my father had given me for my tenth birthday began losing time. Every time it wound down and stopped, the hands were always in the same position as those on the clock in my dream: ten minutes before midnight.

I had assumed it was my own death that I was being warned of, since the dreams came in the week just prior to my operation. I thus said tearful goodbyes to both Mother, who barely stayed in the room long enough to listen, and to Father, who told me how foolish I was to put such stock in dreams.

At first it seemed that he was correct: I did not die in the operating theatre, although my heart faltered under the effects of the ether and actually stopped for several long seconds, giving the doctors a fright. Nor did I die in the days that followed.

On the fifth night after my operation, when I was already on the mend, my father died—at ten minutes before midnight. That was when I realized that the dream had been about his death and not my own—something I should have realized from the start, since my father was a watchmaker by profession.

I still wonder if there is anything I might have done to prevent his death. Perhaps if I had been able to view the future more precisely, I might have provided him some warning.

"Is it possible to control these premonitions, or to deliberately contact the spirits of the dead?" I asked Chambers.

He nodded slowly.

"Can you teach me how?"

"Perhaps—but it remains to be seen whether you have the intelligence and discipline that are required." He said it with a hint of superiority that suggested he had both in ample measure. "At least you have one of the necessary ingredients: the raw talent. I must say that your own story, while incomplete, is quite fascinating."

That brought me up short, like a horse whose reins have been pulled in. Why was I confiding these intimate details of my life to a total stranger? I gave Chambers a hard look, wondering for a fleeting moment if he was also a student of mesmerism.

There was one thing Chambers had yet to tell me. "What paranormal phenomena are you observing in the North-West Territories?" I asked.

"The same as yourself," he said, eyes twinkling. "The disappearance of the McDougall family—and the Manitou Stone."

I blinked in surprise. "You've... heard of it?"

"I've heard of many strange occurrences in the Dominion of Canada," he answered cryptically, "most of them originating on the prairie. That's why I came west. I intend to gather scientific evidence of paranormal activities in the North-West Territories for publication in our journal, and wish to speak to those who have witnessed them first-hand. When I heard that you would be conducting your own investigation at the Victoria Mission, I thought that we might combine forces and share whatever information we collect. I am quite an expert on the subject of the supernatural, and will no doubt be of the utmost assistance to you."

He leaned forward on his umbrella, eager for my reply.

"That will not be possible," I sputtered. The last thing I wanted was this arrogant know-it-all meddling in police business.

"But why not?" he cried.

"Any evidence I collect must remain confidential. If a crime has been committed—if the McDougalls have indeed been kidnapped or killed—there will be details that only those who committed the crime will know. To reveal them to the general public—and especially to have those details published in a journal—would seriously jeopardize any North-West Mounted Police investigation."

"But I have tools for investigating the paranormal that you do not," Chambers insisted. "In addition, any account I write would not be published for several months, until after my return to England. Finally, I could teach you to hone your own psychical powers. Surely those facts must sway your decision."

The yearning to know more about my talent warred with my policeman's oath. In the end, my sense of duty won out. "I'm sorry: no. This is a police matter."

Chambers suddenly tucked his umbrella under one arm and clapped his hands together. "Oh well done, Corporal!" he crowed. "You're everything I would expect in a Mounted Policeman. I look forward to working with you."

"Working with me?" I echoed, surprised by his audacity. "But I just told you that no civilian–"

"Indeed—but I am not a civilian." Chambers straightened, and touched the handle of his umbrella to his bowler hat in mock salute. "Special Constable Arthur Chambers, at your service, Corporal Grayburn."

I was dumbfounded. "You—a special constable?"

"Indeed. I was engaged for a term of service with your famous force while in Winnipeg on a lecture tour. The rate of pay offered was rather poor—just one dollar and twenty-five cents a day— but the work sounded interesting: to serve as a consultant for the creation of a special division within the North-West Mounted Police—a division whose investigations into the paranormal would parallel those of the Society for Psychical Research."

He reached into his jacket and pulled out a letter. I could see a bold signature at the bottom that I recognized at once: Sam Steele's.

Chambers continued: "When Sam wrote to me in Winnipeg, asking me to take passage up the North Saskatchewan into the wilds of the North-West Territories so that I could meet him, I readily agreed. How could I turn down an old friend, especially one so illustrious as Mr. Steele? Later, when he asked that I instead proceed upriver to rendezvous with you at Fort Pitt and provide whatever assistance I could with your investigation, I was delighted to have a chance to prove myself in the field. I do hope you don't mind my little subterfuge, but I thought that I should test my abilities as a plain-clothes agent."

I stood with my mouth open, surprise and irritation filling me in equal measure. I wasn't certain which to be more annoyed by: the realization that Chambers had duped me, or the fact that his salary as a special constable was more than my own rate of pay.

I realized belatedly that he was holding out his hand, expecting me to shake it. I said the only thing I could: "Welcome to the force, Special Constable Chambers."

◄—►

The steward came round to our cabins later that evening, letting us know that the riverboat would arrive at the Victoria Mission the next morning. I sat up until well past eleven o'clock, smoking my pipe and reading the pamphlet that Chambers had given me. Despite the raucous fiddle music that drifted up from the deck below through my open window, the pamphlet had my rapt attention. I devoured every word.

"The Unseen World" described, in much the same words Chambers had used, not only the astral plane that he'd told me about earlier, but also a world beyond that: the ethereal plane. This third plane of existence was the source of the forces essential to magic.

While all humans had a second "body" that existed on the astral plane, and while many people exhibited psychical abilities to a greater or lesser degree, apparently these talents could be used only for observation and not to affect the physical world. The astral plane was no more than a mirror—a reflection of both our own physical world and of the ethereal plane. It was the source of visions and premonitions, only.

For magic, something other than psychical talent was required: willpower.

Only those humans whose willpower was of exceptional strength could command the forces emanating from the ethereal plane, and by doing so, work magic. They did so by controlling the "etheric force" that flowed through all three planes of existence: ethereal, astral, and physical. This etheric force sounded like a kind of electrical current, invisible and undetectable by any scientific instrument. Its flow was thought to be influenced by features in the physical world, the most significant of which was the moon.

I paused then to consider what I had read. Without having heard the evidence of the supernatural that Steele had gathered, I might have dismissed Chambers's pamphlet as the work of a crank. The stuff about the astral body made sense to me, especially in light of my own experiences, but the part about spirits and magic sounded far-fetched.

Knocking the ashes out of my pipe, I looked out the window of my cabin. The moon had risen, and the half of it that was illuminated was a mass of craters. I noted how different the moon was, these days, from the one I recalled from my youth: it had none of the smooth, wide "seas" that I remembered seeing as a boy. After being struck by a comet in October of 1877, the moon had begun to turn its heavily cratered "dark side" toward the Earth. According to the astronomers' calculations, the moon would complete this rotation, exposing the full extent of its dark side to us by the spring of next year, and then would continue turning round, showing us its usual face in another seven and a half years.

As I stared at the cold, silent orb, I mused on the briefing that Superintendent Steele had given me. He'd been collecting evidence of the paranormal dating back to 1881—the year in which the barracks at Fort Macleod were washed away. Had magic blossomed in the world even before that?

I listened to the gears that drove the riverboat's paddlewheel, hearing them with a new ear. My father had always dismissed perpetual motion as a scientific impossibility. What if it was magic that had turned the "impossible" into the possible? I touched my troubled stomach gently. What other miracles might magic offer?

I finished reading the pamphlet. It was fascinating as a philosophical speculation but offered no practicalities of any sort; it was vague in the extreme when it came to the details of magic. It did not tell me what I most wanted to know: how magic actually worked. I wondered whether Chambers himself knew.

I felt a shudder run through the riverboat as it was nudged into shore, in preparation for being tied up for the night. Deciding at last to retire, I hung up my jacket and peeled off my boots and riding breeches. As I did so, I felt a lump in my pocket and drew from it the wad of bills and coin that were my winnings from the poker game. I'd forgotten all about them, but now an idea occurred to me. Four Finger Pete's wife had said that she needed medicine for a sick child, and obviously was in want of the money with which to purchase it. The traders at Victoria Mission were well stocked with medicines, and with the money I held in my hand she could easily buy whatever remedies her child required. Her own husband wouldn't give her the money— but I could.

I pulled my uniform back on, then sat and carefully counted the shinplasters. There were a good number of the twenty-five-cent bank notes: more than twenty dollars worth. I smoothed them out, then picked up the hymnbook that had been left in my room and tucked each note into a separate page of it. I would pass the hymnbook to the Peigan woman and instruct her to be sure to consult it for comfort this evening, adding a cryptic comment about "God's bounty" or some other clue as to its contents. With luck, her husband would not be peering over her shoulder when she did so.

I emerged from my cabin into the saloon, then passed out onto the promenade and found the stairs that led to the lower deck. As I descended them, a loud, rhythmic tapping noise assaulted my ears. The Metis that were playing their fiddles had been joined by others of their race, who were dancing. Their boots made loud clicking noises that carried above the sound of the perpetual engine, which was kept running even after it was disengaged from the paddlewheel for the evening. The dancers must have driven nails into their soles.

I passed the group, looking discreetly away as one of the Metis hid a bottle under his coat, and continued searching the lower deck for Four Finger Pete and his wife. Night had finally fallen, and it was difficult to distinguish between the crowd of Metis and half-breeds whose blankets filled the spaces between the cargo stowed on the lower deck, but at last I heard Four Finger Pete's gruff voice coming from behind a stack of crates. His voice was raised in a shout that easily carried over the volume of noise that filled the lower deck—and over the sound of a young child crying.

"Shut that brat up so I can get some sleep," he bellowed. I knew instantly that the words must be directed at his wife. "You make her be quiet, or I will."

A woman's voice replied, speaking what sounded like a mixture of some Indian language and English. The voice was too low for me to make out the words. Then I heard a sharp crack, like a hand striking flesh. I pictured the gambler striking his wife across the face as he had earlier, and suddenly saw red. I decided then and there to carry through on my previous threat, and teach the brute a lesson. I unsnapped the flap that held my revolver in its holster, just in case it was required, and picked up my pace.

I heard a scuffling noise as I approached the stack of crates. The child's wail suddenly choked off.

"There!" Four Finger Pete cried. "That's shut her up."

"You there!" I said briskly as I rounded the crates. "Stop that at–"

The explosion of a gun going off boomed in my ears. In the flash of light that accompanied it, I saw Four Finger Pete's wife holding a child in one hand and a short-barrelled pocket revolver in the other. The gambler's hands were locked around the child's blanket, which looked as though it had come loose in a struggle, but now his hands fell to his sides. The reason was immediately clear: more than half of Four Finger Pete's face was missing. The bullet had torn his jaw clean away. As the body fell to the ground, leaking blood, I saw that the gambler's holster was empty.

Four Finger Pete's wife spun to face me, a wild expression in her eye. I thought for a moment that her husband's blood had splattered her, then saw that her nose was swollen and leaking blood. The hand that held the revolver was still raised; smoke drifted from the gun's barrel. As our eyes met, my mind registered the fact that the fiddle playing and tapping of the dancers had stopped. The only sound was the steady gurgle of the perpetual engine.

I stared at the woman, wondering for a heart-pounding moment if she was about to shoot me as well. The Indians have a morbid fear of hanging, and one who has committed murder will do anything to avoid being taken into custody by a member of the police. I wondered if I could draw my own revolver in time— and if I'd have it in me to shoot so pitiful a figure as the woman who stood in front of me. When that pistol in her hands had gone off, sending Four Finger Pete to meet his maker, I had seen in an instant that she had only been defending her child from its lout of a father. I couldn't help but marvel at the bravery of this meek and downtrodden member the weaker sex—although it shouldn't have surprised me. I have heard tales of women running into conflagrations, or attacking wolves with their bare hands, when the lives of their children were at stake.

As if suddenly realizing that she held a gun in her hands, the Peigan woman dropped the revolver. It thudded into the expanding pool of blood at her feet. In that same instant, she rushed forward and pressed her face into my chest. The child in her arms let out a small whimper, but otherwise remained still. It didn't appear to be injured—it must have been weak with fever.

My reaction was instinctive: I put my arm around the woman to comfort her. She stood no taller than my chin, and I could smell the scent of her hair as she sobbed against my chest. I am embarrassed to admit it now, but I had a reaction to her then that was purely sensual, as I felt the press of her soft body against my own and stroked her hair. It seemed, in that moment, not to matter a jot that she had just shot her husband, and that a child was cradled in her arms. A very sick child: even through the fabric of my jacket, I could feel the heat of the child's fever.

I heard the sound of running footsteps, and pulled gently away from the Peigan woman as the other passengers on the lower deck ran to where we stood. I could feel that my face was flushed, and was glad that darkness hid it.

The Metis and half-breeds exclaimed in alarm as they saw Four Finger Pete's lifeless body.

"*Mon dieu!*" one exclaimed. "Murder!"

"His wife 'ave shot 'im," another guessed.

"If she committed murder in front of a police officer," another added, "she will surely hang."

"*Non*," said the first. "See how he regards her. He cares for her."

I turned to face the crowd. "I saw the entire incident. It was self-defense. This man—" I gestured at the body "—struck his wife and child repeatedly, then drew his revolver in a rage, with murder in mind. In the resulting struggle, the revolver discharged, and a bullet struck him. His death is not a murder, merely an unfortunate accident, brought about by his own hand."

The passengers muttered. Despite the weight my uniform lent my words, they obviously didn't believe me—not fully. The Metis were a suspicious lot, especially now that their leaders were urging them to open rebellion. They had no love of the police.

Then Chambers stepped forward out of the darkness. "I saw it as well," he said. "The gambler drew his weapon and tried to kill his wife. It would be this innocent woman who lay dead before us if this brave officer of the law had not intervened."

I turned, surprised, and nodded my thanks. Chambers touched the silver handle of his umbrella to his hat in acknowledgment.

The murmurs of the passengers had changed in tone. They nodded, staring now at the body with the same look that jurors will give a condemned man.

"Will one of you please fetch the captain?" I asked. "And the rest of you, please move on. There's nothing more to see here." I leaned down and grabbed a blanket that had already become soaked with blood and flipped it over the body, covering the gruesome remains.

Reluctantly, murmuring to each other and casting looks back over their shoulders, the crowd obeyed. Chambers shooed the last of them away, then vanished into the gloom himself.

The child began to cry again. Four Finger Pete's wife adjusted its blankets, jiggling it gently in her arms and speaking softly to it in Peigan. Wiping away the blood that had finally stopped flowing from her nose, she pressed a cheek against the child's brow to check its fever.

Suddenly realizing that I still held the hymnbook, I handed it to her. She at first shook her head, refusing it, but accepted it when I opened it a little to show her the bank notes inside.

"For medicine," I said, choosing simple words that a woman with only limited English would understand. "For your child."

Her dark eyes widened, then filled with tears. Embarrassed, I looked at the child in her arms instead. It was too dark to see much, but I could tell that the child was a girl, about a year old, with her mother's Indian features and her father's pale blonde hair. The child's eyes were mere gleams in the darkness as she stared silently up at me. Strange though it might seem, I had the feeling those eyes were taking my measure, as an adult's might do.

I tore my gaze away from the child. "Don't worry—I'm not going to arrest you," I told Four Finger Pete's wife. "It's bad enough that your child has lost her father. I don't want to cause her to be bereft of a mother, as well."

She shook her head. "Pete not her father."

"Oh," I said. "I see."

Some other man had fathered the child, then—which could very well have been the reason why Four Finger Pete treated his wife so unkindly, and cared so little for the girl's welfare. I shook my head sadly. Despite his wife's infidelity, it was no excuse for brutality.

The captain arrived then, tousled as if roused from sleep, and I was kept busy explaining what had happened and discussing what would be done with the body of Four Finger Pete when we arrived at our destination the next morning. The gambler's wife shook her head mutely when we asked if Four Finger Pete had any next of kin; I supposed it would be up to the traders at Victoria Mission to bury him, now that Reverend McDougall was missing and there was no one to conduct a Christian burial.

Once that was decided, it was time for me to write a report: not to Q Division, since there was clearly nothing paranormal about the shooting of a husband by his wife, but a regular police report of an accidental death. Before I retired to my cabin to set pencil to paper, however, I made sure that the version of the incident told by Four Finger Pete's wife—whose name, I only learned now, was Emily—would match my own. I repeated for her what I had told the other passengers: that Four Finger Pete had drawn his weapon, and that it had accidentally discharged.

When I was done, she stared solemnly at me. "Thank you," she said. "I say that. And I also say this: you good man. Do not stay this land. Do not stay here, or when Day of Changes comes, you will be made go."

I stared at her, wondering if I had understood what she had just said. She spoke only broken English, and I did not speak enough Peigan to ask her what she'd meant. Nevertheless I thanked her before proceeding to my cabin.

It never occurred to me to ask who the child's father was, but I doubted that Emily would have had the nerve to seek the affections of another man while her husband was still alive. I guessed that she must instead have been ill-used by Four

Finger Pete, perhaps given over for the night to one of the men he'd lost a hand of poker to, or prostituted to a trader in exchange for whisky.

Later, I would come to realize how wrong my guess had been.

—

Chapter III

The *North West* reached Victoria Mission early the next morning.
First ashore were two of the riverboat men, carrying the body of
Four Finger Pete. As they descended the creaking gangplank, a
white bird that had been sitting among the reeds along the shore
startled and winged its way into the air. The men carrying the
body made their way up the bank toward the settlement, sweating
in the hot sun. They were followed by a crowd of spectators, old
and young: the dozen or so settlers who lived near enough to
Victoria Mission to meet the riverboat, and a handful of traders
from the fort, on hand to take delivery of the crates of tea, flour
and salt pork that filled the *North West*'s lower deck.

Four Finger Pete's wife followed the canvas-wrapped corpse
ashore, carrying her daughter, who was bundled in a blanket.
The Peigan woman's nose was swollen, and there was a purple
bruise on one side of her face, but her eyes were free of tears.
While the riverboat men made their way to the settlement itself,
followed by the curious crowd, she turned and headed in the
direction of the trading post. I presumed that she would buy the
medicines she needed for her child first, and then attend to her
husband's burial after that. I planned to visit the trading post
later myself, to see if the traders had any decent tobacco in
stock.

Just before Emily disappeared into the trees, she turned and
looked directly at me, as if I had called out her name. My breath
caught in my throat: I wondered if thought transference was at
work.

I lifted my haversack and strode down the gangplank,
glancing back with amusement as Chambers oversaw the

unloading of his steamer trunks, valises and boxes from his cabin. Just as he had each day of our river voyage, he had changed into a fresh suit of clothing: today it was a Norfolk jacket in brown serge, matching trousers, and boots with button gaiters. He'd replaced his black derby with a brown one; the black band around it matched his black silk tie. I wondered if he'd chosen the jacket because its cut matched that of the red serge jacket that I wore.

"Go on ahead," he called out to me. "I'll catch you up in a moment."

I smiled and waved back at him. I had every intention of doing just that. Even though Chambers had backed me up by attesting to my version of what had happened the night before, he was a civilian. He might be knowledgeable about psychical phenomena, but I was the expert on physical evidence. I didn't want him mucking up what little of it might remain here.

The riverbank at Victoria Mission was heavily treed, with a trail leading up to the half-dozen homes that made up the settlement. The Methodist church was easy to find; I simply followed the two riverboat men at a discreet distance as they carried the body of Four Finger Pete up to a tiny graveyard that had been hewn from the forest. I waited while they set the body down, watched them speak to the crowd and point at the ground, and saw the settlers suddenly disperse. I guessed that the riverboat men had asked for volunteers to bury the body and had found none.

I continued down the trail to the church itself. With a peaked roof, it was a one-story rectangular building made from square-cut logs that had been chinked with mud and whitewashed. Although it was a Sunday, the church doors were closed and the building was silent; the Methodists had yet to send another minister to replace McDougall.

I circled around the depression in the soil where the Manitou Stone had stood. It was a squarish patch of bare soil, dry and dusty, with a fringe of grass around the perimeter. The sides of the hole had not been disturbed, leading me to conclude that the Manitou Stone had not been dragged away; it must have been lifted straight up. Yet there were no adjacent tree branches to which a block and tackle could be attached. I wondered how the stone had been carried away; from Steele's report, I understood it to weigh close to four hundred pounds.

The door of the church was not locked, so I opened it and stepped inside. Three wooden pews provided seating for about twenty people; I set my haversack down on one of them so I could wander about unimpeded. At the front of the church was a raised platform, on which sat a preacher's pulpit. A stack of leather-bound hymn and prayer books lay on a shelf to one side of the platform. The shelf was dusty, but the books were not, suggesting that they had been restacked there recently. Several of the covers were badly stained, as if the books had been thrown in the mud.

On the other side of the platform stood a melodeon. The small organ had a stool behind it; lying on the floor next to it was a book of *Gospel Hymns Consolidated* that had fallen from the melodeon's music rack, and some splinters of wood.

I saw the reason for the wood splinters immediately: the melodeon had several deep gouges in it, as if someone had chopped it with an axe. A number of the keys were missing, and several of those that remained were stuck in the down position. I could see a chip of stone wedged between two of the keys, and concluded that an Indian tomahawk must have wrought the destruction.

I placed a hand upon the silent keyboard, my fingers falling naturally into a C Major chord. During the year that I had attended church in an effort to appease my mother, I had been taught the rudiments of the instrument by the minister's wife. I could still remember the shiver of excitement I'd felt when the church's massive organ filled the air with strident music as my fingers struck the keys. It was no wonder the Indians feared organ music with such superstitious dread.

I picked up the music book and leafed through it, noting the strange squiggles that someone had penciled in under the words to several of the hymns. I couldn't read the script myself, but knew it was an "alphabet" that served to render the Cree language into written form. Translating the hymns must have been a laborious task; I could see that the McDougalls had put a good deal of work into their efforts to convert the local Indians.

The McDougalls had come to this spot to minister to the Cree in the early 1860s, more than a decade before the riverboats began their service. Back then, they had been the only white people in the area, and the annual trip east to Fort Garry and back for supplies had taken four long months. John McDougall had been just 21 years old then—just a year younger than I had been when I joined the North-West Mounted Police. Like me, he had left Ontario to embark upon a new life in the Territories while still in his early twenties. Unlike me, he had done it in the company of his family, and under his own name.

Although McDougall was said to be popular among the Indians and had helped to convince them to sign Treaties Six and Seven, he had never returned their Manitou Stone. It had sat in the front yard of this church, a constant thorn in the side of the Cree who passed it on their way into the place of worship. Given the attacks on the melodeon and prayer books, I doubted whether the Indians' embracing of Christianity had been more than superficial. The thought brought a wry smile to my lips; just as I had done as a boy, they had briefly donned religion like a cloak, then cast it off again.

I wondered whether Reverend McDougall was still alive, perhaps held captive in an Indian camp with his wife and six children, and whether he was preaching to the Indians this day, which was a Sunday, but it didn't seem likely that the McDougalls still lived. Patrols had visited every reserve and Indian camp in the area, but reported no trace of the family.

The dark and silent church had yielded up few clues. I scooped up my haversack and walked back out into the heat and sunshine, and saw that the riverboat men had abandoned Four Finger Pete's body in the tiny graveyard. I wiped perspiration from my brow; it was already a warm morning and the heat was just going to get worse. I wondered who would be coerced into burying the corpse in this weather. I hoped the chore wouldn't fall to me; I didn't relish the thought of being the one to lay to rest a man whose killer I had let go free. If, as Chambers said, our astral bodies really did continue to exist after death in an unseen world that was a shadow of our own, the ghost of Four Finger Pete might be watching me even now.

I heard movement among the trees that bordered the graveyard, and for a moment imagined a vengeful ghost lurking there. Instead, I saw Chambers picking his way carefully through the bushes and grimacing each time one of them brushed against his coat. He flicked away a twig that had caught on his jacket, then looked up and noticed me. Immediately he clasped his hands behind his back and began walking briskly back and forth through the graveyard, studying the markers there. As I approached, he bent down to take a closer look at one of the gravestones. As he stood again, I heard him muttering under his breath: "Just a sister," and, "No, not close enough."

"Chambers," I said as I walked toward him, making a wide circle around Four Finger Pete's canvas-wrapped corpse. "I have a question for you. Can a ghost have any effect on the physical world?"

Chambers squatted in front of another grave marker and shook his head, not bothering to look up from the white marble tombstone he was reading. "No," he said. "Ghosts pass through solid objects—even people—as if they were not there."

That offered me some relief, although I didn't like the reference to ghosts passing through people. I noticed that Chambers had used the same word I had: ghost—and had not "corrected" it to astral body this time. Nor had he answered in his usual longwinded, lecturing manner. He was obviously very intent upon the grave marker—but not so intent that he knelt directly upon the ground. Instead of dirtying his trouser knees, he squatted in a precarious position, reading the words that had been engraved at the bottom of the slab of white stone.

I stepped around to the front of the tombstone, curious to see what had arrested his attention so. The grave was that of a woman: Abigail McDougall, who had died on April 11, 1871, at the age of 23. Below this information, in flowing script, were the words "Blessed are the dead who die in the Lord."

Chambers laid his hand on top of the stone and stared off into space at a point somewhere beyond me. I glanced nervously in that direction, wondering if he'd seen Four Finger Pete's ghost, but saw only the church, sitting in its clearing among the trees. There weren't any unusual cloud formations overhead; the sky was a clear, solid blue. When I looked back at Chambers, his eyes were closed.

"What are you doing?" I asked. Without realizing I was doing so, I had dropped my voice to a whisper.

Chambers's eyes opened. "Trying to contact John McDougall's wife. Please—be silent."

"Do you think she's dead?"

Chambers looked at me as if I was an idiot. "Of course she is," he said. He patted the tombstone. "This is her grave."

He must have noticed my confused look, for he elaborated: "Abigail was John McDougall's first wife—an Indian woman. Her father was an Ojibway, but also a Methodist minister. Even though McDougall remarried a year after Abigail's death, there's a good chance she's watching over her husband still. She may be able to tell me where he is."

I was surprised and annoyed that Chambers's briefing appeared to have been more thorough than my own. I hadn't known that McDougall had married twice.

"The dead can see the living?" I asked. Again my thoughts were drawn to Four Finger Pete. I wondered, too, if my father were watching over me now, and what he would think of the strange direction my career with the North-West Mounted Police had taken. Here I was, standing with a psychic investigator in a graveyard, watching as he prepared to begin a conversation with a ghost.

"Please do be quiet," Chambers said. "I need complete silence to concentrate."

His eyes closed. I couldn't resist one last remark, if only to take a verbal jab at him. "So you're a medium, then? Have you spoken with the departed before?"

"I am a student of thought transference," Chambers hissed back. "And I'm trying to put it to work now, to contact Abigail McDougall on the astral plane. I'd like to establish contact before anyone from the settlement comes to disturb us, so please do go on about your job and let me do mine."

My eyes narrowed. I was a corporal, and he merely a special constable—a civilian, temporarily contracted by Q Division. I was half of a mind to tell Chambers to go to the devil, but he'd spoken earlier as if Superintendent Steele was a personal friend of his. I didn't know whether that was true, and I liked to believe that the Superintendent was above taking sides with a man who was in genuine need of being taken down a peg or two, but I didn't want to take any chances.

I left Chambers to his tombstone and walked down the forested trail that led to the McDougall residence. When I was about half way down the trail, I spotted Four Finger Pete's wife, Emily, making her way through the woods with her daughter in her arms. She was walking slowly, looking around her as if lost.

In the light of day, I was struck by the colour of the child's hair—which was almost white—and the pallor of her skin, which was lighter than my own. The blanket in which the girl was wrapped had slipped down, and I saw her face in daylight for the first time. She had Indian features and wore a buckskin dress and beaded moccasins like her mother, but her eyes were a pale pink. That was when I realized that the child was an albino.

I suddenly remembered the briefing Steele had given me, back in Regina. When listing the magical phenomena that had been reported in the North-West Territories, he'd mentioned an Indian woman who gave birth to a blonde-haired child: a stillborn infant who had been raised from the dead. Had that tearful mother been Emily, and was this the resurrected child in her arms? It seemed too much of a coincidence to be true.

I hurried toward the pair. As I approached, Emily wrapped the blanket around her daughter, but not before I had noted the child's fever-flushed cheeks, sweat-damp hair, and utterly listless appearance. The infant lay limp in her mother's arms, only occasionally stirring or whimpering in a soft voice. Emily rocked her and said something soothing in Peigan.

I paused, wondering how I could broach the indelicate subject of childbirth with a woman. "Your daughter looks like a fragile child. Has she always been that way—since the day she was born?"

Emily looked up at me with a strange expression on her face. I saw the same combination of fear and determination on her countenance that I had seen the previous evening, after she had shot her husband.

"I hope you were able to purchase some medicine from the traders," I continued. "A good patent medicine should set your child on the road to recovery—although I expect you'll also want to combine it with your own remedies. I understand that Indians have many powerful medicines. I'd like to learn more about them, some day."

Emily's response was noncommittal. "White man medicine good. Birth hard, but white man medicine save me." She glanced around the woods with a distant look in her eye, tilting her head as if she was listening for something.

"Yes, but what about Indian medicine? I hear there are Indian women who can effect miraculous cures."

I watched her keenly for a reaction, but didn't see one. Either Emily hadn't understood what I had said or she really wasn't the woman whose child had been raised from the dead. My hopes of being introduced to an Indian medicine woman faded.

"I couldn't help but notice the colour of your daughter's hair and skin," I added. "Albino children must be quite unusual among your race."

Emily tucked the blanket more tightly around her child and her face grew guarded. I realized then that she might think that I found her child freakish. Indeed, that was not the case. The girl might be pale as straw, but her features had the same delicate beauty as her mother's did. I cast about for something else to say.

"Is she feeling any better?"

Emily nodded. "She be well soon. Medicine come soon."

I assumed that meant she would be purchasing medicine from the traders, after all.

Emily's daughter whimpered and reached a soft pink hand out of the blanket. Instinctively, I stuck out a forefinger and let her grip it. The child's palm was hot and moist with sweat.

Emily stared at me, her brown eyes pleading for me to let her be on her way. Her face still bore the marks of the beating Four Finger Pete had inflicted upon her. If she'd been my wife, I'd have given her anything she wanted—not used rude fists to bruise such a lovely face. I suddenly noticed how close Emily was to me, and how warm the day had become.

"Your girl is a dear little child," I said, withdrawing my finger. "What's her name?"

"Iniskim."

It must have been a Peigan word; Emily, it seemed, had given her daughter an Indian name. I noticed that she was trying to keep her daughter's face covered by the blanket, and that my proximity was disturbing her. I decided to give this beautiful, tragic woman no further discomfort by dwelling on the subject of her daughter. I instead decided to be helpful.

"Are you looking for the graveyard?" I asked. I pointed down the trail. "Your husband's body is just over there. They should be laying him to rest presently."

Emily nodded and murmured something in Peigan that might have been a thank you. I watched as she hurried away down the trail toward the graveyard with graceful steps. As she did, she began singing to her child. The song was a simple chant of the kind the Indians favour, and was presumably a comforting lullaby, yet hearing it sent a cold shiver down my spine.

I wondered what would become of the woman and her child. I supposed she would return to her tribe, now that her white husband was dead. I watched her a moment longer, and toyed with the idea of going after her—although to what end I could not say. Reluctantly, I turned away.

I continued along the trail to the McDougall house, which proved to be a simple two-story structure, built of the same squared-off logs as the church, with a stovepipe emerging through the roof. Like the church, it was deserted. As I stepped up onto the porch I heard an unusual chirping sound, and paused to listen to it. The morning was too far advanced for birds to be singing, and evening was too far off for the chirping of crickets. The noise was muffled, as if the creature making it was inside a hollow tree trunk. I listened for a moment, but before I could identify it as belonging to either bird or cricket, the sound stopped.

I pulled my report book and a pencil out of my haversack in order to make notes. Then I pushed open the front door of the house.

I could see immediately why Corporal Cowan had reported signs of a struggle. The kitchen in which I stood looked as if a whirlwind had struck it: tables and chairs were smashed to splinters, broken crockery was strewn across the floor, and one window was broken with its curtains torn. Flies buzzed around mouldy lumps on the stove and floor, and the smell of spoiled food filled the air. Unlike the church, the McDougalls' home hadn't been cleaned up.

I took a good look around the kitchen, the back room, and the two upstairs bedrooms. The destruction was concentrated on the main floor; upstairs, everything looked peaceful, as though the family had just gotten out of bed. On one side of a curtain that divided the upper floor into two bedrooms was a double bed with nightclothes neatly folded upon it; on the other were two rumpled double beds that had been pushed together. A child's rag doll lay on one of the pillows, and a washbasin still held soap and a whitish crust from the evaporated water. A wardrobe on the parents' side was filled with neatly folded clothes, and none of the children's possessions had been disturbed.

Downstairs, the cupboards were still filled with sacks of flour, tea, and salt—even a bottle of spirits. It didn't look as though anyone had looted the place—which was in keeping with the Indians' strange sense of right and wrong: they would happily steal a horse, but would refuse to take food from a larder, even when hungry.

Giving the main floor one last scrutiny, I found no evidence of spilled blood, bullet holes, or spent cartridges. There were gouges aplenty in the walls, table and lower stairs, but they didn't look like the tomahawk slashes I'd found on the melodeon. They looked more like scrape marks than axe chops.

I also noted in my report book that several scraps of clothing of different sizes were scattered about; it almost looked as though they had been torn off the persons wearing them, yet none were bloody. I also noticed two other oddities: a large dent in the thick metal of the cast-iron stove, and a peculiar puncture in the wall next to the front door. The hole was as wide as the circle one can make with thumb and forefinger, and quite deep—too large to have been made by a bullet. When I stuck a finger in to feel its shape, my finger went all the way in.

Slipping my report book back into my pocket, I decided to smoke and think. I took the pipe out of its case, screwed mouthpiece into bowl, and filled the bowl with tobacco. I lit it with a Lucifer match and took several quick draws, coaxing the tobacco into a cherry-red glow.

"'Allo in there!" said a man's voice from outside. "Are you Corporal Grayburn of the Nor' Wes' Mounted Police?"

I stepped out through the front door onto the covered porch and saw a young man standing at the edge of the clearing that surrounded the house. He was a strapping lad in his late teens, with long dark hair and a face and hands tanned by the sun. He wore a workman's shirt, trousers, and moccasins, and his waist was wrapped with one of the bright red sashes that the Metis use to carry loads while portaging. I didn't recognize him as a riverboat passenger; I guessed that he must be one of the traders from the fort. He held a piece of paper in one hand.

"I 'ave a telegram *pour vous*," he said.

I beckoned the lad forward. He was at least thirty feet away, but even at that distance I could see his eyes widen. "Oh *non!*" he exclaimed, making the sign of the cross upon his breast with his free hand. "I dare not, or I will vanish like the others. *Monsieur* must come 'ere, instead."

I sighed in exasperation. I'd just proven him wrong by walking into the house and emerging unscathed, but Metis superstitions run deep. "You can see with your own eyes that there's no danger," I scolded, pointing at the house behind me with my pipe stem. "Bring me the telegram at–"

It was no use. Instead of doing as I had bid him, the fellow bent down and placed the piece of paper he held on the ground. He tarried only long enough to place a rock on it as a paperweight, then fled into the woods.

I shook my head, understanding now why the McDougall house hadn't been disturbed. The locals obviously held it in superstitious dread.

I strode out to the edge of the woods and picked up the telegram. It was from Superintendent Steele, and, like him, was brisk and to the point:

> CASES SIMILAR TO J. M. CASE REPORTED ACROSS NWT: SETTLERS NEAR BROADVIEW, WOOD MOUNTAIN & BATTLEFORD; CPR ROAD CREW AT TRACK'S END NEAR CALGARY; PASSENGERS & CREW ON FERRY AT CLARKE'S CROSSING, & 4 MEN & 1 SGT. FROM MAPLE CREEK DETACHMENT WHILE ON PATROL ALONG INTERNATIONAL BOUNDARY LINE. REPORT YOUR PROGRESS AT ONCE.

I stared at the telegram, the pipe in my hand forgotten. Steele's message was cryptic, since he'd sent it by telegraph via a civilian operator, but I knew instantly what it meant. People were disappearing from widely scattered locations all over the prairie. Even our own North-West Mounted Police, it seemed, were not immune. Both Steele and I had assumed that the McDougalls' disappearance was a single, isolated case, but apparently it was not.

I wondered if anyone I knew was among the men who had gone missing from my former detachment. I'd kept my own company while I was stationed there, but there were among the detachment men whom I respected and liked.

The telegram, according to the date and time recorded by the operator, had arrived in Victoria Mission less than an hour ago. Steele obviously wanted answers, and as quickly as possible, yet I had very little to tell him. The Manitou Stone was indeed gone, as were the McDougalls. Beyond that, I could shed no more light on the case. I folded the telegram and tucked it inside my shirt pocket.

As I contemplated the disappearances, I wondered if the missing men were dead or alive. I was glad that, were I to die in some isolated spot on the prairie, I wouldn't be dumped ingloriously in the nearest graveyard like Four Finger Pete. As a member of the North-West Mounted Police, I was ensured a proper burial.

A shiver ran down my spine then. How morbid my thoughts had become! Deliberately tearing my musings away from the grim prospect of my impending death, I instead pondered what response to give to the telegram. As I stood sucking on the stem of my extinguished pipe, I heard the chirping noise again. With so many questions crowding my mind, I was at first inclined to ignore it, but my intuition told me not to. So strong was the feeling, I tucked my pipe into my pocket, not even stopping to clean it and pack it away in its case.

This time, I could tell where the chirping noise was coming from: a tree a short distance from the house. As I walked closer to the tree, I saw a peculiar object wedged in a hollow in the trunk. Then the noise stopped. For a moment I wondered if I'd merely imagined it. I used a stick to pry the object free, and it fell to the ground. I heard the strange chirping noise again— once, softly—and I instinctively reached down to pick the object up, cradling it in my hand as carefully as a fledgling bird.

The thing was an amulet of some sort: a ball of leather not quite big enough to fill my hand, strung on a leather thong meant to go about the neck. Half a dozen mottled brown feathers had been stitched to the bottom of the ball and hung from it like a fringe. I could hear the chirping noise again; it seemed to be coming from inside the ball, which was made from a thin strip of leather that had been wrapped around and around some object.

My curiosity piqued, I peeled back one end of the leather and began unwrapping it. As I unveiled the object that lay within, the chirping noise stopped.

The ball didn't contain an insect, as I had suspected. Instead it contained a strangely shaped stone.

I'd never seen anything like it. Definitely stone—it was hard and heavy—the object curved in on itself like a snail shell. The spiral was ridged, and the stone of which it was formed had a shiny surface like the inside of an oyster shell, but yellowish-green. As I held it in my hand the stone gave one last chirp—a loud, strident sound, unmuffled by leather—then fell silent. No amount of jiggling it back and forth on my palm could get it to make the noise again.

I had no idea what the stone was or what it signified, but I had a hunch that it was somehow connected with the McDougalls' disappearance. And my hunches were rarely wrong.

I heard a crashing noise in the woods and turned to see Chambers running toward me. When he reached me, he was quite out of breath.

"I've found it!" he cried. "The McDougall grave."

I misunderstood, at first. "Another one?" I asked. "Which McDougall is it this time? Don't tell me there's another wife buried in that graveyard."

"No!" Chambers said. "Not an old grave: a new one. There's freshly turned earth, down by the riverbank."

I shoved the oddly shaped stone and its leather wrappings inside my trouser pocket, next to my pouch of tobacco. "Show me."

I followed Chambers through the woods for some distance. We headed upriver and at last came to a spot where the river had cut a steep bank before shifting its course. We clambered down onto a gravel bar, and Chambers pointed at what looked like a cave in the bluff, an opening as large as a livery stable door. It looked as though someone had been digging inside the cave; a scattering of dark black soil had been thrown out across the gravel bar for some distance.

"I was able to make contact with Abigail McDougall on the astral plane," Chambers said excitedly. "She came to me as the sound of a woman singing. I asked her to show me where her husband was, and the singing led me to this spot. I'm certain the bodies lie just inside that cave. All you have to do is walk in and dig them up, and the case is solved. What an amazing journal entry this will make!"

I didn't share Chambers's certainty. He'd probably heard Emily singing to her daughter, and then stumbled across the cave by accident as he tried to locate the source of the sound. Corporal Cowan's report had made no mention of a cave—had the McDougalls been killed and buried here, surely our scout Jerry Potts would have been able to follow the tracks of their killers to this spot.

There was something ominous about that hole, however: I fancied I could feel a chill breeze sighing out of it, even though I stood a good twenty feet away. The trees on the bank above the cave seemed suddenly filled with shifting shadows, and the gurgle of the river behind me reminded me of the blood that had bubbled out of Four Finger Pete's body after he was shot. As I stared at the cave, the sun on my back utterly failing to warm me, I had a strange dread of entering that dark passage. The feeling was nearly as strong as the premonition I'd had on the day George Johnston had gone up the trail and been killed in my place, but it was different, somehow. I wasn't certain I would die if I entered that cave, but I had the feeling that I wouldn't come back if I did—which made no sense to me whatsoever.

Chambers stared at me, hands on his hips. "By Jove," he said in a bemused voice. "Don't tell me you're too squeamish to dig up a month-old body. I'd expected a North-West Mounted Police officer to be made of sterner stuff!"

I wheeled on him, and glared him down. "I'm no coward," I gritted at him. Ignoring the warning bells that were ringing in my mind, I strode closer to the cave, then knelt to examine one of the clods of earth that lay just outside its entrance. The soil felt moist and cool.

Chambers watched me, bouncing slightly on the balls of his feet like a racehorse anxious to begin its run.

"This is freshly turned earth," I told him. "If the McDougalls' bodies were concealed here a full month ago, these clods should either have dried up, or been melted away by the rain."

Despite my assertions of bravery, Chambers must have thought I was making excuses—either that, or his excitement got the better of him. "Very well, then—I'll do the job myself. I was the one who solved the mystery, anyway. I really can't see why you policemen were so baffled by it."

I jumped up and tried to catch Chambers's arm as he strode into the cave mouth, but he was too quick for me. I started to go after him, but suddenly found myself rooted to the spot by an overwhelming dread. Gritting my teeth, I found myself questioning my own manhood. *Was* I a coward? No, I told myself sternly. I was simply heeding a warning voice—one that the impetuous Chambers refused to hear. The same warning voice that had saved me from an Indian bullet, all those years ago.

Sweat trickled down my temples as my sense of duty warred with my premonition of danger. Inside the cavern, I heard Chambers say: "Oh! Isn't *that* curious." I could hear him moving about inside—he didn't seem to be in any danger. I could still hear his footsteps over the soft gurgle of the river behind me.

No—not birds. The curious stone I'd collected was once again chirping softly. I thrust my hand into my pocket and drew it out, but as soon as I did, the noise stopped. I stared at the stone as it lay on my palm. I'd half expected to see some strange transformation, but the stone was just a stone, as silent as any of those I stood upon. I shoved it back into my pocket.

My tobacco pouch had fallen from my pocket. I picked it up, then pulled out my pipe and refilled it with a fresh pinch of Imperial Mixture. It took two matches to light the pipe, but after a puff or two my hands became steadier.

"Chambers?" I called out. "Have you found anything?"

A distant voice replied: "Not yet. The cave goes quite a way in."

I waited a moment more.

"Chambers?"

I thought I heard a muffled reply, but couldn't be certain. I stepped closer to the cave mouth, shivering as I did so.

"Chambers?"

As I came to the very mouth of the cave, I fancied I could hear a curious rumbling sound inside it. The noise was almost like that of falling water, and I wondered if a stream lay within the gloomy depths of the cave. The angle of the bank overhead screened the interior of the cave from the sun; I could see no more than a few feet inside, to a point where the cavern—which had more of the appearance of a mine tunnel than of a natural cave—curved around a bend.

"Chambers!" I shouted into its depths. "Can you hear me? Come out of there at once!"

I puffed nervously on my pipe. Something had happened to Chambers; the feeling was growing upon me by the minute. Was he lying somewhere inside the cave even now, injured and unable to call out?

I felt a pang of shame. I, a police officer sworn to his duty, had done nothing to stop Chambers from entering a place of potential danger. I let him go into the cave alone, just as I had let poor George Johnston ride away up the trail to his death. I must say I didn't like Chambers much, but dislike should never stand in the way of a policeman doing his duty.

My mind was made up: I was going inside, even if my doom lay within. First, however, I pulled out my police report book and tore out a fresh page. I quickly noted the date and time, and recorded a description of the curious stone I had found, my meeting with Emily, my conversation with Chambers in the graveyard and his claims that he had followed Abigail McDougall's ghost to this spot, and my impressions of the cave. Then I folded it and wrote upon the top in block letters:

TO THE FINDER OF THIS LETTER. PLEASE CONVEY
IT WITH ALL DUE HASTE TO SUPT. S. STEELE, NWMP
HEADQUARTERS, REGINA.

I debated a moment, then added: A REWARD SHALL BE PAID UPON DELIVERY. I thought that, given the urgency of his recent telegram, Steele would not complain about a cash expenditure.

I placed the letter on a large rock where someone would easily find it, then used another stone to weigh it down. Then I took a branch and wedged it into the gravel, hanging my hat upon it like a flag. The gold trim around the edge of the pillbox hat sparkled in the sun, and was certain to catch someone's eye. Short of running through the woods to the settlement to deliver the letter to the traders and then running back to this spot again—during which time an injured Chambers might well die—it was the best I could do.

I squared my shoulders and faced the cave, my pipe clenched grimly in my teeth. I took a step forward—then paused, just on the threshold, as something white caught my attention. Was that a feather, tucked into a crevice at one side of the cave? I looked closer, and saw that the lower shaft of the feather was wrapped in red wool. The feather seemed to have been deliberately placed in this spot, and I had the overwhelming sense that this was significant. I was reminded of Chief Piapot's pipe, and the single eagle feather that hung from it.

On the day that Sergeant Wilde and I had confronted Piapot at the end of the CPR tracks, the chief had lifted his pipe in a ritual gesture before rising to speak to us. I'd seen Indians do the same when they invoked their gods. I suspected it was some sort of protective gesture, like a Catholic making the sign of the cross.

Whatever was in the cave, I wanted all of the protection from it I could get. I raised my own pipe in front of me, then moved it to the left, then above my head, and then to the right, as Piapot had done that day. At first I felt slightly foolish doing it, but by the time I was done it felt natural, not odd at all. I took one last draw on the pipe, then knocked the rest of the tobacco out, took the pipe apart, and put it inside its case. Only then did I feel ready to enter the cave.

I stepped inside, and immediately noted the change in temperature. The cave was quite a bit cooler than the air outside. The walls were of gravel-leavened earth; I could smell fresh soil, as if it had been recently dug—and something else: a faint, musky smell. The floor of the cave was soft underfoot; I could see Chambers's boot prints clearly. I also saw a second pair of footprints, made by someone small and light on their feet and wearing moccasins. That person had walked this way earlier; Chambers's boot prints overlapped many of the moccasin prints. I drew the only logical conclusion: for some reason, Emily had entered this cave ahead of us.

The muffled rumbling sound I'd heard earlier was coming from deeper inside the cave. I struck a match as I reached the bend, beyond which the sunlight did not penetrate. I held the burning match above my head, breathing in its sulphur smell. The light was feeble, but it was sufficient to show me that the cavern continued on for some distance, descending slightly into the earth.

I followed the cavern, squatting every now and then to strike another match and look at the footprints on the floor of the passage. The walls around me were as regular as those of a mine tunnel, but without timber supports. I wondered how it had been dug—and what was keeping it up.

I came to another tunnel joined at an angle to the one I was in, like a tributary feeding into a stream. I looked into it and saw a profusion of hoof prints, all so large that they could have been made by only the largest of plains creatures: the buffalo.

I decided to carry on the way I had been going, along the main tunnel, and head toward the rumbling noise. Chambers's boot prints and the moccasin prints led in that direction, and I saw spent matches upon the ground underfoot: more evidence of his passage.

I continued on for a few steps more, striking another match. I was more than halfway through my box of matches already, and was trying to decide whether I should turn about at this point and use the remaining matches to illuminate my way back. Then I saw a roundish, misshapen object lying in the tunnel up ahead. I walked over to it and squatted down on the ground, lowering the match to illuminate it. There was no mistaking the brown derby with its black satin hatband, even in its current state. The derby was crushed and mud-smeared; it looked as though someone—or something—had trod upon it.

"Chambers?" I called out, my voice muffled by the soft earthen walls of the tunnel. "Where are you?"

The match went out. Shivering in the sudden darkness, I quickly lit another. I walked a pace or two more, looking for Chambers's boot prints, but saw none. The floor of the cavern was completely covered in buffalo hoof prints now—and in something else, I saw to my horror: shreds of clothing that looked as though they had been torn apart by wolves.

I had to light yet another match to get a closer look. My inspection confirmed what I suspected, and only added to the dread I felt. The torn clothing included scraps of brown serge that had been a Norfolk jacket, the cloth from a shirt, and a scattering of buttons that had come from trousers, next to the remains of a button gaiter. Like the clothing I'd found in the McDougall home, all of it had been torn to pieces, yet there was no blood upon any of it. I picked up a scrap of serge and caught the scent of Chambers's cologne and a whiff of Brilliantine, despite the fact that the air all around me smelled strongly of a musky odor that could only have been buffalo.

As I set the scrap of jacket down again and lit another match, I spotted something that chilled my heart: a tiny buckskin dress and one beaded moccasin, just large enough for a year-old. The clothing was intact—not torn like Chambers's garments—but had been trampled. I touched the tiny moccasin gently, wondering what terrible fate had befallen the poor, sick girl who had worn it. I hoped that Emily had merely removed Iniskim's clothing to ease her fever, and that mother and daughter had managed to escape the tunnel before the buffalo whose hoof prints were at my feet had swept through it. I didn't see any of Emily's clothing, which lent weight to my hope.

I pressed forward, making my way through the darkness mainly by feel, in order to preserve my store of matches. I trailed my hand along the right wall, and more than once felt it plunge into the empty space of another tributary tunnel. Each time it did, I lit a match and searched for footprints, but all I saw was a mass of hoof prints that filled the tunnel from one side to the other. I decided to keep to the main tunnel.

As I moved onward, the tunnel I was following slowly began to ascend. The musky smell was stronger now; the air was filled with the odour of the shaggy buffalo. Yet the animals that had produced the odour seemed to be as invisible as ghosts.

The hairs at the back of my neck were prickling, and a shiver coursed through my body. I fancied that I could feel a chill wind stirring my hair; it seemed to be flowing from somewhere behind me. Yet when I lit a match, the flame did not flicker, but burned with a steady light. Whatever current was flowing through this tunnel had no physical effect.

My match went out. In that same instant the rumbling noise I had been hearing became magnified. It was not only coming from the tunnel in front of me now; it was also coming from the tunnel behind—and the ground underfoot was trembling. A trickle of dirt from the roof of the cavern sifted down onto my shoulders. Was the roof about to cave in?

I fumbled to get another match lit, but in my haste, the box fell from my hands. Matches spilled around my feet. I immediately crouched and scooped them up, but I could not find the box. I tried striking a match on my boot, with my fingernail, and on my brass buttons, but it would not light.

The rumbling that was coming from behind me was almost upon me now, although the sound was nearly eclipsed by the hammering of my own heart. I was about to be trampled to death by what sounded like a herd of buffalo, charging toward me at top speed through the utter darkness of the tunnel.

No—not utter darkness. I could see a dim light, somewhere down the tunnel in front of me.

Abandoning my matches, I turned and ran. The ground underfoot trembled as if an earthquake was shaking it, and it was all I could do to keep my footing. I ran blindly, my hands stretched out in front of me, letting my instincts tell me where to turn. More than once I crashed headlong into the soft walls of the tunnel, then staggered away, spitting dirt. All the while, the sound of buffalo running behind me grew louder and louder— now I could hear the snorts of the great beasts and smell their breath as the rush of their approach pushed a hot breeze against my back.

The patch of light in front of me was growing brighter. Rounding another bend, I could see an opening ahead: a cavern mouth, with blue sky and sunshine beyond it. I ran toward it, my lungs aching as I struggled to run up the tunnel, which had developed a steep upward slope. I could not pause: the rumbling was almost upon me.

I nearly wept with relief as I ran the last few steps and burst out of the tunnel and into brilliant sunshine. Then I realized my mistake: I had not reached a place of safety. The rumbling noise I'd heard inside the tunnel was still all around me, filling my ears like the roar of an ocean. I jumped to one side as a dark and monstrous shape hurtled past: a buffalo.

I whirled around, and saw that I stood upon a grassy plain that was filled with the shaggy beasts. Dust hung in the air in thick clouds and the earth shook with the rumble of their passage. An entire herd was thundering past me, and more buffalo still were spilling from the tunnel I'd just emerged from, flowing up and out of it like a living fountain. I leaped this way and that, dodging the charging monsters as they roared past. I saw a flash of something white hurtling toward me, and threw up my hands in alarm. It veered suddenly back the way it had come, treading heavily upon my foot as it turned, and then it was lost in the dust and noise.

By some miracle, I stumbled in the direction of a pile of stones and brush, favouring my bruised and throbbing foot. The buffalo flowed to either side of the obstruction like a river around a rock, turning it into a crude shelter. I sagged gratefully into this place of safety, panting from my exertions.

At last able to look around me, I saw that my place of refuge was one of several piles of stones, set up at regular intervals like the posts of a fence. The buffalo were streaming between them; every time the herd veered to the side, a figure would leap up from behind a screen of brush and whoop and wave a blanket, forcing the buffalo back into the herd. Beyond the piles of stones, other Indians were riding back and forth on horses, shooting arrows into the few buffalo that were bold enough to hurtle past the waving blankets. Despite their efforts, one or two of the great beasts escaped, and thundered away.

I had no idea where I was. I knew only that I'd somehow blundered into the middle of a buffalo hunt.

The last of the buffalo herd thundered past me, leaving dust hanging in their wake. I stood, taking care to remain behind the pile of stones, and watched them rumble away. They charged up a slight incline, then suddenly disappeared.

So did the noise of their hooves.

In the stillness that followed, I heard a number of the mighty animals bellowing in pain, and the excited whoops of Indians. Those Indians I'd seen waving blankets earlier were now all running toward the spot where the herd had disappeared. Those who were on horseback finished dispatching the few buffalo that were still within range, then rode after their tribesmen.

I looked back at the hole I'd emerged from, and shuddered. Nothing on heaven or earth could persuade me to go back into that gloomy tunnel. Instead, I turned and ran after the Indians.

It took me a few moments to get to the spot where the buffalo herd had disappeared. I skidded to a stop just in time. Yawning before me was a precipice; another step or two and I would have plunged to my death. The slope of the ground had hidden it from me until I was almost upon it; I could see why the panicked buffalo had charged right over the edge.

Below me was a scene of carnage. An entire herd of buffalo, close to one hundred of the mighty beasts, lay strewn upon the rocks below. They had fallen more than fifty feet to their deaths, and those that the fall had not slain were being filled with arrows by the Indians below. As I watched, one of the shaggy beasts staggered to its feet, then collapsed with a bellow as an arrow found its throat.

One of the piles of stones and shrubs was nearby, just at the edge of the cliff. I squatted down behind it, screening myself from the view of those below.

Several dozen Indians were swarming over the downed buffalo like ants. The men whooped and danced, their bows held high in their fists, while the women set about the task of butchering the great beasts. Arms bloody to the elbow, they thrust their knives into the thick, shaggy hides, peeling them back from the steaming flesh. One of them plunged her hand deep inside the body of a horned bull, then pulled out what looked like its heart. She handed it to an Indian brave, who ate it raw, blood running down his cheeks and chin. Other Indians—those who had leaped out from behind the rock-and-brush blinds to wave blankets and frighten the buffalo toward the edge—now were climbing carefully down to join the others below.

The herd, small though it was in comparison to those that blackened the prairie in days gone by, was substantial; I wondered where it had come from. In the past I had seen buffalo bones in such large numbers that they turned the prairie as white as snow for many miles, but in recent years had only rarely seen a herd of this size. The buffalo were nearly gone from the plains, hunted to the very last animal, both by the Indians who traded their hides for rifles, food and whisky—and by the white man, for sport. Soon the Indians would have to settle down on their reserves and become farmers, as the government had been trying to persuade them to do. For the moment, however, the Indians could still hunt; the slaughter below would keep them in meat for several months.

As I watched the women cutting strips from the animal's haunches, it took me a moment or two to realize that there was something odd about the dead animals below. Many of the buffalo had light-coloured coats. Although the animals were clearly adults by their size, their shaggy pelts were the yellow-brown colour of newborn buffalo calves.

Something was very wrong here. I could feel it in my bones. Suddenly not wanting to be seen by the Indians, I backed away from the edge of the cliff.

I went back the way I had come, walking between the piles of stones that formed a funnel through which the buffalo had charged. I looked around for Chambers, wondering if he had made it the last few yards through the tunnel to safety after losing his clothing. If I didn't find any sign of him up here, I supposed I'd have to find a source of light and go back into the tunnel itself, to see if his body lay somewhere within. I didn't relish the thought.

Strangely, although I could find the pile of rocks and brush I had taken shelter behind after emerging from the tunnel, I could not find the opening in the earth itself. I walked back and forth across the area where the buffalo had been stampeded, but saw only hard, bare prairie, dotted here and there with yellow grass that had been crushed under buffalo hooves. Nowhere was there any sign of a cave.

Perplexed, I stood with my hands on my hips, slowly turning in a circle to survey the prairie. There were no trees anywhere, and no sign of the North Saskatchewan River or Victoria Mission. The tunnel I followed must have been longer than I thought.

I heard a swishing sound and a dull thud, and turned around to see what the noise was. I was startled to see an arrow, its head buried in the ground at my feet. I looked up—and saw an Indian standing behind one of the piles of stones and brush some distance away, holding a bow in his hand. I had barely time to fumble for my revolver before he knocked another arrow and shot it.

This one did not miss. It tore a painful crease in my upper thigh as I twisted to yank my revolver out of its holster.

My reaction, however, had saved me. While I could feel blood leaking down my hip, the arrow had glanced off the strange stone in my pocket as I turned, and had been deflected just enough so that it did not skewer my leg.

The Indian lowered his bow and began walking toward me. I could see that his quiver was empty. He cast his bow aside and drew from the belt at his waist a slender stick with a single black feather attached to one end. As he approached, walking slowly and deliberately, he held it above his head and waved it at me, laughing and taunting me.

That was when I recognized him, by his lynx skin bonnet with its five eagle feathers: Wandering Spirit, the Indian who had killed Sergeant Wilde and, reportedly, the Indian agent Quinn— and who was about to do the same to me. His feet were bare, and aside from his breechcloth and cap he wore only a fringed buckskin shirt that had been painted with large black circles and trimmed with fluttering eagle feathers. He strode toward me, eyes glittering with malice, a cruel smile twisting his lips.

My police training took over. "Stop right there!" I yelled, brandishing my revolver. "You are under arrest."

He ignored me.

I decided that no further warning was required; the man had already wounded a police officer. I aimed my revolver and fired.

Wandering Spirit just kept walking, not even picking up his pace. My bullet had missed.

I shot thrice more—and missed all three times. Cursing my revolver—the Enfield was notorious for its inaccuracy—I took more time with my fifth shot, steadying my hand by holding my wrist as I fired. Wandering Spirit waved his coup stick at me dismissively, as if I were an annoying fly that he was about to swat with it.

With only one bullet left in my revolver, I forced myself to wait until Wandering Spirit was no more than a pace or two away. I pointed the barrel of my revolver straight at his chest and squeezed the trigger. The gun roared and spat flame and smoke. This time, I saw the bullet strike the shirt Wandering Spirit wore. He paused just long enough to brush the flattened lead aside. His laugh was cold and derisive, as he looked me in the eye.

I was sweating so badly that the first cartridge I pulled from the pouch on my belt slipped from my fingers and fell onto the ground. Backing away from Wandering Spirit, I cracked open the cylinder of my revolver. I just managed to push a single cartridge into a chamber before the back of my leg struck something: one of the piles of stones and brush. The arrow that was still hanging from my breeches caught on the brush and tore free, spilling the contents of my pocket to the ground and causing me to gasp as it ripped a fresh gash in my thigh. Forced to a stop, I slammed the cylinder shut and pointed the revolver at Wandering Spirit.

Wandering Spirit said something to me in Cree. Then he raised his coup stick.

Before he could strike me with it, however, a second Indian appeared, materializing out of thin air as if he had heretofore been invisible. He was a short, stoop-shouldered fellow in his senior years, his face scarred by pockmarks. He wore buckskin trousers and moccasins that were heavily beaded, and a bearskin cap from which three eagle feathers hung. Hanging from a thong around his neck was a gigantic bear's paw, its flesh shrivelled and its claws a dull yellow. I recognized him as Big Bear, the rebellious Cree chief who had refused to sign a treaty or settle on a reserve.

Big Bear's face was seamed with wrinkles; he looked at me with squinting eyes. I had the sense, from the intensity of his stare, that these were eyes that missed nothing.

When the curious stone that had spilled from my pocket chirped, Big Bear glanced at it, then laid a hand upon Wandering Spirit's raised arm. With his other hand he pointed at me, saying something in Cree. I understand only a little of the language, but I heard the words "buffalo" and "earth."

I stood, waiting for Wandering Spirit to strike me, my revolver wavering. I had only one bullet and two targets—and one of them was impervious to bullets.

Wandering Spirit continued to glare at me, but was listening intently to what the other Indian had to say. His voice, although respectful, was filled with barely suppressed anger as he answered. I thought I heard the name of Chief Piapot, and wondered if Wandering Spirit recognized me from our encounter of one year ago. If so, I hoped he remembered that it was Sergeant Wilde who had kicked over the tepees.

I decided that this was not the time to try to question Wandering Spirit about the murder of Tom Quinn or to charge him with assaulting a police officer. While some constables in the North-West Mounted Police had been known to face down entire Indian camps alone, arresting men despite overwhelming odds, I knew that bluster would not save me here. It certainly wasn't going to cow a man who had brushed away bullets like flies. I knew I was powerless—that I could only watch and listen while this pair decided whether or not to kill me. Lowering my gun, I waited, my thigh throbbing from the stinging cut the arrow had delivered. My stomach was a painful counterpoint, my guts cramping as if the arrow had lodged there, instead.

As Big Bear spoke, I thought I heard another name I recognized: Iniskim. Acting on a hunch, I decided to plead my case. I said the first thing that came into my head.

"I know Iniskim." I held my hand low, at knee level, as if patting a small child on the head, then pointed to my own eye. "The little girl—the one with pale hair and eyes. She was sick; I gave her mother money for medicine. Is Iniskim here?" I pointed at the ground, repeating her name and the Cree word for "here," then added, "Is Emily—is her mother here?"

I hoped that Emily would speak in my favour. It was not unknown for an Indian woman to petition for the life of a white man.

Big Bear and Wandering Spirit stared at me, frowning as if puzzled. I wondered if they spoke any English at all. I continued to talk quickly, gesturing all the while and listening to the sounds of the whoops that were coming from below the cliffs, where the buffalo were being butchered.

"I'm not here to interrupt your hunt, or to move you to a reserve," I told them. "I'm just looking for someone who's gone missing: a man by the name of Arthur Chambers. He went into a cave that led for some distance underground." I gestured again at the ground, and saw that my hands were still filthy with soil from my blind run through the tunnel. "The tunnel led here, to the middle of your buffalo run. I'm hoping that Chambers—and Emily and her daughter Iniskim—weren't trampled, that they managed to...."

I paused then, realizing how foolish I sounded. Big Bear continued to stare at me a moment more, then bent and picked up my tobacco pouch. He sniffed at it, then pulled a pinch of tobacco from it and showed it to Wandering Spirit.

"Yes," I said, nodding. "It's tobacco. Would you like a smoke?"

I reached into my pocket for my pipe. Wandering Spirit tensed and raised his coup stick higher, but Big Bear shook his head. I pulled open the case, cracked it open, and assembled the stem and bowl of my pipe.

"Here," I told Big Bear. "Go ahead. Have a smoke."

For a long moment, the chief merely stared at the pipe. Then he reached out and took it.

Wandering Spirit grunted and spat on the ground. Then he abruptly turned on his heel and strode away, heading toward the cliffs. As he left, I could hear him muttering under his breath. Even if he hadn't recognized me from our meeting of a year ago, he'd certainly remember me now.

Big Bear tamped tobacco into the pipe and lit it. He raised it in four different directions, as Piapot had done, then took a long draw. Releasing the smoke slowly through pursed lips, he handed me the pipe. Then he bent down and picked up the curiously shaped stone, carefully using my tobacco pouch to pick it up and folding the pouch shut as he stood.

I jammed the pipe between my teeth, puffing nervously. I wasn't entirely certain why, but I could see in Big Bear's eyes that my life was to be spared. I opened my lips to thank him....

He was gone.

One moment the chief had been standing there—the next he had disappeared. All that remained of him was the puff of smoke that he'd blown from his lips a moment earlier.

I looked wildly around. Big Bear hadn't ducked behind the pile of stones and brush that I stood next to, and there was nowhere else within a dozen yards for him to hide. He had simply vanished, taking the curiously shaped stone and my tobacco pouch with him.

I stood a moment longer, listening to the Indian voices coming from below the cliff. By all accounts, I should have arrested Wandering Spirit. Shooting arrows at a police officer is no small matter. Yet I was still shaken by what I had just observed. I'd seen one man stop bullets and another turn himself invisible. Of what possible use could a revolver and the authority of the law be against the forces of magic? It would hardly serve my commanding officers for me to die in a futile attempt to assert my authority.

I decided to return to Victoria Mission and telegraph Steele at once. Perhaps then a proper search could be mounted for Chambers, Emily, and her daughter.

There was just one problem: I had absolutely no idea in which direction the settlement lay.

⋇—⋇

I had a notion that the tunnel I'd entered at Victoria Mission had curved predominantly to the southwest, and so I kept the afternoon sun at my left shoulder and trudged northeast. It was a long hot walk up and down rolling hills, without a tree in sight. Despite the fact that my pillbox hat had provided only scant protection from the sun, I mourned its absence as the sun beat down upon my bare head. Eventually I pulled my sweat-soaked undershirt off and draped it over my head.

The only pools of water I passed were crusted with salt; I knew that drinking this alkaline water would at best fail to slake my thirst, and at worst would cause my stomach to cramp even worse than it was already. My mouth became as dry as the dust my boots were kicking up, and at last I gave in and quenched my thirst by drinking the last of my Pinkham's, which was in the haversack I still had slung over my shoulder. The alcohol in it made me slightly inebriated; perhaps that was what caused me to hallucinate. I kept imagining eyes upon me, and more than once I fancied that I saw a large shape, following me.

I pushed these thoughts from my mind, ignoring them as I did the false "ponds" that heat shimmers were creating. I kept hoping to catch sight of the telegraph line, or to hear the hoot of the riverboat on the North Saskatchewan River, but nary a landmark nor a guiding call presented itself. I trudged along, favouring my injured foot. I'd been relieved to find that the injury was no more than a blood blister where the edge of my foot had been squeezed against my boot by the force of the hoof that had trod upon it. I was lucky to have no broken bones.

Eventually, after walking for nearly three hours, my way was blocked by a creek. I scrambled down its bank and splashed its water over my head, then drank deeply. Thankful for its cool relief, I rose to my feet, shaking the water from my hair like a beast.

As I stood on the muddy bank, trying to decide which direction to go in, I had the distinct sensation that something or someone was behind me. Whirling around, I saw that, this time, it was no mere hallucination. Standing on the top of the bank was a great, shaggy beast: a buffalo. I hadn't heard it approach; its heavy footsteps must have been masked by the gurgle of the creek.

Buffalo generally ignore humans; the more canny among them flee, fearing the hunter's bullet. This one merely stood and stared at me. I saw then that it had a scrap of black cloth around its massive neck, and wondered if this was one of the few buffalo that had been domesticated. Yet it looked wild enough. Its great chest heaved, as if it had just run across the prairie, and there were sticks and burrs in its hair. Like the buffalo I had seen the Indians butchering, this one had hair that had a peculiar yellowish tinge, despite the fact that it was a full-grown male.

As I watched it, the beast let out a half-strangled bellow, then trotted down toward the creek, all the while fixing me with its large black eyes.

The creek was at my back, deep and swift enough to trip me. If the beast decided to charge, there was nowhere for me to go. I reached for my Enfield, thankful that I'd remembered to refill all six chambers with bullets.

As if it understood what a revolver was, the buffalo jerked to a stop. It stood, eyeing me warily from about thirty feet away. Even at that distance, I could smell its pungent pelt—and something sweet underneath that musky odour. Flies buzzed around its unprotected hindquarters; the buffalo kept flicking its tail, but the appendage was too short to provide any real deterrent to the insects. The buffalo looked at me with a strangely pleading expression; I had the distinct impression that it was asking me to end its torment. I understood its anguish; one of the flies had landed on my bare hand and taken a bite from it, leaving a small but bloody hole.

I decided to draw my revolver and fire it. With luck, the noise would frighten the buffalo away. I pulled the revolver from my holster—and in that same instant the buffalo gave another of its strange sounding bellows. As if struggling to get the noises out, the beast let out a series of long bellows and short grunts, punctuated by a furious pawing of one of its forefeet. Fearful that it was working up the nerve to charge, I raised my revolver and fired it into the air, then lowered the revolver at the ready, in case the buffalo thundered my way. The beast immediately turned and bolted away.

I climbed the bank cautiously, peeking over the ridge to see where the buffalo had gone. I could still hear its hoof beats, although it had disappeared behind another hill.

I holstered my revolver, looking down at the furrows the buffalo had dug in the ground with its hoof. Then I froze, unwilling to believe my eyes. These were not random scratches; they were deliberate marks. In clumsy block letters, they spelled out a single word: HELP.

As I stood, regarding this strange missive with wonder, I heard the sound of hoof beats. I looked up, expecting to see the buffalo, but instead was greeted with the sight of a North-West Mounted Police constable, galloping toward me.

"Hello there!" he called out over the sound of his horse's pounding hooves. "I heard a shot. Is there any trouble?"

The fellow was about my age, with dark hair and a full beard. Like many members of our force, he wore a Stetson rather than the official pillbox hat, and his feet were clad in beaded moccasins instead of riding boots. He pulled his horse up next to me, unwittingly causing it to trample the letters the buffalo had scratched in the ground. I looked up at him, my mind was whirling as I struggled to make sense of what I had just seen. Had that really been a black silk tie around the buffalo's neck—a tie identical to the one Chambers wore? The faintest hint of Brilliantine still hung in the air, confirming my suspicions.

"Who are you?" the constable asked. "And what are you doing out here on the prairie, on foot?"

"Corporal Marmaduke Grayburn," I replied automatically. Then I added: "I'm lost. Can you tell me where the Victoria Mission settlement is?"

The constable's eyes widened. Then he laughed. "You are lost, by God. Victoria Mission is three hundred miles to the north. The only settlement around here is Fort Macleod, six miles down the creek."

Despite the fact that I'd slaked my thirst, I suddenly felt dizzy. Three hundred miles? Had I really traveled that far under the earth? It didn't seem possible. The tunnel had seemed a mile long, at the very most.

"Do you want me to show you to the fort?" the constable asked.

I nodded mutely, then at last found my voice.

"I think I'd better speak to your commanding officer," I said. "Something very odd has just happened."

✦—✦

Chapter IV

A report disbelieved—Contacting Steele by aerograph—
Unsettling news—A ghost story—Dreams of bones and birds—A
chance meeting with Jerry Potts—On the buffalo trail—Another
disappearance—My wild ride—Kidnapped!

Superintendent Cotton sat ramrod stiff in his chair, listening with a doubtful expression on his face as I made my report. He was every inch the officer, with moustache carefully groomed, hair neatly trimmed and combed flat against his head, and impeccable uniform. I could see that my account of settlers and missionaries being turned into buffalo, impossibly long tunnels through the earth, and invisible Indians was something he was hard-pressed to believe. I could hardly blame him—until the recent turn of events, I wouldn't have believed it myself.

"That's a fantastic tale, Corporal Grayburn," he said. "It sounds like an Indian legend, which leads me to give you this caution: If the Indians are telling children's stories about human beings turning into buffalo, you'd do better to ignore them. The love of notoriety is well developed in the Indian character—they'll say anything to make themselves sound important. The Indians have an enormously exaggerated idea of their own supernatural powers, which are really nothing but parlour tricks, performed by amateur conjurers."

"Superintendent," I said slowly, reminding myself to keep my rising irritation in check. "I'm not repeating legends told around a tepee fire. These are things I saw with my own eyes. Special Constable Chambers–"

Cotton leaned forward to skewer me with a glare. "Where is your evidence?"

I glared at him, then realized that insubordination would not further my cause. I glanced ruefully down at my torn pocket, which had held the one piece of evidence I had collected. I had yet to mention the curious stone I'd found, and the chirping noises it had made. Like the tunnel in the earth from which I'd emerged, it too was gone—all I had left was the leather thong it had been wrapped in. The feathers attached to it had become quite mangled in my pocket, and the whole thing now looked like something a cat had shredded. The stone hardly seemed worth mentioning now, especially when I couldn't really explain, in any logical fashion, my hunch that it was connected with the case.

"I have none, sir," I replied with a sigh. I shifted on my chair, and felt the pull of the bandages the police surgeon had bound my wound with. "But Superintendent Steele can confirm that supernatural forces are indeed at work in the North-West Territories. That's why he formed Q Division: to investigate the recent spate of disappearances, and other paranormal occurrences."

Superintendent Cotton drummed his fingers on the table at which he sat. They were short and blunt, their squared tips matching the set of his shoulders.

"I've heard that Steele was setting up a new division—supposedly some crackerjack force of hand-picked men." Cotton's eyes lingered on my dirt-grimed jacket, and the torn, bloody hole in my riding breeches. "Judging by the wild tale that you've just told me, it sounds more like a crackpot division."

I sat bolt upright in my chair, my face hot with anger. "But you've seen the evidence yourself!" I cried. "When the first Fort Macleod was washed away by that sudden deluge, and seven men died."

"A flash flood. Nothing more."

I glared at Cotton, seeing now that nothing I could say would convince him. He reminded me of my father: unwilling to believe in anything that didn't fit his notion of the way the world was ordered. I ground my teeth. Cotton had obviously spent too many years in the militia; it had forced him to see only in neat little parade-square rows.

I could see that I was on the verge of angering the Superintendent, when what I needed was his assistance. To get it, I had to present him with something that he could set his sights upon.

"There is still the matter of Wandering Spirit's assault on me," I said in a steadier voice, gesturing at my bandaged thigh. "And the disappearance of Mr. Chambers. I would request, sir, permission to set out with a patrol at first light, to arrest Wandering Spirit and to search for our special constable."

The Superintendent's eyes narrowed. "I don't need to be told my job, Corporal. A crime has been committed, and an arrest shall be made. A patrol will be sent out—but one of our own men will lead it. We're quite capable of bringing our Indians to justice without the aid of Q Division."

"But sir!" I protested. "You don't realize what you're–"

"Corporal Grayburn!" Cotton shouted. "That's enough!"

I sat on the edge of my seat, fists balled in my lap in frustration. How could anyone possibly arrest a man who was impervious to bullets, and who could kill with the touch of a coup stick? I considered myself quite adept at dealing with Indians, and yet I'd only escaped death by a hair's breadth. I shuddered at the thought of what might befall a less experienced policeman. Yet I could see by the flinty look in Cotton's eye that further protests would do more harm than good. I sat in silence for a moment, listening to the faint *clatter-clack-clacking* of the perpetual motion wheels that generated power for the electric bulbs illuminating the office, and trying to ignore the ache in my stomach.

A thought occurred to me: perhaps if Steele intervened....

"Sir?" I asked.

"What is it now, Corporal?"

Cotton's patience had almost reached the end of its tether. I chose my words carefully. "I would also request that I be allowed to use one of the fort's aerographs to relay a message to Regina. My Superintendent will be wondering why I didn't respond to his telegram this morning." I glanced outside the window of Cotton's office. It had been dusk by the time the constable and I had ridden the six miles back to the fort on his horse, and now it was fully dark. The moon was round and full; a perfect night for sending an aerograph.

Cotton's shoulders relaxed a little. "Very well. I'll get Constable Browne to show you to the aerograph operator. When you're done, you can bunk down in the men's barracks. I believe there's a spare bed; see the quartermaster for a blanket."

I stood and saluted while the Superintendent called the constable to his office.

Constable Browne led me out of the building that housed the Superintendent's office and past the recreation room, where I heard the clacking of billiard balls. I glanced in and saw men drinking cold cider and smoking their pipes, and heard the buzz of male voices raised in companionable conversation. While Browne collected the civilian who operated the fort's aerographs, I bought tobacco at the bar and sat down with my pipe to write my report to Steele. I wrote slowly, composing my message with care. The aerograph was a much more secure way of sending messages than the telegraph, but sometimes aerographs went astray. Just in case this one did, I couched my report in language that only Steele would understand. I didn't want a lost report to be the basis for alarm.

As I wrote the message and enjoyed my first decent smoke in weeks—the bar sold Capstan Full Flavoured by the tin—a wagon pulled up outside. A teamster with a mailbag over his shoulder strode into the room, and there followed the usual hubbub and excitement that follows the arrival of the mail.

After a few minutes, Browne returned with the aerograph operator, a young fellow by the name of Bertrand whose portly girth and thick-lensed spectacles would have rendered him medically unfit for service as a policeman. I decided that he must be a civilian employee of the force.

I nodded hello. "I've just about finished my report. Won't be a minute."

Bertrand gave me the kind of look an officer gives a recruit who is late for picquet duty. "You interrupted my reading," he said in a petulant voice. Then he glanced down at my report and added: "I've better things to do than wait for constables who spell *buffalo* with an *e* on the end of the word."

I felt an angry flush spring to my cheeks, but didn't give him the satisfaction of a response. Instead, I crooked an arm around the paper I was writing on and finished my report to Steele. Bertrand, meanwhile, looked around the room with an air of smug superiority, all the while uttering several loud complaints about being made to stand and wait.

I folded the paper in two and rose to my feet. "Done."

Bertrand reached out to take it, but I jerked the paper back. "Sorry," I said. "This report is for the eyes of my Superintendent only. I'll have to place it inside the aerograph myself, Bertrand, so you'd best show me to it."

He pursed his lips angrily, but led me out of the recreation room and across the parade square. We walked to the northeast corner of the fort, where a bastion stood. After ordering me to knock out my pipe, Bertrand climbed the stairs, wheezing all the way up. I followed him, taking the stairs easily and shaking my head at the poor physical specimens they were letting into the force these days.

At the top of the bastion were two of the wonders of the modern military age: a Gatling gun, its perpetual motion mechanism softly humming; and an aerograph.

The latter looked like a miniature version of the air bicycle I'd ridden to Regina, but with hollow brass tubes in which a message could be placed, instead of seats for riders. Its hydrogen-filled balloon was about a foot long, and was affixed to a railing by means of a wire. It floated in the night sky, propellers whirring, straining at its tether like a dog on a lead.

"Where's the message going?" Bertrand asked.

"To headquarters."

Bertrand stared at me if I'd just said something stupid. "All the way to Regina?" He shook his head. "Medicine Hat has a telegraph. Your message can be relayed from there."

"No! I can't run the risk that the Metis will cut the line again. This report is urgent; it must go directly to Steele at once. Calibrate the aerograph for Regina."

Bertrand met my stare for a moment, then turned his back on me and winched the aerograph down to the bastion. "Cotton's going to hear about this," he muttered. "He'll see to it that your division pays the extra cost."

Bertrand pulled a slim leather case of what looked like watchmaker's tools from his pocket and began tinkering with the aerograph, carefully adjusting the mechanism that drove its miniature wings and propellers. He'd pushed his glasses up his face so that they rested on his forehead; I realized that he was working entirely by feel. He paused to wet a finger and hold it up to test the wind, then continued with his work.

Despite the man's odious nature, I was intrigued. The moon was bright enough that I could peer over his shoulder and watch as he set the angle of the tiny gyroscopes inside. The gimballed wheels within wheels—each a perpetual motion device—spun gently as his thick fingers brushed against them.

"What are you doing?" I asked.

"Adjusting the sensors." His nasal voice was edged with a touch of irritation, and I wondered if my presence had set the machine off-kilter. Yet he couldn't resist the urge to boast. "Not just anyone can be an aerograph operator. It takes a special touch and a keen mind to align the navigational mechanisms. Each has to be precisely aligned with both the Earth's and the Moon's magnetic fields, and calibrated to take into account large sources of iron, which can throw the device off course. If it's done incorrectly, the aerograph could miss its target by dozens or even hundreds of miles. Fortunately, I have a photographic memory and have studied all of the known sources of magnetic deviance in the North-West Territories. There's a direct current of magnetic force between Fort Macleod and Medicine Hat—that's why our detachment was selected as an aerograph post—and from there the device can follow the rails to Regina."

I wanted to challenge him on his preposterous claim to a photographic memory that extended to cover all of the North-West Territories, but kept silent, not wanting to interrupt his delicate work. I retreated to the other side of the bastion and leaned against the Gatling gun, waiting for him to finish. After a moment or two, he seemed satisfied with his adjustments. He nodded his head so that his spectacles fell back onto the bridge

of his nose, pushed them into place over his eyes, then held out
a pudgy hand. "Give me your message."

I did so, and watched as he rolled it up, then opened the tube
at the heart of the aerograph and slipped the report inside it.
Bertrand screwed the end on the tube, then unhooked the
aerograph from its tether. He closed his eyes, aimed the
aerograph toward the west, and let it go. It flew straight and
true, and I let out a sigh of relief, thankful that my strange effect
on mechanical devices had not impeded its course. As the
aerograph disappeared into the night, Bertrand turned and
walked heavily down the stairs to the ground, ignoring me as if I
had ceased to exist.

I waited atop the bastion until the sound of miniature wings
flapping and propellers turning faded away. Anxious though I
was to know what Steele's orders would be, I knew I had a long
wait ahead of me. The aerograph would take several hours to
wing its way over the four hundred miles between Fort Macleod
and Regina. Even if Steele was awake and read the report directly,
it would be hours more before his return missive winged its way
back, via aerograph, to Fort Macleod. It would be mid-afternoon of
the next day, at best, before Steele's reply reached me.

Still dry from the long day's march across the prairie, I
decided to find something cold to drink. I returned to the
recreation room, purchased a large bottle of cold tea, which had
jokingly been labelled "Fine Old Rye," and settled into an
armchair. I listened idly to the buzz of conversation around me.
The topics were the usual ones: the men groused about their
officers, about the lack of women, and about the heat. I perked
up when I thought I overheard the word "ghost" and saw the
fellow who had uttered it holding up a newspaper. The other
constables all laughed, as if he'd just told them a joke. I was just
about to get up from my chair when the fellow took his leave of
the others and crossed the room to sit at a table near my
armchair.

He was a constable, although his jacket was so faded and
dusty that the chevron nearly didn't show. His sunburned face
and casual manner marked him as a long-time member of the
force. He lay a crisp-looking copy of the *Battleford Post Journal*
that must have come in tonight's mail on the table, then opened
up a tin of peaches and began eating them. On a whim, I stared
at the newspaper, silently imploring him to offer it to me.

My attempt at thought transference must have worked. The
fellow looked up and stuck out his hand.

"I'm Daniel Davis," he announced. Then he realized that he
was still holding the spoon in his hand and grinned. He touched
it to his forehead in a mock salute. "Otherwise known as

'Peach.'" He winked, and lifted the can. "They cost a fortune to ship up from Fort Benton, but I love them."

"I'm Grayburn. My first name is Marmaduke—and you shorten it to 'Duke' at your peril. If you're done with your newspaper, could I borrow it?"

Constable Davis gave me the strangest look when I introduced myself, but he handed the newspaper over to me readily enough. As I began to read, I could feel his eyes boring into me. I lifted the newspaper, setting it between us like a screen.

The newspaper was typeset in the typical fashion, with long columns of text punctuated here and there with block-letter headlines in the same size of type. For this reason, the item that was of import to me did not catch my eye for some time. I only noticed it after I glanced at an illustration on the page, which showed a clean-shaven Mountie in a pillbox hat and military jacket. The illustration was so poorly drawn it might have been any beardless member of the force. Then I noticed the headline beside it: NORTH-WEST MOUNTED POLICE CORPORAL MISSING.

Wondering if another member of my former detachment had disappeared, I quickly scanned the article. My pipe nearly fell from my mouth when I saw my own name and realized that the illustration was meant to be me. According to the article, which was as vague as it was inaccurate, "Special Constable C." and I had been spirited away to the underworld by the ghost of an Indian woman named either Abigail or Emily McDougall, in revenge for being unable to save her dying daughter. The writer concluded that the spate of disappearances that had been occurring across the prairie were the work of malevolent Indian ghosts who yanked unsuspecting settlers into the hereafter.

I shook my head in disbelief. How was it possible that the newspaper had come across the story of my disappearance from Victoria Mission so quickly? Someone must have found the letter I'd left for Steele at the mouth of the cave, read its contents, and reiterated them to a journalist: that much was clear. Yet that had been just this morning. Even if the story had been relayed by telegraph this very day, how could the newspaper containing the story be in my hands when it took four days for the mails to travel by wagon from the Medicine Hat train depot to Fort Macleod, the most western of North-West Territories detachments?

Feeling eyes on me, I lowered the paper and saw that Constable Davis was still staring at me. "The man who went missing: that's you, isn't it?"

I nodded mutely. Then I looked down at the newspaper, and at the date at the top of the page: August 11—two full weeks later than I thought it was.

"What is today's date?" I asked sharply.

"Why, it's the sixteenth," Davis replied.

Today was August 16? That meant that nearly three weeks had elapsed; yet every sense told me that no more than a day had passed. I felt my face go pale.

Davis leaned forward and placed a steadying hand on my shoulder. "Are you all right, Grayburn?"

"Yes. Fine." I answered automatically, folding the newspaper. My mind was elsewhere. I was fearful that my days among Q Division were numbered. I'd let an account of my investigation fall into the hands of the general public, and now the newspaper was stirring things up. If I weren't careful, every settler in the North-West would be looking over his shoulder for fear of ghosts. Steele would not be impressed.

There was a chance, however, that my discoveries thus far might outweigh this error. If what I had seen today was real, and not some grand illusion, the missing settlers were being turned into buffalo, which then were slaughtered and eaten by the Indians. I wondered if the McDougalls were among the buffalo I saw being butchered at the bottom of the cliff. The shaggy bull whose heart the Indians had cut out may have been the missionary himself.

I shivered. The poor souls might as well have been dragged by ghosts into the netherworld that Sergeant Wilde and I had ridden to; it would almost have been a kinder fate.

"Do you believe in ghosts?" Davis asked.

"You can't believe everything they print in the newspapers," I told him, mindful of Steele's instruction to discuss my assignment only with officers. "The *Journal* obviously was in error on this story—as you can plainly see, I am not missing at all. I just lost count of the days it took to make the journey here from Victoria Mission. I must have suffered sunstroke."

The answer seemed to satisfy him. He nodded as I rose from my seat, but then added something that stopped me in my tracks: "The Indians certainly do believe in ghosts. I've seen them go without food rather than pass by the spot where a 'ghost' has been spotted."

I sat back down. "When was this?"

Davis quickly warmed to his tale, obviously enjoying the telling of it. "A year ago, I was escorting an Assinaboine band north to their reserve at Battleford. We were just about to ford the Saskatchewan River when the entire band stopped dead in its tracks. More than a thousand men, women and children squatted on the sand and refused to cross because they thought they saw a ghost on the other side."

Davis shook his head. "I crossed the river myself, and ordered the carts that held the government provisions across as well, but the Indians refused to budge, even when I broke open the stores and brewed up tea. For an entire day the Indians just sat there, even after I threatened to dump their food in the river. The next morning everything was all right again. The 'ghost' was gone, and the Indians crossed the river."

I leaned forward, intrigued. I wondered if Davis, like me, had blundered into the after world. "Did you see the ghost yourself?"

Davis laughed. "It wasn't a ghost. It was an animal: a buffalo calf with the lightest hair I've ever seen, almost milk-white. Just a wobbly-legged little wretch that had been separated from the herd, judging by the lost look in its eye. It seemed to be looking for its mother, and was bleating piteously. The Indians saw its white coat, and mistook it for a ghost."

A feeling of restlessness settled over me. There was a connection here; I could sense it. When I'd emerged from the tunnel near the buffalo jump, I'd also seen a flash of something white. It had been smaller than the buffalo that had thundered past me, about the size of a calf. The painful blister its hoof had left on my foot assured me that it was very real—not a ghost at all.

"Did you find any hoof prints on the shore where you saw the white calf?"

Davis gave me a strange look, as if I'd asked a very odd question.

"Not a one—but that doesn't prove that it was a ghost."

I suspected otherwise, but I kept my own counsel.

"What month was this?" I asked.

Davis replied at once. "I remember the date well: May, 24—the Queen's birthday. I was wishing I could have been celebrating it with the others at the mess, instead of being stuck out on the prairie, herding a bunch of superstitious savages."

I thought back to what Steele had told me. The woman in the report he had collected had to have been Emily; the facts all fit. A Peigan woman gives birth in May of 1883 to a child with pale hair and skin. The child is stillborn, its soul presumably flown to the Big Sands that is the Indian equivalent of Purgatory. On a sandy riverbank, Indians see the ghost of a white-haired buffalo: Iniskim's astral body, which for some reason took the form of a buffalo. A day later, a medicine woman uses magic to bring the stillborn infant to life, and the ghost on the river is gone.

Just over a year later, the child is seriously ill. Emily carries Iniskim into the cave near Victoria Mission, and Chambers and I follow. When I emerge from the other side of the tunnel, I see a flash of white, something I now realize must have been an albino buffalo calf: Iniskim, now transformed into a buffalo, body and soul.

Intuitively, I knew what must have happened. Iniskim, it seemed, had been about to die a second time in her short and unhappy life, this time of a fever. In desperation her mother had carried her into the cavern, and the girl had been transformed into a buffalo calf. Somehow, this had saved her. Was that what Emily had been talking about, when she said there was "medicine" at Victoria Mission? Why had she chosen this drastic course of action when I'd provided her with another alternative? I'd given her twenty dollars—why hadn't she used the money to buy medicine from the traders?

"You said the Assinaboine saw this ghost on the banks of the South Saskatchewan," I prompted. "Where were you, exactly?"

"I don't recall," Davis answered. "It wasn't a ford that we usually took—it was a crossing suggested by one of our scouts: a sand bar in the river, somewhere between the South Saskatchewan's confluence with the Red Deer River and the ferry crossing at Saskatchewan Landing. It was the only time I ever went that way; I'd be hard pressed to find the spot again. Why do you ask?"

I gave what I hoped was a nonchalant shrug, trying to hide the pang of disappointment that I felt. I'd been just at the edge of something important; I could sense it.

"Just idle curiosity. I like a good ghost story as much as the next man. What's the name of the scout who led you to the ford?"

Davis frowned. "I think his name was Many something-or-other."

"Which detachment is he attached to today?"

Davis shrugged. "I don't know."

I sat back to think about what I'd just heard. Steele had said that a Peigan woman—whom I now knew to be Emily—had given birth to her albino daughter at Fort Qu'appelle, more than one hundred and fifty miles east of the South Saskatchewan. Why had the buffalo-shaped ghost of the stillborn Iniskim appeared on a river hundreds of miles away?

I asked Davis more questions, but it soon became clear that he could add nothing more to his strange tale. The rattle of billiard balls, the drone of voices, and Davis's cheerful smile were starting to bear down upon me. I needed to be alone, to think. I had too many unanswered questions, too many leads. Everything seemed to be connected: the disappearance of the McDougalls, Wandering Spirit's attack on Dickens, Emily and her daughter, Wandering Spirit and Big Bear, the buffalo... but how, and why? Which should I investigate first?

I decided to let geography decide for me. Whatever clues remained at the ford where the white buffalo calf had appeared two years ago, the confluence of the Red Deer and South

Saskatchewan rivers lay more than two hundred miles northeast of my present location. Even by air bicycle—which Fort Macleod did not have—it would take an entire day to reach, and then still more time to follow the more than one hundred miles of river that lay between that point and the ferry crossing at Saskatchewan Landing. It would take me days or even weeks to find the crossing that Davis had mentioned—assuming I could find it. And even then, what could I reasonably expect to discover after such a length of time?

Closer at hand were Big Bear and Wandering Spirit, but I wouldn't be able to leave until morning for the buffalo jump—which I learned had the rather gruesome name of Head Smashed In. I could join the patrol that would be sent out from the fort, but even if Wandering Spirit and Big Bear had not decamped by then, how was I to force any answers out of a man who had nothing to fear from bullets, and how was I to locate a man capable of becoming invisible? Tracking Big Bear down would be like trying to catch the wind.

There was also the matter of Chambers to deal with. After being transformed into a buffalo he had pleaded with me for help. I was the only man in the whole of the North-West Territories who would know him for the man he was, and not just some "dumb beast," fit only for shooting. I had no idea where Chambers was now, but at least I had a starting point: the spot where he had scratched out the word *help* beside the riverbank. Yet how was I going to convince Fort Macleod's scouts that tracking down a buffalo was important, especially when Superintendent Cotton already thought I was a crackpot? What would they do when I started talking to the shaggy beast?

As I pondered, my stomach began to ache again. If this was typho-malaria that was cramping my intestines, it was taking the devil's own time to run its course.

It was time for some painkiller. I handed the newspaper back to Davis and rose from my chair.

"I'm tired," I said. "I think I'll turn in."

Davis waved goodbye with his spoon. "Pleasant dreams."

⋈—⋊

My dreams that night were anything but pleasant. I dreamed that I stood at the bottom of a rocky bluff, knee-deep in animal bones. From somewhere up above came the sound of a flute and the tramp of tiny feet. I recognized it at once: the music of the Pied Piper, a bedtime tale that had always filled me with terror when I was a child. Whenever my father read me that story of little children marching to their doom, I'd stuff my ears with cotton and hide under the bed for the rest of the night.

I clapped my hands over my ears, trying to blot out the sound, as dust rained down on my head.

A stone fell from up above and bounced, with a sharp crack, off a buffalo skull at my feet. I recognized it as the oddly shaped stone I'd found in the woods near the McDougall home. It chirped as it flew through the air, bounced again, and vanished.

Up above, the *pit-pat* of rat feet became the thunder of hooves. The sound reached the lip of the bluff, and then buffalo began to spill over the edge above. As the animals fell, they became human—women and children screamed and men cried out in terror as they rained down upon me. I threw up my arms to protect my head, certain that a heavy body would land upon me at any moment.

Suddenly, all was silent. Lowering my arms, I looked around. I still stood on a jumbled heap of bones, but this time, they were human. Skulls peered up at me, chunks of greying flesh still clinging to the bone. As I watched, horrified, a crow settled on one of the skulls and began to peck out what remained of one of its eyes.

I saw other animals skulking through the bones, stopping now and again to worry the bits of flesh that clung to them. A lynx sank its teeth into an arm and dragged it to one side; a bear picked up a thick thighbone with its paws and bent it until it cracked, releasing an ooze of marrow that it slurped like honey with its tongue. Foxes, gophers, and mice scurried in and over the bones, and even a deer paused to nibble at the withered flesh on a skull as it if were lichen on a rock. I backed away in horror from this unnatural feast, trying not to draw their attention, but my foot trod upon a dry bone that snapped with a loud crack.

All of the animals looked up. Their eyes held a keen intelligence that was greater than any animal's, and something more: a hunger. I realized then that the grisly repast they had just enjoyed was not enough. They wanted more. They wanted my flesh.

Nervously, I backed away. With each step I took, the animals crept forward, coming ever closer until they formed a half-circle around me, eyes gleaming and mouths chanting. The bear held the spiral-shaped stone to his mouth with one gigantic paw, and was playing it like a flute, leading the other animals forward. As I stumbled backward, I heard someone calling from up above.

"Take it! Throw it up to me!"

The bear and I looked up at the same time. Standing at the top of the cliff, silhouetted by a bloody sun, was a buffalo with yellow-brown hair. The animal had the usual shaggy beard, but its cheeks were bare, as if they had been neatly shaved, and a growth of hair on its upper lip resembled a moustache. Although

I had not been looking at the buffalo when it spoke, I knew its mouth had not moved. Its words had come to me via thought transference.

Before the bear could react, I plucked the stone from its paw and hurled it up to the buffalo. Chambers caught it in his hand. He stood, a naked man silhouetted by the sun, and raised the stone in his fist in a triumphant salute.

I laughed in delight, but my joy was short-lived. Even as I watched, the stone that Chambers held above his head grew. In the space of a heartbeat it was as large as his fist, then as large as his head. His arm sagged under the weight of it—and then the stone suddenly became as big as a buffalo. Chambers had only enough time to give one short gasp of surprise before he vanished beneath its crushing weight.

On top of the stone now stood a buffalo calf, its legs still wobbly, and its eyes large and pink. The calf's hair was a pure white, wet with the juices of the womb and streaked with the blood of its birth. Behind it, framing its snorting head like a halo, was the full moon.

I realized that I had something tucked under my arm: a newspaper. I unfolded it and tried to read the front page, but the headlines wouldn't hold still. I could only make out a single word that kept changing every time I looked at it: MISSING, VANISHED, DISAPPEARED, GONE.

Then the text below the headline began moving. The neat columns of letters broke apart and re-formed into crude stick figures like the ones the Indians paint on their tepees. Around the outside of the page, forming an enclosing circle, were stick men with lines radiating from their heads like the feathers of Indian war bonnets. Inside the circle they formed were other stick figures, these ones without feathers. They seemed to be arranged in a spiral, and about half way along the spiral the figures of humans were replaced by squarish animal figures with four stick legs, curved horns protruding from their heads, and short tails: buffalo. The spiral ended at the centre of the page, where a large black blot of blood had fallen upon the paper. I realized that my nose, which Four Finger Pete had broken, was dripping ink.

I stared at the page, knowing that I should be able to read it, but frustrated that I could not. Somehow I knew that it held a message of great import. Yet the stick figures meant nothing to me. I was an uneducated child who had not yet learned his letters.

I searched the unfamiliar page for anything I could understand. I at last found in an upper corner the only words that remained intelligible: a date. Even as it disappeared, I committed it to memory: September 15, 1884.

Memory echoed in my ears then, in the form of a woman's voice. I heard again the words that Emily had spoken as we stood next to the body of her husband on the deck of the riverboat. She had warned me of the "Day of Changes," and at last I could guess at the meaning of her words. In less than one month's time, when the moon became full again, each and every settler in the North-West Territories—more than seven thousand souls—would be turned into a buffalo. Only Indians would be spared.

I dropped the newspaper and looked around me. The animals had changed into white crows. These sprang into the air and began flying toward the top of the cliff, their wings flapping in unison.

As I watched, I felt something moving in my hands and instinctively released it. An aerograph rose into the sky with the creak and flap of mechanical wings, following the crows. Just as it reached the top of the cliff, the aerograph suddenly swerved. Its air bag caught on one of the white buffalo's curved horns and tore wide open. Now the aerograph was falling. Flail as its mechanical wings might, it was doomed.

I was doomed.

I had become the aerograph—and I had no wings. I fell toward the stone on which the white buffalo stood, drawn toward it by the invisible force of gravity, flailing my useless arms and screaming as I tumbled headlong through the air. The stone drew me to it like a magnet. I crashed into it with tremendous force, feeling my metal bones bend and break, my airbag clothes tatter as they were torn apart.

Now I lay between the buffalo calf's hooves, staring helplessly up at it. One hoof lifted, then paused just above my stomach as the animal considered my fate. Above it, winging their way in a tight spiral toward the moon, the white crows screamed for blood. I could feel fever-heat radiating from the hoof above me as it settled onto my stomach, pressing down with painful force, and I mumbled a protest through bloodied lips.

"No," I croaked. "Please. I tried to help you. No–"

I woke up to a hand shaking my shoulder. Sitting up, I found myself in an unfamiliar barracks. I nearly doubled over as pain punched through my stomach like a fist. Clutching the spot above my scar with one hand, I grabbed the hand that was offered me and gripped it tightly until the worst of the pain had stopped.

I looked up into the worried eyes of Constable Davis. Like me, he was dressed only in his undergarments. The barracks were dark, and I heard snores and the deep breathing of men in slumber coming from the bunks all around me. An empty bed, its blankets thrown back, was next to mine. Moonlight slanted in through the windows, illuminating the room with a pale white glow. Outside the window, a full moon hung in the sky; the sight of it set my heart to pounding. I felt dizzy, disoriented.

"What day is it?" I gasped.

My question took Davis aback. "Why, it's the sixteenth," he said. Then he glanced out the window. "Or rather, the seventeenth, since it's now past midnight."

I sighed with relief. The Day of Changes was not yet upon us.

"Are you all right, Grayburn?" he asked. "I heard you groaning in your sleep, and then you called out for help. Are you ill?"

Realizing that I was still gripping my stomach, I moved my hand away. Wincing at the pain that gnawed at my guts, I gestured at my haversack. Davis handed it to me.

"Just a bout of typho-malaria," I said as I fished the bottle of patent medicine from the pack. "Several of the men at my detachment have it; the water at Moose Jaw is miasmic. I've just got a mild dose—nothing a little painkiller won't manage. No sense in incurring a hospital stoppage if I can still perform my duties."

I took several good swallows of the Pinkham's, and after a moment felt a warm glow begin to replace the ache in my stomach. The young constable nodded, yawned, then crawled back into bed. I heard the crackle of the straw in his mattress.

"I don't know what the bastards in Ottawa are thinking," he muttered. "Docking a man's pay just because he's sick just doesn't seem fair to me."

"Nor to me," I said, taking another swallow of painkiller. "So please, keep my infirmity to yourself, would you?"

"I will," he said.

—

I lay in the dark for some time after that, listening to the other constables breathing. I was jealous of these men who slept so soundly; every time I tried to drift back to sleep I was awakened by the pain in my stomach, and imagined I heard Chambers's voice calling to me. Was he somewhere out on the wide prairie even now, confused and befuddled by his buffalo form, praying I would come to his aid? My dream seemed to be urging me to cure him—but warning that any cure I effected might prove fatal.

At last, giving up on sleep, I rose from bed and pulled on my breeches. I stepped outside the barracks and tamped some Capstan into my pipe, then struck a match and drew until the tobacco was cherry red. Leaning against the rough wooden wall of the barracks, I looked across the parade square that was bathed in moonlight. I tried to imagine the prairie in ten or twenty year's time. Two decades earlier, there had been nothing on this spot but windswept prairie and a few tepees. Now there was a bustling police detachment. A hundred miles to the north lay Calgary, the current terminus of the CPR line. The town had only been surveyed last December, but already it had a population of 500. The *Calgary Herald*, a newspaper whose printing press had arrived by train only last month, was already boosting the town—claiming it would have a population of more than 1,000 before the year was out, and was further predicting a population of 5,000 in a decade's time.

I glanced up at the moon, its "dark side" now bathed in light. If my dream were truly a prophetic one—and I had no reason to believe it was not—then in one month's time the moon would be beaming down on a very different world. I tried to picture Fort Macleod, Calgary, and all of the other outposts and towns of the North-West Territories, large and small, with buildings vacant and silent. Nothing but ghost towns would dot the prairie then: ghost towns, and tepees, and the skulls of buffalo that had once been men, women, and children.

"Heya, *napikwan*. Gotta smoke?"

I started and dropped my pipe, which landed with a shower of sparks on the wooden boardwalk at my feet. Beside me, a stoop-shouldered man bent down to pick it up. When he handed it back to me, I recognized him at once by his short stature and the drooping moustache that matched the slouch of his shoulders: Jerry Potts, the most famous—and notorious—scout in the whole of the North-West Territories. At forty-seven years old he was nearly twice my age, but I say with no shame that he was easily twice the man I'd ever be.

It seemed, in addition to precognitive dreams, that I also had a talent for running into just the person I most needed to meet. I decided to take advantage of it.

"Hello, Potts," I said, passing the half-breed my tin of tobacco. I watched him pull a pipe from the pocket of his frayed trousers and light up. Potts might wear the pants, jacket and hat of a white man, but his soul was pure Indian. The knife that hung in a beaded sheath from his belt had taken more than a dozen scalps from his enemies, and I knew that under his jacket, against his hairy chest, was the skin of a black cat that Potts had killed because he dreamed that its hide would protect him. He might well have been right: even though he'd taken a musket blast in the face during the last big confrontation between the Blackfoot nation and the Cree—the battle that Piapot dreamed would lead to his own death—Potts had walked away with only a powder burn. I wondered if the cat skin also gave him the ability to pad along so silently in his moccasins.

"Potts, will you help me track someone?"

The man beside me grunted. I couldn't tell if it meant "yes" or "no."

"Tonight?" I asked.

Potts squinted up at the moon, thinking. Then he yawned. I could smell liquor on his breath, but he was steady enough.

Suddenly inspired, I added: "There's a bottle of Lydia Pinkham's Painkiller in it for you, if you'll ride with me right now."

"Where?"

I smiled. "Earlier today, I saw a buffalo about three miles up the creek. I want you to track it from the spot I last saw it."

"Gonna shoot it?" Potts asked.

"No!" I exclaimed. "I just want to... to find it. Once we do, you can return to the fort. I'll find my own way back."

Potts stared at me a moment, then sucked on his pipe. "Lotsa Cree," he said, each word a puff of smoke.

"Yes," I answered. "Big Bear's band is camped nearby."

Potts spat.

We stood in silence as I puzzled out what he had been getting at. Potts wasn't noted for his loquaciousness, but the clues were plain to anyone who knew his history. His mother was a Blood Indian, and Potts himself had two Peigan wives. Both of those tribes were part of the Blackfoot Confederacy—and the Blackfoot and Cree were mortal enemies. It would come as no surprise to me if more than one of the warriors in Big Bear's camp was a vengeful relative of a man Potts had scalped.

I indicated my bandaged thigh. "One of Big Bear's warriors shot me today. Maybe we'll run into him."

I saw a sparkle in Potts's eye that told me I'd said just the right thing. Potts nodded, then said, "Let's go."

I stepped into the barracks and hurriedly dressed, not wanting to give Potts time to change his mind. As we made our way across the parade square to the stables, I checked my watch. Assuming it was running properly, the time was nearly four o'clock. Already the eastern horizon was brightening; it would be dawn soon, and Superintendent Cotton would be sending out a patrol to arrest Wandering Spirit—a patrol that would presumably require Jerry Potts to track the man down. I knew I'd catch hell for taking the force's most valuable scout out on what Cotton would see as a "wild buffalo chase." I just hoped that he would allow me to contact Steele before clapping me in the guardhouse for desertion of duty and misappropriation of a police horse.

Potts and I saddled up, then led our horses out of the stables. We were challenged by one of the constables on picquet duty, but a little bluster on my part convinced him that no sane man would be setting out at four in the morning except under orders.

We headed west, across Willow Creek. The horse I was riding—a grey mare—was a playful beast that liked to repeatedly plunge her forefoot into the water, splashing for all she was worth. By the time I managed to spur her across the creek, my riding breeches and jacket were soaking wet. Potts just glanced back at me, not even cracking a smile at a sight that would have evoked gales of laughter from any other man.

We rode in silence for some time. Then, remembering that Potts's own two wives were Peigan, I asked a question.

"I met a Peigan woman earlier toda... ah... earlier this month," I said. "Her name is Emily. She's the wife of a white man, a gambler by the name of Four Finger Pete. Do you know her?"

"Nope," said Potts, without even looking back over his shoulder.

I spurred my horse to come level with Potts. "The woman had a daughter—a girl with pale skin and white hair."

I waited for a reaction, watching Potts out of the corner of my eye, but his face remained impassive.

"The daughter was named Iniskim. The word sounds Peigan. What does it mean?"

Potts grunted. At first I thought he wasn't going to answer me. Then he said: "Blackfoot word." After a moment more, he added: "Means 'Buffalo Stone.'"

I suddenly guessed the connection and leaned across my saddle toward Potts as our horses walked, side by side.

"I saw a strangely shaped stone. It curved in upon itself, like this." I crooked my index finger, imitating the curve of the spiral-shaped stone I'd found near the McDougall home. "Is that what a buffalo stone looks like?"

Potts grunted. I thought I'd seen a slight nod of his head, and took his answer to mean "yes."

I fell silent, thinking about my dream. In it, the curious stone I had found had returned Chambers to his human form. My waking mind now acknowledged what I had intuitively known all along: the stone had the power to transform people into buffalo, and vice versa. But how?

Thinking back to my confrontation with Wandering Spirit and Big Bear, I realized that the chief had avoided touching the stone; he'd used my tobacco pouch to pick it up. Had he been afraid to touch it? If the stone could transform with a touch, why was I able to hold it in my bare hand?

The stone's magic also seemed to work at a distance. The stone had been in a tree outside the McDougall home, yet from the evidence I'd seen, it looked as though the McDougalls had been transformed all at once as they sat at breakfast inside their house. Like maddened beasts, these newly created buffaloes had charged about their home, seeking an escape—which explained the torn clothing and destruction I had seen inside the lower floor of the building, and the hole in the wall near the door where a horn had gored the wood.

"The buffalo stone is magical, isn't it?" I asked Potts. I knew he was superstitious, and that he would have believed any stories he'd heard about the buffalo stone; he wouldn't find my questions odd, as a white man would. "What does it do?"

Potts grunted derisively, as if the answer was obvious. "They call buffalo."

They? I frowned. "Is there more than one buffalo stone?"

Potts merely grunted.

I thought of Iniskim's pale skin and hair. "Do the stones call white buffalo?"

Potts gave me a sharp look. "White buffalo leads the herd. Napi sends it."

"How?"

"Same as any other thing. It's born."

For Potts, it was a long-winded statement—and an informative one. Napi was the Blackfoot creator: the equivalent, in the Indians' eyes, of the whites' Christian God. Did that mean that Iniskim was some sort of Christ child?

"Could the white buffalo be born as a human?" I asked. "As a girl child? And then be transformed into a buffalo when it–"

Potts gave me a quick, uncomfortable look, then dug his spurs into his horse's flanks. The animal trotted ahead, putting an end to our conversation.

I wondered if I'd said too much. I had no idea where Potts's loyalties lay. He had worked for the North-West Mounted Police for ten years, and given loyal and faithful service during that time, despite his love of liquor and the scrapes it got him into—but he was a half-breed. He might very well rejoice if the white settlers were all transformed into buffalo. For all I knew, he might be in league with the Indian shamans who were plotting this transformation.

By now, the sun was up and it was full daylight. We were riding along the grassy bank of the creek, with no cover in sight. I slowly lowered the reins I held until my right hand was against my horse's neck, close to my holstered Winchester. Even as my hand brushed the butt of the rifle, however, Potts glanced back over his shoulder, wary as a cat. I gave him a nervous smile, and moved my hand away.

The odds were not in my favour. I'd heard the stories that had given rise to Potts's infamy. Once, seven Crow Indians had attacked him; four of them were armed with rifles. Potts had killed all four and sent the others fleeing for home. Another time, three Indians had lain in ambush and killed Potts's cousin, capturing Potts himself. Pretending to let him go, they'd shot at his back, but missed and knocked his hat off instead. As he fell from his saddle, Potts had drawn his revolver and killed all three.

If Potts's sympathies did lie with the Indians, and if he decided from my questions that I already had learned too much, I was a dead man. On the other hand, he may have just been relating to me stories that he'd heard as a child at his mother's knee—just as my own mother had read me stories of pixies and sprites when I was a boy. It made me wonder now if pixies and fairies were also real.

Potts reined his horse to a stop. I tensed, but then relaxed when I saw him dismount and peer intently at the top of the riverbank. I pulled my own horse up, and looked down at the soft ground. I saw buffalo hoof prints, the prints of a shod horse, my own boot prints, and furrows in the ground. This was the spot where Chambers had scratched out his message, and where the constable from Fort Macleod had found me.

"Strange tracks," Potts said.

"They were made by the animal I'm looking for," I told him. "Can you track it?"

Potts climbed back on his horse without answering. He turned his horse in the direction that Chambers had run, after I'd frightened him with my revolver shot. Realizing that Potts was already on the trail, I kicked my horse forward.

The tracks circled back to the creek again, then crossed it. I got a second soaking from my mare as she splashed her way across. We rode in silence for several miles, heading due east across the open prairie.

By mid-afternoon, I found myself wondering if Chambers had walked all the way back to Regina, to scratch out a plea for help in front of Steele himself. On several occasions the hoof prints disappeared, but Potts always picked up the trail. We rode on through the afternoon, past prickly pear cactus in full yellow bloom and clumps of pungent sage. We startled an elk that was grazing—when I saw it my heart leapt, mistaking its dark shape for a buffalo and thinking we'd found Chambers at last—and for a while we were followed by a curious coyote. But there was no sign of any buffalo.

By sunset, when we stopped to water the horses and have another quick meal of biscuits and pemmican, I estimated that we'd ridden nearly forty miles. Potts was his usual taciturn self as we unsaddled and hobbled the horses. Watching him as he made a small fire to boil water for tea, I couldn't tell if he was getting restless or not. I decided not to ask if he'd rather turn back; I didn't want to put any ideas in his head. Instead I wanted to give him an incentive to stay.

As we unrolled our blankets in silence, listening to the coyotes yip in the distance, I offered Potts my spare bottle of Pinkham's. He pulled the cork and threw it away, then drained one-third of the bottle in a long swallow. Wiping his drooping moustache, he gave the briefest of appreciatory nods.

"Tastes good," he said.

I supposed it did to a man who was used to the "firewater" the traders brewed up for the Indians. That was vile stuff indeed. It contained enough red pepper and vitriol to give a man a stomach ache worse than my own, and enough iodine, "for colour," to stain a man's moustache a bright red.

As Potts drank the painkiller down, I took a swallow from my remaining bottle to quell the pain in my stomach. The biscuit and tea weren't sitting well; cramps gripped my guts like a vice. The arrow wound in my thigh was also stinging; although the arrowhead hadn't done more than tear open the skin, the day's ride had caused the shallow wound to begin seeping blood. I was gambling that we'd find Chambers and get back to the fort tomorrow; there wasn't enough painkiller left to see me through more than one more day.

Potts wasn't one for conversation, and so I sat and stared at the tiny fire, lost in my own thoughts. I wondered if Superintendent Cotton had sent a patrol out to arrest Wandering Spirit this morning, and how those men had fared. I also wondered if Superintendent Steele had responded yet to my aerograph message. I knew I should have waited for his reply, or at the very least sent further word of my discoveries to Steele, but some compulsion was forcing me to chase after Chambers instead. I couldn't say why, but searching for him seemed more urgent and important than waiting for Steele's orders.

I heard a clink, and looked up to see that Potts had finished his own bottle and had cast it aside. I quickly tucked my own bottle away in my saddlebag. When Potts pulled out his revolver, my eyes widened.

"Potts," I said slowly. "I can only give you the one bottle of painkiller. I need this one for–"

My words choked in my throat as Potts's revolver belched flame, but it wasn't me he was shooting at. Instead, his bullet shattered the empty bottle he'd just tossed aside. I swallowed down my relief as he squinted an unsteady smile at me.

"I can shoot," he told me. "Even drunk." He squinted at my face. "If you had a moustache, I'd trim it with a bullet."

I'd heard of this game: it was one Potts used to play when he was south of the border to test the mettle of the Montana gunslingers. I ran a hand nervously across my upper lip, glad for once that I was incapable of growing a proper beard. Even though it had been more than a day since I had shaved—nearly three weeks, if the days that sped by magically while I was underground were to be counted—I had only a patch or two of stubble on my face.

"Thanks, Potts," I said in a careful voice. "But I'm tired. I'm going to turn in."

I lay down on the ground, resting my head on the saddlebag that held my remaining bottle of painkiller. After staggering off to relieve himself, Potts also stretched out. As the sky darkened and the stars twinkled overhead, I heard him begin to snore.

Although I was bone weary and drowsy with painkiller, I slept fitfully. I dreamed that I stood on a wide expanse of prairie, lost and alone, shivering in a cold wind. All around me the yellow grass was bent, rippling like waves as the wind shifted it this way and that. Every now and then I caught sight of footprints as the grass parted. I saw the small, bare footprint of a human child, and then the grass covered it again. The grass parted, and I saw the heavy indentation of a buffalo hoof. Then the grass shifted and it was gone.

Tracks were all around me, hidden by the grass. I knew that all of them were heading in the same direction, but I couldn't tell which. The wind was a multitude of voices, whispering in chorus for me to follow this invisible trail.

I dropped to my knees and searched, but each time I parted the grass to look at a footprint I had seen only a second ago, it had already disappeared.

I imagined I heard Chambers calling out to me, and the sound of a lost girl crying. I don't know whether it was a dream or reality, but I vaguely remember waking up and looking out across the moonlit prairie, and seeing a small white shape moving through the grass. It might have been a small white buffalo, it might have been a cloud on the horizon, or it might have been a ghost, haunting my dreams.

When I woke up the next morning, Potts was gone. So was my horse. I scrambled out of the blankets, cursing the half-breed scout, certain I had been abandoned now that he'd gotten the liquor I'd promised. At least he'd left my saddle, rifle, and saddle bags behind, although I was damned if I knew how I'd carry them all. Strangely, Potts had also left his own saddle and tack behind. I supposed he must have been too drunk to saddle up.

I pulled on my boots, picked up my Winchester, and slung my saddlebags over my shoulder. I stared ruefully at the saddle and tack, which I'd have to leave behind. I was miles from the nearest police detachment—it was going to be a long, hot walk back.

Then I heard the sound of pounding hooves coming from the west. I looked up and after a moment recognized the rider: Potts, galloping furiously. Just behind him, being led by a rope, was another horse, which I recognized as my grey mare. In the distance behind them were smaller clouds of dust: more riders.

I stared, wondering what was going on. What trouble had Potts gotten himself into during the night? Waving my Winchester in the air, I signalled to him. No need—he was riding straight for me.

Potts yanked his horse to a stop a yard or two in front of me. He was riding it bareback, guiding it with his knees. He held its mane in one hand and the lead rope that was around the neck of my horse in the other hand. His face was covered with a sheen of sweat and blotched by dust; under it, he looked a little green from the drink he'd had the night before. As his horse stood, flanks heaving, he glanced back over his shoulder—not nervously, but with the wary look of a cat that a dog is trying to tree.

"Potts!" I yelled. "What's happened?"

"Cree stole our horses," he said. "I got 'em back."

I stared at Potts, incredulous. All of the Indian tribes are notorious horse thieves; we police have the hardest time convincing them that stealing horses is a crime. The Cree must have crept into our camp last night while we slept. Perhaps they'd heard Potts's pistol shot and come to see who we were, then decided to relieve us of our horses. I'd been sleeping lightly, and yet I hadn't heard a thing. How had Potts, in his inebriated state, been so alert?

Something on Potts's belt fluttered in the morning breeze. I looked closer, and saw a fresh scalp dripping blood onto his leg. Potts must have spotted the look of revulsion that crossed my face; he gave me a grim look, as if deciding whether to add my unruly red-blond locks to the grisly trophy at his belt.

The riders who had been following Potts were closer now; already I could hear the drumming of their horses' hooves. I squinted, and the clouds of dust resolved themselves into more than a dozen dark shapes. A chill swept through me as I realized that an entire war party must be on Potts's trail. After what Potts had done—at least one man must be dead, judging by the scalp on his belt—they wouldn't be in the mood to listen to reason, even from a North-West Mounted Policeman. I could try to pacify them by arresting Potts and announcing that I was charging him with murder, but it probably would do no good—and Potts wasn't the sort of man to submit meekly to the law. He'd rather be taken dead than alive.

I turned and grabbed my saddle.

"No time," Potts gritted.

"But–"

"Ride now or die."

Potts dropped the lead rope and spurred his horse away. I started to saddle my horse, but she was nervous, and skittered away. Now I could hear the war whoops of the approaching Cree.

I was a seasoned rider, but I knew I'd never outrun the Indians if I had to ride bareback. "Damn you!" I cried, grabbing the horse's lead rope. "Hold still."

I heard the crack of a rifle. A bullet whizzed past me. Another slammed with a dull thud into the leather of my saddlebag. The mare shied away, and nearly tugged the lead rope from my hand. Giving up on my saddle, I threw it aside and scrambled awkwardly onto her bare back as more bullets buzzed past my ears like angry wasps. There was no time to pick up my saddlebags and rifle; I left them where they lay. I'd need both hands just to stay on the horse's back.

There was no need to dig in my spurs. With the first touch of my heels, the mare leaped forward. She was sweaty from her gallop across the prairie, but at least she hadn't had a man on her back. She still had some speed in her. As the Indians behind me whooped and howled like wolves that have scented blood, the mare shot forward like a cannon ball. I gripped as tightly as I could with my knees, clung onto her mane and the lead rope, and hunkered down low, praying that a bullet wouldn't find my back.

I rode hard, keeping my eyes on Potts, who had drawn a good distance ahead and to the left of me while I had been frantically trying to saddle my horse. He rode up a rise that was dotted with trees, then disappeared down the other side. I twisted around, trying to see how close our pursuers were. Close!

I was just about over the rise when my horse shied violently as a bird flew up from a bush. Somehow, I managed to hang on. The mare topped the rise and charged down the other side toward a wide expanse of slow, deep water that I knew must be the Bow River. I clung to her for all I was worth, teeth rattling as I yanked on the rope around her neck, trying to stop her before she plunged into the river. Fording it would do no good; the water would slow us down, making me a perfect target. I caught just a glimpse of Potts—and wondered why he was riding the other way, up the bank—and then heard a ragged volley of gunshots behind me.

The mare skidded to a stop at the river's edge and stood with flanks heaving. Behind me, hidden by the riverbank, a battle raged.

My mind raced as I tried to think what to do. My Winchester was gone but I still had my revolver, holstered at my hip. Potts was obviously making a show of it, probably using his favourite tactic of riding straight back at the enemy in an effort to startle them. My best chance would have been to ride as hard and fast as I could along the riverbank, and leave the half-breed to his fate—but that was the coward's way out.

There was only one thing to do: turn around and brazen it out. Perhaps the Indians would respect the red tunic I wore and the revolver in my hand.

If not, my tunic would be even redder, soon enough.

I drew my revolver. Behind me was silence. Potts had either gotten away—or he was dead.

I yanked the mare's lead rope to turn her, but she had other things in mind. She'd lowered her head to drink in the few seconds that I sat catching my breath, and now that she'd gotten over her fright, she got up to her old antics. She raised her forefoot and brought it down with a splash in the water, soaking my leg, then whinnied in delight.

I heard the sound of hooves on the riverbank above. Twisting to take a look, I saw the tips of a feathered war bonnet coming into view above the bank. Heart pounding, I spurred the mare and yanked the lead rope hard—but instead of turning she reared up on her hind legs and came down with both forelegs in the water, sending up an even larger splash than before.

It caught me by surprise. Bereft of a saddle and stirrups, and unable to steady myself, I toppled sideways. It probably saved my life. I heard the crack of a rifle shot as I tumbled from the mare's back and heard the whiz of a bullet pass my ear. Then I fell headlong into the river. Water closed over my head.

I thrashed my way into a sitting position, wiping water from my eyes with one hand and feeling about in the muddy river bottom with the other. My revolver was gone. Something was splashing in the water next to me: it was the mare, still enjoying her game.

I heard the click of a rifle being cocked, and as the mare moved to the side, I at last saw the fate that awaited me. Standing on the shore next to their panting ponies were a dozen Indians, with rifles pointed at my chest and an angry look in their eyes. There was only one thing in my favour: they hadn't shot me yet.

I stood up with as much dignity as I could muster, ignoring the water that was streaming from my sodden uniform. I steeled my voice and fixed them with a stern look.

"I am a North-West Mounted Police corporal," I told them. "If you shoot me, other red coats will come, and hunt you down and hang you like dogs."

The Indians laughed. It wasn't the response I'd expected.

I heard the sound of another horse, and braced myself. For a moment I thought it was Potts, coming to my aid. My heart lifted, then sank again as I realized that the Indians were singularly unconcerned by the sound. In another moment, a familiar rider came over the rise and trotted his pony up to the edge of the river.

Big Bear pointed a wiry finger at me, and then at my mare, who still stood at the river's edge, splashing a forefoot into the water.

"You come," the chief said in barely recognizable English. "Come horse." Then he added something in Cree—a long, rambling speech.

I understood only one word, and it was in the language of his enemies.

Iniskim.

◄—►

Chapter V

A meeting of chiefs—Inside the shaking tepee—Animal spirits—
Two more disappearances—Flight into darkness—Writing On
Stone—Wise advice from an owl—Trapped!—A fortuitous arrival

The Indians did not bind me, but I was their captive just the same. For three long days we rode south, fording the Belly River and crossing two coulees that lesser rivers had carved into the rolling prairie. All during that time braves rode at either side of me, watching with wary eyes lest I try to spur my horse into a gallop. Even had I been inclined to test my mettle against a dozen warriors, I would have had little chance of success. I had lost both my Winchester—which I thought I saw one of the Indians carrying—and my revolver. The Indians had even taken my boots, forcing me to ride in stocking feet.

I kept hoping that Potts was alive—that he would appear to blaze bullets at my captors and provide me with an opportunity to escape. At the very least I hoped he was tracking us. At one point I saw a moving shape that might have been a man—or merely a large animal—but there was no clear sign of Potts. I wondered if he was lying dead on the prairie. One of the horses the Cree were leading looked suspiciously like the one Potts had been riding, but I never got close enough to it to see if it had an S—the brand that all police scouts' horses are marked with—on its shoulder.

There were a dozen Cree in all. Big Bear rode near the head of the band, as did Wandering Spirit, who was mounted on a tall grey mare with fluttering eagle feathers tied in her tail and mane. All were men, traveling light without tepees or travois—a war party, I suspected. None of them seemed to speak any English—either that, or they were simply not inclined to answer my questions. They pretended not to recognize the name McDougall, and simply grunted and looked away whenever I demanded to know what was going on and where they were taking me.

We ate very little, just a mouthful of pemmican each noon and night. By the end of the third day, I was light-headed with hunger. The constant ache of hunger had joined the incessant pangs in my stomach. More than once I found my eyes tearing and I wished heartily that I still had my painkiller. I'd even settle for the traders' firewater—anything to dull the pain. I struggled to keep my face composed; I didn't want the Indians thinking I was frightened of them. My continued survival probably depended as much on not appearing a coward as it did on anything else.

The first two nights we camped out under the open skies, with only the tiniest of campfires to warm us. I'd lost my blankets, and had only my jacket to fend off the night's chill. Sleep was difficult, especially since the braves took it in turn to sit and watch me all night. When it was Wandering Spirit's turn, I deliberately rolled over so that my back was toward him. I didn't need to be a student of thought transference to feel his hostile intentions as his eyes bored into my back. I ignored him as best I could, but found my eyes drawn to the moon, which had passed its zenith and was starting to wane. When it was full again, the Day of Changes would come. I chafed at my captivity, wishing I could make my way back to a police detachment. I needed to tell Steele what I had learned before it was too late.

On the third evening we arrived at a bluff overlooking a river that meandered back and forth across a flat, grassy plain. The slope that lay between this plain and the ridge on which we halted our horses was a maze of sandstone that nature had sculpted into fantastic shapes. Large domes of darker stone capped burnt-orange pillars that were pitted with holes. Birds swooped in and out of these small, smooth-walled caves, delivering insects to their cheeping nestlings. Between these rocky spires, the sandy soil was dotted with tufts of grass and the occasional stand of stunted trees.

I recognized the river at once from its colour: that of dark brown tea diluted with milk. The Milk River flowed east to west, not ten miles from the American border. The coulees leading to the south through the maze of sandstone columns on the opposite side of the plain had been a favourite hiding place for American whisky smugglers for decades.

I thought we would make our way down to the river to water the horses, but instead Big Bear signalled his men to turn and follow the bluffs. After another mile or so, I saw why: ahead was a large number of Indians, already unsaddling their horses and turning them out to graze on the dry grass. There must have been a hundred of them—all men, and all armed. They seemed to be in two large groups, each keeping a little apart from the other. As we rode closer, several of them discharged rifles into the air and whooped. Others welcomed our party by beating wide flat drums and chanting. Several cast suspicious looks in my direction as our group dismounted.

Leaving one of his warriors to watch me, Big Bear strode forward and clasped the arms of a fellow I recognized at once by his long, hawkish nose and square jaw: Chief Piapot. Close by was a tall, distinguished looking fellow with a long, proud face and aristocratic bearing: the Cree chief, Poundmaker. His hair, which hung to his hips, was tied back in a red bandanna, and a scalp lock at his forehead was wrapped with a tuft of glossy fur that looked like mink skin. He stood taller than the other men and carried a fearsome war club in which three knife blades were embedded.

I also recognized, from my days patrolling out of Fort Walsh, the Cree chiefs Little Pine and Beardy. Little Pine was old and wrinkled, bent over a walking stick and peering about through squinting eyes as if he were having difficulty seeing. Yet despite his infirmities, he had a proud bearing.

Beardy—a nickname he'd been given due to his straggly chin whiskers—wore leggings trimmed with jingling silver buckles. On his head was a fur hat topped with a single eagle feather, its tip tufted with red wool. Like Big Bear, Beardy had been reluctant to sign a treaty and settle down on a reserve. And like Piapot, he'd tried to stop the influx of white settlers to the prairies. Just four years ago, the North-West Mounted Police had to deal with Beardy's tribe when it tried to impose a toll on travelers using the Carlton Trail, harassing and threatening those who would not pay.

As Big Bear approached, Beardy raised his right hand to the sky in the Indian salute. It seemed this was to be a council meeting of the Cree chiefs. I wondered if they had come together to meet with Louis Riel, or one of his emissaries. I'd heard the Metis leader was back in the North-West Territories, trying to goad the Indians into a rebellion, but I didn't see Riel or any of his men among the crowd.

As I was studying the second group of Indians—the ones who stood several yards apart from the Cree chiefs—I noticed something odd. Several of them were wearing leggings painted with diagonal black stripes: the hallmark of a Blackfoot warrior. All of them were casting dark, suspicious looks at the Cree and held their weapons at the ready, as if they expected a fight to break out at any moment.

Standing in front of this second group were three men, who, from their bearing, I took to be chiefs. The most imposing of the three wore his hair loose to the shoulder and had hollow cheeks and narrow, watchful eyes. His shirt was fringed with fluttering black feathers under each arm. He carried an eagle wing, mounted on a handle like a fan, in one hand. Beside him stood one of his braves, holding an umbrella over the chief's head to shade him from the sun.

Standing just behind this chief and to his right, in the position reserved for secondary chiefs, was a stocky man with drooping eyes and a down-turned mouth. His eyes were shaded by a Liberty hat that had an eagle feather jutting out the back, but I could see that they were fixed malevolently upon the Cree warriors. His jacket was open, and on his bare chest were jagged red scars that must have come from the sun dance, an ordeal in which braves pierce themselves with sticks attached to rawhide thongs, then dance until these skewers tear free. I winced, thinking that these ancient injuries must have hurt even more than the pains that even now wracked my stomach.

The third chief wore on his belt a round leather shield painted with the figure of an antlered deer. An impressive headdress of eagle feathers crowned his head in a ring, standing straight up in the shape of a top hat, with strips of white fur hanging down on either side of his head like thick strands of hair. He stood aloof with arms folded against the trade beads that draped his chest, his eyes fixed on some distant point. When he did deign to look at the Cree chiefs, his expression hardened. It was obvious that he did not care for them much.

I turned to the Cree warrior who was guarding me, and pointed the foremost of these three men out, making the Indian sign for "Who?" The brave responded by gesturing toward his feet: the chief was a Blackfoot.

I stared at the head chief again, and noticed a stuffed crow's head peeping from the top of the feathered war bonnet he wore. I realized then who he was: Crowfoot, leader of the Blackfoot Confederacy. What was he doing here, at a meeting of Cree chiefs?

The brave beside me pointed at the chief next to Crowfoot—the one with the scars on his chest—and made the Indian sign for the Blood tribe, drawing his forefinger across his lips from left to right. He spoke the fellow's name slowly in Cree, repeating the name twice. Fortunately the words were simple ones that I could understand: Red Crow. Then he pointed at the chief with the shield, rubbing the knuckles of his right hand into his cheek to make the Indian sign for the Peigan tribe. This chief's name was also a word I understood: Mountain.

I looked back and forth between the two groups of warriors in amazement. The Cree and the Blackfoot Confederacy tribes were sworn enemies. According to reports from missionaries that worked among the Blood tribe, Chief Red Crow was just looking for an excuse to fight the Cree, and hoped that Riel would persuade the enemy tribe to rebel. That way, he could slaughter Cree with the government's blessing.

Red Crow scowled at the Cree chiefs as if waiting for them to make a move, and his warriors milled restlessly behind him. I was thankful for the Indian custom of proving one's manhood by waiting for the enemy to take the first shot—it seemed to be the only thing preventing immediate bloodshed.

When the Cree chiefs were done greeting each other, they turned toward the three Blackfoot Confederacy chiefs. Crowfoot was the one they approached first. Poundmaker greeted him, and when Crowfoot returned the salutation, I thought I heard him use the word "son." The two seemed on very friendly terms, despite the traditional animosity between their two tribes, and it took me a moment to realize why. Then I remembered the stories I'd heard about Poundmaker: that he'd spent a portion of his childhood as a captive in a Blackfoot camp, and had come to be adopted by its chief. I now realized that chief must have been Crowfoot. It explained why Poundmaker was taking the lead, and not Big Bear. Poundmaker could speak both Cree and Blackfoot—and had an ally in the enemy camp.

After Poundmaker finished speaking with Crowfoot, Big Bear formally greeted each of the Blackfoot Confederacy chiefs in turn, then waved forward one of his men who carried a hide bundle. Big Bear solemnly unwrapped the bundle, then gestured for Crowfoot to take what lay inside. The Blackfoot chief lifted from the bundle a long, straight-stemmed pipe with the figure of an animal next to its high, narrow bowl. The pipe was carved of white stone, and smudged with red ochre. Crowfoot turned and showed it to his warriors, who shouted their approval, then he handed it to Red Crow. The Blood chief held it up in turn, then passed it to Mountain—who handed it back to Poundmaker, instead of to Big Bear. Poundmaker's eyes widened, but he quickly composed himself and handed the pipe to Big Bear, who gave Mountain a glowering look.

It must have been a deliberate slight. Mountain's tribe and Big Bear's people had fought each other in one of the bloodiest battles in Indian history, just fourteen years ago. It was a miracle that their warriors had not already come to blows here today, and that Big Bear was containing himself in the face of this insult from his traditional enemy. If ever there was a peace pipe, this must be it.

I paid close attention to all that was going on around me. At our meeting in Regina, Steele had told me that Big Bear had been working to unite the Cree tribes with the Blackfoot Confederacy. I'd thought this ridiculous at the time, but here I saw evidence of his efforts with my own eyes.

When the chiefs concluded their lengthy and very formal greetings, they turned and began to walk along the bluffs, away from the assembled warriors. I glanced at the brave who had been detailed to watch me; his attention was fixed on the chiefs. Tired and hungry after three days of riding, I decided it was time to make my appeal.

"Chief Poundmaker!" I said as I strode forward. "I am Corporal Grayburn of the North-West Mounted Police. I have been brought here against my will by Chief Big Bear, and I must protest that–"

I saw movement out of the corner of my eye and ducked just in time to avoid a rifle barrel swung at my head. The warrior who had been assigned to watch me shouted angry words in Cree, then lifted his weapon, cocking it. Big Bear spun around and shouted something. I saw him waving his hands in the air and running in our direction as I grabbed the barrel of the rifle, forcing it to the side. The rifle spat flame, and I heard startled shouts from the assembled chiefs as a bullet flew in their direction. The brave with whom I grappled snarled at me, his face twisted with anger.

Then Big Bear was beside us. With a strength I had not expected in so short-statured and wizened a man, he yanked the rifle out of both of our hands. He said a few curt words to the brave, who slunk away like a whipped dog, then stared angrily up at me. Then he spoke to the other chiefs, gesturing at me repeatedly.

Poundmaker translated his words into the Blackfoot language. The others listened, then stared at me and shook their heads, muttering. I didn't need to understand the Blackfoot tongue to read the threatening looks in their eyes. Red Crow picked up his hat from the ground—I wondered if the bullet had knocked it off his head—and gave me a look that could have split stone.

I had no idea what Big Bear was saying, but it was clear that he wanted me at this council, and that the other chiefs were reluctant at best, openly hostile at worst. Then I heard a word I recognized—one that Poundmaker didn't have to translate: Iniskim. I nodded my head vigorously. I didn't think the Indians were going to harm me, but I was still in a sticky situation, and mentioning the child had saved me once already.

"That's right," I said. "I know the Indian girl named Iniskim. She... became a buffalo calf." Feeling somewhat foolish, I raised forefingers to the sky and touched my thumbs to the side of my head, imitating a buffalo's horns. I used the Cree word for it: "*Paskwawimostos*—buffalo."

The chiefs stared at me for several long moments. Mountain was nodding his head and Crowfoot had a thoughtful look on his

face, but Red Crow glowered suspiciously at Big Bear, as if I were
a dog that the Cree chief had trained to do a trick. Poundmaker
was the first to break the silence. He conferred with the other
chiefs in a low voice until Red Crow reluctantly nodded, then
said something to Big Bear. I could see the chiefs had reached a
decision.

"You come," Big Bear said, repeating the curt instructions
he'd given me three days before on the riverbank.

Every eye was on me, and more than one rifle was pointed in
my direction. I heard an uneasy murmur sweep across the
crowd. I followed Big Bear and the other chiefs, wondering what
would happen next.

Only a handful of warriors from the hundred or so that had
assembled above the Milk River followed us. Wandering Spirit
was one of them, and he made a point of walking next to me and
glaring. In addition to his spotted buckskin shirt and lynx-skin
cap, he was wearing an amulet on a thong about his neck. It
looked as though it was made from a piece of squared-off bone.

I blinked in surprise as I recognized the "amulet" for what it
was: a chipped rectangle of ivory—a key from a piano. Then I
realized which instrument it had to have come from: the
melodeon in the church of Victoria Mission.

I gave Wandering Spirit a hard look. If I lived through this day,
I fully intended to return with a patrol to arrest him on charges
of murder and assaulting a police officer. I'd see him hang.

Wandering Spirit must have heard my silent vow. He raised
his hand, his fingers hooked like claws. My breath caught in my
chest as I recognized the gesture for what it was: a reminder of
the magical wound he'd given Inspector Dickens.

I expected him to kill me on the spot, but the sidelong look
that Wandering Spirit gave his chief told me why he did not: I
was still under Big Bear's protection.

I wondered again why Big Bear had brought me here. I knew
that the Cree chief was involved in the disappearances that were
plaguing the North-West, and I suspected that these other chiefs
were also involved—or soon would be. I made careful mental
notes, carefully adding up the evidence against them. As I
thought about it, however, I wondered what charges I could
possibly lay. I doubted that British law had a statute that
covered the forcible transformation of humans into beasts. Even
if there were, what magistrate or jury would believe my evidence?
I could only hope that Steele was preparing for this contingency.

The group of chiefs and warriors adjourned along the bluffs to
a lone tepee that had been set up overlooking the river. The
whole of the tepee was painted a dusky red, save for a band of
blue at the top and a circle of stick-figure animals, painted in

black around the bottom. These crude drawings bore an unsettling resemblance to the figures I had seen in my dream.

Big Bear said something to the braves who had accompanied us, and then the chiefs, together with Wandering Spirit, filed inside the tepee. I tried to enter it myself, but as soon as my hand touched the door flap one of the braves—the fellow who had carried Poundmaker's umbrella—knocked it aside. Apparently I was to remain outside with the six warriors—three Cree, and three from the Blackfoot Confederacy—who had accompanied the chiefs. They squatted on the grassy bluff, rifles across their knees, and motioned for me to join them.

I took another glance at the tepee, inside which voices were murmuring. I supposed my chance to speak to the chiefs would come when I was summoned inside. I found a large flat stone to sit on, and checked my watch. Assuming that the watch wasn't running fast or slow again, the time was just about nine o'clock. I decided to give the chiefs no more than an hour before demanding an audience with them.

I passed the time by filling and lighting my pipe and watching the sun go down, listening intently to the voices inside the tepee for any words I recognized. From out of the top of the tepee drifted smoke that was tinged with the sweet smell of burning sage.

As I smoked, I debated what to do next. As a lone policeman in a camp of a hundred armed Indians, I had no hope of making any arrests. I'd be lucky to get out of here with my scalp still attached to my head. Yet I could give the chiefs a strong warning, and remind them that they'd face years of imprisonment with hard labour, at the very least, if they harmed a member of the North-West Mounted Police. Perhaps through bluster and bravado I could convince them to let me go.

When I checked my watch again I found that it had stopped working. It had to be at least nine o'clock, however, since the hands had stopped at five minutes before the hour. The sun was just slipping below the horizon, painting the sky a bloody pink, when from inside the tepee came the sound of a drum and a rattle. A voice rose in a chant, and then another, and soon a chorus was filling the air. I could pick out Poundmaker's deep, stentorian tones and the wheezing voice of Little Pine. I couldn't make out any of the words—my grasp of the Indian languages was too tenuous—but the chant seemed to be a jumble of Blackfoot and Cree.

I rose to my feet, and the warriors squatting on the ground rose to flank me, rifles still held in the crooks of their arms. I showed them my watch, then looked pointedly at the tepee, which was already starting to shake from the fervour of those inside. For all I knew, the chiefs would go on for hours. During a sun dance, the Indians will carry on for days, not stopping until they drop from exhaustion. I was tired and hungry and my stomach felt as if it had twisted into a knot—I'd reached the end of my patience, and wasn't very keen on the prospect of sitting up all night.

"This has gone on long enough," I told the fellow with the umbrella, who sat closest to the tepee door. "Big Bear forced me to ride across the prairie for three days, and now has kept me waiting for an hour outside his tepee. Either I speak to the chiefs now, or I'm leaving. You can try to stop me from entering the tepee if you like—but you'll have to put a bullet in my back to do it." I winced as another spasm of pain wracked my stomach, then added: "Quite frankly, I don't really care if you do."

I expected them to prevent me from entering, but instead they untied the flap of the tepee. Then they backed cautiously away, as if expecting something dangerous to burst from within.

The tepee was shaking now; the painted buffalo hides that made up its covering were vibrating like a struck drum. Even the poles that supported it were rattling against one another. I noticed that the warriors' eyes widened every time they glanced at it. When I placed my hand on the door flap, they all drew back another pace. I shook my head at their timidity. Regardless of what kind of weird ritual was going on inside, I was going to get on with my investigation, one way or another. I bent down low, and pushed my way in through the door flap.

It took my eyes a moment to adjust to the dim light inside as the flap closed behind me. The interior of the tepee was lit only by a small fire that had burned down to glowing coals, and the light that passed through the thick, ochre-painted walls of the tepee was a murky red. I could just make out Poundmaker sitting directly opposite the opening, beating on an ornately carved, bowl-shaped drum. Big Bear sat in the position of honour on his right, followed by Piapot, Beardy and Little Pine, who was closest to me. To Poundmaker's left sat chiefs Crowfoot, Red Crow, and Mountain. Wandering Spirit sat closest to the tepee's entrance, as if guarding it. Each of the men had stripped down to his breechcloth, and they were chanting in unison to the beat of the drum. Little Pine shook a rattle, and Crowfoot fanned the coals with his eagle wing. The smell of burning sage was nearly overpowering, and the hot smoke stung my throat and lungs.

Behind the chiefs, the walls of the tepee fluttered and rippled like a sail in a strong wind. The poles were shaking, rattling against one another where they met at the apex of the tepee, as if an earthquake were jiggling them up and down. Yet the ground underfoot was firm and I knew that the air outside was still. I felt the hairs on the back of my neck rise: magic was at work here. Whatever its purpose was, I was certain it couldn't be good. I decided to put a stop to it.

Every one of the Indians had his eyes fixed upon the glowing coals at the centre of the tepee. Not one of them had looked up at me, although all must have noticed my entrance. It was hot inside the tepee; I could feel sweat running down my sides, under my jacket. I bent over and yanked the rattle out of Little Pine's gnarled hands.

"This is an illegal gathering," I told them in as stern a voice as I could muster. "I order you, in the name of the Queen, to stop it this instant."

The chant faltered to a halt. The Indians all looked up at me at once. I dropped the rattle on the ground; it rolled toward the fire pit and Beardy caught it just before it toppled into the coals. Wandering Spirit shifted; I saw his feather-tipped coup stick in his hand. Behind him, the sides of the tepee continued to shake.

Smoke from the fire stung my eyes, making them water. I was having trouble seeing in the dim light; the cross-legged chiefs wavered and blurred like figures underwater, but although the air was clearer down where they sat, I wasn't about to give up the advantage of height. I blinked my tearing eyes and tried to focus on Big Bear's hunched form. I kept talking, even though I knew he spoke no English. Perhaps the force of my words would be enough, or perhaps thought transference would convey my meaning.

"Big Bear, unless you want to feel about your neck the noose that you so fear, I suggest you order your men to release me at once. I also order you and Wandering Spirit to turn yourselves in to the nearest North-West Mounted Police detachment for questioning in connection with the disappearance of–"

Poundmaker suddenly stood and raised his club. The three knife blades embedded in the end of it gleamed red in the firelight. The coals were also reflected in his eyes, which no longer looked human; instead they were small and fierce. I took an involuntary step back, and found my shoulders pressing against the side of the tepee.

I swallowed and raised my hands, preparing to fend off any attack. "Poundmaker!" I shouted. "Stop! Murder is a hanging offence!"

The Cree chief stepped around the campfire, menace in his eyes. Then his club swept down—but I was not its target. Instead it struck the drum he still held, tearing it open. In that same instant, all of the Indians cried out at once, their voices a blend of strange cries, howls, and roars.

A similar cry erupted from my own lips. Then I lost control of my body. It twisted and shrank, and my hands were forced down to my sides. My face broadened and flattened, and the skin all over my body erupted into itches as if hair were growing at a terrific pace. The tepee around me, its glowing red sides still shaking, loomed large overhead as I shrank. I tried to shout, but my lips had become hooked and hard, and produced something that sounded like a bird's hooting cry. Terrified, I looked around me with eyes that felt as if they were stretched wide with fear. The interior of the tepee had been very dark, but now it seemed as bright as day, although everything was in shades of black and white.

I blinked, amazed by what I saw. The Indian chiefs had disappeared. In their places were animals. Directly in front of me stood a mink, its paws and head just peeping above the remains of a torn drum. To its right loomed a gigantic bear with a human hand suspended on a thong about its neck. On the other side of the mink was a large black crow. It stared at me with unblinking, beady eyes. Nestled within the black feathers on the top of its head was what looked like a tiny, shrivelled human head.

Other animals were ranged around me in a circle. To my left were an eagle, a fox, and a mouse, which scurried away behind the fox; to my right a gopher, and a deer with broad antlers. Nearest the door flap was a lynx. Without warning, it took a slash at me, and only by jerking aside at the last instant did I avoid the blow. The lynx's claw tore a hole in the side of the tepee, through which blood-red sunlight spilled. Then the bear reared up on its hind legs and roared. Cowed, the lynx slunk back into a crouch.

The other animals stared at me, and for a frozen moment I was too surprised to do anything but blink. They stood ranged around me in a half-circle, like the animals I'd seen in my dream. The only difference was that I stood not at the base of the buffalo-jump cliff but inside a tepee.

Something else was different from my dream: I was no longer a man. My skin was covered in feathers, and my arms had become wings. My eyes were large and round, and when I opened my mouth to speak, all that emerged was the hoot of an owl.

What's happened to me? I hooted, my feathers ruffling in alarm. *Where am I?*

We have entered the spirit world, the mink answered. *We have taken on spirit form, and can understand each other now.*

It was true. The mink was speaking Cree, but I understood it as if I spoke the language fluently.

Ask him where she is, the crow cawed in Blackfoot.

Who? I hooted.

My granddaughter, the deer said in a soft voice. *She is lost.*

I shrugged my wings and moved my head slowly from side to side. I had no idea who they were talking about.

He knows nothing, the lynx growled. *And he knows too much. Mistihaimuskwa was wrong to have brought him here. We should kill him now, before he does any more harm.* The lynx raised a paw and flexed it, and sharp claws sprang from the pads. I saw that a tiny black feather was tied to one of its claws.

The bear growled the others into silence. *This red coat has powerful medicine. He came through the earth and was still a man. He touched the buffalo stone and was still a man. He saw Iniskim, and waved her back into the earth.*

The bear pointed a claw at the eagle. *You, Piapot, sensed the power of his spirit a year ago and warned us of him. Yet when you tried to knock him from the sky with a thunderstorm, he escaped you.*

I looked at the eagle, and saw a spark of lightning flash in its eye. I suddenly realized that it was Piapot who had directed the thunderstorm that had buffeted the air bicycle over Regina. The Indians must have been watching me for some time. But why?

The bear nodded toward the lynx, then added: *Kapapamahchakwew was also powerless against him. When he tried to send the red coat into the land of the dead, the red coat would not go.*

The lynx growled softly and flattened its ears. Its claws—and the black feather that was tied to one of them—retracted back into their pads.

The fox cocked its head, and stared at me with its tongue lolling. *Now we see why this red coat is so powerful: he stands before us in the form of an owl. We all know what that means.*

What? I hooted in alarm. *What does it mean? What are you going to do to me?*

Do not be afraid, the bear growled. *I brought you here because you said you knew where Iniskim was. Tell us how to find her, and we will guide you back to the world of men and let you live. You will not be harmed; you have my word on this.*

The mink stared fiercely at me. *If you refuse to tell us, we will leave you here in the spirit world. You will never find your way back, and your body will sicken and die. Now, where is Iniskim?*

I suddenly realized that Iniskim must have been the granddaughter that Mountain said was lost. The albino girl was obviously very important to the Indians, and I could guess why: Iniskim, named after a stone that could "call buffalo," must be a vital part of the magic that would turn every settler in the North-West Territories into buffalo with the coming of the next full moon. I chided myself for not seeing it sooner: I should have realized that much from my prophetic dream. In it, on the Day of

Changes, a white buffalo calf had stood atop the large boulder that the spiral-shaped buffalo stone had grown into.

The large boulder....

I suddenly realized what else the Indians needed to enact the Day of Changes: something much more powerful than the small, spiral-shaped stone that had been used to transform the McDougalls into buffalo, which worked only if it were touched. The Indians also needed the Manitou Stone.

They'd already admitted that Iniskim was lost. She must have been the flash of white I'd seen after following the tunnel from Victoria Mission. According to Big Bear, Iniskim had fled back into the tunnel when I'd startled her.

I thought back to my dream of three nights ago, and the overpowering sensation I had of being lost and alone on the prairie. Iniskim must have turned down one of the many side tunnels and emerged from the earth somewhere else—at some distant point where the Indians couldn't find her.

I wondered if she were the only thing that was missing.

Where is the Manitou Stone? I hooted.

The animals looked at one another, not answering my question. The mouse nervously groomed its whiskers, the lynx flattened its ears again, and the other animals' sidelong glances at one another confirmed my guess. The Manitou Stone hadn't been hauled away from the churchyard at Victoria Mission: it had disappeared.

The Indians had probably intended to transport the Manitou Stone back to its original resting place, and had presumably used magic to move it. That magic, however, had gone awry. According to the briefing Steele had given me, the stone had been taken by the McDougalls from a hill near the Battle River. If it had returned to its original place on the hilltop, the Indians could have found it easily enough—but like Iniskim, the Manitou Stone hadn't gone where it was supposed to.

The bear confirmed my guess. *We do not know where the Manitou Stone is now.*

The lynx growled, but the bear waved a paw, silencing it. *Where is Iniskim?* the bear repeated.

The other animals stared at me, waiting for my answer. I opened and closed my beak, as if searching for the right words, while my mind raced.

I understood now why Big Bear had prevented Wandering Spirit from killing me on that day beside the buffalo-jump cliffs, and why he had forced me to accompany him here to the council of chiefs after our paths had crossed a second time. He'd misunderstood what I'd said when I first spoke about trying to help Emily and Iniskim, when I'd asked their whereabouts. He'd thought, with his limited grasp of English, that I was telling him that I knew where they were. The Indians were desperate to find Iniskim so they could work their magic, so my life had been spared.

One thing didn't make sense, however. I knew that the Indians could transform people into buffalos without Iniskim being present. When the McDougalls were transformed, the girl had been nowhere near Victoria Mission. During our poker game on the *North West*, Four Finger Pete had said that he'd come from Fort Garry, a journey of several weeks. Emily and Iniskim would have been traveling with him at the time the McDougalls disappeared. Nor could Iniskim have been at all of the widely scattered disappearances Steele had mentioned in his telegram.

If the Indians had worked their magic without Iniskim on these occasions, why did they need her to be present at the Manitou Stone?

Something occurred to me: perhaps they didn't. Perhaps they only needed Iniskim to *lead* them to the Manitou Stone. That was why they wanted to find her, and desperately enough that they were willing to let a policeman—a white man—witness their council—and their magic.

A chill ran through me as I realized that I was doomed, no matter what I said. If I told the truth, I would demonstrate that I was of no use in finding Iniskim and I would be killed. If I told them I knew where Iniskim was, they would drag me to whatever spot I named, then kill me when they realized I had lied. I steeled myself; betraying fear to the Indians would be a fatal mistake. I even managed a smile, as I imagined what Jerry Potts would have done, if he had been the one captured. He'd probably spit in their faces like an angry cat.

My time was running out. I decided to spend the moments that remained wisely. I would do all I could to dissuade the Indians from using their magic. I would plead for mercy—not for myself, but for the innocent settlers who would be transformed into buffalo and slaughtered.

I know about the magic you intend to work with the Manitou Stone, I told the animal-chiefs. *I am asking you not to do it—to put a stop to the Day of Changes.*

The mink shook its head. *It must be done. On the Day of Changes, the buffalo will return and the Indians will live the life that the Creator intended them to live.*

I looked up at the bear, hoping for a more sympathetic response. *They aren't buffalo! They're human beings. They have the bodies of beasts, but the minds of men.* I thought of Chambers and the plea for help he had scratched in the riverbank—of the frightened look in his eye. *Think how terrified*

*they must have felt as they plunged over the cliff to their deaths
at Head Smashed In. Some of them were children—mere babes.*

The bear dropped to all fours and roared in my face, its hot
breath flattening my feathers. *What do your people care about
children dying? For many winters, ever since the buffalo began to
disappear, our people have gone hungry. In the worst winters we
hunted and ate anything that remained—even gophers and
mice—but it was not enough. Our people starved. Those chiefs
who had taken reserves turned to your Great White Mother for
help. Even though our children and elders were dying, when we
asked for the food that had been promised in the treaties—
promised in return for our land! — your people said no. They said
that if we did not work, we would not be fed. Yet, how can a man
work when he is so weak that he cannot even carry his rifle?*

The lynx growled its agreement. *Quinn was the worst. He
always said no.*

So you killed him? I asked.

The lynx nodded, and bared its fangs in a smile.

I shook my own head in dismay. Wandering Spirit had just
confessed to Quinn's murder, but even if I lived to testify, no
jury would ever believe me unless they themselves had
witnessed this Indian magic first hand—and by then it would be
too late.

We could kill all of the white men, if we chose to, the lynx
growled. *Even though you have built iron horses and metal birds
that fly, our magic is stronger than yours.*

The eagle nodded. *Both the Indians and the white man can
hear the Creator's voice, but the Indians are the best listeners.*

War is something I counselled against, the bear rumbled. *It
will only bring sorrow and death to both sides. I know this,
because many years ago, when I traveled below the medicine line,
I had an ugly dream. I saw a spring shooting up out of the ground.
I covered it with my hand, trying to smother it, but it spurted up
between my fingers and it ran over the back of my hand. It was a
spring of blood. Indian blood.*

My eyes widened in realization. It seemed I wasn't the only
one who had prophetic dreams. Big Bear was right: if there were
an Indian uprising, his people would lose the battle. The
Canadian militia outnumbered and outgunned them. Yet, now
that the Indians had magic on their side, they outgunned us. All
of the bullets and canon shells in the Dominion wouldn't stop
the Day of Changes.

*I have heard stories from those who have traveled beyond the
prairie in the direction of the morning sun*, the crow said. *The
whites there are as thick as flies in summer. Mistihaimuskwa
dreams true. As men, the whites would eventually defeat us, no*

matter how brave our warriors were, but as buffalo, they will not be able to use their thunder sticks against us.

The Day of Changes will be much kinder to your people, the bear added. *Not all of those reborn as buffalo will be needed for food and hides. Some will be free to roam the plains. It will be a different life than they have been used to, but not a cruel one. It is a better way than war. And it will mean that we will not have to go hungry through another winter.*

The McDougalls are dead, aren't they? I asked. *You transformed them into buffalo, stampeded them through the tunnel in the earth, and drove them over a cliff. You gave them no warning.*

The mouse peeped out from behind the fox. *What warnings were we given?* it squeaked. *The spotted disease came and killed us without warning. The traders we extended a hand of friendship to did not warn us that they would kill all of the buffalo. The Long Knives south of the Medicine Line give us no warning when they slaughter our people, and you red coats are no better!*

The eagle screeched its agreement. *You, yourself, helped the men who bring the iron horse to steal our land.*

I felt my feathers bristle. *The Mounted Police are not like the American soldiers,* I said. *We treat you fairly. The Queen's law is the same for Indian and white man alike.*

When a white man and an Indian quarrel and come to blows, it is the Indian who finds himself with shackles on his feet, the deer said quietly.

I started to hoot my indignation, but a part of me recognized the truth in his words. In my years with the North-West Mounted Police, I'd met more than one magistrate who refused to believe the testimony of an Indian, especially when it came in halting English or was garbled by a translator. I wanted with all my heart to believe that justice was being served, but in truth I had seen it falter many times. The solution, however, was neither war, nor magical transformation. All that was needed was for the Indians to settle down and become respectable farmers—the testimony of a productive citizen is always given more weight— and to learn to speak English. I could never before see why this had been so difficult for them, but I was beginning to understand. Why adopt the white man's language and ways if you believe the Day of Changes is coming? I needed to put a stop to their magic, but what could I do? I had been transformed into an owl and was trapped inside a tepee with creatures larger and fiercer than myself.

I felt the tips of my wings clench in frustration—and suddenly realized that this was something that wings did not normally do. Were those fingers I felt, instead of feathers? I turned my head slowly from side to side, looking around the tepee. Given the fact that we had been transformed into beasts, I expected to see piles of torn clothing at our feet, but the ground was covered only by robes and blankets.

I began to wonder if I had truly been turned into an owl, or whether Poundmaker's magic had altered only my senses and not my physical form. My arms certainly felt like wings, and when I brushed them against my sides they seemed to touch downy feathers, rather than the rough serge of my jacket. My feet felt bare, even though they must still be clad in woollen socks.

I glanced around, looking for a weapon I could use to fight my way out of the tepee. Poundmaker's war club lay on the ground beside the drum, but it was too far away for me to reach. Even had it been within my grasp, I couldn't be certain that I could grip it; my fingers were as stiff and splayed as wing feathers. Then I spotted a soft leather pouch near Big Bear's feet and recognized it as my tobacco pouch. I suddenly realized that it held the best weapon of all.

The animals were talking again, the lynx insisting that I did not know Iniskim's whereabouts and should be killed, the bear equally insistent that I could lead them to her. Even the grey-furred mouse was squeaking; it stood beneath the deer on its two hind legs, trying to get the larger animal's attention. Soon all of the animals were talking at once. I hopped closer to the bear, flapping my wings as if I wanted its attention. To my surprise, I actually rose into the air. My perceptions were still very much in the spirit world—and if the same were true of the others, they would not be able to see through my feathers. When I settled to the ground, I let one wing droop over the tobacco pouch. I felt a familiar, hard lump inside.

Now I needed a distraction. I turned my head back over my shoulder to look at the deer, which I guessed was Mountain, the chief who had carried a shield painted with a deer design. He had a personal stake in all of this—the Peigan chief had called Iniskim his granddaughter, and whether he had intended the term literally or not, he was probably related to Emily. That was probably why he'd agreed to meet with his enemies, the hated Cree. I'd noticed his dislike for Big Bear earlier, and now I intended to use it to my advantage.

Once I had the deer's attention, I turned back to the bear. *I'll tell you where Iniskim is—but only you. That way, I'll know I won't be killed. Tell the others to leave. I do not trust them, and nor should you.*

The bear pondered this a moment, then glanced at the other animals. The mink and crow nodded, but the deer protested, as I had expected.

I'm staying, it said. It folded its legs beneath it, flopping down on the ground.

A muffled squeaking came from beneath the deer. My attempt at a distraction had worked even better than I'd planned—the deer had accidentally sat on the mouse. In the ensuing commotion as the mouse extricated itself, I wrapped my talons around the buffalo stone. Then I leaped backward.

The lynx growled and lashed out at me with its claws, but missed. I held the spiral-shaped stone in front of me, menacing the lynx with it.

Stay back! I told the animals. *Or I'll touch you with the stone and turn you all into buffalo.*

I was gambling that this was true—that our current transformation was illusional, and that they would fear the more tangible and lasting transformation wrought by the buffalo stone. I wondered if I should try to turn them all into buffalo and put a stop to the Day of Changes, here and now, by using the stone, but there were too many of them. I'd never be able to touch them all with it.

Anger flared in the lynx's eyes. Although the other animals were hesitating, it was clear from the flexing of its claws that it was about to attack.

Just as the lynx sprang at me, I flapped my wings and rose into the air. I aimed for the tear in the tepee wall, folding my wings tight against my sides only at the last moment and squeezing through the hole. Bursting out into the night air, I beat my wings for all they were worth.

They didn't carry me any further. Instead of flying, I landed in a sprawled heap on the ground, knocking the wind from my lungs. It seemed I had found my way out of the spirit world on my own. I was a man again. A lump lay under me: the buffalo stone. As the warriors who had remained outside the tepee leaped to their feet, I grabbed the stone and scrambled upright, holding it out in front of me like a weapon.

"Stay back!" I yelled, repeating the warning I'd given inside the tepee. "Stay back or I'll turn you into buffalo!"

The tepee had stopped shaking, but the door flap rustled. The Indians outside had tied it shut again. Fingers fumbled at its edges, clumsily untying the flap from within. I didn't want to be here when the chiefs—or animals, or whatever was inside that tepee now—emerged.

I turned and ran.

It was dark, and my human eyesight seemed poor, indeed, compared to the owl-vision I had just moments ago. I ran in the worst possible direction: toward the bluffs. Only when I suddenly felt nothing but air beneath my feet did I realize my mistake.

Fortunately, the fall was a short one. I hit a patch of sandy ground, bounced, and rolled. Rocks clattered around me, and dust filled my mouth and nostrils. I tried to stop myself from tumbling, but the slope and the loose ground prevented me from getting a grip. Suddenly I was in the air again. I twisted around like a cat, trying to get my feet under me, and saw a patch of something darker below: trees. Then I was among them. Branches tore at my jacket and breeches and leaves whipped across my face. For a moment my fall was arrested as my jacket caught on something—and then the jacket tore free. I landed in a heap, knocking the wind from my lungs. Sparkles of light danced before my eyes, and something painful was under my chest. I turned my head, spat dust from my dry mouth, and feebly wiped away the spittle. That was when I realized that my hand was still clenched tight around the buffalo stone.

The world was still spinning. Up above and to my left, I heard shouts and excited voices. I tried to rise, but my body was as limp as a rag doll. My jacket and undershirt had been torn from my body in my descent through the trees, and my upper body now was naked. Whatever was causing the pain under my chest seemed sticky; it held me to the ground. I hoped the stickiness wasn't my own blood. I managed to roll over onto my back, and felt a tearing in my skin. I turned my head, and saw a clump of prickly pear. The cactus was smashed flat and several of its pads were torn away; I could feel their spines sticking into my flesh, holding them to my chest. I lowered my head again, resting the back of it against the ground. Something white drifted down from the trees above. At first I thought it was snowing, but then I realized I'd fallen into a grove of cottonwood.

I lay on my back for some time, unable to rise. At any moment I expected the Indians to descend the slope and come for me—either to kill me or to recapture me, depending upon who found me first—but although I heard voices coming from the darkness above for some time, they never came any closer.

I am not sure if minutes or hours passed by. Eventually my strength returned. I sat up and pulled the cactus pads from my chest, grimacing as the spines tore free. The tiny puncture marks burned like the points of hot matches. A number of spines remained deeply embedded in my chest; but I didn't want to waste precious time pulling them out. Not with the Indians looking for me.

I rose to my feet and glanced up the slope. I'd fallen a good thirty feet in that final tumble through the trees, and the bluffs rose even higher beyond that. All was quiet above. The Indians could be anywhere, however. I peered around at the shadows under the trees, imagining Wandering Spirit lurking there. If the warrior was the first to find me, I was a dead man.

The river wasn't far away, but I didn't relish the thought of crossing it. I would be too exposed to the eyes of those above on the flat, grassy plain that led to the river, and would be a perfect target as I slowly forded the water. I decided instead to make my way west, parallel with the bluffs. There were one or two small detachments along the U. S. boundary line; if I could reach them I would be safe.

I made my way, shivering, through the maze of sculpted sandstone. I had no jacket and one leg of my breeches was torn and fluttering. Walking in my stocking feet, I had to tread carefully to avoid sharp-ended twigs and the numerous clumps of cactus. Fortunately, the moon was rising. It was still three-quarters full. However, this meant that anyone searching for me would have an easier time of it.

Just as I started out, a rock tumbled from up above. I pressed myself against a spire of sandstone, fearful that someone had found me. I clenched my only weapon—the buffalo stone—tightly in my hand, even though I knew it would do me little good if someone chose to shoot at me from the bluffs above. I waited there until I was shivering, but the attack I anticipated never came.

I took a deliberately winding path after that, staying well inside the canyons between the spires of rock. The ground was broken and rolling, and several times I had to climb up a slope and scramble down the other side. It was slippery climbing on the sandy soil, especially with the buffalo stone still in my hand. I used holes in the stone walls as natural handholds for a time, but once when I put my hand inside a deeper hole, I felt something slither over my fingers and out onto the ledge I was trying to climb onto. I could not let go of my handhold for fear of falling, and so I used my free hand, which held the buffalo stone, to strike the snake and knock it from the ledge. Only after my heart stopped pounding did I realize that it had probably been no more than a garter snake, since I hadn't heard any warning rattle. I counted myself lucky that the stone, which had brushed against the snake as I struck it, hadn't turned the animal into a buffalo, or it would have knocked me to the ground.

I avoided the holes after that.

The fear that had spurred me earlier in my wild run from the tepee left me drained and exhausted when it ebbed. The knot of pain in my stomach was back, and the hunger that lay beneath it was a dull rumble. My lips were dry; I yearned for water. Yet I daren't go near the river. Not yet.

As I slid down yet another slope, I thought I heard a whispered voice. I froze, listening, but heard only the sifting trickle of sand. I hoped it had been just my imagination, and not one pursuer whispering to another. I looked up at the spires of rock that surrounded me, but saw no one.

Standing in one spot only caused me to start shivering again. I decided it was best to keep moving. I glanced around, trying to find an easy path, and saw that the easiest route led past a wide cliff of flat sandstone. I began moving toward it.

I stopped abruptly after just two steps. A moment ago, the cliff face had been dull and smooth. Now I could see lines scratched into it. They had appeared as if by magic. I tried to tell myself that it was only the angle of the moonlight that had changed, that I had moved into a position where the shadows that filled the grooves in the rock became visible, but a tingling sensation at the back of my neck as my hairs rose told me otherwise.

As if drawn by a magnet, I moved closer to the cliff face. The scratches in the stone began just above my head; I reached up a hand to touch them. The sandstone was soft, and a piece of it sloughed off under my fingers, shattering into sandy fragments as it hit the ground with a thud. I jerked my hand away and looked around, fearful that the noise might be heard by my pursuers.

I had to step back to see the entire cliff. I expected to see stick figures or other primitive Indian carvings, but the scratches in the sandstone seemed to be only a random jumble of crisscrossing lines. I shrugged, and was just about to continue on my way, when something stopped me. Out of the corner of my eye, I saw something that made sense among the scratches: a word, in capital letters. THOMAS.

It had been years since I had used my real name, but the sight of it carved there in the cliff stopped me cold. Logic would put it down to chance—some settler or hunter named Thomas must have carved it there—but my intuitive mind insisted that I pay attention. This was something more than mere coincidence: it was a message, aimed at me. Yet I couldn't read it. The moon was bright, but the canyon in which I stood was filled with deep shadow. I could barely make out my surroundings, let alone the markings on the cliff.

As I stood staring up at the cliff in the darkness, I wished I hadn't lost my jacket, which had my pipe in one of its pockets. There's nothing like a good smoke to steady the nerves and help one concentrate—and I couldn't concentrate, not with my stomach cramping and my flesh scraped raw by my tumble down the bluffs. How I wished for some Pinkham's—even a mere drop of the stuff would be a welcome balm.

I started to fold my arms across my naked chest, but quickly drew them away as they drove deeper the cactus spines that were still embedded there.

The night air was chilly against my skin, yet it was nothing compared to the shiver that rushed through my body when a hoot echoed from the cliff above. My heart pounding, I looked up. Inside one of the caves that pockmarked the cliff something stirred. A head swivelled, and large round eyes looked down at me. Then the owl launched itself from the cliff, and flapped away into the night.

"I wish I had your eyes," I whispered, watching the owl as it flew away.

Yooo... dooo....

I blinked in surprise. Had the owl actually spoken to me in words I could understand?

It seemed no stranger than anything else that had happened to me this night. I wondered if my earlier transformation into an owl had rendered me capable of communicating with these birds—and that thought gave rise to another, even more peculiar notion.

When Poundmaker had worked his magic inside the shaking tepee, he said we had entered the "spirit world." Presumably this was the Indian name for what the Society for Psychical Research called the "astral plane." Somehow, Poundmaker's magic had caused our perceptions to shift to our astral bodies.

According to Chambers's pamphlet, our astral bodies should have been human in form, mirror images of our physical bodies—yet each of the Indians in the tepee had appeared as a different animal. Now that I had time to think about it, I could guess why. Indians believe in guardian spirits—powerful animal spirits that watch over and protect them. The Indians go through elaborate rituals to seek them out, going out into the wilderness and doing without food and drink and sleep until the spirit appears to them and forms a mystic bond with them.

I'd always thought these rituals to be superstitious nonsense or the product of hallucination, but now I knew otherwise. Magic really did exist. So too did spirits, like the bear that watched over Big Bear, the mink that guarded Poundmaker, and the lynx that was the guardian spirit of Wandering Spirit. When our perceptions had been shifted to the astral plane, each of the Indians had either assumed the same shape as his animal guardian spirit—or had merged his astral body with that of the spirit. We'd spoken to each other not in the diverse tongues of men, but in the universal language of the spirits.

It made sense, but one thing still baffled me. Why had I been transformed into an owl? I'd never even seen an owl, aside from the pictures in the storybooks my mother had read to me when I was a child. Was it possible that a guardian spirit watched over me too? Could some mystic bond have been forged without my knowing it?

Chambers had said that sensitives could see with their astral bodies. Did that mean that I could merge with it in astral space and use its all-seeing eyes to read the markings on the cliff?

I tried to concentrate, imagining that I was an owl. I even set the buffalo stone down on the ground and held out my arms like wings, stretching out my hands until my fingers ached. I hooted, I hunkered down like an owl on a branch, and I forced my eyes open wide, turning my head slowly from side to side, but nothing happened. The night just grew darker, the cliff in front of me more indistinct.

I dropped my arms to my sides. I was exhausted, hungry, and thirsty—and aching in a hundred different places. I couldn't do it.

I winced, and grabbed at my midriff as my stomach cramped. This cramp was a bad one; it nearly doubled me over. The movement caused me to look at the cliff from a new angle. Just as I was squeezing my eyes shut, I saw another word.

MANITOU.

My eyes widened, and in that moment the word disappeared back into the gloom. I straightened as the stomach cramp eased, and cursed my involuntary reaction. If only I'd kept my eyes half-squinted shut....

No, that wasn't it at all. What was it that Chambers had said, during the guessing game on the riverboat? He'd talked about how discomfort contributed to a successful result. The anxiety I felt at being surrounded by spectators on the riverboat had augmented my ability to guess which card would appear next. Would another form of discomfort—physical pain—increase my chances at using my astral body to view the cliff in front of me?

I raised a hand to my chest and located one of the cactus spines. With a vicious tug, I yanked it free. Then I found another, more deeply buried than the last. As I wrenched it out of my flesh, I felt a trickle of blood roll down my bare chest. My eyes began to water. I forced them open wide, refusing to blink.

By the time I'd pulled a half-dozen spines out of my flesh, my body was flushed. I no longer felt the cold night air. It was as if my skin were wrapped in a gauzy covering of soft, downy feathers....

There! Was the air really getting brighter? Whatever the reason, I could see clearly now. Straining not to blink, I yanked the last cactus spine out of my chest and stared up at the cliff. The message scratched upon it was plain to me now. I read the words eagerly.

MANITOU STONE SITS ON APPARITION TRAIL.

"A clue!" I whispered under my breath—one that would surely lead me to the Manitou Stone, if only I could puzzle out its meaning. Yet I wanted more. I not only needed to know where to find the stone—but how to destroy it when I did. That way, the Day of Changes would never come.

Other words were carved at an angle to the rest of the message. I turned my head to read them.

BIRTH AND DEATH ARE THE BEGINNING AND END OF THE TRAIL. TO END THE DAY OF CHANGES, START AT THE BEGINNING. CLOSE THE....

The message ended in a broken patch of stone. My heart sank as I realized that the crumbling indentation was the spot I'd touched earlier. I cursed my own stupidity and searched the cliff face for the conclusion of the message. There was none. The words I'd already read were the only ones on the cliff.

Close the what? I wondered. Try as I might, I could not come up with the answer. The only thing that sprang to mind was "close the door"—but that didn't make any sense. Worse yet, the words on the cliff were fading, becoming meaningless cracks and lines once more.

The cliff before me seemed to tilt to one side, and I realized that I was swaying on my feet. Excitement and exertion had taken their toll; it was all I could do to keep my eyes open. The night now was as dark as it had been before; my mind was fully back in my physical body and could no longer perceive with an owl's keen sight. If I pressed on, I'd probably tumble off another bluff. I needed somewhere protected to wait out the night.

I looked around and saw a larger hole in one of the spires of sandstone. I approached it carefully, and used a stick to prod around inside. Satisfied that there were no rattlesnakes within, I crawled inside. The hole was just large enough to accommodate a man who assumed a curled-up position. I crawled into it, and rested my head on my arm.

A wind had started to blow, and as I listened to it I realized that it would be erasing my tracks across the sandy soil, making it harder for the Indians to find me. I thanked whatever was responsible, be it God or guardian spirit. As I lay there, thinking of disappearing footprints, I was reminded of my dream of being lost on the prairie. I wondered if Iniskim had at last emerged from the tunnels that ran under the earth. Was she wandering alone somewhere, lost and confused?

Back in the tepee, I'd been certain that I had no idea where the girl might be, but now that I had time to think about it, I had a hunch where she might be headed. According to Constable Davis, the white buffalo calf that I'd surmised was the "ghost" of the stillborn Iniskim—and which I now knew was her astral body in animal form—had been spotted by the Assinaboine on the banks of the South Saskatchewan River. If Iniskim had gone there once before in astral form, she might return to the spot again, now that she had actually been transformed into a buffalo.

For a few moments, my excitement at having figured out where Iniskim might be headed kept me awake, but eventually exhaustion overtook me. My eyes closed, and I was lulled to sleep by the whisper of blowing sand.

✛✛✛

When I woke up, my knees and elbows were hot. It took me a moment to realize why: the sun was well up in the sky and its rays were slanting into the hole in which I lay. I clambered out and stretched the stiffness out of my arms and legs. My mouth was dry and my hair dusty. I scratched an itch on my chest, and my fingernails came away with dried blood from the cactus-spine punctures.

Through a crack between two pillars of rock I saw a patch of green grass and the milky-coloured river that wound across it. A lone bird soared in the distance, above the sandstone bluffs on the far side of the river. I didn't really want to risk venturing out into such open country, but if I didn't drink something soon I would become faint. When I relieved myself, my urine emerged as a deep yellow trickle. I needed water.

I reached into the hole I'd slept in and retrieved the buffalo stone. I stared at it, tracing a finger around its spiral. In the sunlight the stone shone metallic gold and green. I rolled it in my hand, wondering how its magic was triggered. When I'd first found the stone, it had been encased in a leather-thong wrapping, which I'd discarded. Big Bear had marvelled at the fact that I could touch the bare stone and not be transformed into a buffalo, and the other Indians had recoiled from it.

I made my way cautiously down through the maze of rock toward the river. I paused just before the spot where the canyon opened onto the grassy plain. Birds swooped back and forth overhead, and from either side came the sounds of nestlings cheeping, snug inside holes in the rock. I also heard the rustle of grass beside the river as the wind stirred it, and the yip of a coyote off to my right. Another coyote answered it from the left.

I stopped, suddenly realizing something. Coyotes sleep during the day. Those weren't animals: those were Indians, signalling to one another.

I looked wildly around. Had they spotted me? A noise like the scuffing of a foot came from somewhere above and behind me.

I spun around, and thought I saw the tip of a rifle that was pulled quickly back behind a rock.

Maybe it was just a branch moving, I told myself. Maybe they hadn't found me, after all.

Then I saw a tiny flash of sunlight from the cliff that rose to my right. The Indians keeping silent, signalling to one another with mirrors—and they were close. There was no other direction for me to go in, save out onto the open grassland.

I searched the grassy plain ahead of me for a hiding place, but there was none. I glanced behind me again. There was no further sign of the Indians. I gripped the buffalo stone tightly in my fist, trying to decide whether to make a stand in the canyon—where they could shoot me from above, like an animal in a pit—or try to flee across the open grass toward the river. As I stood there, my mind whirling, I heard a peculiar sound: the *whuff, whuff, whuff* of wings.

There! Just flying into view, on the far side of the river, was the "bird" I'd seen earlier: an air bicycle, with an operator sitting at the controls. He had to be a police officer—perhaps even one from Q Division. Had Steele himself come to rescue me?

I leaped to my feet and waved, but the operator did not see me. Instead he turned the air bicycle so that its balloon presented its full length to me, and began to follow the Milk River.

He hadn't seen me! In another moment, the air bicycle would be well beyond my reach.

Screwing up my courage, I ran for the mouth of the canyon. As I burst out into the knee-high grass, running for all I was worth, I heard a shout behind me, then the crack of a rifle. I have no idea how close the bullet came—the wind in the grass and my own thudding footsteps hid the sound of the bullet striking. I ran as hard as I could, zigzagging back and forth to present a more difficult target. I tried to shout to the operator of the air bicycle, but the exertion of my run left me almost breathless. A second rifle shot, however, got his attention. I saw a goggled face turn toward me, and I waved my hands above my head, imploring him to land.

I was halfway between the bluffs and the river now, and my legs felt as if they were on fire. I didn't stop, however. Forcing myself onward, I ran straight for the air bicycle, hoping that it would stop for me.

The air bicycle dipped slightly.

Another rifle shot rang out. I saw the operator glance at the cliffs and begin to adjust the trim of his machine.

No! Throwing every ounce of will I had into it, I silently urged him to land.

I don't know whether I accomplished thought transference or whether the operator simply took pity on the scene below: a half-naked white man, running wildly across the grass and being shot at by Indians. Whatever the reason, the air bicycle descended and landed. With my last ounce of strength, I climbed up onto the rear seat. Strapped all around it was a collection of five-gallon coal oil tins. I perched atop them and clung on for all I was worth.

"Thank you," I gasped. "You've saved my life!"

"Not yet," he gritted. As he adjusted the angle of the wings, sending us flapping up into the air, a bullet smacked into one of the coal oil tins below me. Immediately I smelled a pungent odour: alcohol. A spray of bright amber liquid arced from the hole the bullet had created, falling in a stream toward the ground.

"Damnation!" The operator wrenched around in his seat to stare at hole. "You're a bloody expensive bastard to rescue."

He shoved a lever to one side, and the air bicycle tipped violently. I assumed that it was an evasive manoeuvre, but then realized that he'd set us at an angle to stop the flow of alcohol.

As we rose at this awkward angle into the sky, I clung to the air bicycle's frame with one hand and peered down at the ground. Our ascent was agonizingly slow; it seemed it was all the air bicycle could do to lift the two of us. On the bluffs below stood an Indian holding a rifle. I thought it might be Wandering Spirit, since the figure wore what looked like a fur cap and patterned shirt, but we were already too far away for me to be sure. He raised his rifle to his shoulder and fired, but the shot must have gone wide.

As I watched, the Indian suddenly scrambled down into the canyon, out of sight.

The operator of the air bicycle turned and handed me a handkerchief from his pocket.

"Here!" he shouted. "Stuff that into the hole."

I did as he'd ordered, reaching down and poking the handkerchief into the bullet hole with a finger. The job was made more difficult by the fact that I still held the buffalo stone, but I managed to plug the leak in the tin. The flow of alcohol slowed, then stopped, and the operator trimmed the air bicycle so that it was flying level again. I was glad to have an even perch to sit upon; the ground was already more than a hundred feet below us.

I peered at my rescuer. Judging by his rough attire and heavy beard, he was a man of the frontier. He wore blue wool pants that looked like American military trousers with the stripes torn off, a buckskin shirt, and well-worn boots. His moustache and beard were as wild and untrimmed as his hair, which had been bleached by the sun. He wore no hat—only an operator's goggles.

I decided that this was a man who meant business: a bandolier hung across his shoulder, and a rifle was tucked into a metal case bolted to the front of the air bicycle frame, just ahead of his seat. Having seen and smelled his cargo, I knew him to be a whisky smuggler—and a wealthy one, if he could afford an air bicycle. Contempt for his profession warred with my gratitude at his having saved me.

"What happened to you, and where in blazes are your shirt and boots?" he asked, glancing back at my bruised and bloody chest. "Why were those Indians after you?"

I gave him only part of the truth. "Another fellow and I were out buffalo hunting, and tangled with Indians when they tried to steal our horses. The Indians captured me and took my boots, but I escaped from them last night. I made my way into one of the canyons in the sandstone bluffs, and hid there the night."

"That was smart," he said. "The Indians are afraid of *Aisinaipi*. They won't venture into it at night." He laughed, then added with a wink: "Too many evil spirits."

"*Aisinaipi?*" I asked. "Who or what is that?"

"It's a Blackfoot word. It means 'Writing On Stone.' The local tribes carve drawings into the soft sandstone cliffs, then pretend the spirits did it. They scare each other around the campfire by insisting that these spirits will kill folks who venture down into the canyons at night. They say *Aisinaipi* is a place of visions and magic. It's superstitious nonsense, but at least it saved your skin."

I knew otherwise. Magic really did exist: I had seen magical writing on the cliff with my own two eyes. How else to explain a message that exactly answered my unspoken questions—and in the English alphabet, no less.

I decided to change the subject. "What's your name?"

"Cochrane."

The name sounded familiar to me, but I couldn't place it.

Cochrane set his controls so that we would continue flying level, and turned to give me a better look. "Who are you?"

Suddenly I realized where I'd heard the operator's name before. Two years ago, a patrol out of Fort Walsh had arrested a whisky smuggler by the name of Cochrane. The name wouldn't have stuck in my mind, except for the fact that the fellow was a former North-West Mounted Policeman—one who had, upon completion of his term of duty, turned to a life of crime. He was fined one hundred dollars and released. The experience obviously hadn't taught him any lessons. As I recall, he'd headed south, back to Montana.

I glanced at the rifle in its case.

"Cochrane," I said in a level voice. "My name is Corporal Marmaduke Grayburn of the North-West Mounted Police."

I heard him swear softly under his breath.

"You have been caught in the act of smuggling spirits into the North-West Territories. Normally, I would arrest you, but I am prepared to make you this offer. If you will agree to a brief engagement as a special constable with the force, I will utterly ignore everything I have seen today." I nodded down at the coal oil tins.

Cochrane's eyes hardened behind his goggles. He moved a hand to the controls. "I could tip you off your perch. The fall would kill you."

I gripped the frame of the bicycle a little tighter. "It would," I agreed. "But how long do you think it would take our men to put two and two together, once they've spotted you on your machine? A police officer is killed in a fall out of thin air—and a known criminal is seen flying an air bicycle. It shouldn't be too hard for even the dimmest sub-constable in the force to puzzle out. You don't want to hang, do you, Cochrane?"

Cochrane swallowed, as if already feeling the noose about his neck. He shook his head.

"What do I have to do?"

I smiled. "Fly me to the detachment at Medicine Hat. Then you're free to go."

⋈—⋈

Chapter VI

We were half way to Medicine Hat, passing over rolling prairie at
a height of about four hundred feet, when I heard the crack of
rifle shots. Leaning out to the side to peer around Cochrane, I
saw a cloud of dust, raised by the hooves of a small herd of
buffalo. Six of the shaggy beasts were running flat out across the
grass, pursued by three riders who were firing at full gallop.
I saw one beast go down, bellowing as it crashed to the earth,
and then another. The other animals veered this way and that in
a desperate bid to escape.

I noticed then that two of the animals had yellowish-brown
hair, like the coat of a newborn buffalo calf. One of these animals
suddenly doubled back to charge the riders, weaving to avoid
their rifle shots. I watched, horrified, knowing that this was no
mere beast, but a human being in buffalo form, fighting
desperately for his life. As a rifle cracked and the buffalo went
down, I gulped, wondering if I had just witnessed the death of
someone I knew.

I tapped Cochrane on the shoulder. "We've got to land."

He glanced down. "You want to join in the hunt?"

"No!" I cried. "I want to save those poor brutes. We must land!"

Cochrane gave me a strange look, then nodded and pulled a
lever. The angle of the air bicycle's wings changed, and we began
to descend. I had seen a calculating look in his eye as he glanced
back at me, and suspected that he intended to take off again as
soon as I was on the ground, but being stranded was a chance I
had to take if I was to save the poor wretches below.

I watched in trepidation as we descended. One of the hunters
saw the air bicycle's shadow on the grass, and waved a rifle over

his head. Cochrane waved back. The other two hunters were intent upon their game. The two brown buffalo fell, and then the second light-haired one also collapsed in the dust. I groaned, thinking we were too late, but as the hunters dismounted and ran over to this animal, it leaped to its feet and charged them. I cheered, seeing that it had used its human cunning to fool them into thinking it was dead, but my joy was short-lived. Quick as lightning, one of the hunters raised his rifle to his shoulder and fired thrice in quick succession. The animal went down at his feet—for good, this time.

The air bicycle touched the ground, bounced once or twice, then settled. The hunter who had waved to us—a Metis fellow with a huge moustache and bushy black eyebrows, wearing a buckskin vest beaded in the Indian fashion—dismounted from his horse and strode over to us.

"'Allo!" he called out, looking up at the balloon from which the air bicycle was suspended. "Your balloon *bicyclette*, she is a fine looking...."

He stopped in mid-stride as he saw that I was half-naked, then started to laugh. "*Mon dieu, Monsieur*, are de winds so strong that they 'ave torn off your shirt?"

I ignored him. Jumping down from the coal oil tins on which I was perched, I ran toward the nearest of the light-haired buffalo—the one that had put up so heroic a fight. The buffalo stone was still in my hand. "You don't realize what you have done," I shouted at the Metis over my shoulder. "But you will soon enough. This isn't a buffalo that you shot. It's a man."

I stopped and looked down at the great beast. Its tongue hung out of its mouth and blood welled from a bullet hole in its neck. Flies were already buzzing around the wound and landing on its soft brown eyes. I steeled myself for the worst, knowing that when the transformation came, it would not be a pretty sight. For all I knew, this might be a beautiful woman cut down in her prime.

I knelt and touched the buffalo stone to the animal's forehead.

Nothing happened. The buffalo remained a buffalo.

I stood, stunned. What had I done wrong? Perhaps the stone had to make contact with a particular part of the body. I touched the stone to a hoof, to the spot over the chest where the heart lay, to the mouth. Still nothing.

Behind me, I heard nervous laughter.

"Your friend," the Metis said. "He is crazy, perhaps?"

The other two hunters were standing a short way off, watching me with a mixture of amusement and puzzlement on their faces. I glanced behind me and saw that Cochrane had shoved his goggles up onto his forehead for a better look.

I ran over to the other light-haired buffalo. The creature was still warm, the wounds in its side still bleeding. One leg was bent at an angle under it, the splintered bone protruding through the flesh. I touched the stone to the dead beast.

Once again, nothing happened.

I stood slowly, then looked in puzzlement at the spiral-shaped stone in my hand, trying to figure out why it had done nothing. Perhaps the stone's transformative powers only worked on living things.

The hunters laughed again and I glared at them, tempted to strike them with the stone. They needed to be shown what they had just done. They were murderers—even if they didn't know it.

I must have had a wild look in my eye. The Metis closest to me—a young lad with beardless cheeks—looked nervously at me. He shifted his grip on his rifle, raising it slightly.

Sighing, I lowered the stone. These men were not murderers. They did not realize what they had done.

I walked back to the air bicycle, the hand that held the buffalo stone hanging at my side. Cochrane hadn't abandoned me after all; his curiosity had gotten the better of him.

I heard a sniff; the Metis hunter closest to the air bicycle had caught the scent of the whisky. He licked his lips. I glanced at the saddlebags on his horse, then back at him. The fellow looked about my size.

"Have you a change of clothing?" I asked. "I'll trade you the whisky that remains in the punctured tin for a shirt and a pair of moccasins."

"Done!" the Metis said with a smile. He began rummaging in his saddlebags.

"No you won't!" Cochrane protested, twisting around on his seat to prevent me from unhitching the punctured tin.

"I'm on the ground now," I reminded him in a terse whisper. "All I have to do is get these fellows to take me to the nearest detachment and report what I've seen, and there will be a warrant out for your arrest. Let me give them this whisky, and I'll keep quiet."

Cochrane thought about that a moment. Grumbling, he unfastened the punctured tin from the air bicycle, then lifted it and sloshed its contents back and forth. It didn't sound like there was much whisky left inside; that probably made his decision easier. When the Metis handed me a buckskin shirt and worn-looking moccasins, Cochrane handed him the tin. The Metis' grin stretched to the ends of his moustache, and he waved his fellows to him with a whoop.

I pulled on the shirt and moccasins. The heavy buckskin shirt irritated the punctures on my chest, but at least my nakedness was covered now. I climbed up behind Cochrane.

"Right," I said. "On to Medicine Hat."

Cochrane set the wings to flapping and the air bicycle rose into the air. "I'll fly you to the outskirts of town," he said. "But no more stopping to trade away my whisky. Agreed?"

I grinned. "Agreed."

When we were level and winging our way northeast again, Cochrane turned on his seat. "What was that you said? That business about buffalo being men?"

"It's rather a complicated story. And you probably wouldn't believe it."

He glanced at the buffalo stone, which I still held clenched in my fist. "What's that in your hand?"

I debated a moment, then decided to tell him the truth. I'd observed his curiosity, and hoped that if I whetted it some more, he would agree to land again, should we see another fair-haired buffalo.

"It's a buffalo stone," I answered. "It has the power to transform human beings into buffalo. I thought it could also do the reverse—that it could undo these transformations. I seem to have been wrong."

He made no reply; he probably thought I was a madman. We traveled in silence for a time. I listened to the flapping of the wings and the rush of air, lost in my thoughts as I watched the sausage-shaped shadow of the air bicycle sweep across the prairie below. Perhaps the buffalo stone had lost its power. Perhaps only Indians could work its magic. Perhaps....

I glanced down at the grassy prairie that rolled in gentle hills like an ocean below us. I had the distinct impression that our course was off—that we should be headed more to the right. I noted the position of the sun, and saw that the air bicycle was indeed pointed to the northeast, the direction in which Medicine Hat lay. Yet the feeling that we had strayed off course was growing stronger by the minute.

I tapped Cochrane on the shoulder and pointed to the west. "We need to go that way."

"Not if you want me to take you to Medicine Hat," Cochrane protested.

"Turn the air bicycle," I insisted. "We need to go to the west, just for a little while. There's... something in that direction I need to see."

I was thankful that Cochrane didn't ask what it was. I couldn't have said myself what inner voice I was following, or where it was leading me. All I know was that when Cochrane changed course, my sense of unease lessened dramatically.

After a few minutes we passed over a coulee with a small creek at the bottom of it. About a dozen buffalo stood in it, drinking the muddy water. When the shadow of the air bicycle passed over them they broke into a bellowing run, splashing away down the coulee. One of them, however, stood its ground and craned its massive head back to look up at us. As its dark eyes searched the heavens, I felt compelled to meet their gaze. I stared at the great, defiant creature and saw that it was lighter than the rest.

"There!" I cried, pointing it out to Cochrane. "Land the air bicycle next to that one."

"All right—but I'll have to circle 'round so we're parallel with the coulee first."

I didn't stop to wonder why Cochrane was suddenly so willing to land. I watched the light-haired buffalo as we circled over the coulee. The other animals were long gone by now, having at last run up one of the banks and thundered away across the prairie. I watched the animal below, realizing now that its silent call was what had led me to this spot. I hoped it was Chambers, but I didn't see any fabric around its neck. If this was Chambers, he'd lost his black silk tie.

As we circled, the buffalo began to run back and forth in a seemingly random manner, but I soon realized that its movements had purpose. It was stamping out a word in the dust. As I recognized the first letter—an *H*—my heart pounded in my chest. I knew I'd found my missing special constable.

"Chambers!" I yelled. "Hang on. I'm coming."

The beast glanced up at me, a hopeful look in its eye.

As soon as we landed, I sprang off the back of the air bicycle and ran toward the buffalo, the stone in my hand. The beast stood perfectly still, watching me as it squatted on its haunches. Just as I was about to touch the stone to the buffalo's forehead, I hesitated, remembering my dream. If this was Chambers, would transforming him back into a man kill him?

As if sensing my hesitation, the buffalo suddenly lurched to its feet and bellowed. I jerked back from it, the hand holding the stone still raised. Behind me, I heard the metallic click of a weapon being cocked. I whirled around and saw Cochrane shouldering his rifle.

"Don't shoot!" I shouted. "It's a man."

Then I realized my mistake. Cochrane's rifle was pointed at me, not at the buffalo. The coulee I stood in was a rugged, desolate spot. If Cochrane had it in mind to murder me and leave my body here, he'd probably get away with it. I had foolishly neglected to tell the Metis who I was, and was no longer wearing my uniform. Even if a police patrol stumbled across my body, they'd have no way to identify it.

Fortunately, Cochrane had not yet worked up nerve enough to shoot. Slowly, not wanting to startle him, I lowered the hand that held the buffalo stone. Out of the corner of my eye I saw the buffalo take a step forward to meet it. Then the stone touched its great, shaggy head, just between the horns.

A cry came from the great beast's lips—a human cry—and suddenly the massive creature that had stood beside me was gone. In its place was a naked man, bent over in the dust on his hands and knees, tousled black ringlets hiding his face. He looked up—and in the same instant that I recognized Chambers's sweaty and dust-grimed face, I heard Cochrane gasp.

"Almighty God!" he croaked. "You were right. It *is* a man."

The rifle hung forgotten in Cochrane's hands. He stared with a dumbfounded look at me, the stone in my hand, and the naked man beside me.

Chambers climbed unsteadily to his feet. I caught him as he nearly fell—he was not yet used to standing on just two legs—and helped him steady himself. He was unclothed and reeked of sweat, and his beard and moustache were unkempt. His mouth worked for a moment, as if he had forgotten how to speak. Then he found his tongue.

"Th-th-thank you," he whispered. "I've been t-t-trying to find you for d-d-days."

The sincerity of his gratitude moved me to compassion. Two weeks ago, I'd have savoured the sight of the pompous Arthur Chambers swooning like a girl and expressing his humility in a stutter as bad as Dickens's, but now all I could think of was the immensity of the ordeal he had just been through. I was careful not to let the buffalo stone brush against Chambers—I didn't want to put him through another transformation.

I nodded at Cochrane. "Special Constable Arthur Chambers, I'd like to introduce you to Mr. Cochrane, who is also a special constable under temporary contract with the North-West Mounted Police. Mr. Cochrane will be flying us to Medicine Hat, where we can telegraph Superintendent Steele. You'll soon have a hot bath and a soft bed to rest upon, Chambers."

Cochrane was still muttering under his breath, his eyes wide. "That buffalo. It became a man. When you touched the stone to the buffalo, it became a man."

I helped Chambers toward the air bicycle. "Pull yourself together, man," I told Cochrane in a brusque voice. "In Q Division, we see sights like this every day." I gave Chambers a wink, then turned back to Cochrane. "Now take us to Medicine Hat."

That seemed to bring Cochrane around, but his reply wasn't what I wanted to hear. He shook his head. "I can't," he said. "The machine won't lift three men plus cargo."

"Right." Leaving Chambers to stand on his own, I dropped the buffalo stone to the ground and yanked the rifle from Cochrane's hands. It was already cocked. I fired the first bullet into the nearest tin, then continued shooting until whisky was streaming from every container. Cochrane leaped from the air bicycle and tried to grab the rifle back, but I shouldered him aside. I noticed that his foot nearly landed upon the buffalo stone.

"Watch out!" I warned. "If you tread on the stone, you'll be turned into a buffalo."

It was an exaggeration—I'd seen Big Bear pick up the stone with my tobacco pouch and not be transformed, and knew that Cochrane's boots would protect him. Unaware of this fact, he jumped back as quickly as if he'd nearly trod on a rattlesnake.

I made sure the rifle was empty, then handed it back to Cochrane. The air was pungent with whisky and gunpowder. A forlorn look on his face, Cochrane dejectedly shoved the rifle back in its case.

"Come on," I told Chambers. "Climb aboard. We'll be in Medicine Hat in no time."

◄—►

Superintendent Steele leaned over a table in the office he'd commandeered from the officer in charge of the Medicine Hat detachment. Chambers and I sat across from him. Spread on the table between us was a map of the North-West Territories that was covered in small red circles—the disappearances—and a red X that marked the original resting place of the Manitou Stone. Beside the map were two thick folders stuffed with reports, and beside them was Steele's Stetson hat. Further down the table— well out of harm's way—was the buffalo stone, tucked safely inside my tobacco pouch. I carried it with me still, everywhere I went. We couldn't run the risk of anyone accidentally touching it.

"We've had dozens of reports of disappearances," Steele said in a grim voice. "Settlers have gone missing from their homesteads, telegraph surveyors have vanished, leaving their equipment behind, and a train engine was found rolling along the track without a soul on board. Some of our own officers have gone missing, as have some influential men. Two Indian agents and a magistrate are among those reported missing, presumed transformed. Even Jerry Potts seems to have disappeared off the face of the earth—there was no trace of him, dead or alive, where you last saw him, Grayburn. And if Potts can go missing...."

Steele paused to collect himself, then continued. "The actual number of persons to go missing in each case is small—the largest group was a dozen men—but there's no way we can keep this quiet any longer. We've managed to keep the transformations themselves from the public, but word is getting out about the disappearances, and people are becoming frightened. They're whispering of Indian massacres and unmarked graves."

Chambers and I listened quietly to this grim news. The pair of us had been deposited at the outskirts of Medicine Hat two days ago by Cochrane, who had sworn to keep silent about what he had seen. After reporting to the detachment and telegraphing Steele, we had been ordered to wait for the Superintendent's arrival by train. I'd kept my word and said nothing about Cochrane and his illegal cargo, and had urged Chambers to do the same. The smuggler had probably returned south for another load of whisky, but that was a minor concern. I just hoped he was keeping his promise—that he wasn't spreading wild tales about North-West Mounted Policemen turning buffalo into men.

I was back in uniform, and feeling better for it. I'd also managed to pick up a bottle of Pinkham's from a doctor's office in town, and at last the wrenching pain in my stomach had been dampened down. I hoped that Steele didn't smell the patent medicine on my breath and mistake it for liquor. I didn't want to be labelled a drunkard, like Inspector Dickens.

A clock on the wall chimed. Steele stared through it, stroking his moustache as he voiced his thoughts aloud. "We need to find the Manitou Stone. It has to be the key. If we can get one of our field pieces within range of it, we can blow the stone to bits. That should stop the Day of Changes."

He turned to me. "I hope you're correct in your guess that the albino calf can lead us to the Manitou Stone. Based on the strength of your prior premonitions, I've already acted upon your speculation. I've ordered a patrol from the Swift Current detachment to search along the South Saskatchewan River for the calf, but there's more than one hundred miles of riverbank to search. Are you sure you can't be more specific about the location where her 'ghost' appeared, Grayburn?"

I shook my head. "Constable Davis said only that the crossing lay somewhere between the Red Deer River and Saskatchewan Landing. If we could find the Indian scout that led him to the ford—"

"We're trying to find him," Steele said. "We've questioned Many Spotted Horses and Many Mules and have sent for another scout from Battleford whose name begins with Many, but without a full name it's going to be tough to track down the right man."

I thought over our progress so far—or lack thereof. A patrol had been ordered to the bluffs overlooking Writing on Stone, but

had found no Indians there. The chiefs and their warriors had all
departed, leaving behind only a fire pit and the circle of stones
that had weighted down the edges of the shaking tepee. Their
tracks led in several different directions; I guessed that the
chiefs had gone their separate ways and would not meet up
again until the Day of Changes was nigh.

There had also been no further activity at the buffalo jump
where I had emerged from the tunnel. The patrol that
Superintendent Cotton had dispatched to the cliffs found
evidence that the Indians beat a hasty retreat from that spot,
and nothing—neither Indian nor buffalo—had been seen in the
area since. Despite the fact that settlers were still disappearing,
if they were being driven through tunnels in the earth as the
McDougalls had been, they weren't emerging at those cliffs. It
didn't surprise me; I had a hunch that the tunnel's exit was in
some new location now, hundreds of miles away.

The only sensible course of action seemed to be that which we
were already taking: searching for Iniskim.

"We've got twenty-three days before the next full moon," I said.
"With luck, one of our patrols will spot the albino buffalo calf and
she'll lead us to the Manitou Stone."

"All well and good," Steele said. "Unless Big Bear and the
others have already found her. If they see our patrols, all they
need do is drape a hide over the calf, and it will look like a pony
or a large dog from a distance. It's an old Indian trick; I've seen
them cover their own horses with hides when they hunt buffalo,
and fool the herds into thinking they're buffalo, as well."

"Blood knows blood," Chambers muttered.

Steele and I both turned. It was the first time Chambers had
spoken during our meeting. Chambers looked like his old self,
with cheeks shaved and hair freshly Brilliantined, wearing an
expensive cutaway suit and polished boots. Yet he was quieter
than he had been before his brief tenure as a buffalo—less prone
to lecturing and more thoughtful. He sat with his hands folded
on the table, contemplating them with a quizzical look that
suggested that he was still getting used to their human form. His
fingernails had cracked like well-worn hooves; even a trim by the
town's barber hadn't cleaned them up entirely.

After a moment, Chambers lifted his head. "In the graveyard
at Victoria Mission, I contacted the spirit of Abigail McDougall.
Her singing led me to the cave that her husband had been driven
into—the one in which I...."

A shudder coursed through his body.

"It was Emily you heard singing, not McDougall's wife," I gently
reminded him. "We know that Emily entered the cave with her
daughter, and I heard her singing after I spoke to her in the woods."

Chambers's hands clenched. "I know what I heard—and whose spirit I contacted. It was Abigail McDougall. I saw her as plain as I see you now: an Indian woman, covered in pockmarks and weeping for her departed husband."

"Abigail McDougall did die in the smallpox epidemic of 1870," Steele noted.

I pointed out something that should have been obvious. "The same smallpox outbreak scarred Emily. Surely, she was the one you heard, Chambers."

The fire in Chambers's eyes went out. Slumping back in his chair, he lapsed back into a brooding silence. I was sorry to have questioned his abilities, but I felt it my duty to report the truth as I saw it.

I started to apologize, and he shook his head. "I only mentioned the ghost of Abigail as an example of using thought transference to contact the astral plane," he muttered. "It is Emily's spirit we need to contact now, if we wish to find her daughter."

"But she's not dead," I protested.

"She must be," Chambers insisted. "She went into the tunnel, was transformed into a buffalo, and was driven over the cliff and slaughtered. She's dead."

"No she's not!" I shouted.

"Corporal Grayburn!" Steele's voice cracked like a whip. "Button that lip. I want to hear what Special Constable Chambers has to say."

I could feel my cheeks burning, and realized belatedly that I had done what a good investigator should never do: I'd let my attraction to a woman get the better of me. I vowed to make no further retort, and hoped that Chambers wouldn't contradict what I'd written about Four Finger Pete's demise in my report.

Steele's voice softened. "Now then, Special Constable Chambers," he prompted. "Tell me why we should contact Iniskim's mother."

Chambers sat up a little straighter in his chair. "If Emily is dead, her astral body is no longer constrained by her physical body. She can wander the astral plane at will. Like most 'ghosts,' she'll be drawn to the person she cared for the most: her daughter. Emily can lead us to Iniskim—or at the very least, she'll know where the girl is."

Steele leaned across the table toward Chambers, his posture radiating enthusiasm. "Contact her, then. Call up her spirit and talk to it. Get her to tell us where Iniskim is."

Chambers shook his head. "Alas, it isn't that simple. In order to contact a specific ghost, a link with that person is required. I would need an article of Emily's clothing, or some other personal effect, before I could attempt to call her."

Steele mused a moment. "The Peigan woman and her husband were traveling by riverboat. If what Corporal Grayburn surmises is correct—that Emily deliberately entered the cave at Victoria Mission—she wouldn't have carried all of her luggage into the cavern with her. Perhaps she left something behind on the *North West* or at Victoria Mission. I'll send a telegram at once, to have both searched."

I wanted to protest. I knew in my gut that searching for Emily's clothing and holding séances to contact her ghost wasn't going to get us anywhere, but I didn't dare allow myself to lapse into another outburst.

Instead, as Chambers and Steele discussed the prospects of contacting Emily's ghost, I mentally listed the facts that pointed to her still being alive. When I'd entered the tunnel at Victoria Mission, I'd found Chambers's torn clothing in its depths, and Iniskim's tiny dress and moccasins, but nothing of Emily's. If the woman had been transformed into a buffalo, her clothing would have been torn to pieces. I should have found scraps of her dress and moccasins somewhere on the floor of the tunnel.

It seemed more logical to conclude that Emily had for some reason remained in human form, despite entering the tunnel— but if so, where was she? Had she blundered up one of the tributary tunnels? Was she underground even now, wandering alone through the darkness, wondering if her daughter was dead or alive?

I stared at the map. The red circles on it reminded me of the pockmarks on Emily's face. I touched a hand to the paper, imagining that my fingers were stroking her skin. I trailed my fingertips over the map in a gentle circle....

I gasped as a sudden realization hit me. Then I peered more closely at the circles of red that marked the disappearances. Each was neatly labelled in Steele's fine penmanship with a date—and those dates had a definite pattern. I rose to my feet and crossed the room, grabbing the pen and inkwell from the commanding officer's desk. Returning to the map, I dipped the pen in the ink and began tracing a blue line across the map, joining up the marks according to their dates.

Both Steele and Chambers stopped to stare at me.

Steele swore, and started to grab for my hand. "That's my only map!" he cried. He stopped when he saw what I was drawing: a spiral. Its ever-diminishing curve enclosed a large blank space at its centre, just north of the CPR line and south of the South Saskatchewan River.

"By God," Steele said. "I hadn't noticed that before. What does it signify?"

I stared at the map, wondering that very thing. The line I'd drawn passed through each of the circles, spiralling inward in a counter-clockwise direction as it joined up the more recent disappearances. The only circle that didn't line up with the spiral was the one at Victoria Mission, site of the earliest disappearance. Then I saw why: had I begun drawing the line at the X that marked the stone's original resting place on the Battle River, the curve would have gone in the right direction. I took the pen and corrected the line.

Steele leaned over the map eagerly. "What about the other end of the spiral?" he asked. "If we can plot its course in the other direction—inward—we can predict where the Indians are most likely to strike next. Then we can prevent them from using their fiendish magic to transform anyone else into buffalo."

I dipped the pen once more in the ink, studied the spiral for a moment, then drew a few short strokes at the innermost end of the line. I was able to extend the spiral a little further, but I soon saw that it would be impossible to complete it. The problem was that the spiral was far from perfect: its curves bulged outward on an east-west axis. The distances between the loops were uneven, and the curves were irregular.

"This is the best I can do," I told Steele. "From this point, the line could continue inward along any number of different angles. I can only sketch the line's direction with any hope of accuracy to the point where it crosses the river."

I paused, then, and peered more closely at the map. With a thrill of excitement, I saw that I'd just extended the spiral across the South Saskatchewan—the very river on whose banks the "ghost" of Iniskim had been spotted, two years ago.

I pointed at the spot. "Look here! You see this point? This is the only place where the spiral could possibly cross the river between Saskatchewan Landing and the South Saskatchewan's confluence with the Red Deer River—the rest of the spiral would all be south of the river, after this point. This has got to be the place where Constable Davis forded the river and saw Iniskim's ghost."

Steele clapped me on the back. "Well done, Corporal. I'll order the patrol that's searching the South Saskatchewan to make for the spot posthaste."

Chambers just stared at the map.

"This line," he mused, touching his finger to it. I hadn't blotted the ink, and his finger came away wet. He wiped it against his neatly pressed trousers—a sure sign that he was not his former self. "It looks like a ley line."

"A what?" Steele asked. Like a good investigator, he was alert to every clue.

Chambers looked up. "A ley line. It's a current of etheric force that exists solely on the ethereal plane, but with links to the physical plane. Ley lines typically flow along and around natural terrestrial formations in the physical world: along rivers, through valleys, and around hills and mountains. Mankind has tried for centuries to direct their flow, with mixed results. Stonehenge is but one example."

I had no idea what Chambers was talking about, but he was starting to sound like a professor again. Strangely, it no longer irritated me.

Steele asked the obvious question: "What is Stonehenge?"

Chambers smiled. For the first time since being returned to his human form, he was truly enjoying himself. "Stonehenge is a gigantic megalith." He paused expectantly.

I obliged him: "What's a megalith?"

"A gigantic structure made of stones placed one upon the other. The pattern was believed to be magically significant by ancient druids."

I frowned. I had no idea what "druids" were, either, but Chambers was wound up now, and wasn't waiting for questions.

"The Society for Psychical Research has studied Stonehenge for some time," he continued. "We believe it to be a gateway that channels etheric flow. Through its many apertures, the flow of etheric force is refracted and redirected, to spread out like the invisible spokes of a wheel, across all of England."

"What has that got to do with the spiral that Grayburn drew?" Steele asked. His tone was slightly irritated; he was a man who expected answers he could understand.

Chambers stared at the map, his brows furrowed. Then snapped his fingers.

"The spiral begins with the Manitou Stone, and is almost certainly a ley line. The Manitou Stone must work in the same way that the boulders of Stonehenge do: as a channel for etheric force. This energy is being used to augment the powers of the buffalo stone, allowing its magic to be used at a distance. The Indians tested this on the McDougalls, and it apparently worked, despite the fact that the Manitou Stone no longer sat in its original position on the ley line. Had the Manitou Stone been in its proper place, the Day of Changes might have occurred then and there.

"The Indians tried to use magic to move the Manitou Stone back to the place the McDougalls had taken it from, but something went wrong. It's my guess that the Manitou Stone wound up somewhere other than the place the Indians intended, and that they are searching for it still. In the meantime, they're trying to initiate the Day of Changes using other, less significant points along the ley line. Hence, the rash of disappearances, all of which correspond to the spiral."

Steele digested this information, then nodded toward the end of the table, where the spiral-shaped stone lay nested in my tobacco pouch. As he regarded it, his lips pressed together in a grim line.

"The disappearances continued, even after Corporal Grayburn recovered the buffalo stone," he said. "There must be more than one of the blasted things."

"That's true," I said, remembering Jerry Potts's assertion that there were many such stones. "But there's only one Manitou Stone—and only one ley line."

"So we hope," Steele said grimly. Then he turned to Chambers. "The Manitou Stone marked the beginning of the spiral, before the Indians tried to move it. Could it have wound up at the spiral's end point?"

"It may have, indeed," Chambers peered at the map, then stabbed a finger at the place where the spiral crossed the South Saskatchewan. "The most logical place for it to have wound up is here—at the spot we presume Iniskim to be heading. That's why she made for it once before: she had a premonition that this is where the Manitou Stone would one day be. It must be the spiral's end point."

Steele nodded eagerly. "By God, if the Manitou Stone is at the ford, I'd best lead a patrol to the spot myself. Well done, Chambers!"

Chambers beamed under the praise. I still had doubts, however. If the Manitou Stone had come to rest on the banks of the South Saskatchewan, surely the Indians could have guessed where it was long ago. The Assinaboine were allies of the Cree; at some point over the past year, Big Bear must have heard their stories of the buffalo calf "ghost" that was spotted at the ford. He would have come to the same conclusion that Chambers just did.

I stared at the map. The spot on the South Saskatchewan River wasn't necessarily the end of the ley line—the spiral I'd drawn still had a lot of room at its centre, and looked incomplete.

One other thing nagged at me: the fact that Big Bear was using the ley line's energy to transform people into buffalo. How could he do this if he didn't know the spiral's route?

A thought occurred to me, as I stared at the uneven spaces between the lines I'd drawn and the strange bulging of the curves. I wondered if something was wrong with the spiral—if something had deformed it to the point where it no longer followed its true course. Perhaps the Indians didn't know where the spiral was now. The spate of disappearances marked on our map may not have been attempts to trigger the Day of Changes. They might instead be the Indians' way of using magic to plot the spiral's course.

As I thought about what Chambers had just said about ley lines, I was reminded of another conversation. The whole discussion of ley lines was vaguely familiar. I thought back to Bertrand and the brief mention he'd made of magnetic fields, as he was calibrating the aerograph.

"Are currents of magnetic force the same as lines of etheric force?" I asked.

"Similar, but not the same," Chambers said. "Etheric forces have an organic flow; while magnetic forces just run north-south. That's why we have four cardinal directions: north, south, east, and west."

East-west. That was the way the spiral bulged. Bertrand had also mentioned large sources of iron, which could throw an aerograph off course. That was why the aerograph followed the CPR line.

I suddenly realized why Piapot had been so defiant about the railway being built across Indian land. "That's it!" I shouted.

Both Chambers and Steele turned to look at me.

"The railway line. It's thrown the shape of the spiral off. That's why the Indians don't know where the Manitou Stone wound up. Even if the ford would normally have been the spiral's end point, the Manitou Stone may not have wound up there. It was thrown off course by the deformed ley line, and overshot its mark. I have a hunch that it's somewhere in here, instead."

The three of us stared at the blank space inside the innermost arm of the spiral. It was more than sixty miles across, a barren expanse of sandy ground and alkaline lakes that had yet to be settled. Few trails crossed it, and little was known about it. Searching it for a boulder that stood only as high as a man's waist could take months, and we had only three weeks.

"The ford is still our best starting point," Steele said. "I'll lead the patrol there myself."

"Sir," I said. "I'd like to be part of that patrol."

Steele shook his head. "Sorry, Grayburn. I want you where you'll be of most use to Q Division: here in this detachment, close to the CPR line. If our other patrols find any light-haired buffalo, we'll need you on hand to transform them back into human beings again."

Damnation! I didn't want to sit idle in Medicine Hat. I also didn't want Steele to think I was disobeying his order.

"Sir," I said in a measured voice, "even if you do find Iniskim, your patrol may be attacked by Indians intent on capturing her. You'll need a way to prevent them from using her to find the

Manitou Stone. I can use the buffalo stone to transform Iniskim back into a little girl again. That should blunt her worth to the Indians; I'm certain of it. You're best to have me on the spot when the albino calf is found."

I wasn't sure, of course, that I wanted to use the stone on Iniskim. If I transformed her back into a little girl, would her fever return? I didn't want to be responsible for a child's death.

Steele thought a moment, then nodded. "Very well."

Chambers scrambled to his feet as Steele began gathering up the maps and reports. "Superintendent! You'll need me as well. If the Manitou Stone is at the ford, a tremendous amount of etheric force could be spilling out into the physical plane at that point. Ley lines are dangerous, and there isn't a single man in Q Division with any idea of how to deal with them except me. You'll require my knowledge and expertise."

"Quite so," Steele said.

I walked to the end of the table to collect the pouch that held the buffalo stone. Holding it in my hand, I stared at Chambers, pleased to see that he was his old self again. I knew he was right: with his knowledge of ley lines, he was the best man for the job of finding and destroying the Manitou Stone.

Remembering the dream I'd had of the buffalo jump and Chambers's demise under the Manitou Stone, I prayed the job wouldn't wind up being his last.

◄—►

Steele spent the rest of the day organizing the patrol. He chose six regular constables from the detachment, and conscripted Medicine Hat's aerograph operator over the protests of the detachment's commanding officer. He told all of us to be ready to set out at dawn the next day. He planned to lead the patrol himself, using the detachment's air bicycle to reconnoitre.

Steele didn't want to include a scout on the patrol—they were all either Metis or half breeds, and their Indian blood made them questionable allies in our endeavour—but I convinced him that it was necessary. We needed a man who not only knew the uncharted territory between here and the South Saskatchewan, but one who could track buffalo hoof prints, should any be found.

Steele wished heartily for Jerry Potts, but the man was still missing, presumed killed by the Cree. Steele instead settled upon Louis Leveillee, a Metis who had also served with the mounted police since 1874. Leveillee was half Cree, but his French ancestry predominated. Tall and greying, and in his late sixties, Leveillee was polite to a fault and as loyal to the North-West Mounted Police as Potts was presumed to be.

When we turned out on the parade square the next morning, Leveillee turned a wary eye to the skies above. Rain had been falling steadily all night, and the clouds overhead were grey and thick. It looked as if a deluge was about to begin at any moment. The horses we sat upon whickered and shifted their footing uneasily, their hooves making sucking noises in the mud. Already rainwater was trickling down into my jacket, despite the non-regulation Stetson I wore.

Steele stood beside a cart-mounted device that was pumping hydrogen into the balloon of his air bicycle, one careful eye on the balloon's pressure gauge. Mounted on the cart were several large brass drums, each lined with glass and filled with sulphuric acid. A central drum, connected to the others by glass tubes, held iron shavings onto which the acid dripped. The resulting chemical reaction produced hydrogen, which escaped through rubber hoses into the air bicycle's balloon. The hoses were carefully sealed to prevent any gas leakage; all I could hear was the gentle clatter of the perpetual motion device that drove the pumping mechanism.

Leveillee slopped his way across the parade square, nearly losing a boot in the mud. He bowed before Steele, doffing his sodden cap.

"*Excuse moi*, my dear Superintendent," he said. "Forgive me to impose, but the sky, she looks unsettled today. I fear a storm. Perhaps if we wait–"

Even from where I sat on my horse, I could see Steele's moustache bristle. "We've already been delayed half an hour, and I don't want to waste any more time. A little rain isn't going to stop us. We'll set out at once."

Leveillee gave a graceful shrug. "As you wish, Superintendent." The scout hadn't pressed the issue—but as he walked back to his horse, I could see that he was still casting worried looks up at the heavens.

I glanced in the same direction and thought for a moment that I saw a round black spot among the rolling masses of vapour. My heart nearly faltered as my imagination took flight. Was that the malevolent eye of a thunderbird, looking down at me? But then the eye took on the rosy tint of dawn, and I realized that it was no more than a hole in the clouds.

Even so, I didn't want to take any chances. Steele had impressed upon me the need to report any hunches or premonitions to him immediately. I wasn't certain that vague, uneasy feelings qualified, and Steele had been irritated once already by Leveillee's hesitation—but orders were orders.

"Superintendent," I called.

A grumble of thunder drowned out my voice. I saw that Steele hadn't heard me. He flicked a finger against the balloon, listened with a look of satisfaction to its tight *thrum-thrum*, then twisted shut the valve on the sulphuric-acid drum nearest to him. He waved at two constables who stood sheltering in the doorway of the stables to drag the cart away.

Although I'd fortified myself with painkiller that morning, my stomach felt as though it were tied in a knot. The uneasy feeling had grown into a certainty that something bad was about to happen—but I had no idea what.

The constables began to drag the sulphuric acid cart away, muttering expletives under their breath as they forced it through the thick, gooey mud. Then one of them slipped and fell against the cart. I heard the sound of breaking glass, and the faint hiss of escaping gas. The constable stood up, cursing aloud and holding his hand. Blood welled through his fingers.

The gas... I looked wildly around to see if anyone was smoking. No, that wasn't it: the hissing noise slowed, then stopped.

The constable who had fallen against the cart had cut his hand quite badly. Blood was flowing from it and his face had gone pale. The other man who had been pulling the cart took a look at the wound, then began shouting for someone to call the detachment's surgeon. I nodded to myself. This mishap had probably been the source of my earlier unease. If this was the worst that was going to happen, all would be well.

The thought made me look up. I saw that the reddish hole in the clouds was still there. It looked even more like a circle, and it was even redder than it had been before.

Suddenly, I realized my mistake. The "hole" was in the western sky—and the sun was rising in the east. That *was* an eye up there: the eye of Thunderbird.

It blinked, and I saw a bolt of lightning streak from it, striking the prairie no more than a mile away. I suddenly realized what it intended.

"Superintendent!" I bellowed. "Get away from the air bicycle." I turned my horse and waved an arm frantically. "Get away, everyone!"

Steele reacted immediately. He took one look at my wild expression and began to run. The mud, however, slowed him down, making it impossible for him to move quickly. Each step was an eternity for him; he floundered like a man in a nightmare.

I dug my heels into the flanks of my horse and charged to where Steele floundered. "Climb on!" I shouted. With agility amazing in so large a man, Steele clambered up behind me.

"Ride," he gritted. "Ride!"

We did.

The explosion came before we'd made it two hundred feet. I saw the bolt of lightning streak from the sky, and then the flash of exploding hydrogen blinded me. A wave of heat washed across my back, and I heard a man's shrill scream.

My horse bolted, but after a moment I got it under control. I turned the panicked animal back in the direction of the parade square, rode up as close to the ruined air bicycle as I dared, and reined my horse to a halt. Even before I did, Steele was off its back and running in the direction of the air bicycle. The hydrogen gas had been consumed in an instant, but the fabric of the balloon was blazing—as were the uniforms of the two constables who had been pulling the cart. Steele knocked them both to the ground, then rolled them in the mud to smother the flames. I saw them rise to their feet a moment later, and was sorry that my premonition of impending danger hadn't been clearer or come sooner—but they did not seem to be badly harmed. The thick serge of their uniforms had protected them from the worst of it.

I looked around me, and in the gloom counted eight men on horseback. The patrol had all been seated on their horses, ready to depart, and this had saved them. I ran through the list in my mind: six constables, a scout, an aerograph operator, Chambers.... There should have been nine men in the patrol, besides Steele and myself. One person was still unaccounted for—and then I saw why.

A horse had been knocked over by the force of the explosion; as I watched, it struggled to its feet, then bolted away. A moment later, a man rose from the spot where the horse had fallen. I did not recognize him at first, so covered was he in mud, but as soon as he curled his lip in disgust and tried to use the falling rain to wash the mud from his clothes, I had to smile.

"Chambers," I called out. "Are you all right?"

He blinked up at me, his eyes white against the brown mud. "I am," he said. Then he looked ruefully down at his suit. "I wish I could say the same for my jacket and trousers. They cost more than sixty dollars!"

Steele stood beside the twisted wreckage of his air bicycle, fists on his hips. Amazingly, one of its perpetual motion wheels was still turning, filling the air with a *click-clatter* noise. Steele glowered at it, then kicked the wheel with a mud-gummed boot. The wheel stopped.

I gulped. I'd never known Steele to lose his temper before. When he looked up at me, however, there was a determined gleam in his eye.

"The Indians seem to know that we're coming." He smiled. "Good. That means we're on the right track."

I heard another grumble of thunder, and glanced up at the sky. It was still cloudy, but the lightning had stopped. The thunder was retreating away into the distance, and there was not an eye to be seen among the clouds.

Steele looked around and spotted the scout. "Leveillee!" he shouted. "It seems you were right, after all. We'll leave this afternoon, instead."

◄—►

Our patrol didn't leave that afternoon—nor even that evening. No sooner had Steele traded his air bicycle for a horse than the aerograph operator and three constables were struck down by a bout of typho-malaria. The constables could easily be replaced, but Steele wanted to send dispatches as swiftly as possible back to Inspector Irvine, who was personally monitoring Q Division's progress in this case. The nearest replacement operator—Bertrand—was at Fort Macleod. Even though our own operator was able to struggle from his sick bed and send a message to Bertrand, ordering him to Medicine Hat at once, it would be three days before his replacement arrived.

Steele decided to depart without an aerograph operator—only to have his plans thwarted once again. This time, it was the horses that fell ill. One after another, they succumbed to trembling fits. The veterinary surgeon shrugged his shoulders, claiming he'd never seen anything like it before, and that they must have been poisoned. Steele responded by arresting every half breed and Indian within a mile of the detachment. Even the gracious Leveillee was temporarily placed behind bars.

It didn't do any good. When he sent a telegram, calling for replacement horses to be sent, a response soon arrived declaring that all of the horses in the nearby detachments had succumbed to the strange malady as well. Horses would have to be sent in by train from the nearest unaffected detachment—Moose Jaw—and organizing their shipment would take another three days. We might as well wait for Bertrand.

Chafing at the delay, Steele did what he could to mobilize his forces. He telegraphed Maple Creek, ordering that detachment to limber up its nine-pound muzzle-loader and stand by. The limber was one of those powered by a perpetual motion device, and could travel swiftly over open prairie. If the Manitou Stone did turn out to be at the place where the spiral crossed the South Saskatchewan River, it would be a simple matter of sending a rider back to Maple Creek to alert the artillery crew, and the gun could be driven to the spot within twenty-four hours.

Just in case the Manitou Stone had wound up elsewhere on the ley line, Steele sent telegrams to every detachment that was close to a spot where a disappearance had taken place, requesting the commanding officers to search the area for large or unusual boulders, and to use their field guns to blow these stones to pieces.

As might be expected, the commanding officers responded with a barrage of questions. Why were they being given such strange orders? What was this new division—which they had barely heard of—up to, and under whose authority was the Superintendent acting? Steele had to come up with a plausible reason for his orders, and wound up weaving together fact and fiction. He explained that the stones were of religious significance to the Indians, and that they were to be smashed in order to demoralize the Indians and to make them think twice about supporting the much-anticipated Metis uprising. When Commissioner Irvine himself backed up Steele's orders, the commanders at last agreed.

Never one to sit idle myself, I used the time to send a telegram to the detachment at Fort Qu'appelle. I addressed it to Acting Hospital Steward Holmes, the fellow who had delivered the stillborn Iniskim and seen her alive several months later. I hoped that he could shed some light on the medicine woman's identity, and urged him in my telegram to find out everything he could about her.

I told Steele we needed to find and question the medicine woman about the Day of Changes and Iniskim's role in it. Secretly, however, I hoped to persuade her to cure the cramps that had wracked my gut for the past six weeks. Although I was able to carry out my duties, the lingering of this bout of typho-malaria was starting to worry me. I wondered if I would ever be free of it.

The return telegram from Holmes was a disappointment, however. It simply reiterated what he'd said in his report to Steele.

Convinced that there had to be something more, I asked Steele if I could again see the report on the birth and resurrection, and read through it carefully. I found one detail that Steele had neglected to mention: according to Holmes, the birth had been a difficult one. I knew that already; Emily had told me as much herself. Holmes's report added something more, however. Emily had lost a great deal of blood while giving birth, and at one point Holmes was convinced that he'd lost her. Yet even though he'd been about to give her up for dead, along with her child, she'd lived.

I thought my efforts to find the medicine woman had come to an end, but then I heard that a scout by the name of Many Eagle Feathers had been ordered to report to Medicine Hat for questioning. I didn't pay him much attention at first: he had been

hired by North-West Mounted Police just six months ago, and
turned out not to be the scout who had guided Constable Davis
and the Assinaboine. He wasn't the man we were looking for.

He was half Blood Indian, though—the same tribe that the
medicine woman who healed Iniskim was from—and he'd briefly
spent time in a Blood camp, after his father had died. I decided
to ask if he knew of the medicine woman, even though the odds
were against it.

I caught up to Many Eagle Feathers as he was getting ready to
ride back to his detachment. He stood outside the blacksmith's
shop, watching the farrier shoe his horse. That surprised me—I
thought that all half-breeds rode unshod ponies, as Indians did.
This fellow, however, looked more white than Indian. He had
close-cropped hair and wore trousers and a jacket. His only
Indian accoutrements were his moccasins and a string of trade
beads around his neck. Suspended from them was a silver
crucifix, and beside it an amulet bearing the image of one of the
Catholic saints. When I hailed him, and he greeted me in
flawless English, I started to doubt that he'd have any
information for me at all. Still, it was worth a try.

I motioned him away from the ringing clangs of the farrier's
hammer. "Many Eagle Feathers, can I have a word with you?"

"My name is Peter," he said.

He must have changed his name in the six months since he
signed on as a police scout. I supposed he had adopted the
Christian faith only recently. "Peter, then—can we talk?"

He nodded.

"I'm looking for a woman from the Blood tribe. I'm wondering
if you know her."

"Maybe. What's her name?"

"I don't know," I said. "But she's a powerful medicine
woman—so powerful that she can cure any illness—even bring
people back from the dead."

The scout merely nodded, as if I hadn't said anything out of
the ordinary, and fingered the cross that hung around his neck.
"Only Christ can raise the dead. God's is the only true power;
medicine men are false prophets."

"This was a medicine *woman*," I reminded him. I had no desire
to get into a religious debate; I knew from observing my parents
that it only led to anger and tears. "She was in Fort Qu'appelle
last summer."

"I've never been to Fort Qu'appelle."

He'd replied a little too quickly, the way a guilty man will when
questioned about a crime.

"There was a girl born in Qu'appelle in May of last year—a
stillborn. This woman brought her back to life."

Peter merely shrugged, but his silence and his refusal to meet my eye were speaking volumes. He knew something and didn't want to tell me. I could see that I needed to be more persuasive—but how? Then I noticed a puckered scar on the inside of his forearm, just peeping out from the bottom of his sleeve. I thought about how much the wound must have hurt, and that gave me an idea.

I pointed to my stomach and doubled over, as if wracked with pain. It didn't require much acting; my eyes had already begun to water as a wave of nausea gripped me. "I'm ill," I told Peter in a lowered voice as I straightened up. "I need to find the medicine woman so she can cure me."

It took Peter a moment to meet my eye. When he did, his expression was guarded. He pressed his lips together in thought. My hopes lifted—I was certain he was going to tell me what I needed to know—but then he shook his head.

"You should pray," he advised. "Perhaps God will hear you, and send a saint to heal you. They are very powerful."

I could see that even my impassioned plea wasn't enough. Peter wasn't going to help me find the medicine woman. Why was he so reluctant to talk about her? I could guess by his carefully neutral expression that he knew the woman. I stared at him, and after a moment I realized that he had crossed his arms in such a way as to conceal his scar.

"I've got to go," he said. "The farrier is finished with my horse."

He was right. The ringing of the hammer had stopped.

"Wait." I grabbed Peter's wrist and yanked up his sleeve. His scar ran all the way up to his elbow on the inside of the forearm, and looked as though it had been made by a knife. It had probably been a bloody wound—very nearly fatal. Yet there were no stitch marks.

"This medicine woman healed you, didn't she?" I guessed. I glanced at his crucifix. "And the priests told you that it was the work of the Devil."

Peter jerked his hand away and gave me a frightened look. "She is the Devil."

"So you do know her!" I cried. "Well I don't care if she is, or if she has horns and a pitch fork. I want to be healed by her."

Peter thought about this for a long moment. "I know the woman," he said slowly. "Her name is Strikes Back."

Relief washed through me like a dose of Pinkham's. "Where is she now?"

He shrugged. "I don't know."

"Which of the Blood bands is she with?"

"None of them. Strikes Back is a half-sister to Chief Red Crow; she used to travel with his band, but she had a fight with him many years ago and has gone her own way since."

It was all I could do to contain my excitement. Of the chiefs that had been present in the shaking tepee, Mountain had described Iniskim as his granddaughter, and now Red Crow turned out to be related to the medicine woman who had used her magic to restore life to Iniskim. Was Strikes Back part of the plan to effect the Day of Changes—or, given her animosity toward Red Crow, was she working to prevent it?

"What was the fight about?" I persisted.

Peter's earlier hesitation was gone. Now that the stopper of fear had been removed, he proved to be a font of information.

"About ten years ago, Strikes Back learned that Red Crow had kept some of the horses that should have been given to her husband when she married. She became angry and shot them."

"She shot the chief's horses?" I asked. It was an incredible act of defiance among a people who valued horses above all else—even more so for a woman. I'd already seen one demonstration of an Indian woman's mettle when Emily shot her husband, but that had been a desperate act to save her child. I still imagined women to be the weaker sex, not prone to such acts of violence.

Peter chuckled. "If you met Strikes Back, you'd understand. She's a woman with a man's heart. She rides and hunts buffalo as well as any man, and is as tough as a man. I heard that she was once found in a snowdrift, frozen to death. They carried her back to her tepee, thawed her out beside the fire, and she came back to life."

"Where did she go after leaving Red Crow's band?"

"She married a white man—a trader. She lived with him in the trading post at Fort Macleod for many years. That was when I met her—and she healed me."

Fort Macleod! I'd been there only a few short days ago.

"Is she there still?"

Peter shook his head. "She quarrelled with her husband more than a year ago and walked away, leaving him and their four children. That was the last anyone saw of her."

"What was the trader's name?"

"Davis."

That took me aback. "Any relation to Constable Davis? The one they call 'Peaches'?"

"Not that I know of."

"Did you have to pay Strikes Back to heal your arm?"

The scout gave me a strange look, but before I could interpret it, the farrier walked Peter's horse over to us. Peter paid him for the shoeing, then swung up into his saddle. "I'm still paying her," he muttered, making the sign of the cross upon his breast. Then he kicked his horse into a trot.

"With what?" I asked, running after him. "Money? Furs? Trade goods? What did she want?"

His horse increased its pace and galloped away in a cloud of dust. I thought for a moment about chasing after him, but realized that it would do no good. If he'd wanted to tell me more, he would have.

I walked back to the blacksmith shop, kicking the dusty ground in my frustration. Then I noticed that the horseshoes of Peter's horse had left a peculiar pattern. I called the farrier over, and pointed it out to him.

"He was a strange one, all right," he said. He scratched his beard with the clawed end of his hammer, then shrugged. "Not your typical Indian scout, at all. He must be a really religious fellow. He wanted to re-shoe his horse, even though the shoes were brand new. He wanted me to use nails with cross-shaped heads. He says they're for good luck. Maybe he thinks they're gonna help his horse to walk on water."

Laughing at his own joke, the farrier walked away. Peter had already ridden out of sight to the north, on his way back to the Battleford detachment. I wondered if the cross-studded horseshoes really did bring protection—if there really was something to Peter's newly adopted Catholic faith. Raised by a sceptical father, I'd been brought up to believe that religion was just so much superstition. It was balderdash—just like premonitory dreams, and magic. Except now I knew that magic was real.

Peter was gone, but he'd given me a starting point for finding the "manly hearted" Strikes Back: Fort Macleod. Another possible source of information was coming from that very detachment, even now. I just had to wait for him to arrive.

◄ — ►

That night, I had a strange dream. I was standing in a graveyard, much like the one at Victoria Mission. All around me were mounds of freshly turned earth, each of them a grave. All were marked with rough wooden crosses, except for one, which had a tombstone. Curious as to whose grave it might be, I walked over to read the inscription.

There was none: the tombstone was a solid black slab of stone, with nary a word upon it.

A burning curiosity filled me—whose grave was it? With the sudden insight that comes upon one sometimes in dreams, I realized that the tombstone was weighing down the person who had been buried here. I had only to lift it and she would rise to the surface, revealing her face to me.

I bent down and grasped the stone, then gave a mighty tug. Despite its weight, it came up easily in my arms, revealing a hole in the earth. I saw movement below, and realized that the occupant of the grave had unexpectedly become animated. Suddenly terrified, my thoughts filled with wild imaginings at the horrific form this morbid creature might take. I ran from that spot, still holding the tombstone in my arms. The corpse hauled itself out of the grave and followed me, running low and swift to the ground like a beast. Its feet had become hooves, and they were striking the ground with a *tick-tick-tick-tick* noise that was counting off the seconds to my death.

I staggered onward, then realized that I was running in a circle. The empty grave lay directly in my path. Unable to stop myself, I plunged headlong into it. As I fell, the tombstone rolled back into place, sealing the grave shut—but not before I caught a glimpse of a buffalo, haloed by the moon, staring down at me with a smile on its lips as my doom descended upon me....

I woke up in a cold sweat, my legs flailing. Something was indeed ticking in the darkness, and for a wild moment I fancied that it was part of my dream. I slammed a hand down upon it—and the ticking stopped. I realized belatedly that it was only my watch—that it had inexplicably started working again.

I rolled over and pulled the blanket up closer to my chin. Then slumber found me once more.

The next morning, Bertrand at last straggled in to the Medicine Hat detachment on one of the few horses from his unit that had not been struck down by illness. He was surprised by the warm greeting I gave him. As he climbed down from his horse, complaining loudly about chafed calves and saddle sores, I invited him into the mess and bought him a glass of cider. As soon as he was settled I asked him if he knew of a white trader named Davis who had married a Blood woman. I hoped he could tell me more of the history of Strikes Back.

Bertrand was quite curt and gave me a suspicious look, but he did know the full name of the fellow—D. W. Davis, an American out of Montana. Bertrand also added one key fact: Strikes Back had deserted her husband in May of 1883. He even remembered the date: Victoria Day.

On that day, the trading post had just received a shipment of tinned goods that would be used to enliven the annual celebration of the Queen's birthday. Bertrand had gone to the trading post to pick them up, and found the jilted husband of Strikes Back smashing bottles of cider against a wall.

As I put the two stories together, something gave me pause: the dates. How could Strikes Back have been in Fort Macleod and in Fort Qu'appelle on the same day? The two settlements were four hundred and fifty miles apart. It simply was not possible—unless magic was involved.

I knew from personal experience of one way a person could travel a great distance by magic: by passing through a tunnel like the one I'd entered at Victoria Mission. I wondered if Strikes Back had walked into a cave at Fort Macleod and exited it later that same day at Fort Qu'appelle. Time flowed at a different rate in the tunnel than it did above ground. In my case, nearly three weeks had sped by while I walked through the tunnel. Strikes Back, an accomplished medicine woman, had been able to produce the opposite effect: only a few hours had elapsed while she'd made a journey of several hundred miles.

It seemed logical to conclude that Strikes Back had used the tunnels to reach Fort Qu'appelle, but one thing puzzled me. Upon entering the tunnel, why had she not been transformed into a buffalo?

Just like me, Strikes Back must have been able to pass through the tunnels without being transformed. And so had Emily, since I didn't find any shreds of her clothing next to those of Chambers. I sat and thought about that, as Bertrand drank his cider. What commonalty did Strikes Back, Emily, and I share?

As pain clenched my stomach, I suddenly knew the answer: all three of us had nearly died at one point in our lives. My heart had faltered on the operating table, Emily had nearly died of blood loss while giving birth to Iniskim, and Strikes Back had been frozen in a snowdrift. For one brief moment, each of us had a foot inside death's door. Perhaps because we had already been "reborn" once, the magic that turned humans into adult buffalo with the light-coloured coats of newborn calves no longer worked on us.

That would explain why I could handle the buffalo stone, and why it had not transformed the dead buffalo back into human beings again. Its transformative magic only worked on living creatures. People like myself, who had "died" at one point in our lives, were counted among the dead.

One question remained, however. I'd seen Big Bear carefully pick up the buffalo stone in my tobacco pouch. He'd obviously feared its magic—which must work on white and Indian alike. Why then, when the Day of Changes came, were the Indians so confident that only whites would be turned into buffalo?

What protection did the Indians have that white people did not?

As I was pondering the question, my eyes fell on a pair of antlers that had been mounted as a trophy on the wall. They reminded me of the deer form that Chief Mountain had taken, when Poundmaker's magic sent those gathered inside the shaking tepee into the spirit world.

Suddenly, I realized why the Indians would not be affected by the Day of Changes. Every Indian had a guardian spirit—a protector in animal form. The magic of these animal spirits might not be able to prevent the transformation wrought by actually touching a buffalo stone, but it was a shield against the less direct magic of the Day of Changes.

I wondered if whites, whose only "guardian spirits" were angels in human form—and saints, like the one on the amulet around Peter's neck—would be afforded the same protection by these guardians. Somehow, I doubted it. The McDougalls had been devout Methodists, and yet their faith had not protected them.

An even more startling epiphany struck me: if we were unable to prevent the Day of Changes from occurring, I, the only white man with an animal guardian spirit, would not be transformed into a buffalo. I personally had nothing to fear from the Day of Changes. Like the Indians, I was immune.

A spasm of pain gripped my stomach, reminding me that I was not immune to all things.

When I'd joined the North-West Mounted Police, I'd been driven by a thirst for adventure and the desire to spend my life doing something more than working at a humdrum job in a tobacco shop. Over the past five years, however, a sense of duty had grown in me as I realized that I was bringing law and order to what had once been wilderness. I was not merely having adventures—I was helping to forge a new land. If I could prevent the Day of Changes from occurring, I would have the satisfaction of having accomplished something truly noble and enduring before I died.

I rose to my feet, intending to report my conclusions to Steele at once. Just at that moment, however, he strode into the mess. Before I could utter a word, he ordered Bertrand to set his cider down and get back on his horse, and told me to mount up.

"Healthy horses have arrived at last!" he cried. "We can finally ride north."

I followed Steele outside into the square, giving him a quick summation of my thoughts as I trotted along beside him. Across the parade square, two constables were tying up the dozen horses that had been shipped by boxcar from Moose Jaw. I stopped in my tracks as I recognized a gelding that was a familiar dun colour. The ochre handprint was long since gone from his flank, but I knew the bronco at once by the familiar defiant toss of his head. As if sensing my eyes upon him, the horse yanked hard on the lead rope, ripping it from the hand of the man who was trying to tie him to the rail.

"By God," I said to Steele. "That's my old horse, Buck!"

Steele's grin seemed to reach to the very tips of his moustache. "I know. I thought he might come in handy. Would you like to ride him?" Without waiting for my answer—he knew it would be yes—he turned to shout at the other men who would be part of the patrol. "Boots and saddles, men. Mount up!"

I ran to get my saddle, grinning all the way. Buck had seen me safely out of the Big Sands—the Indian purgatory. I had no doubt that he'd see me through whatever else came my way.

⋈—⋈

After three long days on the trail, we were finally approaching the spot where the spiral on the map crossed the South Saskatchewan River. The sky was free of clouds, and the air was still and hot. I rode near the back of the patrol, next to Bertrand, who had trailed behind the others throughout our ride. The aerograph operator sat on his horse like a loose sack of oats, complaining bitterly about his aches and pains and the dust that collected on his thick-lensed spectacles. The back of his shirt was drenched with sweat—I wondered how one man could have so much water in him—and his hair was plastered to his forehead. He smelled like a man who had not washed in three months—not just three days.

I reined in Buck, letting Bertrand get well downwind of me. After a moment his horse disappeared behind a rise; all I could see of him were the two aerographs that he'd tied to his pommel. I would have thought that he'd carry them in a box, but he said their mechanisms were too delicate. Instead, they bobbed along a few feet over his head, hanging from their sausage-shaped balloons with mechanical wings gently flapping and noses pointed in the direction of Regina.

When they, too, disappeared below the rise, I kicked my horse forward. I heard voices up ahead, and as I topped the rise I saw that we'd reached the South Saskatchewan River. It lay before me in the bottom of a wide valley. Nearly as wide as a small lake, it was studded with gravel bars. A faint trail led down to the river's edge; the patrol was winding its way down along it, their thirsty horses trotting toward the water. I laughed aloud at the sight of Bertrand's flabby body bouncing this way and that; he had no idea how to use his stirrups.

I reined Buck to a stop and looked around. Judging by the gravel bars and the way the river slowed and widened, we'd come to the ford that Davis had spoken of, but I saw no sign of the Manitou Stone—just a jumble of smaller river rocks along the water's edge. There was no sign of Iniskim, either. Leveillee had been told to keep a careful eye out for the tracks of a buffalo calf, but the scout hadn't seen any during our journey. The only tracks he'd spotted were those of a lone rider, who had crossed at an angle to our path earlier that day. It wasn't an Indian pony, Leveillee said: the hooves of the horse were shod.

The rest of the patrol were letting their horses drink. Two of the constables had dismounted, and were lifting off the pack horses the crates of dynamite we'd brought along, just in case we found the Manitou Stone. Steele trotted back and forth behind the rest of the men, pointing out the areas across the river he wanted searched. That was the logical place to start: according to Davis, Iniskim's ghost had been spotted on the north side of the river when it had made its appearance two years ago. We just had to find the way across.

Leveillee had already ridden his horse into the river and was using it to test the water's depth. Bertrand, meanwhile, had dismounted from his horse and sprawled on the sandy riverbank. He looked too exhausted to care that his horse was untended. Fortunately, it was a placid animal and merely stood in the river, drinking.

Chambers had dismounted. He squatted by the river, trailing his fingers in the water as if he were trying to read it like Braille.

Steele glanced in my direction. "Corporal Grayburn!" he shouted. "What are you doing up there? Have you seen something?"

I started to shake my head. Then a flash of white caught my eye. My heart raced—but then I realized that it wasn't a white buffalo calf, after all. It was something small and square that fluttered in the breeze about five hundred feet to my left, at the base of an outcropping of rust-coloured rock.

"Maybe," I shouted back at Steele. "I'll let you know."

I turned Buck to the left and rode along the rise. The white object turned out to be the fluttering pages of a book. It lay in a clump of grass, its pages flipping back and forth in the breeze. Someone had left a marker in it, and as the wind rustled the pages again, the piece of paper came free. As it blew past me, I recognized the bookmark as a twenty-five-cent shinplaster.

I dropped the reins and leaped down from the saddle. Sweeping up the book, I saw that it was a collection of hymns. With trembling hands, I opened the front cover. The hymnbook was inscribed with the name Frederick Baldwin—it was the very same book that I'd given to Emily on board the *North West*.

My eyes ranged up and down the river. "Emily!" I shouted. "Are you here?" I turned toward the bluffs and cupped a hand against my mouth. "Emily!"

I heard pounding hooves. Glancing back at the river, I saw Steele spurring his horse up the bank toward me. When he reached me, I held up the hymnbook.

"Sir! This hymnal is the one I gave to Emily. She couldn't have carried it here if she'd been turned into a buffalo. That means I was right—she must be a woman still. She's alive—and looking for her child."

Steele nodded, only half listening. His eyes were fixed on the outcropping of reddish rock behind me.

"Amazing," he exclaimed. "From up here, it doesn't look like anything at all." He nodded benevolently down at me. "Good job, Grayburn. If you hadn't drawn my attention to it, I'd never have noticed."

He waved at the rest of the patrol. "Corporal! Send the scout up. If we're going to find buffalo tracks anywhere, it will be up here."

I turned around and looked at the rocky outcropping. It appeared natural enough, but for a moment I wondered if I'd missed something—whether the tunnel through which Emily must have walked to this spot lay open behind me.

It didn't. The bluff was just an outcropping of stone, one of many along the riverbank. The only thing that made it stand out from the rest, as far as I could tell, was that it seemed to contain a fair amount of iron, judging by the rust stains on its surface.

Steele grinned broadly down at me from under the shadow of his Stetson. "Don't look so perplexed, Corporal. All you need do is ride down to the river, and you'll see what I'm talking about."

I shoved the hymnbook into my pocket and did as instructed, passing Leveillee on the way down. When I reached the river, where the rest of the patrol stood pointing, I turned my horse around. Only then did I see what Steele had been so excited about. From this vantage point, the rocky outcropping looked exactly like a buffalo's head. It had two jutting stones where the horns should be, and was the same reddish-brown colour as a buffalo skin.

As I dismounted and let Buck drink from the river, Chambers walked over to me. He stared up at the outcropping with one palm raised, as if he were feeling for a source of heat. River water ran down his fingers and dripped from his wrist.

"The flow of etheric force is strong here," he said. "That buffalo-shaped rock appears to be channelling it."

I didn't feel a thing—and the sceptic in me wondered if Chambers did. He hadn't even noticed the rock until it was pointed out to him, and now he was claiming that it emitted energy like a beacon. Even so, I nodded in silent agreement. The outcropping projected a sense of strength and protection. I could see why the ghost of the stillborn Iniskim would be drawn to it. The massive buffalo head would have drawn her like a magnet.

As I mused on this thought, my eye fell on Bertrand. The aerograph operator was struggling with his horse, trying ineptly to unsaddle it. The two aerographs were still tied to the pommel, and when he at last wrenched the saddle from his horse's back they were yanked down past the animal's face. Spooked by the sudden movement, the horse reared and lashed out with its forefeet. Bertrand staggered back, nearly collapsing under the heavy saddle.

Instead of helping Bertrand, the constables laughed and whooped, enjoying the spectacle. Then one of the horse's feet struck the saddle, knocking it from Bertrand's arms. He toppled backward into the river, dropping the saddle on the sand.

The constables laughed all the harder.

The horse's kick must have loosened one of the wires that tethered the aerographs. Like a suddenly released kite, one aerograph soared into the air. Constables scrambled this way and that, trying to grab its wire as a dripping Bertrand, his thick glasses askew on his face, screamed insults at them from the river. The aerograph floated over all of their heads, trailing its wire past their grasping hands.

Instinctively, I grabbed for it as it sailed past me. I caught the very end of the wire, and quickly twisted my hand so that it wound around my wrist. I smiled as the other constables cheered. I noticed that the wings of the aerograph had sped up as soon as I grasped the wire. That didn't surprise me—but something else did. The aerograph was no longer pointed east, in the direction of Regina. Instead it seemed to be straining to go to the west, its propellers turning ever faster and wings flapping out a frenzied beat. It wanted to be set free....

I let it go.

The aerograph picked up speed, as if it had been caught by a strong gust of wind. It zoomed up at a steep angle, directly toward the spot where Steele and the scout stood. Their backs were to it at first, but then one of their horses spooked. The two men saw the aerograph just in time, and ducked out of the way as it soared past their heads. The machine slammed into the rocky outcropping, its bag bursting with a loud pop.

Although this was the first time I had stood in this spot beside the South Saskatchewan, I had the strangest sense that I had seen this comedy acted out once before. Then I realized that I had: but from a different perspective. I'd been dreaming at the time.

Steele leaped on his horse and kicked it into a trot, and within moments was down at the riverbank. His livid face was as red as his jacket. "That was valuable government property!" he shouted. "Who is responsible for its destruction?"

The constables weren't laughing now. They all seemed to be looking at the ground—and at me, out of the corners of their eyes. Steele turned his horse to where I stood, fire in his eye. I could see that I was going to get an earful—and I knew full well why. We'd brought only two aerographs with us, and each could be sent in only one direction: to carry reports back to Commissioner Irvine in Regina. Without knowing our precise location, there was no way for the operator in Regina to send the device back to us again. He could come close by using a map, but maps of this area were hardly precise. It seemed nothing short of a miracle that we'd come to the right spot ourselves. We'd somehow come straight to the very place we were looking for, as if we were birds blown by the breeze—or as if we were aerographs, drawn by an invisible current of etheric or magnetic force.

Even so, I couldn't help but smile. "Superintendent!" I cried.

Steele glared at me. "What is it, Corporal?"

"We don't need Iniskim to find the Manitou Stone," I said, my smile growing larger by the moment. "We can use the aerograph to find it!"

◄—►

Chapter VII

Steele was quick to agree with my suggestion, especially after
Chambers concurred with my conclusions. The buffalo-shaped
outcropping had to be a channel for etheric force, directing and
giving shape to the ley line—and it was clear from its reddish
hue that the rock contained a large amount of iron.

Iron, I concluded, must be the key element that enabled
stones to channel etheric force. For my proof I only had to point
to the CPR tracks, which were interacting with the ley line in so
dramatic a fashion as to seriously deform its spiral shape.
I reasoned that the Manitou Stone must also contain significant
amounts of this metal. Iron was something the aerograph was
naturally attracted to, and so the aerograph would home in on
the Manitou Stone as well.

All that was required was for the aerograph to be calibrated to
negate both the rocky outcropping here at the ford and the
railway line to the south. If the aerograph could be made to
confine itself to the blank spot at the centre of the spiral I'd
drawn on Steele's map, it would lead our patrol to the Manitou
Stone. We'd be able to head straight for the stone, and wouldn't
be slowed down by having to follow the curving spiral of the ley
line. Even if the Indians were ahead of us now, we'd ultimately
beat them in the race to the Manitou Stone.

Bertrand grumbled and muttered about the complex
adjustments that would be required, but Steele would hear none
of it. He ordered the aerograph operator to begin the calibrations
at once, regardless of the fact that it would be dark soon. Steele
was well aware that Bertrand could calibrate his aerographs by
touch, even in pitch darkness, and refused to listen to the
special constable's excuses.

Steele ordered the rest of the patrol to use the daylight that remained to search the area for signs of Iniskim. He also told us to keep an eye out for signs of the four-man patrol that had been working its way west along the river from Saskatchewan Landing; the patrol should have reached the ford ahead of us. It was odd that we'd seen no sign of them.

We soon found out why. No more than thirty minutes after we began searching, Leveillee gave a shout. I was closest to him, and I spurred Buck across a shallow spot in the river and up the opposite bank to the place where the scout was crouched. As I dismounted, Leveillee stood, holding a scrap of red serge and a torn riding boot. I smelled the sickly sweet odour of rot, and in the failing light saw the bloated body of a horse behind some rocks. Pieces of torn clothing were scattered all around, and a tangled bridle hung from a tree branch. All of these items were cast in a lurid glow by the reddish light of the setting sun.

I was glad that Chambers wasn't the one to have found this. He didn't need any more reminders of his own terrible transformation.

Leveillee gestured at the rocky ground. "My dear Corporal, I fear I 'ave nothing but bad news. You see these tracks? Four men ride toward the river, down the slope 'ere, several days ago. They 'ave not dismount; there is no boot print 'ere. Instead only hoof print of horse that is panic. Then buffalo print—more than two, perhaps t'ree or four animal—and horses fall: 'ere... and there... and there...."

The scout looked around thoughtfully. "Something very strange 'appen 'ere. Horses scatter—but buffalo run in a bunch down to river, even though they 'ave fear, too. You see that? Buffalo so frighten, he make night soil there."

Leveillee walked around, pointing at marks on the ground that were invisible to my eyes. "One horse drag his leg, go this way some distance and probably die, one run this way, and one run that way. Fourth horse, he has broken legs and die, as you can see. As for men riding horses..."

He held up the scrap of red serge—the arm of a jacket, split open from shoulder to cuff—and waited for me to provide an explanation. He had been told nothing about the Day of Changes, but the look in his eye suggested that he had figured out for himself what had happened here at the ford.

"Those poor wretches," I muttered, looking around at the torn clothing. "They were turned into buffalo."

Leveillee nodded, and placed the sleeve and boot gently on the ground. He seemed relieved to learn that someone else had reached the same conclusion that he had—that he was not going mad, after all.

I heard hoof beats behind me, and a moment later Steele and two of the constables reined their horses to a halt beside us. Leveillee bowed to the Superintendent, then repeated what he had just told me, once again allowing the facts to speak for themselves.

Steele nodded, offering no explanation for what had happened here. The constables next to him looked uneasily at the scraps of uniform and dead horse, then shared a nervous glance. They'd been told only that we had gone out to search for a large boulder that the Indians held sacred, and that we were also looking for a rare albino buffalo calf. They'd been warned to expect strange sights and to be prepared for a possible Indian attack. They hadn't been told about the Day of Changes, but could see with their own eyes that something strange and terrible had happened here.

Their nervous glances were infectious; soon I too was glancing over my shoulder. If the Indians who had transformed the Swift Current patrol into buffalo were still lurking about the ford, these constables would learn of the dangers of the Day of Changes soon enough.

Steele's eyes darted about, taking in the scene, then came to rest on the scout. "Are there any moccasin prints?"

Leveillee shook his head. "None."

"What about on the other side of the river?" I asked. I slid a hand into my pocket to touch the hymnbook, wondering if Emily had witnessed the transformation of the patrol. "There must have been moccasin prints near the rock shaped like a buffalo head."

Leveillee shook his head solemnly.

"Are you certain?" I asked. "You didn't spend much time searching up there."

"I assure you, my dear Corporal, dere were none."

Steele stared out into the gathering gloom, as if the sheer intensity of his gaze would bring the missing patrol back. The sun had slipped below the horizon, and although the moon was up, it was a mere sliver that cast little light. In another two weeks it would be full—and the Day of Changes would be upon us.

"Those—buffalo—are injured," Steele said. "Can you track them?"

Leveillee touched a finger to his hat. "But of course, my dear Superintendent. I already 'ave. Tracks go toward the river—then stop."

"Were there none on the other side?" Steele asked. "Or up and down the river?"

Leveillee shook his head sadly. "I 'ave seen none when I ride across. Tracks just... stop."

"At the river's edge?" Steele asked.

"No. Well before."

"Just like at Victoria Mission," I said softly.

Steele heard me. "Quite right, Corporal Grayburn. Which means the buffalo must have disappeared underground, into a tunnel."

"Are we going to search for them, sir?" I asked.

Steele hesitated. I could imagine what he must be thinking. He'd ordered the patrol to this spot—orders that had resulted in the loss of four men. There was only a slim chance that they were still alive. By now, they had probably been driven over a cliff and slaughtered.

Like any military commander, Steele had to sacrifice the few for the many. He answered as I expected him to. "We'll find the Manitou Stone first. Once it's dealt with, we'll mount a search."

I nodded, and Steele ordered the men to regroup on the riverbank.

There had been no tunnel at the point where the buffalo tracks ended. Like the tunnel that had opened to receive the McDougalls at Victoria Mission, it had closed up again once they were driven into it.

The tunnel at Victoria Mission had opened a second time, however. When Chambers and I found the cave near the river, the clods of earth at its entrance were fresh. The tunnel had only reopened, it seemed, when Emily approached. It was as if she had a key....

I suddenly remembered the white feather that I'd seen tucked into a crevice at the cave mouth, and guessed what Emily had used to open the tunnel: a "key" in the shape of a feather. She'd left it behind at Victoria Mission after entering the tunnel there, and the cave had remained open, allowing Chambers and myself to follow her. I could only suppose that she must have expected to be transformed into a buffalo, along with her daughter, and not to have need of the feather again.

Emily had emerged here, at the ford—presumably slipping out of the tunnel when a cave was opened to receive the four Mounties who had been transformed into buffalo. The hole in the earth had then sealed itself shut.

The tunnel mouth had to be on the north side of the river, at the spot where the buffalo hoof prints had come to a sudden halt. Yet I'd found the hymnbook on the opposite side of the river, near the buffalo-shaped outcropping of rock. Emily must have crossed the river and walked up to the outcropping, knowing that it had some special significance for Iniskim. Then, after carrying the hymnbook all the way through the tunnels, she'd abandoned it. Had something—or someone—

surprised her up on the bluff, causing her to drop the book in alarm?

Leveillee hadn't found any sign of Emily's moccasin prints. Had they somehow been erased? And, if so, what other tracks had vanished with them?

One other thing also puzzled me: why had Iniskim's ghost come to this spot, a year ago, instead of heading for the Manitou Stone? According to Indian lore, the Manitou Stone held the most powerful magic of all. Chambers had concluded that it must be the ley line's key point.

When I realized what the answer must be, I chided myself for not thinking of it sooner. One year ago, when Iniskim died at birth, the Manitou Stone had been sitting in front of McDougalls' church at Victoria Mission—it had no longer been part of the ley line. Iniskim's ghost had been drawn instead to what must be the second most powerful point on the spiral: the buffalo-shaped outcropping on the riverbank above the ford.

When our patrol was together again, I pulled Steele aside from the other members of the patrol and repeated my conclusions for him in a low voice.

Steele's nod was as decisive as his reply. "We won't find Iniskim here, then—she'll be making for the Manitou Stone directly. We'll have to trust to the aerograph to find it before the Indians do."

Chambers had strolled over and heard the last of our conversation, and was quite animated by it. He insisted that Steele pull out his map, then pointed to the spiral I'd drawn.

"Just as I thought," he said. "The buffalo jump at Head Smashed In is also on the ley line. I suspect that all of the tunnels through the earth also follow the spiral. If we can find a way to open a cave, here at the ford, we can follow the tunnel to the Manitou Stone."

I told him about the feather I'd spotted at the cave mouth at Victoria Mission, and his eyes gleamed. Then I reminded him of the difficulties. "A feather is the key, but we don't know what type of bird we need or which of its feathers to use, let alone the spells to trigger its magic."

I paused then, as a shudder of pain passed through me. I touched a hand to my stomach. My time was running out—my discomfort was increasing with each passing day—and that reminded me of something.

"Opening the tunnel isn't our only problem," I told Chambers. "Time passes more quickly down there. I was inside the tunnel for what I thought was less than a day, yet nearly three weeks passed in the world above. Even if we did succeed in opening a cave and used it to reach the Manitou Stone, there's no guarantee we'd get there in time. The Day of Changes may already have come and gone."

Steele had been listening carefully to our exchange. He looked first at Chambers, then at me. "Corporal Grayburn is right. We won't attempt to use the tunnels unless we're forced to. The aerograph is still our best hope of finding the Manitou Stone. Let's see how Special Constable Bertrand is making out with it."

Chambers, still lost in thought, wandered back to where the other men were resting, and I followed Steele to the spot where Bertrand sat. The aerograph operator had removed himself from the others, and had his tools scattered around him. The aerograph's wire was tied firmly around a rock, and as Bertrand gently adjusted the delicate gyroscopes, the aerograph strained this way and that, like a dog trying to pick up a scent. Its wings sped up a little as I approached. I took a step back, not wanting to send it off kilter.

"Have you got it calibrated yet?" Steele asked.

"It isn't easy, you know," Bertrand said in his irritating nasal tone. "You've no idea of the complexities. This area hasn't been properly charted, and while I can calculate the amount of iron in the railway line and its sidings by multiplying the mileage by the thickness of the rails, I also have to take into account the metal in the trains themselves—which means factoring in their schedules. Then there's the matter of how to estimate the exact amount of iron in the buffalo-head rock. I can do the calculations in my head—I graduated top of my class in mathematics and have a perfect memory for figures—but it's going to take time."

Bertrand shook his head and sighed as if the weight of all of the iron in the world were resting upon his shoulders. Then he picked up his case and began putting his tools away.

"I was hired as an aerograph operator for Fort Macleod, not to roam about the Territories on a wild buffalo chase," Bertrand said. "It's impossible to work under these conditions. I haven't had anything to eat but cold biscuits, I'm half lame from riding that nag of a horse, I'm exhausted and in need of sleep, and people keep pestering me with questions. 'Is it ready? Can we ride out yet?' I've about reached my limit. I've half a mind to let the aerograph smash itself into the rock, like the other one did."

He tucked the last tool away and tied the case shut. "I'll finish the calibrations in the morning."

I saw Steele stiffen, but to his credit as a commander, he kept his emotions in check.

"Special Constable Bertrand," he said, every word carefully controlled. "Not a man in this patrol has had a hot supper, and not one of us—myself included—is going to rest until the

Manitou Stone is found. Anyone who doesn't do his duty will be charged with mutiny, and will be dealt with in the same manner that the army deals with mutineers. Do I make myself clear?"

I saw that Steele's hand was resting upon his holster. Bertrand saw it too. After a moment's thought, however, his chin came up defiantly.

"You need me," Bertrand said. "No one else can operate the aerograph."

"I'll continue without it, if I have to," Steele answered. "Special Constable Chambers is one of the best men to have come out of the Society for Psychical Research; he can follow the ley line by feel. If that fails, Corporal Grayburn's prophetic dreams will lead us to the Manitou Stone. We won't reach it as directly as we will if we use the aerograph, but we'll get there."

I kept a straight face and nodded gravely, as if conjuring up a prophetic dream was something I did every night. It was nonsense, of course. My dreams came when they pleased, not at my command, and I could no more control their subject matter than I could their frequency. Yet Steele's bluff worked. Whatever fresh complaint Bertrand had been about to utter, he suddenly thought better of it.

"Give me a few minutes more," he said. "I'll get it done—but I'm going to file a formal complaint with Commissioner Irvine when this is over."

I would have laughed out loud, had I not been so disgusted with the man. Bertrand had been briefed about the Day of Changes and knew full well the calamity that would befall the North-West Territories in sixteen days.

I couldn't imagine how Bertrand would deal with true discomfort, like the pain in my stomach that burned like constant, slow coals. All I wanted, right now, was to slip away and drink some of the Pinkham's that I'd stashed in my saddlebag. I hoped I'd get the chance soon.

Satisfied that Bertrand would complete his calibrations, Steele turned on his heel and motioned for me to follow him. "Corporal Grayburn."

"Sir."

"As soon as the aerograph is ready, I'm going to set out with the patrol. I want you to remain here at the ford, with Leveillee and Constable Moody. He's a new recruit—he signed up just six months ago—but he's a steady hand. He grew up on a farm in British Columbia, where they have to contend with trees as big as houses when clearing the land, and he knows a thing or two about stumping powder and setting explosives. I'll leave you with one of the crates of dynamite. In the morning, have Moody blow that outcropping apart. That should put a dent in the ley line."

"But what of Bertrand's calibrations?" I asked. "Won't the destruction of the outcropping throw the aerograph off course?"

"Set off the charge at eight o'clock precisely," Steele instructed. "I'll keep an eye on the time, and instruct Bertrand accordingly."

I nodded my acknowledgement of his orders.

"While Moody is setting the charges, have Leveillee continue to search for any sign of the white buffalo calf," Steele continued. "If you find Iniskim's hoof prints, send Moody ahead with a dispatch as soon as he's blown the outcropping. If you don't find any sign of Iniskim by noon, however, leave the ford and ride after us. Bertrand says the aerograph will need to be recalibrated every half-dozen miles or so, so we should be traveling slowly enough for you to catch up."

"And if we sight Iniskim herself?"

"Follow her as closely as you can without startling her. If you can catch up to her, you know what to do."

I touched my hand to the jacket pocket that held the buffalo stone. "Yes, sir."

"Any further questions?"

"What about Special Constable Chambers? Are you taking him with you?"

Steele must have heard the tension in my voice. "You're worried about that premonitory dream you told me about, aren't you?"

I nodded. "The Manitou Stone holds special danger for Chambers, sir. I fear it will kill him, as it did in my dream. If you find the stone, I'd recommend that you don't let him anywhere near it."

Steele glanced at Chambers, who, together with the other men, was resting near the horses, waiting for Bertrand to finish his calibrations. Steele had warned them against lighting a lantern or kindling a fire, in case there were Indians about, and so they were supping on cold biscuits and pemmican. The sun had long since set, and the men were no more than dim shadows in the gloom. Chambers was sitting on one of the two crates of dynamite we'd brought along, and for some reason this sent a shiver through me.

"I'll leave Special Constable Chambers with you," Steele said. "He wanted to study the buffalo-shaped outcropping; perhaps he can learn more about the ley line and how best to disrupt it. Keep an eye on him; he's too valuable an asset to lose."

"I will," I said, vowing to make sure that Chambers was nowhere near the dynamite when it was lit.

◄——►

It took Bertrand more than an hour to finish calibrating the aerograph. By that time, it was completely dark. Steele ordered five of the constables to mount up, and the patrol set out. Once again, the aerograph was tied to Bertrand's pommel; I could hear its propellers whirring as it pulled at the end of its wire like a bloodhound on a leash. As he crested the riverbank, Steele waved farewell with his Stetson. I saluted his silhouette as the patrol disappeared into the night, heading southwest.

The four of us who remained—myself, Chambers, Leveillee, and Constable Moody, the new recruit who looked as though he'd lied about his age to join up—retired to the spot Leveillee had chosen to bed down for the night. It lay on the north side of the river and was well sheltered by some large rocks that screened us from view of anyone using the ford. The night was very dark; the moon had waned to a mere sliver. On the far side of the river, the outcropping loomed against the night sky, blotting out the stars.

The scout had dug a hole in the ground, which I assumed was for use as a privy, given his fastidious nature. When I returned from checking on the horses, however, I saw that he'd kindled a small fire of buffalo chips in it. I told him to put the fire out, but he insisted that we were well in cover, and reminded me that he'd seen no trace of Indians at the ford.

If I'd been as hot-tempered as Sergeant Wilde, I'd have kicked out the fire then and there, but instead I let this minor breach of discipline pass. The dynamite was well away from the tiny fire, and the dried dung gave off only a faint red glow, like coals. The night air was chilly; it wouldn't hurt to brew up some hot tea.

While the water was boiling, I pulled out my pipe and filled it with the last of my Capstan's Full Flavoured. As my fingers brushed against the buffalo stone that was nestled in my tobacco pouch I felt eyes upon me. I looked up to see Leveillee staring at the pouch, but wasn't sure if he was waiting for me to share some tobacco with him, as was customary, or if he had seen the stone.

I folded the pouch and tied it shut. "Sorry," I told the scout. "That's my last pipeful. There's none left."

I was telling the truth, but the scout's eyes narrowed slightly. The buffalo stone made a large bulge, and it was clear that the pouch contained something. Leveillee, however, was too polite to press the issue. He pulled out his own pipe—a chipped clay with a short stem that must have produced a hot draw—and lit up what smelled like a mix of tobacco and willow bark, which the Indians often smoke. He puffed on it as he made and served our tea.

As we drank from steaming cups, I noticed Constable Moody glancing out into the darkness. He at last worked up the nerve to ask a question. "Corporal Grayburn, is it true that the Indians have magical powers? They say that Q Division was formed to fight conjurers and bad medicine men."

His eyes were wide above his beardless cheeks as he awaited my reply. I was tempted to deny the existence of magic, but he'd already seen the aftermath of what had befallen the other patrol—he'd been one of the constables who had ridden with Steele to the spot where Leveillee had found the torn clothing and dead horses. I couldn't think of a lie that would prove any more comforting than admitting the truth. I exchanged a glance with Chambers, who nodded.

Leveillee crossed himself, then stared into the fire. I should have realized that the scout, like all good Frenchmen, was a member of the Catholic faith. It made me think of the half-breed scout Peter, who had so utterly rejected his people's beliefs. Would half-breeds, too, be transformed by the Day of Changes?

I turned back to the young recruit and, in an attempt to bolster his courage, said, "The Indians have magic, it's true, but Q Division will know how to deal with it. Special Constable Chambers is an expert in the field of magical energies and ethereal forces, and I have no little experience myself. You're safer here with us than you'd be if you were back in your bed at the detachment."

I gave Chambers a pointed look. "Indeed so, Constable," he agreed, winking at me behind Moody's back. "The corporal and I are quite capable of handing any magical calamity, large or small."

"But what are we doing here?" Moody said. "And what happened to the other patrol? It looked as though their clothing had been torn apart. It must have been a horrible way to—"

"They didn't die," I said quickly. "At least, we think not."

"They were changed into buffalo, weren't they?" Moody said.

That shouldn't have startled me, but it did. I realized that Moody had either overheard Steele and me, or like Leveillee, had drawn the correct conclusion from what he had seen.

"Will the Indians do that to us, too?" Moody asked.

Chambers answered the question before I could. "The other patrol ran afoul of magic, but the Indians who wrought that magic are long gone from here. Be thankful you remained here, with us. Steele and the others are much more likely to run into them than we are."

I hoped Chambers was right about the Indians not being anywhere nearby. I might be immune to their transformative magic, but they certainly had other conjurations that could affect me.

"We can't tell you any more than you've already guessed," I said to Moody, making sure I caught Leveillee's eye as well. "The details are for the ears of Q Division only. All you need to know is that, if the Indians try anything, I have the means to counter their magic."

"But–"

"No further questions, Constable," I said. "That's an order."

I thought I saw Leveillee's eyes flick to the pocket I'd placed my tobacco pouch in, but couldn't be certain. He touched a hand to his chest, and nodded sagely. I wondered if he carried some sort of Indian amulet there, like Jerry Potts and his protective cat skin.

We finished our tea in silence, and then spread out our blankets. Chambers had somehow contrived to pack a pair of stylish silk pyjamas in his saddlebags, and was pulling them on over his long underwear. The young constable guffawed out loud, but Chambers ignored him. He went through what must be his evening routine, brushing his hair and moustache until the smell of Brilliantine filled the air, then neatly folding his clothes and lining his boots up next to them. Leveillee was more polite, bidding Chambers a pleasant good night while hiding his smile behind a hand. Like me, both Moody and Leveillee were going to sleep fully clothed, with boots on—or moccasins, in the case of Leveillee. I was glad not to have to disrobe; I didn't want anyone to see the scar left by my surgery.

The constable fell asleep instantly; already I could hear him snoring. It didn't surprise me; even for someone as young and healthy as he, it had been a long day's ride. In the distance, I could hear coyotes yipping. I hoped they wouldn't trouble our horses in the night.

"Shall I put out the fire, Corporal?" Leveillee asked.

"Not yet," I said. "I'd like to read a bit first."

I pulled the hymnbook out of my pocket and pretended to read it by the dim red glow of the fire, intending to wait until the others were asleep. The tea hadn't done anything to soothe my stomach; I needed a dose of the Pinkham's that was hidden in my saddlebag. I didn't want Leveillee to see me drinking it, however.

Leveillee nodded and whispered something to himself, then rolled over. Chambers, however, remained propped up on one arm, regarding me. "A hymnal?" he asked with an amused twinkle in his eye. "I didn't think you were a religious man. You told me you gave up church when you were a boy, because it angered your father."

I murmured in a noncommittal fashion, puffing on my pipe and turning the pages. I considered drinking the Pinkham's then and there—Chambers already knew I carried some with me, after all—but Leveillee was probably still awake. If the scout had as good a nose for spirits as Jerry Potts did, he'd smell the Pinkham's in an instant. I'd already insulted him once by not offering tobacco; I didn't want to compound that seeming slight by denying him "liquor" as well.

Something fluttered out of the hymnbook, and out of the corner of my eye I saw Chambers catch it before it landed in the fire. It must have been another of the shinplasters I'd tried to give to Emily. I'd thought the wind had blown them all away.

"What's this?" Chambers asked.

"A bookmark."

"Rather an odd thing to use."

I'd yet to tell Chambers about giving my poker winnings to Emily—there just hadn't been time. I didn't want to launch into the story just then.

"It was the only thing I had at the time," I said.

"A feather?"

That made me look up.

Chambers did indeed hold a feather in his hand. It was about five inches in length and rather bedraggled. It looked like a wing feather from a crow, except that it was pure white.

"It must be Emily's," I said, leaning forward and closing the hymnbook. "This hymnal was the one I gave to her on the *North West*, and the feather looks just like the one she wore in her hair. Now we know how she opened the tunnel at this end. The tunnel would have closed behind her once she emerged—she must have planned to use the feather to re-open the tunnel once she found Iniskim. Either she decided not to use it or...."

I wanted to believe that Emily had simply abandoned the hymnal, but now I wasn't so sure. That feather was her key to the tunnels. I didn't think that Emily would have left it behind willingly.

Chambers's dark eyes bored into mine. "You know what this means," he whispered.

I glanced at Leveillee and saw that his breathing had deepened—he was asleep. I turned back to Chambers. "Steele said we'd open a tunnel only as a last resort, if we couldn't find the Manitou Stone any other way."

Chambers dismissed that idea with a flick of the feather. "That's not what I meant," he hissed. "This feather belonged to Emily. We can use it to contact her ghost."

I opened my mouth to protest that Emily wasn't dead, but suddenly I wasn't so sure. My imagination was starting to form a picture of what might have happened. Emily had carried a similar white feather with her to Victoria Mission, and used it to open the cave there. She'd left it in place, not expecting to need it again, but then wasn't transformed into a buffalo in the tunnel, after all. She'd tried to follow her daughter, but had lost her. She'd used this second, bedraggled feather—the one from her hair—to open a tunnel here at the ford, and had climbed up to the buffalo-shaped rock to look around. She hadn't cared that the tunnel had closed behind her—she knew she could re-open it again—but something had prevented her from doing so. Hoping to use the feather later, she'd hidden it inside the hymnal—but why?

I already knew the answer: a white man's hymnal was the last place another Indian would look for it.

Big Bear and his cohorts must have been here at the ford. They had probably come to search for Iniskim, just as we had. They'd spotted the other patrol, and used the ley line's magic to transform them into buffalo. Then they left, using magic to cause their footprints to vanish—just as I'd seen Big Bear himself vanish on the day he'd prevented Wandering Spirit from killing me at Head Smashed In. Emily's footprints had been erased as well. The only evidence of her that had been left behind was the hymnal.

Only two questions remained: had Emily gone with the other Indians willingly—and was she still alive?

There was one way to find out. I looked at Chambers, who was still waiting for me to respond. "Do it," I whispered back. "Contact Emily."

Chambers held out the feather. In the ruddy light of the buffalo-chip fire, it took on a lurid red glow. "We'll do it together," he said. "As a sensitive—and as someone who has developed an affection for the woman—you stand the best chance of reaching her. I'll tell you what to do."

I set my pipe aside and pinched the feather between thumb and forefinger, taking care not to crush it, while Chambers continued to hold its shaft. Below my hand, I could feel the warmth of our tiny fire.

"What do I do next?" I asked.

"Close your eyes."

I did.

"Now concentrate. Picture Emily in your mind, and call to her."

"Is that all?" I asked. I didn't know much about séances, but what little I'd heard seemed to indicate that they required tambourines and trumpets—and tables upon which the spirits could rap out messages.

"Just call her," Chambers said. "You can speak her name silently, just as you would when trying to attract someone's attention via thought transference—or you can say her name aloud, if that helps you to concentrate. Sometimes speaking aloud is easier, since both your physical and your astral bodies will be saying the name at the same moment. If your plea is impassioned enough, you'll contact her."

I was determined to contact Emily—although I had yet to tell Chambers the true reason why. I was confident that the aerograph would lead Steele straight to the Manitou Stone—that we no longer needed Iniskim to lead us to it. If we did succeed in contacting Emily, I would still ask where her daughter was—but what I really wanted to ask her was how to find Strikes Back.

I concentrated on Emily's name, but nothing happened. I heard no reply—only the faint snores of Constable Moody, the distant yipping of coyotes... and the soft hoot of an owl.

Whooo?

"Emily," I whispered.

Whooo?

"Emily."

Even as I spoke the word, I realized what was wrong. This was the name that Four Finger Pete had given his wife. She had no reason to respond to it any longer.

Whooo?

A name floated into my mind, as gently as a feather. I tried to grab it, but it slipped through my hand like smoke. I tried again, this time imagining that my hand was an owl's foot. My claws brushed against the feather, then caught in its weave and closed....

"Stone Keeper," I said.

I felt a drop of liquid splash upon my hand. I opened my eyes and looked up.

The night seemed brighter than it had before. The thin wisps of smoke given off by the burning buffalo chips were curling back upon themselves to form a leg, a hand, an oval face. I recognized the face at once by the pockmarks that overlaid its beauty, by its sad eyes and the two long braids that framed it. Emily—Stone Keeper—was crying. A tear trickled down her cheek and landed on the coals with a faint hissing noise.

The sound caused Chambers to open his eyes in surprise. He had the presence of mind neither to speak nor to let go of the feather we both still held. By the way he was looking around, I guessed that he couldn't see the woman in the smoke—but when she moved, causing her skirt to rustle slightly, his breath caught. He tipped his head, as if listening.

"Stone Keeper," I said, using her proper name. I vowed that I would never again call her by the name Four Finger Pete had given her. "Why are you crying?"

"My daughter is dying."

I expected her to answer in the broken English I'd heard her use when I'd first met her on the *North West*. Instead, she was speaking in another language—probably Peigan. It didn't matter; just as I had understood the chiefs in the shaking tepee, so I understood her now.

It seemed that Chambers could hear Stone Keeper, as well. "Where is Iniskim?" he asked.

"I don't know," Stone Keeper said. She did not glance in his direction but instead stared straight at me with her sad, dark eyes. "Iniskim is lost. You must help her, Thomas. She must reach the Manitou Stone."

"Why?" Chambers interrupted in a strained voice. "So your people can work their terrible magic? You must know where Iniskim is. Tell us. Now!" The feather I was holding shuddered, and I realized that Chambers's hand was shaking.

I was about to rebuke Chambers for trying to bully Stone Keeper into telling us something she clearly didn't know. After the way she had been treated by Four Finger Pete, it was an unkind approach to take. Then I realized what Stone Keeper had just done. She'd called me by my true name: Thomas.

Chambers hadn't noticed. I glanced at Leveillee and Corporal Moody. Both were still wrapped in their blankets, fast asleep, as senseless as if a spell had been cast upon them.

"Why must Iniskim reach the Manitou Stone?" I asked Stone Keeper.

"If she doesn't, she will die."

"Didn't taking Iniskim into the tunnel cure her fever?" I asked. "I thought that, by being transformed into a buffalo–"

"Taking the shape of a buffalo gave my daughter the strength to run, but in order for her to live, the spirit inside her must reach the spirit world."

"Why?" I asked.

"She was not meant to walk this earth so soon. She must return to the spirit world, if my daughter is to survive."

I was confused. Who was the "she" Stone Keeper was talking about?

Chambers grasped the answer more quickly than I, even though he could only hear Stone Keeper's words, not see her. "Your daughter Iniskim," he said, looking through the smoke rather than at it. "There's a spirit inside her body, isn't there—a spirit forced to enter the physical plane and share her flesh."

Stone Keeper nodded.

"For what purpose?" Chambers asked. "To enact the Day of Changes?"

"Yes, Albert," she whispered. "That is the reason."

Stone Keeper looked quickly down at the coals then, as if suddenly realizing that she was talking to two white men. The smoke from the fire began to resume its natural course, no longer eddying into the whorls that formed Stone Keeper's body. Her face started to fade. I saw that the buffalo chips had nearly burned out; there was very little red among the ashes.

"Stone Keeper, wait!" I said. "If we promise to help Iniskim, will you tell us more?"

The smoke paused.

I touched my stomach with my free hand. In the excitement of having contacted Stone Keeper, I'd been able to ignore the constant pain that filled it, but now the twisting nausea had returned. Leveillee and Constable Moody both seemed to be fast asleep, but just in case they were secretly listening, I chose my words carefully.

"You already know one truth about me, and I suspect you know others," I told Stone Keeper. "Look into my heart and judge whether what I say is true. I want to help your daughter, but I am duty-bound to do everything in my power to prevent the Day of Changes. Is there a way that I can do both?"

A breeze blew across the buffalo chips, fanning them back to a rosy glow. The smoke from the fire thickened into lazy curls.

"Help Iniskim to reach the Manitou Stone so that the one who shares her body can return to the spirit world," Stone Keeper said.

"Will that stop the Day of Changes from coming?" I asked.

Stone Keeper seemed reluctant to answer.

Chambers broke the silence. "It won't stop it," he guessed. "It will only delay it from coming for another nine months, until the spirit can be reborn. Isn't that right, Emily?"

Stone Keeper's downcast eyes confirmed this.

"It takes months for a child to be born," I said. "At least that's something. That should give us plenty of time to destroy the stones that shape the ley line."

"No one can stop the Day of Changes," Stone Keeper murmured. Her eyes rose to meet my own. "Not even you. The medicine men have dreamed it for many hungry winters now: when White Buffalo Woman returns, so will the buffalo."

"Tell us more," Chambers said. The antagonism he'd displayed earlier was completely gone; now his voice was filled with curiosity, instead. "If Constable Grayburn is to help your daughter, he has to know the nature of the spirit that shares her body."

"The spirit inside my daughter is White Buffalo Woman. She once walked this earth in human form, in the days when the buffalo were so many that the prairie was black with them. We have not seen her for many, many winters, yet she watches the herds still—sometimes as a white buffalo calf, and sometimes as a white crow. She has seen the herds dwindle, hunted until there were too few buffalo left to feed our people. She has heard our prayers—and she has prepared for her return.

"It was said that when White Buffalo Woman returned to this earth in human form the buffalo would also return. That time was to come in spring, when the Moon of Eggs was full."

I made a quick calculation. The Indians count moons, rather than months: thirteen moons make up their year. The Moon of Eggs—so named because it is the time when wildfowl build their nests and lay eggs in them—fell in late spring.

Chambers glanced up at the sliver of moon overhead. "The Day of Changes wasn't supposed to take place until after April, when the moon's dark side had completed its rotation toward the Earth, was it?"

"Why then are the chiefs trying to transform the white settlers into buffalo so soon? Why didn't they just wait for the Moon of Eggs?"

"For many winters now, our people have gone hungry," Stone Keeper said. "Many have died, and some even turned *wendigo* and feasted upon human flesh in their desperation to survive. The chiefs needed to find a way to make the Day of Changes come before winter, so that our people would not face starvation again.

"Chief Poundmaker knew that his buffalo-calling stone had the power to change humans into buffalo, and that other buffalo stones also had this power. Chief Little Pine remembered that the Manitou Stone had once marked a medicine line of great power—power that could spread the buffalo-calling stones' magic across the prairie. But the Cree could not use this magic until White Buffalo Woman was summoned to this earth—for that, they needed the help of my people.

"Chief Big Bear began meeting with the other chiefs, and with Poundmaker's help convinced his enemies that the Day of Changes could be made to come early—if the Blackfoot Confederacy and Cree joined their magic. And so the Motoki women began working their medicine upon my unborn child, forcing White Buffalo Woman to come before the moon had fully turned."

I mulled over what Stone Keeper had just said. I had heard of the Motoki before, but only in passing. Mary Smoke had used the word once, in one of her stories, and I'd asked her what it meant. She told me only that it was a sorority of sorts—a group of old women within the Blackfoot Confederacy who were allowed to dance with the buffalo hunters before the men set out to hunt.

Given what Stone Keeper had just told us, I suspected there was much more to it than that. The Motoki were medicine women.

A sudden inspiration struck me. Here was a way to bring the conversation around to the subject I most wanted to ask about.

"Is Strikes Back a Motoki?" I asked.

"No," Stone Keeper said. "But she wanted the buffalo to return as much as any of the Motoki did. She dreamed that my child was still alive inside me—but that it would soon die without her medicine—and came to find me."

I frowned at this news. I had hoped that Strikes Back might want to prevent the Day of Changes, if her hatred of Red Crow was strong enough—but it looked as though she was firmly on the side of the chiefs.

I leaned forward eagerly, at last daring to ask my question. "Where is Strikes Back now?"

"She is dead."

"Dead?" I croaked. The words struck me like a blow. It took a moment for me to find my voice again. "How do you know?"

"I tried to find Strikes Back, when Iniskim first became sick with fever. When I heard that Strikes Back was dead, I did not believe it: her medicine was so strong that I thought she would never die. Then I spoke to a man who had seen her body, bound in buffalo hide and resting in a tree, and I knew it must be true. Strikes Back was dead. Red Crow shot her."

"But why?" I asked. "Red Crow is one of the chiefs who is working to bring about the Day of Changes. Wouldn't he have been pleased with his sister for bringing Iniskim back to life?"

Stone Keeper shook her head. "The Motoki had already selected another woman to give birth to White Buffalo Woman: Red Crow's second wife. By restoring Iniskim to life, Strikes Back prevented this wife from having this honour."

"Can Strikes Back still work her magic, even as a ghost?" I asked.

Stone Keeper shrugged—a gesture she must have picked up from her white husband.

"Where does her body lie?" I asked, wondering if we could use the woman's corpse to contact her ghost.

"I do not know."

"What was the name of the man who saw her body?" I persisted. Perhaps the fellow could lead me to the bier on which Strikes Back lay.

"He was once called Many Eagle Feathers, but he no longer uses this name."

"You mean Peter?" I asked, stunned. The coincidence seemed unbelievable. Peter was the half-breed scout I'd spoken to just a few days ago, when our patrol had been preparing to set out for the ford. Then I remembered that Peter's Catholic faith led him to believe that the Devil was the source of the magic that Strikes Back wielded. It made sense that he would have sought out her body, to make sure that she was dead—but if this was the case, what had he meant by his comment that he was "still paying" her for healing his arm? And why had he spoken of her in the present tense, as if she were still alive?

I suddenly realized something. For all I knew, I might be talking to a ghost, even now. "Stone Keeper," I asked hesitantly. "Where are you now? Are you... alive?"

"I am asleep—dreaming in my father's tepee. He found me at the ford, and forced me to return to his lodge. He hopes Iniskim will come to me. If she does, he will give her human shape again. She will die soon afterward—her human form is too weak to hold two spirits for long—but the chiefs do not care. As long as White Buffalo Woman walks our world in human form when the moon is full, even for a few moments, the Day of Changes can be made to come."

Hearing Stone Keeper talk about her father—Chief Mountain—made me realize that she had left part of her story out.

"How did you come to leave your tribe," I asked softly, "and wind up with a brute like Four Finger Pete?"

The smoke swirled gently as Stone Keeper sighed. "When the Motoki women began forcing the spirit of White Buffalo Woman into my child, I could feel her sicken inside me and realized that she would not be strong enough to carry White Buffalo Woman's spirit inside her. She would die before her first winter.

"I knew that our people needed the Day of Changes to come in order to survive, but I was selfish. I didn't want it to be my daughter who died. I told my father that I had used the woman's root to wash the child from my body—that there was no baby— so the Motoki women would cease their magic. It was a lie, but my father believed it. He wanted to kill me, but my mother persuaded him to give me to the white man instead."

"When Iniskim was born a few months later, I saw by her pink eyes, white hair and pale skin that the Motoki women's magic had worked, after all. White Buffalo Woman's spirit had entered my child. Iniskim had lived long enough to be born, but her body was too weak to hold two spirits, and she died that same day.

"Two days later, Strikes Back gave my daughter life again. She entered the spirit world, and led Iniskim's spirit back to her body, as I had begged her to do. But she tricked me, and did something I had not expected: she also led back the spirit of White Buffalo Woman."

Angered though I was at the news of the duplicity of Strikes Back, I was proud of the way that Stone Keeper held in her grief as she told her sad tale. She was a brave woman who had done everything she could to save the life of her child.

"The medicine of Strikes Back was enough to keep my daughter alive for many moons, but it was not strong enough to do this forever," Stone Keeper continued. "Iniskim sickened, and eventually a fever took hold. I could see that she was about to die a second time. When my husband decided that we should travel up the river, I saw my chance. I would find some excuse to stop at Victoria Mission and go to the Manitou Stone. White Buffalo Woman could use it to leave my daughter and return to the spirit world.

"When I got there, the stone was gone."

I nodded, enthralled by her tale. I could guess the rest, but listened patiently while she concluded her story.

Stone Keeper sighed. "I knew there was only one thing that I could do: enter the medicine tunnel, and allow my child's body to take the shape of the spirit that was within her. With four strong legs, perhaps she could run far enough to reach the Manitou Stone."

Chambers looked across the fire at me. "Do you understand what she's saying?" he asked, staring intently at me across the fire. "That's why Iniskim's astral body was sighted here at the ford, on the day she was stillborn. When the medicine woman restored her body to life, it disappeared—the 'ghost' was led out of the astral plane and back to Iniskim's body. If Iniskim reaches the Manitou Stone before the Indians do, White Buffalo Woman will escape to the astral plane. The Day of Changes will be delayed until spring—and no settlers need be transformed!"

I nodded, realizing that my guess about the Indians needing Iniskim to lead them to the Manitou Stone had been wrong. Even as I spoke to the chiefs inside the shaking tepee, they were already well on their way to finding the Manitou Stone, by testing their transformative magic and plotting out the ley line with each successful transformation.

They didn't want to follow Iniskim to the stone. They wanted to *prevent* her from reaching the stone by capturing her before she reached it. This done, they would transform her back into human form and cause the Day of Changes to occur.

One thing puzzled me, however. Two weeks had gone by since I stumbled out of the tunnel at Head Smashed In, and nobody had seen Iniskim, despite the fact that both our patrols and the Indians from four different tribes were scouring the prairie for her. Even Iniskim's own mother didn't know where she was.

There was only one place she could avoid such an intensive search. She must be under the earth still, inside the tunnels.

I wondered if Indians had continued transforming people into buffalo not just to plot the ley line, but also in the hope that, as the shaggy beasts ran through the underground tunnels, they would sweep Iniskim up with them and bring her back to the surface again.

We had sat in silence for several long moments, and my hand became chilled. I noticed that the buffalo-chip fire was going out. The image of Stone Keeper fluttered like a moth as the last wisps of smoke rose into the air.

"If I find Iniskim, I'll do what I can to protect her," I promised. "You have my word on it."

"Thank you, Thomas," she whispered. "I hope you will live long enough to keep that oath."

A sense of unease gripped me. "What do you mean?"

"Your illness," she said. "It has returned. You are dying, Thomas."

She named the disease, using the Peigan word for it, but I understood it as plainly as if she were speaking the Queen's English: cancer. It was a word that had haunted me for six long years, ever since my diagnosis and operation. Over the past few weeks, I'd refused to acknowledge the true cause of the ache in my stomach, telling myself it was only a prolonged bout of tyhpo-malaria. When the pain grew too fearsome, I'd drowned it in Pinkham's and soldiered on. Yet all the while, I'd secretly known the truth, deep in my heart. Now I prodded my tender stomach with hesitant fingers, searching for the return of an all-too-familiar lump. Was the tumour really back?

Chambers stared at me. "Is it true?" he asked. "Is that why you carry a bottle of Pinkham's with you?" To his credit, he did not draw his hand away from mine, despite the risk of contagion.

I nodded, unable to speak. My eyes were watering; smoke must have drifted into them. I tried to shake off the sense of impending doom that was settling over me, but to no avail. To put it bluntly, Stone Keeper's pronouncement had terrified me. I knew that, this time, I would succumb. There would be no second chance. After my operation six years ago, the doctors told me that they could not repeat the procedure. I wasn't strong enough to endure the strain of a second operation: when my heart had briefly stopped under the anaesthetic, only by a miracle had it started beating again. If the cancer came back, the doctors could not operate to remove the tumour: a second dose of ether would kill me.

"I'm still capable of carrying out my duties," I answered Chambers at last, swallowing hard. I glanced at the ghostly figure of Stone Keeper. "And of doing what I can to save the girl in...whatever time I have left."

The smoke began to drift sideways on the breeze. Stone Keeper's face was resting on her hand now, and the remainder of her body had vanished. She looked as though she were fast asleep. Her face was peaceful, as if a burden had been lifted from her shoulders.

I suddenly realized that one question had remained unasked. "Stone Keeper, who is Iniskim's father?"

Her only answer was to smile sweetly in her sleep as the last wisp of smoke fled up into the night sky.

I'd asked my question too softly. Stone Keeper had disappeared.

I let go of the white feather.

"Is she gone?" Chambers asked.

I nodded.

Chambers gave me a thoughtful look. I thought he was going to ask about my disease, and braced myself for an unpleasant conversation, but his mind was on other matters. "Why did she call you Thomas?" he asked.

"It's a name I used to go by. Why? Does it matter?"

As Chambers quickly shook his head, I remembered something else that Stone Keeper had said. She'd given us her true name—and taken ours in return. I wasn't the only one using an assumed name: Chambers, also, was not who he claimed to be.

"Why did she call you Albert, if your name is Arthur?" I asked him abruptly.

Chambers waved the question away as if it didn't matter. "It happens all the time," he said smoothly. "I've a brother named Albert. We're only a year apart. People are always mistaking us."

I knew that Chambers wasn't telling the truth. Stone Keeper had seen into our hearts: his name really was Albert—and it had been Arthur's name on the pamphlet I'd read. This could only mean one thing: the man in front of me had assumed his brother's identity.

I was rendered speechless by the impossible coincidence. Out of all of the people I might have met in the North-West Territories, out of all of the men who might have been hired by Q Division, the person seated across the fire from me in this lonely spot was someone who had also assumed another man's identity. Because that man was his brother, he even matched the portrait on the back of the pamphlet.

I found my voice at last. "Does your brother approve of you passing yourself off as him, and pretending to be an expert on psychic phenomena?"

Chambers's cheeks flushed. "I'm no charlatan," he said hotly. "I've read every publication the Society for Psychical Research ever printed, and I'm an expert in thought transference. Arthur wouldn't have agreed to let me lecture in the Dominion if I wasn't. I may be self-trained, but that hardly matters, does it? Not when I can produce the kind of results you just saw."

I nodded, but silently wondered how much of a hand Chambers had played in contacting Stone Keeper. He hadn't even been able to see her. Then I remembered that he'd heard and understood Stone Keeper, even though she was speaking in Peigan. That must count for something. Chambers was, at least in part, a "sensitive" like myself.

Chambers couldn't resist taking a verbal jab in return. "Tell me about the real Marmaduke Grayburn," he said. "Does he approve of you passing yourself off as a Mounted Policeman?"

I felt my own cheeks flush. "I am a policeman," I said. "I took Marmaduke's place well before the training began, and I have served honourably ever since. For five years now, I've done my duty to–"

Chambers waved away the rest with a chuckle. He extended his hand. "Let's agree that we're both fully qualified to carry out our respective duties, regardless of what our real names might be. I agree to keep your secret, if you'll keep mine."

I took his hand. "Agreed."

He released my hand clasp, and thought for a moment. He held up the feather. "Iniskim has to be below ground still. If we can open up the tunnel–"

I heard a rustling noise, and shushed Chambers with a finger to my lips. Moody rolled over, then threw off his blankets. He rose to his feet, rubbing his eyes.

"Too much tea," he said with a shy grin. Taking his leave of our camp, he walked a few feet away, into the darkness. I could hear the sound of him passing water, and a moment later, his soft grunt of relief.

Chambers lowered his voice to a whisper. "If we can use Emily's feather to open the tunnel, perhaps you can find Iniskim, and lead her to the Manitou Stone before the Indians find it. I'll ride after Steele, and tell him not to destroy the stone quite yet. That will give you more time to find her. We've got sixteen days still—as long as you don't spend too much time in the tunnels, you'll be back well before the Day of Changes."

I opened my mouth to tell him that no watch I carried had ever counted time accurately, but there was something else nagging at me—a feeling that something wasn't right. Not a premonition, but an awareness that came from my mundane physical senses. I heard a low whicker that sounded like Buck, and then a hissing noise, off in the direction where Moody had gone.

"Chambers," I said. "Constable Moody is taking an awfully long time to–"

The night erupted with a thunderous crash as a flash of light lit up our camp. Blinking, unable to see or hear clearly, I caught the muffled sound of horses whinnying in fear. As clods of earth and burning chunks of wood that looked like boards from a crate fluttered down all around me, I saw Leveillee fling off his blankets and rise to his feet, rifle in hand. He whipped the weapon up to his shoulder, shouting something at the same time. I heard only the words, "*Les savages!*" before a figure hurtled out of the night. Then Leveillee's rifle spat flame—but too late. The running figure came in low and fast, under its barrel. As my ears popped, I heard a swishing noise, like a riding crop whipping through the air. Then Leveillee dropped his rifle and crumpled to the ground.

I scrambled to my feet, my mind feverishly trying to piece together what had just happened. The crate of dynamite had exploded. Constable Moody was nowhere to be seen. A blood-curdling war whoop came from somewhere to my left, and was echoed on my right and behind me. Dark shapes were everywhere in the night. Chambers leaped to his feet, then sprinted away in his pyjamas, Stone Keeper's feather still clutched in his fist.

Where was my rifle? I dropped to my knees to find it, and heard something whistle over my head. When I grabbed the rifle and looked up, frantically cocking my weapon, Wandering Spirit stood above me, a wicked expression on his hideously painted face. One hand held the feather-tipped coup stick he'd just used on Leveillee, the other, a knife whose brightly polished blade glinted in the starlight. Behind him, a figure wearing a feathered war bonnet struggled to drag away a kicking horse.

I shot Wandering Spirit square in the chest, and saw the flame from the barrel of my rifle lick across the buckskin jacket he wore. The flattened bullet fell to the ground at my feet.

I'd been too stunned by the explosion and the sudden attack to think clearly, but now I realized I had reached for the wrong weapon. Wandering Spirit had been smarter—he'd known his coup stick couldn't kill me and had come armed with a knife, as well.

Dropping the rifle, I leaped out of the way of the blade's swishing arc. I shoved a hand into my pocket and dug out my tobacco pouch, but the ties of the pouch were in a tight knot that would not be undone by my fumbling fingers. I looked up and saw the knife jabbing toward me....

The *crack-crack* of a rifle caused Wandering Spirit to glance back over his shoulder at the last moment, and I was able to twist out of the way. I heard a scream from one of the figures near the horses, then another rifle shot and a groan. I saw Wandering Spirit's eyes narrow in anger, and then heard a bullet whine past my own head. The rifle cracked again, and Wandering Spirit's lynx skin war bonnet flew off his head and tumbled to the ground. I wondered if Constable Moody had joined the fight. It couldn't be Chambers—he didn't even carry a weapon.

Whoever was shooting at Wandering Spirit didn't realize that he couldn't be harmed by bullets. I had to act quickly. I dove at Wandering Spirit's feet, knocking him to the ground.

The warrior was as quick and supple as a snake. In an instant he'd twisted around and had his knife at my throat. I wrenched my head to the side and felt the blade scrape across my chin like a razor. I brought my hand up to fend off the blow— and the knife sliced through the tobacco pouch I still held. It also sliced through the palm of my hand with a pain like fire— but now the buffalo stone was in my hand.

Wandering Spirit wrestled me onto my back, slamming my head against the ground. Amid the sparks that washed across my eyesight, I saw his knife descend. I grabbed his wrist with my left hand, but could only halt its descent for a moment. Panting, a victorious grin on his yellow-painted face, he forced the knife down toward my throat. His other hand held my right wrist, pinning it to the ground.

With one last desperate effort, I wrenched my right hand through his sweaty fingers. The buffalo stone, still clenched in my fist, brushed against the palm of his hand. A look of shock and surprise crossed Wandering Spirit's face—and then a tremendous, muffling weight crushed my chest. I was buried under something that felt as heavy as a train engine covered in a coating of spongy wool. Limbs thrashed, gouging the ground all around me, and then the monstrosity was standing above me.

I looked up at the belly of an enormous buffalo, its shaggy hair a pale colour that contrasted with the star-studded sky above. Its face was streaked with a lighter colour, which I recognized after a moment as the remnants of Wandering Spirit's yellow war paint. The beast bellowed its hot breath in my face and tried to stomp me with one of its hooves. Frantically, I twisted myself aside. Then I heard the crack of a rifle firing and the thundering of hooves, and the beast wheeled and ran off into the night. Suddenly all was silent, save for the faint crackling of a piece of the dynamite crate that was still burning beside me.

I lay there, staring up at the stars, still struggling to take a breath with lungs that felt as though they had been crushed

flat. My right hand stung where Wandering Spirit's knife had cut
it. Then something loomed above me in the darkness: the
silhouette of a man. He held a rifle in one hand, its barrel still
smoking, and Wandering Spirit's coup stick in the other. He
flicked it back and forth, watching the black feather at its tip
flutter. Then he whooped.

"Heya, *napikwan*," a familiar voice said. "Good fight, eh?"

I forced myself into a seated position with shaking arms.
"Potts?" I asked. "Is that you?"

Potts grunted, then ambled away into the night. I heard the
scraping of a knife against bone, and realized that he must be
collecting his gruesome victory trophies. I felt around for the
buffalo stone, found it under the remnants of the painted shirt
that had been torn from Wandering Spirit's back during his
transformation, and shoved it in a pocket with my uninjured
hand. Then I staggered over to where my saddlebags lay, and
pulled my spare undershirt out to wrap around the hand that
had the knife slash. After cinching it tight to stop the bleeding, I
reached for my bottle of Pinkham's and took a long drink.

It was almost pitch black, but I could dimly make out Potts as
he bent over the last of the three Indians he'd shot, cutting away
his scalp. Then he walked to where Leveillee lay, and nudged the
other scout's body with his foot.

"Heya, Leveillee," he said gruffly. "Get up."

I heard a low groan, and realized that Leveillee had somehow
survived Wandering Spirit's coup stick. As he sat up, he fished a
hand inside his shirt and pulled out a crucifix. He kissed it
reverently, then rocked back and forth, whispering in French. It
must have been a prayer of thanks; there were lots of "*mon
Dieus*" and "*mercis*" in it.

I realized that Leveillee's Catholic faith had somehow
protected him from the deadly magic of Wandering Spirit's coup
stick—something that went against everything I had been taught
to believe. I'd been raised by a father who strongly voiced his
opinion that all religion was superstitious nonsense, and so I'd
never considered prayer to have any effect other than soothing
the mind. Now I wondered: could religion be a form of magic? I
thought of the half-breed scout Peter, and the crosses he'd had
nailed into his horse's shoes. Maybe they would afford some
protection, after all.

Potts ambled back in my direction, sniffed the air, and eyed
my bottle of painkiller. I handed it to him, and he drank deeply,
wiping the back of his hand across his lips when he was done.
I didn't mind; he was worth every drop.

"Where have you been, Potts?" I asked. "I thought you were
dead."

"Been tracking 'em," he said, gesturing at the three corpses. "Got my horse back. Now I got scalps, too."

Leveillee halted his prayer to look up. "The tracks I saw that we cross on the way to the ford—the horse, she was ride by you."

Potts grunted.

A realization hit me. "You tried to kill Wandering Spirit once before, didn't you—on the bluffs beside the Milk River. That was why he stopped shooting at me—why I was able to escape on the air bicycle."

Potts just shrugged. "Should'a got him. Missed."

"No you didn't," I assured him. "Wandering Spirit has magic that protects him from bullets."

Potts accepted this as if it were an everyday statement. In his world of cat-skin amulets and war magic, I supposed it was.

I looked around. "There was a young Constable with us, by the name of Moody. Did you see him?"

"Yup." Potts flicked Wandering Spirit's coup stick in the direction Moody had taken earlier. "Dead."

My heart sank. "And Special Constable Chambers?" I asked. Then I remembered that Chambers and Potts had never met. "A man with dark curly hair, wearing pyjamas. Did you see him?"

"Yup."

"Where is he?"

"Dunno. He ran away."

I looked around in alarm, cursing the night's gloom. "Do you think the Indians killed him?"

"Nope. No body."

I sighed, exasperated by Potts's short answers. Leveillee tucked his crucifix away and rose to his feet. I offered him the bottle of Pinkham's but he shook his head.

"My dear Corporal," he said, giving me his customary bow. "If *Monsieur* Chambers yet lives, he will return, now that all is quiet. We 'ave only to wait for 'im."

"Can't wait," Potts said.

"Why not?" I asked.

"More Indians coming this way. Too many to fight."

I cursed, realizing that I had only temporarily defeated Wandering Spirit by transforming him into a buffalo. If a chief who possessed a buffalo stone was among the Indians who were approaching, Wandering Spirit could readily be changed back into a man again.

Leveillee was waiting for my orders. Potts had already wandered away, and after a moment I heard the *clip-clop* of horse's hooves and the jingling of a buckle. Potts was saddling our horses, preparing for our departure.

"Come with me," I told Leveillee. Together, we walked in the direction that Moody had gone. We found the young constable only a few paces away from where our fire had been, lying on his back. I squatted for a closer look, and saw that his eyes were wide open. There didn't seem to be a mark on him, but I knew what we'd find if we opened his clothing: a black smudge, just above his heart.

Gently, I closed his eyes. According to what Steele had told me earlier, Moody had only joined the force six months ago. He'd been a policeman for less time than I had been when I'd had the premonition at the horse camp that had prevented my own death.

Even though I probably didn't have much longer to live now, with the cancer returned and a tumour growing in my stomach, I'd had a longer life than Moody. This poor young constable had lost his life in the line of duty, and I was determined that he should get a proper burial.

Leveillee stood just behind me, making the sign of the cross on his breast. Even in the gloom, I could see from his expression that he realized how close he had come to sharing Moody's fate.

"Help me pick him up," I said, grasping the dead constable by his shoulders. "We'll tie him to his horse; you can bury him later, if you get a chance. Ride for Steele, and tell him what has happened. Take Potts with you."

Leveillee nodded. "What about you, my dear Corporal? Are you not coming with us?"

I shook my head.

"What will you do?"

What, indeed? There was only one answer.

"I'll stay behind, and search for Special Constable Chambers. If I don't find him I'll ride after you."

As Leveillee and I struggled to lift Moody's corpse, Potts led our horses toward us. On a lead behind them were four other animals, with Indian saddles on their backs. We wound a rope around Moody's waist and heaved him across the saddle, then Leveillee fastened the end of the rope to the pommel. The young constable's arms and legs dangled to either side limply; it would be a while before he stiffened up.

My wounded hand was pulsing with pain, and the makeshift bandage was soaked with blood. I took the reins of my horse with my good hand and repeated for Potts my plan to stay and search for Chambers for a short time, and to flee if I saw any signs of Indians. Potts grunted his assent.

Leveillee gave me a worried look, then swung up into his saddle. "Farewell, Corporal Grayburn. I will pray *pour vous*."

"Thank you."

I watched them go, then led Buck across the uneven ground, trusting him to find his own footing in the dark. He proved exceedingly adept at this, picking his way along with sure-footed grace while I stumbled over rocks. I made for the spot that Leveillee had pointed out earlier—the place where the hoof prints of the transformed patrol had ended abruptly. Chambers had run in this direction, during the Indian attack. He'd been too panic-stricken to realize what he held in his hand, and what might happen when he reached this spot.

I smelled freshly turned earth, and realized that my guess had been right. Ahead in the darkness lay a deeper patch of black: the mouth of a cave. Chambers had run this way with Stone Keeper's white crow feather clutched in his hand, and the tunnel had opened for him.

I sighed in exasperation. Was I going to have to rescue Chambers a second time? He'd proven himself a coward by fleeing the moment the Indians attacked, and had stupidly run in the worst possible direction. Even though I'd grown close to liking him over the past few days, it was hard to work up sympathy for the man now.

I walked up to the threshold of the cave, then stopped. Why had it remained open? I'd assumed that Chambers had blundered into it in his panicked state, and that the tunnel had closed up after him again. It had seemed the best explanation for Chambers's failure to return to the campsite when the battle was over.

I now saw that I had been wrong.

I glanced down and saw something white beside my boot: Stone Keeper's feather. It was standing upright, its quill embedded in the earth. Had Chambers dropped it in surprise, as the tunnel opened to engulf him? If so, why hadn't he simply walked out of the tunnel again, once his panic subsided? I dropped the reins of my horse and pulled a box of matches out of my pocket. I lit one and held it awkwardly in my injured hand. By its light, I saw that the quill was pushed deep into the ground, as if deliberately forced into it. Chambers had wanted the cave to remain open—but why?

I noticed that my boot was resting on words that had been scratched into the ground with a stick. They were in block letters, just like the ones Chambers had scuffed in the earth with his hoof after he was transformed into a buffalo.

INISKIM HERE.
FOLLO_ _E.

My boot prints had obliterated two of the letters, but the message was plain enough. Chambers hadn't run away in a panic. Somehow, in the instant of the explosive flash that had left me blinking, he'd spotted the white buffalo calf. In a desperate effort to keep her out of the hands of the Indians, he'd opened the cave and led her inside, pausing to leave me a message he knew the Indians couldn't read. He'd done this knowing that he'd be transformed into a buffalo again—a fate he dreaded above all else.

He'd counted on me to defeat Wandering Spirit and to follow him inside.

I couldn't let him down.

I was just about to pluck the feather from the ground when Buck whinnied. Realizing that I might not return, I wondered whether I should remove his saddle and bridle and turn him loose. I rested a hand on him, trying to decide what to do, and my fingers brushed over the rough brand on his flank. I was reminded of the Indian handprint that had decorated his rump after being captured by Indians, and how he'd found his way back to the detachment, all on his own. He'd also led me safely out of the Big Sands. If ever there was a horse whose loyalty and sense of direction I could rely upon, it was Buck.

I decided to take Buck with me, into the cave. The tunnels below were big enough to accommodate herds of buffalo; riding would be the best way to negotiate them. All I had to do was find Chambers and Iniskim—and then we'd head straight for the Manitou Stone, and send the spirit of White Buffalo Woman back to the spirit lands.

—

Chapter VIII

Ride into darkness—A strange transformation—A possible solution—An ominous dawn—Into the pound—A desperate chase—The invisible revealed—An explosive result—Return to the Big Sands—Strong medicine—A mother's grief—A father revealed

I picked up the white feather, then swung up into the saddle. Even as my foot left the ground, I could feel the earth tremble. Buck shied sideways as the earth shook, and clods of soil thudded down like heavy rain from the roof of the tunnel. I didn't have much time.

"Ho!" I shouted, and spurred Buck forward. He stumbled as a section of the tunnel mouth came crashing down, but continued bravely forward. In a moment more, the thudding of his hooves was completely drowned out as a ton of earth and stone crashed down behind us. I heard a few last muffled thumps, and then the noise stopped.

I reined Buck to a halt. For a moment I sat coughing on the dust that choked the air. The darkness inside the tunnel was complete. I held the white feather up in front of my face, close enough to feel my breath on my hand, and could not even see the feather's outline. I pulled the hymn book from my jacket, tucked the feather carefully inside it, and returned the book to my pocket. Then I patted Buck on the shoulder.

My hand touched what felt like a coarse and matted fabric. As I shifted my weight slightly on my stirrups, the saddle beneath me slid loosely on Buck's back. I supposed the saddle pad must have worked its way forward and bunched up—the saddle felt as if something wide and lumpy was under it.

"Bravely done, Buck," I said, moving my hand up to stroke his neck instead. "Now we just have to find–"

Buck's neck was not where I expected it to be—my hand encountered nothing but air. I lowered it, patting around to find the reins, and found that they rested on a neck that was at once too wide and covered in coarse, woolly hair. In that same instant, Buck made a sound—not the delicate *whuffle* of a horse, but the low, heavy snort of a much larger beast.

I reached into my pocket for my box of matches, and struck one.

The yellow circle of light it cast shook as I saw what I was sitting upon. My mount was no longer a horse. Just ahead of the saddle, massive, shaggy shoulders descended to a pair of curving horns. Buck turned his head, and I could see that the bit and bridle were still in his mouth. He looked back at me with a small, round eye and tossed his head, as if impatient to be off. He didn't seem to notice—or else didn't care—that he had been transformed into a buffalo.

As the match went out, I felt the saddle shift. I slipped my feet out of the stirrups, jumped to the ground, and felt under Buck's belly to see why the saddle had come loose. The strap ended in a frayed bit of leather that hung down at his side; so large was Buck's girth that it had snapped during his transformation.

I had no way to repair the saddle. I hauled it from Buck's back and cast it aside, and then removed my saddlebags. I paused only to retrieve my bottle of Pinkham's and put it in my pocket, then took a fistful of Buck's shaggy shoulder. "Easy now, Buck," I said. "There's a good hor... ah, buffalo."

I hauled myself onto his bare back and settled in just at the point where the matted hair ended and his smooth-coated flanks began. Buck stood patiently, snorting and moving his head gently from side to side, his teeth making grinding noises as if he were trying to adjust his mouth to an ill-fitting bit.

I gave Buck a gentle prod with my spurs and he walked forward as obediently as any horse. His gait was different—heavier and more jarring—and the width of his back bowed my legs out even more than usual.

I decided to risk a shout—if being transformed into a buffalo didn't cause Buck to spook, neither would my call.

"Chambers!" I cried. "Where are you?"

I strained my ears, but heard no reply. It didn't surprise me; I assumed that Chambers had been transformed, once again, into a buffalo. He could hardly respond to my shouts. I listened instead for the sound of hoof beats, knowing that he and Iniskim must have been just ahead of me. Perhaps he would hear my call and run back to show me the way.

"Chambers!" I cried again.

I counted my matches by feel. I had only seven left, so I decided to let Buck pick his own way through the darkness. The thud of his hooves soon turned to a *clip-clop* noise; the tunnel must be passing through a section of solid rock. I raised my arm to protect my head, in case there were any low spots in the roof above. A few minutes later, I heard a faint slurping sound, just up ahead. Buck jolted to a halt, and as he did I could hear air whistle in and out through his wide nostrils. He'd smelled whatever I had heard.

I lit another match. Then I gasped.

No more than three or four paces ahead of me, at a place where the tunnel bent sharply, stood a buffalo calf with hair as white as the snow. It looked no more than a year old—already firm on its feet but still small, with only vestigial horns. Its pale pink eyes reflected the light of my match back at me as it looked up—and then it lowered its head once more and an equally pink tongue began dabbing at a body that lay on the floor—a human body.

The match went out.

I dropped Buck's reins and slid down from his massive back. I hurried forward through the tunnel and struck another match. Iniskim shied at my approach, backing away from the body.

I recognized Chambers at once by the silk pyjamas he wore and the smell of the Brilliantine in his dark hair. I was relieved to see that he was not dead; his back rose and fell slightly as he breathed. He lay on his stomach on the stone floor of the tunnel, his face turned away from me. Iniskim had been licking his cheek. I held the match closer, and saw an angry-red bump on his forehead. It looked as though he had struck his head in the darkened tunnel—either that, or he'd been rendered unconscious by a kick from a tiny hoof.

I gently rolled him over, lifting him into a sitting position. As the match went out, I fished the bottle of Pinkham's out of my pocket and pulled the cork with my teeth. I found Chambers's mouth by feel, and pried his lips apart. Then I sloshed a little of the painkiller into it.

Chambers sputtered, then broke into a choking cough. As he felt someone holding him, his arms immediately began flailing.

"Chambers," I said reassuringly. "It's me—Grayburn."

Chambers was patting his body, checking shoulders, arms, legs. At first I thought he was looking for injuries, but then I realized what he was doing.

"You're all right," I told him. "You're still a man."

I heard Buck snort behind me, and the scrape of a large hoof against the ground. A ringing, metallic noise echoed through the tunnel, and after a moment I realized what it must be: Buck was trying to pry off a loose horseshoe. Now that he was a buffalo, the shoes no longer fit his massive hooves.

The bottle of Pinkham's was wrenched from my grasp. I heard a gurgle as Chambers drank. Lighting another match, I saw that Iniskim hadn't strayed. The albino buffalo calf stood a short distance away from us, her eyes already focused on us as if she could see in the dark and had been watching us all this time.

I shook my head in wonder. I couldn't believe that I was face to face with Iniskim at last. A fierce pride filled my breast. Like the proverbial Mountie who gets his man, I'd gotten my buffalo. I was glad, now, that the tunnel had closed behind me—it meant that Iniskim wouldn't fall into the hands of the Indians that Potts had said were on their way to the ford. Now it was up to us to see her safely to the Manitou Stone and prevent the Day of Changes from occurring.

Chambers was sitting up without my assistance. He seemed to have fully recovered from his brief spate of unconsciousness. Ignoring the fact that he was drinking more of my Pinkham's, I rose to my feet. I dropped the match and reached into my pocket to pull out the hymn book. I found the feather by feel, then held it in my hand as I struck another match.

"Iniskim," I said. "This was your mother's."

The white buffalo calf snorted. I realized then that, even if the soul of Iniskim was inside that buffalo body, the girl was too young to understand me. She was barely a year old—and at that tender age she probably didn't speak the language of her Peigan mother yet, let alone English.

I tried again, at the same time attempting to project the essence of my message via thought transference. "White Buffalo Woman, I know that you are looking for the Manitou Stone, so that you can escape from this world. I've come to help you find it."

I wasn't paying attention to the match, which burned right down to the end. I dropped it with an oath and sucked on my burned fingers. As I did so, I heard the *clip-clop* of unshod hooves. A moment later warm breath stirred the feather, and then a soft wet nose nuzzled my hand.

I reached out with my other hand and stroked her head. For the briefest of moments, I imagined that my hand slid across soft human hair, but then a familiar coarseness was under my fingertips again. My hand rested on a buffalo calf—but just to make sure, I struck another match.

Chambers had gotten to his feet and as the yellow circle of match-light filled the tunnel, he stared at Buck.

"By Jove, Grayburn," he said. "Did you really saddle up a buffalo to come and find me?"

I walked back to Buck and inspected his feet. He'd managed to scrape one horseshoe off, but the rest were still firmly in place. He stood placidly, waiting for me to mount him.

"This is no buffalo," I told Chambers. "It's my horse, Buck."

I saw Chambers eyes narrow thoughtfully just before the match went out. "You don't say," he muttered.

I found Chambers's hand and pressed the reins into it, taking back my bottle of Pinkham's. My stomach was twisted in its customary knot of pain—in all of the excitement, I had been able to ignore it until now. I drained what was left in the bottle, then cast it aside. I heard it roll across the stone, then fetch up with a sharp crack against one wall.

"Get on his back, and let him have his head," I told Chambers. "I have a hunch he'll find the way for us. I'll follow along behind, with Iniskim."

Chambers did as I had instructed. I slapped Buck forward and then followed the sound of his hooves, my right hand resting on Iniskim's shoulders as she walked daintily along beside me. In my other hand I held Emily's white feather. If the way ahead was blocked, I hoped that the feather would open it.

We passed a tunnel on the right that opened into the one we were in, but we carried on along the main route, always following the curve to the left. I was counting on us not having to walk too far; according to the size of the spiral I'd drawn on Steele's map, the end of the spiralling ley line—and the Manitou Stone— couldn't have been more than sixty miles away from the ford on the South Saskatchewan.

I could feel that we were close; etheric energy flowed over me like a chill wind, causing the hairs to rise on my arms, and on the back of my neck. My ears were filled with a faint crackling noise that had grown steadily as we passed through the tunnel, and my skin tingled. Strange to think that we were moving through a current of magical energy, and were yet immune to it. Then I realized something.

"Chambers," I asked the darkness. "How did you manage to avoid being turned into a buffalo? Did you know you'd remain a man when you followed Iniskim into the tunnel?"

The answer was preceded with a relieved chuckle. "It was an educated guess," he said. "I knew from observation that the transformative magic didn't work on those who had been 'reborn' once already. I gambled that my previous 'rebirthing' in buffalo form had inoculated me. I won that bet—although I probably would have been more sure-footed on four feet. Iniskim led me a merry chase through the tunnels, and I was going full bore when I ran into that bend in the tunnel. Had I been a buffalo, with horns and a thick skull, I wouldn't have been rendered unconscious."

I mulled that over, listening to the *clip-clip-clip-thud* of Buck's hooves and the lighter *clippity-clop* of Iniskim's daintier feet. With an unlimited amount of time, I could use the buffalo stone in my pocket to inoculate all of the settlers in the North-West Territories, one by one, by changing them briefly into buffalo and then back into human form again—but time was something we had precious little of.

I wondered how much time was passing, up in the world above. I was tempted to slap Buck on the rump and have him pick up the pace, but didn't want to run the risk of Chambers being knocked unconscious a second time—or of him being separated from us. My hand gripped Iniskim's shaggy shoulder more tightly. At least she wasn't going anywhere. She walked along beside me as obediently as a small child guided by its mother's hand.

"Chambers," I asked again. "Why was my horse transformed into a buffalo? When the buffalo stone touched a snake, nothing happened. I didn't think that it would work on animals."

"I was wondering when you would think of that," Chambers said.

Despite his knowing tone, I wasn't irritated. He was the expert on ley lines, after all.

"There seem to be three mechanisms for producing a transformation," Chambers said. "The first—the buffalo stone—is the simplest. It works only upon the physical plane, and must come into direct contact with the physical body itself—the human body. It will not transform animal into animal.

"The second mechanism for transformation is the energy contained in the ley line. The etheric force that flows along it can be used to augment the magic of the buffalo stone, allowing transformations to occur over a great distance. By using this energy, every human being bounded by the spiral—which takes in virtually all of the North-West Territories—can be made subject to the magic of a single buffalo stone."

"Not every human being," I reminded him. "The Indians will be protected by their guardian spirits."

I could imagine Chambers nodding in the darkness as he replied. "Quite so—and why?"

I opened my mouth to answer, but Chambers plunged on before I could speak. "The transformative magic, when spread over so wide an area, is weakened. It must spread across both the physical and astral planes. Encountering a barrier in the astral plane—the body of a protective spirit that stands between that magic and a human being like a shield—it is unable to transform the physical body."

"And that protective spirit must be an animal," I guessed. "A Christian angel or saint won't do the job."

"It would appear so," Chambers concurred. "But perhaps some angels are stronger than others."

I frowned, thinking about the half-breed scout Peter. He'd been raised by an Indian mother and spent time among the

Blood Indians. He'd presumably been given a guardian spirit by his mother. Why did he feel the need for the additional protection of a Catholic saint?

"What's the third mechanism?" I asked, though the answer was plain enough.

"These tunnels," Chambers said, and I could hear the shudder in his voice. "They're the ley line itself—the etheric force flows underground, not above, and is drawn to the surface by the Manitou Stone, and at other power points, like the buffalo-shaped outcropping at the ford. These tunnels are filled with pure etheric force. No living creature—human or animal—can withstand that amount of magical energy, even with a guardian spirit, unless, like you and I, they have already been 'reborn.' In my case, it was my previous 'rebirth' as a buffalo that inoculated me. I can only assume that you, also, experienced a 'rebirth' at some point in the past."

"I had an operation to remove a cancerous tumour," I told him. "I nearly died on the operating table. My heart stopped beating; only through a strenuous effort was the surgeon able to revive me."

"Quite so," Chambers said quietly, a note of sympathy in his voice. He had the discretion not to continue in that vein. Instead he picked up the thread of logic once more. "As I said, pure etheric current flows through these tunnels. As soon as a living creature enters them, the transformation to buffalo form is instantaneous."

"Not at Victoria Mission," I reminded him. "You weren't transformed until you'd gone some distance along the tunnel."

Chambers had obviously been thinking this over himself. He had a ready answer for my puzzle. "The Manitou Stone had been moved more than a month before we arrived at Victoria Mission. It was still possible to open a tunnel at that location, but etheric force only flowed along that tunnel at the point where it joined the main body of the spiral. Had you ridden a horse into the tunnel, it would have been transformed into a buffalo at the same point that I was."

I stopped in my tracks as a thought struck me. "Chambers," I said in a hushed voice. "The Indians could transform animals into buffalo, instead of humans!"

"Of course they could—but only if they drove them down here, into the current of etheric energy itself."

"That's easily done," I said, waxing enthusiastic. "The Indians could open a tunnel and drive a herd of horses into it. Then they'd have plenty of buffalo."

I heard Chambers chuckle. "No—not horses. The cost would be too high. Although there would be a gain in meat, the Indians would lose a valuable source of transport."

"Dogs then," I said, my excitement running high. "Or gophers, or even mice. There has to be some creature that's suitable, and that is found in sufficient numbers. It's just a matter of convincing the Indians that it's feasible. When they see Buck, they'll realize that it's possible to...."

Then I realized my mistake. Increasing the size of the buffalo herds was only part of the Indians' goal. They also wanted to rid the North-West Territories of settlers.

Thought transference must have been at work, for Chambers next words echoed my thoughts. "Convincing the Indians to use their magic on animals, instead of we interlopers, will take some doing, though, won't it?" he asked softly.

I realized that I'd been gesturing with my hands as we spoke, and had let go of Iniskim's shoulder. I patted the air beside me, and found only empty space. The albino calf had trotted on ahead—and I could no longer hear the *clip-clop* of her hooves.

"Chambers!" I said. "Iniskim is gone!"

I heard a snort and the clinking of a bit as Chambers reined Buck to a sudden stop. In the silence that followed, I listened for the sound of Iniskim's hoof beats, but heard none. I struck my second-to-last match, and the smell of burning sulphur filled the air. Holding it high overhead, I looked wildly around, my heart pounding.

There was no cause for alarm. Iniskim was a few yards ahead of us, her nose snuffling against a solid wall of earth where the tunnel had come to an end. As the match burned down toward my fingers, she glanced upward, her pink eyes wide with yearning, and let out a soft bleat. She didn't need thought transference to speak to me—her glance at the white feather I still held in my hand was communication enough.

"Chambers," I whispered. "I think we've arrived."

Chambers nodded down at me from his perch on Buck's broad back. He looked slightly ludicrous in his silk pyjamas, smudged with dirt, his bare feet dangling as he straddled the buffalo. His voice dropped to a whisper as well. "I think you're right. The ground has been sloping upward for some time. The Manitou Stone must be directly above."

I held up the feather. "Shall I?"

Chambers nodded.

I gave Buck a pat for a job well done, then strode forward. I had no idea what we would find when the tunnel opened. The Manitou Stone, certainly—I could feel in my bones that we'd reached the end of the spiral at last. The etheric force, palpable as a chill wind, was pressing against us with all its magical might.

I drew my revolver from its holster, wincing at the pain from my knife wound. The buffalo stone in my pocket was a much better weapon, especially against the likes of Wandering Spirit and his ilk, but I had already decided against carrying it in my hand. I didn't want to run the risk of someone grabbing it and using it to turn Iniskim back into a girl again. I wanted White Buffalo Woman to get safely to the Manitou Stone—and back to the astral plane—while still in the form of a buffalo calf.

"White Buffalo Woman—are you ready?" I asked.

A gentle snort came from the darkness beside me, and a tiny horn nudged the small of my back, as if to say: *do it!*

I touched the feather to the wall.

A crack of light suddenly appeared in front of me as the end of the tunnel split open. Clods of earth rained down on my shoulders, and a trickle of sand fell into my face, forcing my eyes shut. Iniskim trotted out through the falling debris, and I stumbled after her, blinking at the sudden change from darkness to light, even though that light was pale and grey. Behind me, I could hear Chambers cursing and Buck's protesting snorts. Chambers seemed to be having trouble making his mount move forward.

In hindsight, I should have paid attention: Buck not only knew where to go—but where not to go. Instead I ran after Iniskim, not wanting to lose her.

I found myself amid gently rolling hills, under a star-filled sky. The ground underfoot was dotted with white—the dried salt of alkaline lakes—and patches of sand. Tufts of straw-like grass poked up through the ground here and there, sun-bleached and brittle. I looked around me, searching for a landmark, and located the northern star. I turned toward the eastern horizon and saw that the hills there were just starting to glow a faint pink, heralding the imminent arrival of a new day. Peeping up behind them was the moon—a sight that froze me in silent horror. Even though it had only partially risen above the horizon, I could see that it was round and full. The Day of Changes was at hand.

I cast a wary eye about me, searching for any sign of Indians. The open prairie offered scant places to hide, but I had the distinct impression of eyes watching me. I checked my revolver, making sure it was loaded, then listened. From somewhere off to the west came a faint clicking sound, like the *tick-tock* of a watch. I took it to be an omen that our time was running out.

I couldn't see the Manitou Stone anywhere. Iniskim, however, seemed to be able to smell it. After only a moment's hesitation she gave a happy bellow, like a buffalo that has scented a wallow, and trotted with determination toward the east.

Chambers had abandoned Buck. Emerging from the tunnel on foot, he cocked his head to the side and listened, cupping one ear in the direction of the clicking noise. Iniskim, meanwhile, had almost reached the top of the hill. She would be out of sight in another moment.

"Come along," I urged, tugging at his pyjama sleeve. "We can't lose track of her."

"You go on ahead," he said. "I want to find out what that noise is. I'll catch you up."

I paused just long enough to jam the feather in the ground to prevent the tunnel from closing up, then ran after the buffalo calf. She crested a hill, and in the increasing light of dawn her white hair turned a rosy pink. The sight sent a shudder through me.

"White Buffalo Woman!" I cried, running up the hill after her. "Wait!"

As I reached the summit I noticed below what I took, at first, to be a pile of sun-bleached branches on which a round white rock had been placed. Then I recognized it for what it was: a pile of bones, capped by a human skull.

Just as Iniskim approached the bottom of the hill, I heard a faint noise that sounded like an Indian whoop. To my ears it was only a distant echo, but to Iniskim it proved much more startling. She veered away from the pile of bones with a snort of fright and headed south.

I ran down the hill after her, keeping a wary eye on the pile of bones myself. When I saw an Indian suddenly leap out in front of the bones, rifle in hand, I raised my revolver and fired. Only belatedly did I realize that he was no more substantial than a ghost: his face was a ghastly white colour, and a flap of skin that had peeled back from the top of his head hung down across one ear. Dimly, my mind registered the fact that he was an apparition: he'd been killed and scalped. My bullet passed harmlessly through him, knocking a bone from the pile. He fired back—and although his rifle was as insubstantial as he was, I felt my jacket jerk as a bullet tore through its hem.

The ghostly brave let out a war whoop that turned the blood in my veins to ice, and cocked his rifle. If I kept running, he would have a clear shot at my back. Instead, I skidded to a halt, raised my revolver, and fired.

My bullet struck exactly the spot I'd intended—not the ghost himself, but the skull on the pile of bones behind him. In the same instant that the Indian's finger tightened on the trigger of his rifle, the dry skull exploded into a thousand splinters. The ghost disappeared.

The exchange had taken no more than a few seconds, but already Iniskim was well ahead of me. To my left I could see more piles of bones, and corresponding piles on the right.

I immediately recognized them for what they were: the beginnings of a buffalo run. Iniskim was being driven along it—each time she tried to veer east again, something startled her back into the run.

I had no choice but to run after her—circling up the hill behind the piles of bones would cost me too much time. I ran as fast as my feet would carry me, bracing myself for the apparitions that leapt out from the piles of bones on either side and saving the bullets in my revolver for the most menacing of the ghosts.

A ghostly woman whose naked skin was covered in pustular sores ran toward me, trying to wrap an infected blanket around my shoulders, but I dodged under it at the last moment and escaped. An emaciated figure with a bloated belly and a ravenous look in his eye staggered toward me with a knife, but I easily avoided his hunger-weakened thrusts. Another brave, this one's body pierced by so many arrows that he looked like a porcupine, tried to throw a tomahawk at me, but I fired two quick shots at the pile of bones beside him, striking the skull with my second bullet and sending him back to the place from whence he came. Yet another warrior, this one with a belly wound from which entrails hung like streamers, tried to shoot me with an arrow. My shot was a lucky one; it didn't hit the skull itself, but managed to knock out a bone beneath it, causing the skull to tumble from its perch. It was enough—like the other two warriors, the bowman faded away into mist.

The piles of bones were closer together now. Iniskim was approaching the end of the funnel-shaped run, and I had nearly caught up to her. Thick and fast from either side came the shouts and whoops of ghosts, the beating of drums and the bonelike clatter of shaking rattles. Ghostly arrows sailed past my head, and puffs of rifle smoke drifted up on either side of me. I ran on after Iniskim, shouting at her to stop, but my pleas went unheeded. There was terror in the buffalo calf's pink eyes—a terror that drove her on like a goad.

Out of the corner of my eye, I could see that the moon had fully risen above the horizon; it was a ghostly white circle in a sky that was growing increasingly bright. The stars had disappeared, and the eastern horizon was ablaze with reddish light.

Silhouetted atop a low hill to my left, I saw a shape I recognized only from a photograph: the rectangular bulk of the Manitou Stone. From this angle, and with the light of the rising sun behind it obscuring all detail, it looked like the gaping hole left by an open door.

Iniskim ran steadily south. She charged up a slight rise, her head turned longingly toward the Manitou Stone, then disappeared from sight.

The ground was too gently sloping for there to be a cliff ahead, which meant that the run must end in a buffalo pound. Coming from where this enclosure must be, I could hear the slow, steady beating of a drum. I was terrified that I would be trapped inside the pound if I entered it, but I could see no other alternative to following Iniskim into it. My only hope was that I could drive Iniskim out again, and lead her up that hill to the Manitou Stone.

I charged up the ramp and leaped down into the enclosure, then ran over to where the albino calf stood panting and shivering. All around us—plainly visible now that we had entered the enclosure—were the walls of the pound itself. The circular enclosure was nearly a hundred feet across, made from thousands upon thousands of buffalo skulls that had been piled with curved horns interlocking to form a waist-high fence.

At the centre of the pound was a tree, its uppermost branches bent to form a platform. Something or someone sat atop this platform, chanting and beating a drum, but I could not make him out clearly.

Inside the pound, the bodies of four large buffalo lay a short distance from where we stood. Although they were all adults, each had the yellowish-brown hair of a newborn calf. They'd been butchered some time ago, judging by the smell that rose from the carcases. I realized that I'd found the missing patrol—the poor wretches who had disappeared from the ford.

Just outside the pound, ghosts whooped and danced. I took a fistful of Iniskim's hair and tried to drag her toward the ramp, but too late—the ghosts were already piling skulls across the entrance with tremendous speed, sealing us inside. Already the pile was knee-high.

The ramp we'd run along to enter the pound was too high for Iniskim to jump back up to, especially with the gate of bones now atop it. Our only hope was to clamber over the fence itself. Iniskim couldn't climb, however, and I couldn't lift her—a buffalo calf is a heavy creature, weighing more than two hundred pounds. I'd only be able to carry her out if....

It was a gamble I had to take. Holstering my revolver, I pulled the buffalo stone from my pocket. "I'm sorry," I told her. "It's the only way."

The buffalo calf blinked, and looked trustingly up at me.

I touched the stone to Iniskim's forehead, and in the place where an albino buffalo calf had stood a heartbeat before, there now crouched a naked toddler. Her hair was a dull white, her pale skin flushed and blotched with red. I caught her as she crumpled to the ground, and could feel the fever that infused her skin. Her eyes rolled back in her head, and her frail body began to tremble as a sheen of sweat broke out on her forehead.

I scooped her to my chest. "Be strong, Iniskim," I told her. "For just a few minutes more."

Cradling the toddler in my arms, I ran for the side of the fence nearest the Manitou Stone. I ran straight at the wall of bones, shouting my own defiant war cry and praying that my feet would not slip. They didn't—I climbed the stack of skulls like stairs, somehow keeping my balance as the pile shifted beneath me. Then I leaped over the head of a ghost who reached out to grab me with hands that looked as though they had been gnawed by beasts. I flew through the air, envisioning the wings of an owl lending me extra height and speed, then landed, stumbling and twisting my ankle.

It took me only an instant to find my footing again. I ran on, gritting my teeth against the pain of my injured limb. I spared one glance over my shoulder and saw that the ghosts were still single-minded in their task of piling ever higher the walls of the pound, even though their quarry had escaped. One or two, however, were pointing in my direction.

As I ran up the hill, my eye was drawn to a patch of red halfway up its slope. As I drew closer, I saw a body that lay twisted on the hillside, its head crushed like a melon. The red serge jacket and riding breeches it was clothed in told me this was a policeman, but who he was I could not say. I knew only that he was a constable, by the stripe on his sleeve.

I ran on, past a second dead constable, this man lying on his back with his jacket torn open. A bloody hole had been clawed into his chest, over his left breast. A part of my mind registered the mechanism of death, identical to that used against the Indian agent Quinn: this murder was Wandering Spirit's work. Yet I saw no Indians anywhere about—aside from the ghosts behind me.

The ghosts that had driven Iniskim and me into the pound were now surging up the hill, rifles making faint popping noises and mouths screaming war cries. I stepped on something soft— and felt a wash of revulsion as I saw I had trod upon the fleshy arm of Bertrand, who gazed sightlessly up at the sky.

Up ahead, I could see a bird circling the Manitou Stone. With a sinking heart, I realized that it was the aerograph. My idea had worked, and Steele's patrol had followed the aerograph to this spot. Judging by the bodies that lay on the hill, they'd encountered Indians who had put up a stiff fight. I just hoped the Superintendent was still alive.

Although she was barely a toddler, the child in my arms felt heavy as a stone. The hill seemed suddenly very steep, and the Manitou Stone that crowned it very distant. I was hot, as sweaty as if I had a fever myself, and the air came to my lungs in ragged gasps. I struggled upward. Just a few yards more....

I crashed into something I could not see, and was knocked to my knees. A painted buffalo skin fell to the ground, and there, standing before me with his arms crossed upon his chest, was Big Bear. As I staggered to my feet, his wizened face broke into a smile. He let go of the bear's paw amulet that hung about his neck. In the blink of an eye, nearly a dozen other Indians became visible: Piapot, Little Pine, Beardy, Mountain, Red Crow, Crowfoot—all of the chiefs who had been in council inside the shaking tepee, save one. Beyond them, on the other side of the hill, I saw a cluster of Indian tepees.

Hearing a noise behind me, I glanced around and saw that the ghosts had disappeared. Poundmaker was striding up the hill, a newly mended drum in his hand. I now knew who had summoned up the apparitions that had driven Iniskim and me into the pound.

Close behind him was a bare-chested and bare-headed Wandering Spirit, now bereft of his lynx-skin headdress and painted buckskin shirt. Draped over his shoulder was the limp figure of a policeman. I recognized the officer at once by the amount of gold braid on his sleeve and his handlebar moustache: Superintendent Steele. Whether he was alive or dead, I could not say.

Encumbered as I was by Iniskim, I did the only thing I could think of. The buffalo stone was still in my right hand. I threw it at Big Bear, hoping he would dodge to the side, and in the same moment sprinted desperately past him, making for the Manitou Stone.

I got no further than a step or two before I was knocked down from behind. Iniskim fell from my arms onto the ground, and landed a mere two yards from the Manitou Stone. Her eyes opened for a moment and she whimpered, but she was too weak even to crawl. Her eyes closed.

I struggled against whoever had knocked me down, and found myself staring up into Wandering Spirit's angry face. His body smelled musky, like a buffalo's hide. His hand shot out to clasp my injured hand and squeezed, and the knife wound in my palm opened up again. Blinking away the pain, I fumbled with my left hand for my revolver. Wandering Spirit might be immune to its bullets, but I could always use the pistol as a club.

I never got the chance. Wandering Spirit pinned my other arm to the ground with his knee, then formed his free hand into the shape of a lynx's claws. In that instant, I knew I was a dead man. All he had to do was gesture, and my heart would be ripped from my chest.

Big Bear shouted something in Cree, and Wandering Spirit paused. Then the warrior looked in the direction that Big Bear was pointing. I glanced up at Big Bear, who held the buffalo stone in his bare hand. Like me, he now was immune to its magic. I wondered if he had allowed himself to be transformed into a buffalo and back into human form again, in order to inoculate himself. I hoped that it wasn't my transformation of Wandering Spirit that had given him the idea.

I tried to shift Wandering Spirit off, but he had me well pinned, and I was utterly exhausted from my run. Peeking out under his arm at the spot that Big Bear was pointing to, I saw a large, four-legged creature that could only be a buffalo. Something trailed from its mouth: reins. Buck must have finally summoned up his courage and emerged from the tunnel. What he was doing on the opposite hill, I could not say.

"Big Bear!" I shouted, trying to get the chief's attention. "You see? That buffalo was once a horse." I cast desperately about in my mind for the Cree words, and strung them together as quickly as I could, trying to persuade him that it was not necessary to change human beings into buffalo—that animals could be transformed instead. I used the first animal that sprang to mind, a word I knew well: horse. "*Wapastim meskocipayiwin paskwawimostos. Namoya napew maskocipayiwin paskwawimostos, paskwawimostos wapastim. Kitahamakewin*— Stop!"

Poundmaker trudged up the hill at this moment and dumped the limp body of Steele next to me. I tried to call out to the Superintendent, but Wandering Spirit's grip shifted from my injured hand to my mouth. I wrenched my head further to the side—and got an even better view of what Big Bear was pointing at.

It seemed that Steele's wasn't the only patrol to have reached the Manitou Stone. Sitting on the hill on the opposite side of the pound, its muzzle swinging round to point at the Manitou Stone, was one of our nine-pound artillery guns. It must have been the one from Maple Creek, for its limber bore not only the gun itself but also a perpetual motion device. Its pendulum was still swinging back and forth, producing the steady ticking noise I'd heard earlier, but that wasn't what had brought the gun to the top of the hill. The limber had been drawn there by brute force; Buck was yoked to the front of it.

Standing next to the gun itself, working frantically with something he held in his hands, was the pyjama-clad figure of Chambers. As a flame sprang to life on the end of a brand that had been resting on the limber—he must have been struggling to light it with a match—I saw what Chambers intended. He was going to blow the Manitou Stone to pieces!

We were too far away for our eyes to meet, but even so, a silent communication passed between us. I knew that I was

close enough to the Manitou Stone that I might be killed, either
by the explosion of the shell itself or by the shrapnel of
splintered stone. I didn't care. *Do it,* I silently urged him.

With a triumphant gesture, Chambers saluted me with the
burning brand—and in that instant, I realized my mistake. The
gesture was the same one Chambers had made in my prophetic
dream: the one in which the Manitou Stone had crushed him
under its weight.

I threw every ounce of will into one last attempt at thought
transference. *Stop!* I implored him. *It won't work!*

Too late. Chambers had already lowered the flame to the gun,
touching off its powder. It exploded with a tremendous roar and
a belch of white smoke and flame—and a second later it
exploded a second time. I couldn't say whether the gun itself was
faulty and blew apart—or whether the artillery shell, deflected by
the Indians' magic, had somehow doubled back on its course to
blow up the gun instead of its intended target. All I know is that
one moment Chambers was standing there, his body radiating
triumph, and the next both he and Buck were gone. The artillery
piece had disappeared altogether from the limber, which rolled
slowly backward, wheels squealing as it passed out of sight. All
that remained on the hill were two lumps of mangled flesh that
might once have been a buffalo and a man.

I finally succeeded in wrenching my head out of Wandering
Spirit's grip. "Damn you!" I shouted at Big Bear. "That man was
my friend!"

Big Bear ignored me. I saw tears trickle down his wrinkled
cheeks as he picked up Iniskim, and as he gently brushed the
hair from her eyes, I realized that he must have felt regret at the
child's grave illness. He passed the girl to Mountain, then turned
and reverently placed the buffalo stone I'd thrown at him at the
foot of the Manitou Stone. I saw that there was a cluster of other
stones already there: some of them small and spiral-shaped, like
the one I'd carried in my tobacco pouch for so long, others a
dusky red colour, with protuberances that gave them the
appearance of four-legged animals.

This done, Big Bear turned to Wandering Spirit, and made a
curt gesture. I thought it was a signal for Wandering Spirit to
claw out my heart, but instead of attacking, Wandering Spirit
hissed at Big Bear, then hauled me to my feet. I saw that the
Cree chief had his own coup stick, this one tipped with what
looked like a bear's tooth. He advanced upon me, coup stick at
the ready. It looked as though Big Bear wanted the honour of
killing me himself.

The chiefs behind him began to chant and, as their song grew,
a cold wind that prickled like a premonition swept up over the

hill. It swirled once around the Manitou Stone, swept across Steele—who transformed before my eyes into a buffalo, his uniform tearing away from his body like rotten cloth—then spiralled away toward the horizon. My mind was flooded with thousands of anguished cries—and then Big Bear's coup stick flashed toward my chest.

I tried to wrench free of Wandering Spirit's grasp, twisting away in a final, desperate attempt for freedom—only to feel the coup stick touch my stomach instead of my chest. My stomach filled with a pain one thousand times more fierce than the cancerous tumour had ever produced, even when the disease was at its worst—and then I knew no more.

◄—►

I found myself standing in a place very much like the rolling prairie on which I'd just lain, except that everything around me appeared in faded shades of grey. The sky overhead was a uniform, desolate grey, devoid of sun or moon or stars, and the ground underfoot was a similar colour, dotted here and there with crusts of white salt where pools of water had once stood. All around me were endless, rolling hills, with nary man nor beast to be seen. The breeze carried snatches of sound that I took to be voices, but every time I strained to listen, they disappeared into the hiss of the wind.

That wind stirred the grass that tufted here and there like the hair on a mangy animal's hide. Sand blew around my feet in swirls, dusting across the tops of my boots. I realized then that I was still in uniform—although when I looked down at my riding breeches and the serge of my jacket, both were a leaden grey.

Something other than colour was missing. It took me a moment to realize it, but then I figured out what it was. The familiar, gnawing ache that had filled my stomach these past few months was gone. Suddenly frightened, I wondered if I had lost all connection with my body. I slapped my hand against my face, but neither my cheek nor my hand stung. All sensation had departed—I couldn't even tell if I was breathing.

Only emotion remained, and foremost was an overwhelming sense of futility. I had failed utterly to do my sworn duty, and had let my fellow policemen down. Chambers was dead, Steele had been transformed into a buffalo, and the Day of Changes had come, despite my utmost efforts. I wasn't merely visiting the Big Sands this time. I was here permanently—I was dead.

A thought occurred to me: why was I alone? When I'd entered the Big Sands the first time with Sergeant Wilde, we'd ridden into an Indian village populated with the souls of the dead. Yet these ghosts were nowhere to be seen—nor were any others.

Chambers had just been killed; surely his ghost was around here somewhere.

I chuckled grimly, thinking that if Chambers were here with me, he would certainly correct my choice of words. He wasn't a "ghost," he would say in his most imperious voice. He was an "astral body" and I'd do well to get the terminology correct.

According to what Chambers had taught me, the astral body was unfettered by time and space. I didn't have to remain in this dismal, lonely place if I didn't want to. I was free to wander at will.

I was free to fly....

Just as I had done in the canyon at Writing on Stone, I called out to my guardian spirit. It was easier here. After just a moment's thought, I saw something winging its way toward me. An owl drew nearer and nearer—then swooped down into my body, entering my stomach with a tickle of feathers. An instant later I had become the owl, and was soaring over the sandy wasteland with wings outstretched.

Whooo? the owl asked.

I understood its question at once, but it took me a moment to decide upon my answer. I yearned to find Chambers, but instinctively knew he would be of little use here. Knowledgeable though he was about the astral plane, I suspected that the information collected second-hand by the Society for Psychical Research would pale in comparison with the wisdom of someone who regularly walked the spirit world searching for the souls of the dead.

"Strikes Back," I answered.

A tree appeared below me. Cradled in its branches I saw a human-sized bundle: a hide-wrapped corpse. I swooped down and settled on a branch next to it, then used my beak to pluck at the thongs that had been laced around it. After a few sharp tugs, the last thong tore free, and the buckskin robe fell open.

I looked down at the body that lay within. Strikes Back had the same hawkish nose and high cheekbones as Red Crow, and wore her hair in the same style: a single braid that lay across her shoulder, next to the rifle that was tucked in the crook of her arm. For a moment I thought I was looking into the face of a man. Certainly her countenance was grim enough. Yet her body had a woman's curves under her dress, which was decorated at the neck and sleeves with rows of elk teeth.

Suddenly, Strikes Back opened her eyes, causing me to flutter my wings in alarm. Only one of the eyes was intact—the other was a gaping hole. When the corpse sat up, I saw why: a bullet had entered through this eye and blasted its way out of the back of her head, leaving a large and bloody hole.

Her hand shot out and clasped my leg. Forcing myself to stay calm—reminding myself that this was the medicine woman I had been seeking for so long—I met the penetrating stare of her single good eye. Perhaps she could still help me, even though she, too, was now no more than a spirit.

Strikes Back spoke before I did. Although she used her own language, I understood her perfectly.

"Red Owl," she said. "You have come. I dreamed that you would."

There wasn't time to stop and think about the name she'd addressed me by. Somehow, it sounded right—it fit, just like the feathers that now covered my astral body.

"I want you to restore me to life," I said. "You resurrected Iniskim—can you do the same for me?"

"I could lead you back to your body," she answered. "But you would die soon afterward. Big Bear's coup stick has caused the evil spirit in your belly to grow even larger. You would only live a short time with it inside you."

I didn't even think to ask how she knew about the coup stick. Instead I was busy fuming at my own stupidity. If I hadn't tried to wriggle free from Wandering Spirit, the coup stick would have landed on my chest, and might not have killed me. Instead, it had struck my body's weakest spot.

Strikes Back stared at me with her one good eye, as if listening to my thoughts. Then she gave me a wicked grin. "I can teach you how to heal yourself," she said.

"You can?" Had I any awareness of my heart, I was certain I would have felt it pounding in my chest. Strikes Back had just offered me my life.

"I can help you live—but first you must do something for me."

"What?" I asked, suddenly suspicious. The hope that had been surging inside me faded as I remembered the half-breed scout Peter, and his grim comment that he was "still paying" Strikes Back for having saved his life. I wondered what terrible service she would demand of me.

Strikes Back pointed at one of the branches that her bier lay upon. Glancing in that direction, I saw what looked like a chunk of meat impaled upon a bare branch. By the faint pulses that coursed through it, I recognized it at once as a heart—a human heart, still beating—and instinctively knew whose it was.

"Eat it," Strikes Back said.

If my astral body had been capable of sensation, I am certain that my gorge would have risen in my throat.

"You want me to eat your heart?" I said in a horrified whisper.

"It is the only thing that will set me free. Once it is consumed, I can return to the land of the living—I can be reborn. I would have had it destroyed some time ago, but my servant found the power to refuse me. Now I have found another who can consume it for me: you."

I didn't trust Strikes Back. "Teach me how to rid myself of the cancer first."

She laughed—a dry, croaking chuckle. "You are a hard man. Very well then. There is a healing song that weakens the walls between the human world and the spirit world; it will allow you to reach inside yourself and pull out the evil that is the cause of your sickness. Listen: I will teach it to you now."

Strikes Back closed her good eye—the empty socket remained open—then began a slow chant. It was in the Blackfoot tongue, and contained many words that I did not understand, but I could feel the song's power. Even as Strikes Back sang it, the air around us seemed to shimmer. She chanted the song only once, but when she had finished it was as if the song had taken root inside my head. I repeated it under my breath. I had no idea what I was whispering, but I was certain that the chant was letter-perfect. The knowledge filled me with immense joy—now I could heal my cancer!

"Good," Strikes Back said. "Now eat my heart. I cannot lead you from the spirit world until you do."

I swallowed. If Strikes Back was trapped here in the spirit world, then so was I. The healing song would do me little good if I couldn't find my way back to my body again.

I hopped onto the branch where the heart was impaled, and used my beak to take a tiny bite. The heart was fresh, warm meat; blood dribbled down my beak. Somehow I choked the tiny piece down, then glanced at Strikes Back.

Her intense frown told me that it wasn't enough. I had to consume the entire heart.

I did so, bite by bite, forcing the raw chunks of meat down. Only when I swallowed the last piece did the heart stop its quivering beat.

Strikes Back let out a soft sigh. Her body was fading— already I could see through it to the branches behind her. A realization hit me like the chill of ice water: Strikes Back was leaving—and she was not going to take me with her.

"Wait!" I said. "I thought we struck a bargain. You promised to lead me back to my body!"

Strikes Back bared her teeth in a grin. "I made no such promise. I said I would teach you the healing song, and I did. I wouldn't have taught the song to you if I thought you were able to use it. Not to you, Red Owl—especially when you might use it to undo the Day of Changes. Better that you should remain here, lost in the spirit world."

"Me?" I asked. "I could reverse the Day of Changes on my own?"

For just a moment, her gloating expression faltered. Then her good eye narrowed. "That is true," she said slowly. "You have the power within you, but even if you find your body again, I doubt that you will choose to use this power. You want to live—and that is only possible if you use the song I taught you to heal your sickness. If you heal yourself, your power will vanish.

"You have to choose between your power and your life. I think that you will choose to live."

I stared at her, defiantly meeting her eye as she slowly faded from view. Strikes Back didn't know me that well. It was true that I wanted to live, but not at any cost. I didn't want the weight of thousands of poor wretches who had been transformed into buffalo resting upon my conscience. I would rather die doing my duty than live with the knowledge that I was a coward.

In another instant, Strikes Back was gone. I was perched alone on a tree branch, staring down at her empty bier. The rifle still rested upon it, but little else, save for a second pair of moccasins and a knife. The possessions that had accompanied her into the afterlife were few. I avoided touching them, fearful that I would pick up some taint from them.

I was going to fly away from there in owl form, but suddenly had the feeling that this would be a terrible mistake. The landscape around me was featureless; I had no idea in which direction my salvation lay.

I happened to look down through the branches, and saw something I had not noticed before: at the base of the tree, the ground was not the trackless waste it had been at the place where I'd entered the spirit world. The hoof prints of a single horse led up to the tree, then away from it again.

I flew down to the ground—and found myself in human form once more. The owl spirit with which I had bonded seemed to have flown. I squatted down for a closer look at the tracks, and saw something which caused my heart to leap. The horse that had made the tracks was shod—and the horseshoes had been affixed with nails whose heads were shaped like tiny crosses.

Peter had visited the bier recently—and unless I missed my guess, Peter was still alive. Just as I had been living when I'd followed Sergeant Wilde into the Big Sands, so too was Peter now. He'd ridden into this desolate wasteland—and ridden out again. All I had to do to escape from this place was to follow his tracks.

I did so at a run, following the trail of hoof prints away from the tree. In places they crossed a stretch of shifting sand, or were lost among tufts of brittle grass, but by circling carefully around these obstacles I was able to pick up the tracks again.

I followed the trail for what seemed like miles, never tiring and never thirsting. Gradually, I noticed a change in my surroundings. The greyness of the landscape was lifting—I saw a clump of yellow grass here, a patch of blue sky there. The sun appeared in the sky and began to warm my shoulders, and I noticed that the sleeves of my jacket were once again red. My boots were leaving tracks in the sandy soil, and my breathing was gradually becoming more laboured, forcing me to slow my pace to a walk.

As colour and sensation returned, so too did my pain. With each step I took, the agony in my stomach grew. It felt as if a fist were gripping my intestines, twisting them into a hot, tight knot. By the time the world around me returned to normal, I found myself doubled over, barely able to take a step. In another moment I collapsed. I lay on the ground, gasping at the fierce pain, and stared stupidly at my shadow.

After several long moments, I realized that another shadow lay across it—one that was boxy and rectangular. I turned my head, and saw the Manitou Stone looming over me. Fearfully, I glanced around, but saw no sign of Wandering Spirit or any of the other Indians. I'd done it! I had found my body and was back in the land of the living—but for how long I could not say.

A few feet away from me sprawled the body of a large and magnificent buffalo. Forcing myself to my knees, I crawled over to it. I saw with relief that the mighty beast's chest still rose and fell—Steele was alive! I could do little for him, however, since the buffalo stones that the Indians had placed at the foot of the Manitou Stone were gone. I tried to rouse Steele, but even though I gripped both of his horns, his head was too heavy to lift, let alone shake. I had no smelling salts with which to bring him back to his senses, and so I left him where he lay.

I knelt on the ground, both hands folded over the burning ache in my stomach, and looked cautiously around. The sun had risen well above the horizon, and although it was not yet noon, the tepees that I had seen on the far side of the hill were gone. I suspected, by the height of the sun, that at least three hours had passed—time enough for the Indians to have packed up their travois and gone. They'd obviously assumed that I was dead, and left my body to rot.

I ran a hand through my hair, thankful that I had not been scalped, then picked up my Stetson and jammed it back on my head. Someone or something must have been watching out for me.

I stared at the Manitou Stone, wondering what to do next. The aerograph that had been circling it was gone, either taken by the Indians or flown away on its own. Now that I had found my way back from beyond death's door, I had to decide what to do next. I thought over the words that had appeared upon the cliff at Writing on Stone: "To end the Day of Changes, start at the beginning. Close the–"

The message had to be the one I had guessed at earlier: Close the door. It made sense to me, now. I knew now that the Manitou Stone was a portal to the astral plane—one that White Buffalo Woman had hoped to use. Chambers, who knew so much more about ley lines, must have guessed the same thing—that was why he'd tried to use the artillery piece to shatter the Manitou Stone and close the door.

A wave of nausea gripped me then, and I vomited onto the ground. When the wracking spasm had stopped, I saw that my bile was streaked with blood. Strikes Back had spoken the truth—I didn't have long to live. I could feel the tumour in my stomach like a hard, hot lump. Strikes Back had also said I had the power to reverse the Day of Changes, but I couldn't for the life of me think what I might do to bring this about. I wondered if I should just admit defeat and heal myself instead.

Without consciously intending to, I found myself humming the first few notes of the song Strikes Back had taught me. The song died on my lips, however, when I heard a woman's anguished cry. Startled, I staggered to my feet and looked over the Manitou Stone. On the other side of it, I saw the person I'd least expected to find: Stone Keeper. She was on her knees, bent down low with her long dark hair trailing over a tiny, blanket-wrapped bundle. A bloody knife lay by her side. I saw a strand of ash-white hair straggling from within the blanket, and for one horrified moment thought that Stone Keeper had killed her child. Then I saw the blood welling from Stone Keeper's little finger, and realized what she had done. It was the custom, among the tribes of the Blackfoot Confederacy, to cut off the final joint of a finger when mourning the loss of a loved one. I realized that the blanket must be Iniskim's shroud, and that the child was dead.

Emily looked up, and her tear-streaked eyes met mine. She seemed unsurprised to find me there. It was almost as if she had known all along that I would return from the dead—and was absorbed in the fact that her child would not.

"Stone Keeper," I said, falling to my knees beside her. "What happened?"

"Daughter die," she said in a listless voice. "White Buffalo Woman go to spirit world, but too late. Iniskim die." She reached for the knife.

I grabbed her hand before she could cut off another finger joint. "Don't," I said softly. "You've already sacrificed enough."

When she dropped the knife, I unwrapped the kerchief I'd used to bind up the wound in my palm. It was crusted with my own blood, but it was all I had. Taking Stone Keeper's injured hand, I wrapped the cleanest portion of the cloth around her severed finger, then squeezed gently to staunch the flow of blood.

Both of us sat in silence. The pain of my cancer still wracked my stomach, but I knew my agony to be less than Stone Keeper's. She'd lost a child—her only daughter. The chiefs had used the girl, then cast her aside. I supposed that they justified it as the sacrifice of one for the good of the many; Iniskim's death had made possible the Day of Changes, and the newly transformed buffalo would feed their people for years to come. Yet as I sat beside the cold, dark Manitou Stone, staring down at the tiny corpse in its frayed blanket, I cared little for their reasons. I could only see the terrible consequences.

I touched the silky hair that protruded from the blanket, intending to tuck it back inside. As I did, I thought of White Buffalo Woman, who had until recently shared this frail body. I wondered how the spirit felt about the chiefs forcing her to enter the world of men before her appointed time.

Foolish men. If they had only waited, I–

Startled, I jerked my hand away. Had that really been White Buffalo Woman speaking? It had sounded like two voices in one: the husky tones of a grown woman, and the higher pitch of a young girl.

A spasm of pain wracked my stomach, and as I blinked away the tears from my eyes, I suddenly realized what I had just done. Somehow, I had summoned the spirit of White Buffalo Woman herself. I had contacted her by touching something that, until recently, had been as close to her as anything in this world could be: Iniskim's body.

I glanced at Stone Keeper, worried that she would realize what I was doing. I didn't want her to think that I was using the body of her child, as the chiefs had done. Pretending to be completing the job of tucking in the strand of hair, I focused intently upon my silent words, speaking them with all of the effort of will I could muster.

Tell me, White Buffalo Woman. If the chiefs had waited, what would have happened?

There was a long pause, and for a moment I thought she would not answer.

The Day of Changes would have come when it was meant to—in seven moons more—and I would have led the spirits of the dead buffalo back to the living world. They would cover the land so thickly that it would appear black.

I couldn't believe what I was hearing. My fingers tightened on the lock of hair. *If I can reverse what was done today—if I can transform my people back into human form again—will that day still come?*

It will.

Tell me, White Buffalo Woman—how can I reverse the chiefs' magic?

I held my breath, waiting for her reply.

Close the circle.

I frowned in puzzlement. *What do you mean?* I asked her.

There was no answer. With those words, White Buffalo Woman faded from my mind.

Try as I might, I couldn't puzzle out this cryptic message. I could guess part of it—although White Buffalo Woman had used the word "circle," she was probably referring to the spiral. It could be "closed"—made into a circle—by joining up its beginning and end points, but how?

Then I remembered the dream I'd had, before our patrol set out from Medicine Hat—the one in which I'd lifted a tombstone from a grave and run with it in a panicked circle, then fallen into the grave. I looked up at the Manitou Stone, and saw that its general outline matched that of the tombstone in my dream. The answer suddenly became clear: by moving the Manitou Stone back to its original resting place I could close the circle—and reverse the Day of Changes.

I now knew who had written the words I had read upon the cliff at Writing on Stone. White Buffalo Woman had been trying to give me the answer for some time.

"Thank you," I whispered.

I realized now what had to be done. The circle that White Buffalo Woman had spoken of was a metaphor: to reverse the Day of Changes, I had to close the spiral of the ley line. Somehow, I had to haul the Manitou Stone back to its original resting place. This would reverse the flow of magical energy, thus transforming those who had been turned into buffalo back into human beings again.

I had to do this swiftly. The longer those poor wretches remained in buffalo form, the more chance they had of injuring themselves or of being slaughtered for food by the Indians. I had already thought of how I would transport the heavy stone: if the gun limber and its perpetual motion device were not too badly damaged, I could use the limber like a cart. I even knew how I would find the Manitou Stone's original resting place: by following the tunnel back to the other end of the spiral. Best of all, I knew that I could accomplish this Herculean task in just one day.

Strikes Back herself had unwittingly given me the clue. A year ago last May, she had used the tunnels—the currents of etheric force—to travel from Fort Macleod to Fort Qu'appelle in just one day. The Manitou Stone had been at Victoria Mission then, and the flow of etheric current was spiralling in a counter-clockwise direction, down through Fort Macleod in a gentle sweep south of the border and back up into Fort Qu'appelle. Because Strikes Back was traveling with the current, she made the journey in a fraction of the time that was passing in the world above.

By the time I first entered the tunnels, the Manitou Stone had been moved: the current of etheric force was flowing in a clockwise direction. I'd been fighting against the current as I traveled from Victoria Mission to the cliffs at Head Smashed In, and so time had flowed more rapidly in the world above.

With luck, the opening I'd created with Stone Keeper's feather was still in place. Since I now knew the Manitou Stone to be the beginning of the spiral, I could be confident that we would be traveling with the current. If the gun limber could be used to haul the Manitou Stone through the tunnel, we'd close the circle in no time.

Getting the Manitou Stone onto the limber, however, would be no easy task. The stone weighed close to four hundred pounds. Even though the slope of the hill would allow me to position the limber just below it, I'd need Stone Keeper's help to topple the Manitou Stone onto it. She had no reason to help me—there was no gain in it for her. Iniskim was dead, and moving the Manitou Stone wouldn't help her.

Suddenly, I realized that I was wrong. In the premonitory dream, the occupant of the grave had awakened when her tombstone was moved. The dream had contained a second message for me: moving the Manitou Stone back to its original resting place would bring Iniskim back to life.

The Manitou Stone was a portal to the astral plane—one that Iniskim's astral body could use to return to the world of the living, allowing soul and body to become one again. White Buffalo Woman had told me as much herself, when she wrote the words on the cliff face. I could remember her words precisely, as if they had been engraved upon my heart: "Manitou Stone sits on apparition trail. Birth and death are the beginning and end of the trail."

I had to follow the apparition trail—the ley line—to the point that was both its beginning and its end. This would bring about the end of Iniskim's death and the beginning of a new life for her.

Following it would also be a beginning and end for me: an end to life, and the beginning of my death. Now that I had a taste of the afterlife, however, I was ready for it. If an eternity in the Big Sands was to be my fate, I would meet it manfully.

"Stone Keeper," I said softly. "I have spoken to White Buffalo Woman. She told me that, if we can move the Manitou Stone back to its original resting place, Iniskim will be restored to life."

Stone Keeper sniffed. The look she gave me was cold. "You want make Day of Changes go away," she said in a voice filled with bitter accusation.

I couldn't lie. She'd suffered hurt enough.

"That's true," I said. "But it's also true that moving the stone will bring Iniskim back to life. And the Day of Changes will still come—in spring, when the moon has fully turned. White Buffalo Woman will return—on her own terms, this time—and she'll bring the buffalo back with her."

I thought I saw a glimmer of hope in Stone Keeper's eyes. She could hear the certainty in my voice, and must have realized, by my own return from death, that I had powerful "medicine."

"Winter that come will be cold," she said. "Like before, no buffalo. Many people die. What good Iniskim live again, if only starve?"

"I'll see to it that you and your daughter do not starve. I'll be dead long before winter comes, but there is something I can do this very day." I nodded at the buffalo that was Superintendent Steele. "I'll write a note to my commanding officer, instructing that my pension be delivered into your hands, as if you were my wife. I'll say that Iniskim is my daughter, and must be provided for. I'll lie and say that you and I met more than a year ago, and that I fathered the girl during our brief meeting. When my superiors read that, they will be honour-bound to abide by my wishes. Will that satisfy you that your daughter will not starve? Will that persuade you to help me move the Manitou Stone?"

When Stone Keeper nodded, I heaved a sigh of relief. Then her mouth fell open, as if she had just realized something, and she laughed out loud.

"You!" she said suddenly. "You speak true. Iniskim your daughter. We make baby."

I threw my hands up in alarm. "No," I said. "You've misunderstood. It's just a story I would tell my commanding officer—a lie."

Stone Keeper shook her head vehemently. "No. You Iniskim's father. I dream you. Make baby in dream, Red Owl."

When I realized what she had just called me, I nearly swooned. I'd never told Stone Keeper that my guardian spirit was an owl, and now here she was, using the same name that Strikes Back had bestowed upon me in the Big Sands. Then I remembered how naggingly familiar Stone Keeper had looked when we had first met—just like the Indian woman I had once dreamed about.

I stared down at the lifeless body of Iniskim as the realization dawned upon me. I had visited Stone Keeper in my dreams—in astral form. Our two souls had known each other intimately on the astral plane, and here lay the result. I had unwittingly spoken the plain truth: Iniskim was my daughter.

I clutched my stomach as another wave of pain washed through it, and fought down the bout of nausea that followed. Staggering to my feet, I silently vowed to live for at least as long as it took to carry the Manitou Stone back to its original resting place.

The life of my daughter depended upon it.

◄—►

Chapter IX

I walked slowly past the buffalo-skull pound and climbed the opposite hill, my guts twisting in agony with each step. I could feel the cancerous tumour quite plainly now—it was a large, hot lump that visibly distended my stomach. It wasn't just the cancer that was slowing my steps, however—I was also dreading what I would see on top of the hill.

I reached the top at last, and saw the ruts that the wheels of the limber had left in the grass, and the barrel of the gun a short distance away. Buck lay dead on the ground in his makeshift harness, the bit still in his mouth. Chambers lay on his back near the barrel of the gun. One hand still clutched the brand he'd used to ignite the artillery piece. I didn't see any mark upon his body, and for an instant I thought he might yet be alive, but when I knelt on the grass beside him and lifted him in my arms, I could feel something shifting inside him. His chest had been crushed by the weight of the gun barrel, which had then rolled off him. Now that I looked closer, I could see the oily mark it had left on the front of his pyjamas.

I held him a moment more, wishing I had the time to give him a proper burial. Although we had gotten off on the wrong foot in our initial meeting, I had come to like Chambers. After years of keeping to myself, fearful that my fellow policemen might find out about my illness, I had finally found a kindred spirit—a man who had also joined Q Division under false pretences. I suspected that, had Chambers lived, we would have become fast friends.

The agony in my stomach reminded me that my time was too precious to spend grieving. Waving to Stone Keeper, who stood on the other hill beside the Manitou Stone, I turned to follow the limber's tracks.

It hadn't rolled far. It had come to a stop halfway down the hill, one wheel fetched up against a large rock. I was relieved to see that the perpetual motion device was still working. The round brass pendulum that drove the engine's pistons was still swinging back and forth, completing a smooth arc despite the angle at which the limber sat. Its *tick-tock* sounded regular and steady; I wondered why Chambers had used Buck to draw the limber up to the top of the hill.

I saw why in another instant. The perpetual motion device itself was intact, but the main gear that drove the wheels had broken in two. Fixing it would require the services of a machinist and a fully equipped blacksmith's shop, at the very least.

Or would it? I peered closer at the spot where the gun itself had been mounted. The barrel had been torn from its moorings by the force of the explosion that had killed Chambers, but three of the gears that had connected it to the perpetual motion device, allowing the barrel to be rotated and elevated, were still in place. One gear had been twisted back upon itself when the barrel ripped free, and another had several teeth stripped, but the third was intact, save for a very slight warp. It was slightly smaller than the gear that needed to be replaced, but I thought it might do the trick.

It had been many years since I had set foot in my father's watch making shop. When I was a boy, he had at first been proud of my fascination with the workings of the watches and clocks he repaired, and had invited me to the shop, allowing me to look on over his shoulder. After a time, however, he noticed a pattern. Whenever I stood next to him in the shop, the workings of the watch or clock he was working on either sped up, inexplicably, or slowed down—or stopped working altogether. Unwilling to believe that some supernatural force might be at work, he insisted that I must have been tampering with the workings when his back was turned. When I seemingly refused to stop these "childish pranks," I was given a good strapping and banished from the shop.

I never did lose my fascination for machinery, however—and now I had my chance to prove my father wrong. I could be as good as he was.

The limber still had its toolbox, and I set to work with the wrenches and screwdrivers inside it. It took all of the strength I had to undo the nut that held the gear I wanted to remove; I was drenched in sweat by the time I got it off. Gritting my teeth against the stomach pain that made me feel as weak as a girl, I at last worked the bent gear free and shoved the smaller one into its place. I had an anxious moment when the pendulum missed a beat—perpetual motion devices are nearly impossible for the lay mechanic to start up again, requiring a specialist's touch—but by working feverishly to tighten the bolt again, I got the gear in place before the pendulum lost its momentum entirely. When I was finished, I wiped a greasy hand across my forehead and heaved a sigh of relief.

I climbed up into the operator's seat, and cautiously pushed the drive lever forward. The gears engaged with a grating noise and a screech of metal, but the limber lurched forward. In another moment, it was climbing the hill, the pendulum clicking out a steady beat.

I drove the limber down past the pound and up to the place where the Manitou Stone stood. The limber moved only slowly and its mechanism squealed so loud that I wondered for a moment if the smaller gear was up to the strain, but at last it made it to the top of the hill. Positioning it just under the stone, I unfastened from the side of the limber a large iron bar—a tool intended to lever the limber out of mud holes. With Stone Keeper helping me, I levered the Manitou Stone away from its resting place. It teetered for a moment, then fell with a heavy crash onto the limber.

I helped Stone Keeper up onto the seat at the rear of the limber, then passed Iniskim's blanket-wrapped body up to her. I climbed up beside Stone Keeper, stumbling as my foot missed its mark. I was weaker than I thought, my mind clouded from pain. When we set out, I accidentally threw the lever into reverse, and the limber began to roll backward down the hill. Frantically, I shoved the lever in the opposite direction. Behind me, the perpetual motion device seemed almost to sense my urgency, and the pendulum picked up its pace. With a sudden lurch, the limber came to a stop, then began to roll forward again. We were on our way! Soon we'd be in the tunnel, and the going would be smoother.

Something was wrong, however. I could feel it in the vibrations beneath my seat. The perpetual motion device was ticking faster now, and when I craned my head around to look, I saw that the pendulum was swinging back and forth with a distinct wobble. Suddenly, a wrenching shudder ran through the limber. I heard a large *spanging* noise and a clatter as something metal broke—and then the limber was rolling down the hill. Try as I might to stop it, I could not. The perpetual motion device had disengaged, and the brake was not working. The limber hit a bump that sent the Manitou Stone several inches into the air, nearly sending it flying, but it crashed back down onto the limber again. The limber smashed through one of the piles of bones at the bottom of the hill, and then rolled, at last, to a stop. The pendulum was still ticking—but the gear I'd replaced was hopelessly broken.

I cursed, and then began to silently weep. The cursed bad luck that caused every mechanical thing I approached to go awry was my downfall. There was no way I would get the Manitou Stone to its original resting place now—no way for me to save the settlers and bring my daughter back to life. All of my efforts had been for naught.

Stone Keeper shifted on the seat beside me. The blanket in which Iniskim was wrapped had come partially undone in our wild ride down the hill. Stone Keeper tucked the blanket back around Iniskim, then sat in silence, staring straight ahead of her.

Suddenly, her head turned. I heard her gasp, and looked up to see what she had spotted. My mouth fell open as I saw a yellow-haired buffalo descending the hill where the Manitou Stone had stood. There was only one person it could be.

"Steele!" I shouted, waving my arms.

As the buffalo trotted toward us I wiped my tears away with the back of my sleeve, and climbed down painfully from the limber. Steele came to a halt a few paces in front of me, and shook his mighty head, as if in disbelief at the fate that had befallen him. He bellowed, then lashed his tail back and forth in frustration at his inability to speak.

"Superintendent," I said, gritting my teeth against the pain that wracked my stomach. "The Day of Changes came to pass—but there's a way to reverse it. We have to get the Manitou Stone back to its original resting place. We can do this by carrying the stone through the tunnels—but only if you help us."

Steele stood with round, dark eyes fixed upon me, listening with rapt attention. Despite his buffalo body, his mind was still that of a man's. He nodded his massive head. It was clear that he understood my every word.

Quickly, I explained what needed to be done. The traces that Chambers had used to harness Buck to the limber were damaged, but the rope in the limber's toolbox would do the trick. I fastened it to what remained of the traces, then made a makeshift harness. When I was done, I held the loop out for the Superintendent, who stepped neatly into it. I tightened it around his chest, apologizing for the indignity. He shook his head and snorted, as if to tell me that no apology was necessary.

I climbed back onto the limber, by now feeling so weak that I allowed Stone Keeper to help me into my place. Then Steele dug his hoofs into the earth, and with a massive pull hauled the limber into motion.

It didn't take us long to reach the tunnel. Stone Keeper's feather was still sticking in the earth where I'd left it, and a dark hole led into the earth. Either the Indians hadn't realized that the tunnel was open, or they had forgotten about it in their excitement at having successfully brought about the Day of Changes. Steele headed for the cave, hauling the limber along behind him. We paused only briefly, to retrieve Stone Keeper's feather. We might need it to open the tunnel at the other end.

As we entered the tunnel, clods of earth began to fall behind us, sealing us inside. The pendulum picked up its pace again, but this time it wasn't my proximity that was causing it to do so. It flashed back and forth in a *tick-tick-ticking* blur, propelled by the wash of etheric energy that flowed through the tunnel. I felt the hair at the back of my neck rise as a shiver passed through me, and saw that Stone Keeper was also trembling. I laid my hand on her arm—taking care to avoid her hand, with its severed little finger—and gave it a comforting squeeze. She turned her pockmarked face to me and smiled, then looked away.

The limber trundled on through the darkness. Unable to see, Steele had slowed to a walk.

"Follow the curve to the right, Superintendent," I called out to him. "Ignore any side tunnels; they're only tributaries. Keep to the main tunnel."

From the darkness ahead of the limber came Steele's answering snort.

The pendulum on the limber was still in motion, its rapid ticking as loud as a clock in an empty room. After a minute or two, its heavy brass ball took on an eerie blue glow. Sparks crackled across its surface and spun off in spirals like ball lightning. Soon the light they produced, although inconsistent, was enough to see by. Steele picked up his pace, pulling mightily upon the rope and moving at a brisk trot.

How long our journey through the tunnel took, I could not say. I couldn't trust my pocket watch, and the pain in my gut was distorting my sense of time, slowing it to a painful crawl. I spent much of the ride bent nearly double, arms wrapped tight around the throbbing ache that my stomach had become. I felt sweat trickle down my temples, and bloody bile rising in my throat. I told myself that the journey would be a swift one; I could almost feel the current of etheric energy pushing us along. I just had to bear it a little bit longer.

After what seemed like an eternity, Steele's questioning snort caused me to look up. Ahead, I could see a patch of light. It grew steadily brighter, and I could see that it was the mouth of a tunnel, filled with bright sunlight. Beyond the cave mouth, I could hear the rush of flowing water. The tunnel went no further; we must have reached its end point: the spot on the Battle River where the Manitou Stone had originally stood. I was glad that we didn't have to use Stone Keeper's feather to open a cave here; I was feeling so nauseous that I was no longer certain I could climb down from the limber. Only the fact that Stone Keeper was seated beside me caused me to choke down my bile; I was too much of a gentleman to be ill beside her.

The pendulum was acting strangely now, no longer ticking back and forth but instead spinning in a furious circle. It spiralled first in one direction, then another, as if the current of etheric energy that flowed over it were changing direction. Sparks crackled from it in a continuous stream, shifting back and forth through the colours of the rainbow as the pendulum whirled first counter-clockwise, then clockwise, then back again. A peculiar hot burning smell filled the air, stinging my nostrils.

Steele had stopped in the cave mouth, his nostrils quivering. Beyond this exit I saw a gentle, grassy slope leading down to a wide river. The tunnel gave egress onto the crest of a hill. The grass that covered it was being stirred by a stiff breeze that blew it back and forth. A series of tiny whirlwinds seemed to be chasing each other across these bending stalks, and converging on one particular spot: a barely discernible depression in the ground, no more than a dozen yards outside the cave mouth.

"There!" I gritted, clutching my stomach. I pointed at the overgrown depression in the soil. "That must be the Manitou Stone's original resting place."

Steele gave me a questioning look, and bellowed, but I was unable to understand the meaning of his guttural call. His massive shoulders shuddered, as if he were trying to shrug. Then he threw himself against the rope, straining the limber forward.

As we emerged from the cave, the wind caught us full force. My Stetson was torn from my head, and Stone Keeper's hair whipped about her face. The wind plucked at the blanket in which Iniskim was wrapped, producing the eerie illusion that the body inside it was moving. Stone Keeper flipped back the blanket and laid an ear to Iniskim's chest, listening for a heartbeat. When she looked up at me, she shook her head—but there was a gleam of fervent hope in her eye.

My knees began to tremble with cold, as if I were seated next to a block of ice. The cold seemed to be coming from the Manitou Stone. Bending forward, I touched a finger to it—and immediately jerked back my hand as my skin stuck to the stone. Already a thin film of lacy ice was beginning to form on the metal floor of the limber, all around the Manitou Stone. I just hoped that we'd still be able to move the stone—that the ice wouldn't cement it to the limber.

The limber rattled forward, with Steele pulling mightily in the traces. We had only a couple of yards to go. I sighed and closed my eyes, offering up my thanks to whatever spirits or angels were listening that it would all be over soon. In a moment more, I would tip the Manitou Stone from the cart, back onto its original resting place. Iniskim would live, and the settlers would be transformed back into men, women and children once more. Then I could die in peace.

That was when Stone Keeper screamed.

My eyes flashed open just in time to see a familiar figure leaping onto the limber. Like a recurring nightmare, Wandering Spirit had returned, and murder was in his eye. He hit me full force, knocking me backward from my seat. As we tumbled off the back of the limber I caught a glimpse of Stone Keeper clutching Iniskim's body to her breast, and screaming for all she was worth.

We landed in the swirling grass, and somehow I evaded Wandering Spirit's grip and lurched to my feet. I staggered around the side of the wagon, trying to get it between us. Wandering Spirit followed me with the slow, malevolent pace of a lynx stalking wounded prey. He wore only a breechcloth and moccasins now, and his entire body was painted yellow. A knife was sheathed at his hip. His long dark hair, once black as a raven's wing, now had its own war paint: at some point during the last few hours, it had started to turn grey. Wandering Spirit advanced slowly upon me, his eyes filled with malice.

Steele had stopped and was watching us with wide dark eyes. He snorted softly to attract my attention, and I saw that one hind leg was cocked under his belly, ready to deliver a violent kick as soon as Wandering Spirit came into range.

Wandering Spirit was too cunning to fall for that trick, however. Raising his hand above his head, he curled his fingers into claws. Lashing his hand forward, he screamed something in Cree. I felt a flash of hot pain across my lower leg, and collapsed to the ground. The magical attack had torn right through the leather of my boot to reach my flesh; I felt hot blood running down my leg. Within seconds the agony of my slashed leg was as great as the twisting knot in my gut.

Steele was throwing himself back and forth now, trying desperately to break out of his harness and come to my aid. Stone Keeper had jumped down from the limber and stood with Iniskim in the crook of one arm, a wrench in her other hand. She threw the wrench as hard as she could at Wandering Spirit, but the warrior dodged it easily.

Wandering Spirit lashed out a second time, and a line of pain tore its way across my shoulder. He was playing with me, as a cat plays with a mouse.

Steele gave up trying to shed his harness and threw himself forward, hauling the limber after him with a mighty bellow. I saw what he intended to do—circle around and run Wandering Spirit down—but I also saw that he would never be able to get himself turned about in time.

Stone Keeper was still standing in the spot where she'd jumped down from the limber. I waved at her to run.

"Stone Keeper!" I croaked. "Get away!"

She ran in the direction opposite to the one I indicated. Instead of carrying Iniskim to safety, she stopped and laid her upon the ground.

Wandering Spirit's next slash cut painfully across my scalp—just deep enough to sting, and to send a wash of blood down into my eye. Then he drew his knife from the sheath at his hip, and stalked toward me.

The limber rumbled and rattled as Steele turned it around for his final charge. The entire boulder was covered in frost now. The pendulum had stopped emitting sparks, and was stuck fast to the Manitou Stone; a film of ice was creeping up the pendulum's shaft. As I saw this, I suddenly knew what I must do. I staggered toward the limber, shouting at Steele to slow his pace.

He did, and I threw myself onto the limber, using my good arm and leg to crawl up next to the Manitou Stone. Wandering Spirit was after me in a trice. I felt a hand grip my hair and saw the flash of his knife as he raised it—and then the knife jerked violently to one side. It slammed up against the Manitou Stone with a ringing peal, like a needle drawn to a gigantic magnet. In the instant of confusion that followed, as Wandering Spirit tried to tug it free, I arched my body and slammed him into the stone. His bare back stuck to the ice-cold rock, trapping him like an insect on flypaper—but then, with a blood-curdling howl, he tore himself free. Strips of torn skin hung down his back, looking for all the world like the bloody aftermath of the warriors' thirst dance.

I lay on my back, trembling, too weak to move. Flexing his shoulders against the pain of his torn back, Wandering Spirit once again curled his fingers into claws. Steele bellowed a warning and jostled the limber, but I was too weak to move. I was done for.

In that instant, I saw a flash of something moving, just behind Wandering Spirit's head. I heard a dull thud, combined with a crunch, and suddenly Wandering Spirit's face drained of all expression. Slack-boned, he crumpled into a heap next to me, then rolled off the limber, dead.

That was when I saw Stone Keeper, standing on the limber with a wrench in her hand. Slowly, she lowered it, then let it fall

from numbed fingers. Even as I opened my lips to thank Stone
Keeper, she leaped from the limber and ran away.

I sat up as best I could, blinking away the blood that still
flowed from my scalp wound. Steele, still hitched to the limber,
regarded me with a nervous eye.

"I'm still fit for duty, sir," I croaked. "Let's put this stone
back where it belongs."

Steele snorted his approval, then heaved the limber forward.
When we were even with the depression in the earth, I hauled
myself painfully to my feet. There was no way I could lever the
Manitou Stone off the limber now—I was too weak—but that
didn't mean that Steele couldn't do it.

It was the matter of only a few minutes to refasten his
makeshift harness around the Manitou Stone. That done, I
gave Steele the nod. With a mighty heave, he pulled the
Manitou Stone down off the limber. It landed in its spot with a
thump that seemed to shake the entire Earth, and then all was
still.

The very air seemed to hold its breath for a moment. Then,
just as it had done before, a cold wind began to blow. This
time, however, it started far out on the prairie and swept
toward us, spiralling ever closer. As it at last washed over the
spot where we stood, Steele gave a loud grunt and transformed
back into a man again. The magical wind swept past him,
leaving him naked on all fours and shivering as it howled its
way toward the Manitou Stone. The heavy boulder rose into
the air and spun one full revolution counter-clockwise—then
fell back onto the ground and was still.

As I collapsed on the ground, I heard an infant's cry. In
another moment, Stone Keeper knelt beside me with Iniskim in
her arms. The toddler, although small, looked healthy and
well; she sat upright in her mother's arms and looked about
her curiously. Her skin was the natural copper colour of the
Indian, and her hair had turned a lustrous black. There was
none of the knowing expression I'd seen in her eyes earlier—
this time, White Buffalo Woman was no longer inside Iniskim
when she was restored to life. Iniskim looked down at me; a
faint frown pursed her pink lips, as if she wondered who I was.

Stone Keeper touched a hand to my shoulder, her eyes
silently expressing her gratitude. I smiled up at her, and tried
to reach out for her, but my arm fell back to my side as a wave
of pain wrenched my stomach.

Steele knelt on the other side of me and placed a hand on
my uninjured shoulder. He seemed oblivious to his nakedness,
and the fact that his muscular body was covered in dust and
dirt.

"That was a fine piece of work, Corporal," he said, pride and admiration filling his voice in equal measure. "I'll see that you receive a promotion for this."

I glanced up at Stone Keeper and Iniskim, then back at Steele. It was difficult to move my head. My limbs were starting to feel stiff and heavy, and my lips were barely able to form words.

"Promise me... Sir," I whispered. "Promise you'll see... my pension goes to... Emily. She...."

"I'll see that it's done, Corporal—but a pension won't be necessary," Steele said in a falsely hearty tone. "I've no intention of letting you die."

I smiled wanly up at him, knowing that he was lying to comfort me. I'd used up the last of my strength harnessing Steele to the Manitou Stone. I didn't even have it in me to sing the song that Strikes Back had taught me.

"We did it, didn't we Sir?" I whispered. "We stopped... Day of Changes. The Indians can't ever–"

"That's enough, Grayburn," Steele said. "You're badly wounded, and need to save your strength. We're miles from the nearest detachment, and even if there are settlers nearby, they're likely to be quite unnerved by their recent transformations. We'll have to rely upon our own resources to...."

His voice trailed off and he looked quickly over his shoulder, as if something had startled him, then shrugged and turned away. I glanced fearfully in the direction Steele had just looked, expecting to see Wandering Spirit risen from the dead.

It wasn't Wandering Spirit, but Big Bear. The Cree chief stood not three paces away from us, arms folded over his chest. The Hudson's Bay blanket he wore hugged stooped shoulders, and he was staring at the ground. When he looked up at us, I expected to see anger in his eyes, but instead his wrinkled face was lined with sorrow.

Big Bear's lips began to move, and I realized that he was speaking. I could not hear his words, however, and after a moment I realized that I could see right through him. I had no idea whether Big Bear had come to me as a ghost—or whether he had deliberately projected his astral body to this spot in an effort to communicate with me. I only know that I was filled with a burning desire to know what his message was.

Steele apparently did not see the apparition, even though he had felt its presence. He rose to his feet and began searching the limber, obviously intent upon seeing what he could scavenge from it. Stone Keeper was likewise oblivious to Big Bear's presence— although Iniskim pointed a pink finger in the chief's direction.

Staring at Big Bear, I mentally reached out one more time for my guardian spirit. In an instant, I felt something land lightly on my shoulder. A soft voice hooted in my ear, and then began to translate what Big Bear was saying.

I do not understand, the chief said. *When I dreamed of you, Red Owl, I dreamed that you would help my people. That is why I protected you, even though it went against the wishes of the other chiefs. When you brought Iniskim to the Manitou Stone, I thought that I had dreamed true—that the Creator had answered my prayers. You delivered to us the one thing we needed to replenish the prairie with buffalo: White Buffalo Woman.*

Now I see that I was a fool to have protected you. I should have listened to my war chief's words, and let Wandering Spirit kill you long ago. Now my people will go hungry. The winter that comes will be an unnaturally cold one—I have seen it. Many will die, in both the Cree and the Blackfoot camps, and just like before, the food the white man agreed in his treaties to provide us with will not be given. Your man Government is a liar. He has never once given what was promised.

I turned my head to look at Iniskim—my daughter. She might be provided for by my pension, but if the coming winter was as cold as Big Bear predicted, many other children would die—and many mothers like Stone Keeper would grieve. What Big Bear was saying was true. For several years now, those of us who knew the conditions of the prairie first-hand had urged Commissioner Dewdney to increase the Indians' rations—yet these rations had been cut, instead. The anger that rose in me as I thought about this unnecessary hardship gave me the strength to speak.

"The government will have to live up to its treaties now," I whispered back. "You've just demonstrated your might, by changing everyone in the North-West Territories into buffalo."

They have become human beings once more, Big Bear reminded me. *They cannot be changed into buffalo again.*

"That's true—but with Chambers dead, I'm the only white man who knows it."

Big Bear looked startled for a moment, then narrowed his eyes and stared at me thoughtfully. He glanced over his shoulder at Steele, then nodded and moved closer. Even though his voice sounded only in my mind and could not be heard by Steele or Stone Keeper, Big Bear dropped it to a whisper.

You have powerful medicine. You learned the secrets of the Manitou Stone. Your leaders will believe whatever you tell them about it. The words you speak to Government will be believed.

I coughed, and spat as bloody bile rose in my throat. "I won't live long enough to tell the government anything," I said. "I'm dying."

Would you like to live?

I looked up at him warily.

Big Bear touched a hand to the bear's paw that hung against his chest. *You do not need to die. My medicine could help you.*

"Why would you want to help me?" I asked. "I reversed the Day of Changes and thwarted all of your plans." Even as I protested, however, a spark of hope flickered to life inside me.

The apparition leaned closer. *For many winters now, I have been searching for a man who would carry my words to Government. I see now that I dreamed true when I saw that you would be a friend to our people. I will heal you, if you promise to tell one great lie. Tell Government that we could use our magic at any time to change your people back into buffalo again. If you will do that—if you will speak for us—I will use my medicine to help you to live.*

I could feel my heart pounding with excitement at his promise. I would live! Yet it would mean going against my sworn duty and telling my superiors a lie. Or would it? Perhaps I could simply neglect to mention that the settlers were already inoculated— and let my superiors and the politicians draw their own conclusions.

I glanced at Iniskim, cradled in her mother's arms. She was safe enough—but if Big Bear's premonition about the severity of the coming winter were true, hundreds of other children and adults would die. I didn't want the weight of their destruction upon my soul.

I noticed that Big Bear was also looking at Iniskim. His face was creased with lines of sorrow. He tried to touch her, but his ghostly hand passed through her. Iniskim shivered in Stone Keeper's arms, but, to her credit, did not cry. Instead, she stared fixedly at Big Bear with round dark eyes.

I never meant for the girl to die.

I could see by the sadness in the chief's eye that he meant it. "I believe you," I said.

My own children....

I spoke before he could finish: "I'll do it. I'll keep your secret."

Big Bear nodded, then grunted his satisfaction. He touched his bear's paw amulet and laid his other hand to my chest— gently at first, but then he pressed down. As its weight bore down, forcing the air out of my lungs, the words of the song Strikes Back had taught me rushed from my lips.

In some distant corner of my mind I heard Stone Keeper's gasp and Steele's surprised oath. The words came stronger now; I sang them in a steady stream, without needing to stop to take a breath. My vision blurred and sparkles of colour danced behind my eyes, but still I sang. In a moment more, I was sitting up, my entire body vibrating with my song. My flesh seemed thin and translucent to me now, and when I tore open my jacket and looked down, I saw the angry red-and-brown lump that was my cancerous tumour, just beneath my skin.

When I reached the final note of my song, I hooked the fingers of my right hand into the shape of talons and plunged them into my stomach. My insides were wet and hot, and as my fingers slid in past my intestines, a large lump slithered away from them, not wanting to be touched. I used my owl's claws to hook it, and with a mighty tug wrenched it out of my stomach.

I held it up, and with a shock saw that it was a knot of bloody brown feathers. The ball of gore hung wet and dripping in my hand. I have a vague memory of holding it up to show Steele as he ran toward me.

Stone Keeper backed away from me in horror, then let out a shrill scream. After a moment more, blackness claimed me.

∗ — ∗

I didn't see Big Bear again until nearly one month later. I was part of a treaty commission that had been hastily assembled in the wake of the Day of Changes, and Big Bear was the head of a council of dozens of chiefs who had gathered to redraft Treaties Four, Six and Seven—the treaties that covered the area enclosed by the ley line.

This time, the meeting was held at a time and place of the Indians' choosing. The site chosen was a hill near Duck Lake—a spot that Beardy had seen in a prophetic dream. Back in 1876, when the Cree agreed to sign Treaty Six, Beardy had tried to get the commissioners to hold the meeting in this place. They had thought him an ignorant savage, and had ignored his "superstitious" notion.

They weren't ignoring him now.

Tepees were spread out around the hill in all directions, rising up in a colourful display from the snowy ground. Cree, Assiniboine, Salteaux, Blackfoot, Blood, and Peigan had all assembled here in this one place, under the single greatest peace treaty ever forged. Off to one side was a cluster of police and commission tents; beside them were the sausage-shaped bulks of the air bicycles that had conveyed us to this spot. A picquet of police surrounded these conveyances, keeping curious Indians at bay.

The chiefs waited for us at the top of the hill in an immense structure that resembled the lodges that the Indians build for the thirst dance. A circular roof thatched with evergreen branches had been erected around a massive centre pole, and the whole structure smelled of fresh sap. Around its perimeter danced dozens of Indian braves, beating drums and chanting.

Daubed in gaudy war paint, they were bedecked with feathers and fringed buckskin. Their dance seemed to be summoning up a magical energy that pulsed in time with their stamping feet; it crackled in a faint nimbus around each dancer. As we drew nearer, I could feel the hair rise on the back of my neck, and a shiver passed through me. The Indians were demonstrating their magical might, reminding us of the powers they had at their command.

Seated inside the structure, row upon row, were the chiefs of the many tribes, all decked out in their finest clothes. As we entered, my eye was caught by Crowfoot, who wore two brightly polished treaty medals pinned to the front of his dark blue shirt. He was seated in a place of prominence, as were the other chiefs I had met inside the shaking tepee.

The members of the treaty commission walked one by one to the places where they would be seated. The Indians had insisted on talking to our "great chief, the man called Government," and so no less a personage than Sir John A. Macdonald led our entourage. It was the first time I had seen in person the man who had been Prime Minister of our country for so many years— the politician who had founded the North-West Mounted Police. Macdonald had thick curly hair that had long since retreated from his forehead, and an oversized nose whose veins hinted at long use of the whisky I could smell on his breath. He seemed an intelligent fellow, though, and had a rich, gravelly voice that would serve a politician well. If he had any hard feelings for the Indians, he hid them well under a mask of joviality.

Lieutenant Governor Edgar Dewdney followed close behind the Prime Minister. Dewdney was a large man with a white moustache and mutton-chop sideburns that hung like jowls from either cheek. He was dressed for the occasion in a suit and bowler hat, but had a scowl on his face like that of a boy forced to attend a formal occasion against his will.

Dewdney also served as Indian Commissioner for the Territories, and had been responsible for overseeing the Indians' transition to farming. He'd provided them with a fraction of the equipment needed to do the job, and instructors who didn't speak the Indians' languages and who had no knowledge of dry farming. Naturally enough, the crops failed. Now Dewdney was reaping the bitter harvest he had sown.

Behind him was Assistant Indian Commissioner Hayter Reed, a man with sharp eyes, a pointed moustache, and thin hair parted in the middle and combed flat behind a high, balding forehead. He walked with his hands folded against his chest, an unlit cigar clenched in his teeth. Every Indian he passed gave him a hard look. Reed was the man who had cut their rations at the time they were starving. The Indians called him "Iron Heart," and said he had the blood of their children and old people on his hands.

Flanking these officials were a dozen men from Q Division, turned out in full dress uniform and commanded by Superintendent Steele. A host of lesser dignitaries were also in attendance, as well as a handful of journalists. Only one photographer had come to record the scene for posterity—I suspected this moment was something the Canadian public would rather not be reminded of, in years to come.

No Union Jack flew above the proceedings, this time, and no military band played. Instead, when all were settled, the Indians unwrapped a sacred pipe, and passed it around the circle while drums pounded. The Prime Minister puffed it gravely, then passed it on to the Lieutenant Governor. He passed it to Hayter Reed—who looked as though he'd rather be smoking the cigar he'd shoved in his breast pocket—and then the pipe passed on to Steele. The Superintendent took a puff, then passed the pipe to me.

I held up the pipe to the four directions, as was the Indian custom, then took a draw. As I exhaled, Big Bear's eyes met mine. A smile creased his wrinkled face, and then he nodded. I had kept my promise, not telling anyone—not even Steele—that the white settlers were immune to further transformations. Yet even if I had told the truth, it would have made little difference. Those who had been transformed on the Day of Changes had eventually been returned to human form, but in the chaos that resulted in those first few moments there had been dozens of deaths and hundreds of injuries. Lanterns crashed over and untended cooking stoves had sparked fires, causing entire towns to burn to the ground. Trains and riverboats that were suddenly crewed by buffalo, rather than by men, had crashed or run aground. Unable to swim in their new forms, dozens had drowned when they had leaped overboard.

The transformations wrought by the Day of Changes had lasted no more than five hours, but the day's effects were still being felt. In its wake, a panic had gripped the North-West Territories, and there had been a mass exodus for points east and west. Few whites wanted to settle here any more.

When the preliminaries were over, the chiefs got down to business. Piapot was among the first to speak. He pointed an accusing finger at Macdonald, and delivered a speech in Cree that started thus: "When we took our reservations, you made promises as long as my arm, but the next year the promises were shorter, and got shorter every year until now they are about the length of my finger—and you keep only half of that."

When he was finished, it was Poundmaker's turn. His speech was long and flowery, and as he concluded, he hinted at the Day of Changes that was yet to come. "We have returned to the god that we know. The buffalo will come back, and the Indian will return to the life that the creator intended him to live."

I saw Dewdney shudder at the mention of buffalo. I didn't think that he had been in the North-West Territories on the Day of Changes—but he knew full well that he was within the area the magic had affected, even now.

Big Bear did much of the talking after that, but there were several long speeches from other chiefs, as well. They wanted the terms of the original treaties honoured—especially those dealing with the provision of cattle and flour, to stave off winter famine. They wanted their traditional hunting lands kept clear of settlers. Instead of being confined to reserves, they wanted free range over all of the land except that which had already been settled by whites: a narrow strip along the North Saskatchewan River, and along the CPR railway line. The North-West Mounted Police detachments and trading posts that had already been erected in their lands could remain, but all new settlement had to be approved by the Indians.

All of this the treaty commission agreed to. They had little choice—hanging over their heads was the possibility that every man, woman and child in the North-West Territories would be the victim of Indian magic of the most diabolical description. If Sir John A. Macdonald was ever to live up to his promise of joining our fledgling nation with a railway that stretched from coast to coast, he had to accept these terms. He'd promised in 1871 that the CPR would reach British Columbia within ten years, and already the railway was three years overdue. If he didn't want to lose his newest province, he had to keep the North-West Territories open. As long as a strip of land was available for the railway, he would agree to almost any terms.

Unlike the original treaties, upon which the chiefs had made their X marks, this treaty was not written down. All the Indians asked for was Macdonald's solemn promise that its conditions would be upheld. The Indians didn't need paper to hold the white men to their vows—not when they had the threat of magic.

I had thought that the treaty was concluded at that point, but Big Bear had one last demand. He drew our attention to the fact that, when the Hudson's Bay Company had sold the North-West Territories over to Canada in 1869, they had paid the Dominion a sum of 300,000 pounds sterling. This money, he said, should have gone to the Indians, since it was their land. Unless it was paid posthaste, the Indians would have no recourse but to unleash their magic a second time.

As the translator repeated these words, Macdonald's hands began to tremble. I stared at the Prime Minister wondering what he would say. The fee was an enormous one, a far cry from the five dollars per person—and twenty-five dollars per chief—the Indians had been promised under the original treaties. To my amazement, however, the Prime Minister nodded.

"It's a great deal for our government to bear, all in one go," Macdonald told the Indians. "We'll agree to it—but only if we can make it in installments. Will equal payments over the next ten years suit you?"

The translator conveyed the Prime Minister's words, and after only the briefest of murmurs from the chiefs behind him, Big Bear answered. Knowing how the Indians love to debate, I realized they must have anticipated an offer like this, and already decided upon what they would or would not accept.

"Four years," Big Bear said. "No more. My *pawakan* has said it must be so."

I coughed gently, and caught the Prime Minister's eye. "Excuse me, sir, but I think you'll find that Big Bear won't budge on that point. Four is a sacred number to these people, and if his guardian spirit has told him that this is the way it must be, he'll insist on those terms."

Macdonald's eyes narrowed as he stared at Big Bear, and then he sighed. "At least the wee rascal isn't charging interest," he said grimly.

He turned back to the chiefs. "Very well. The government agrees."

The proceedings went on much longer, well into the night. They concluded with Poundmaker, an eloquent orator, repeating the words that the Lieutenant Governor had used himself, a decade ago: "So you have promised, and so it shall be. For as long as the sun shines and the rivers flow."

By the time the negotiations concluded, the moon was up, painting the snow-covered prairie with a ghostly white light. It was nearly full once more—a celestial reminder of the Day of Changes, and the strength of the Indians' magic.

I was stiff from sitting on the cold ground. I rose from the buffalo robe I had been seated upon and repaired to my lodging for the night: a standard white canvas tent of police issue. I entered it and lit the lantern that sat on the rough wooden table beside my bed. I hung my helmet on the centre post and sat on my palliasse to pull off my boots. Outside the tent, the sound of drums and Indian voices raised in celebratory song filled the night. Already the Indians had slaughtered several of the cattle from the herd the treaty commissioners had brought as a sign of good faith. There would be full bellies and much joviality tonight.

The children conceived on this night—and on all the nights hereafter—would never have to go hungry again.

My thoughts turned to Stone Keeper. I had traveled to the treaty negotiations alone; she and our daughter Iniskim were waiting for me back in Medicine Hat. Stone Keeper still hadn't decided whether or not to accept my proposal of marriage, but I had high hopes.

I stripped off my jacket and riding breeches and folded them carefully. The brightly polished buttons on the front of my jacket gleamed gold in the lantern light, as did the sergeant's stripes on my sleeves. Steele had promoted me—even after my confession that I had been serving under an assumed name. He'd merely said that one name was as good as another, and that it was the man that counted.

As I stood in my long underwear and stocking feet, staring at the new stripes on my red serge jacket, I thought of the uniform they'd buried Chambers in. He'd been promoted too—albeit posthumously. They'd buried Chambers in red serge, in full dress uniform. My last act of kindness to him was seeing to it that the uniform was properly tailored and turned out. I'd burnished the buttons myself, and ensured that his helmet was pipeclayed white and his boots were gleaming.

I sat back upon my palliasse, settling myself comfortably upon its straw stuffing, and pulled the blanket up over my knees. I was sleeping comfortably now—the claw wounds that Wandering Spirit had inflicted upon me had healed, as had the knife wound in my palm. My dreams, although sometimes troubled, seemed to contain no more prophetic messages. Strikes Back had spoken the truth: when I'd healed my cancer, my powers of precognition had disappeared.

I pulled open my long johns, and stared at my stomach—something I'd done more than once in the weeks since the Day of Changes. Despite the fact that Steele and Stone Keeper both witnessed me pulling out the bloody bundle of feathers from my abdomen, there was not a mark to be seen on my stomach. It was as if it had never happened. Yet my cancer was completely healed—the police surgeon who had treated my wounds at Medicine Hat had felt no tumour, and the pains had troubled me no more.

Reaching into my kit box, I pulled out my pipe and filled it with a pinch of Old Chum. I puffed on it gently, filling my tent with aromatic clouds of smoke. As I placed my tobacco pouch back inside my kit box, my eye fell on a small square bundle, wrapped in a black silk handkerchief: Chambers's cards. So strong had been my compulsion to possess them that I'd stolen the cards from his personal effects when they were being wrapped up for delivery back to his brother in England. Filled with guilt at my petty theft, I hadn't even looked at them these past few weeks, but now I slowly unwrapped the handkerchief that held them.

The cards still looked the same as when Chambers had used them to test my psychic abilities, that day on the *North West*. A host of priests, fakirs and shamans stared up at me from the face cards, their eyes imploring me to test my powers once more. I shuffled the deck and held the cards in a neat stack, then turned them over one by one, guessing what each might be. No matter how hard I tried, however, I couldn't guess a single one. My powers had deserted me.

Uttering an oath, I cast the cards to the floor. They fell in a scatter around my stocking feet, mostly face down. One of the face cards, however, landed face-up. The character printed on it—a magician in an elegant black suit and top hat, holding what looked like a shell in his hand—caught my eye. I picked it up.

When I gave the card a closer scrutiny, my hand began to shake. I saw something I'd never noticed before. The fellow depicted on the card was the spitting image of Chambers, right down to his dark curling hair, moustache, and the beard worn below the chin, with cheeks shaved. The object in his hand wasn't a shell—it was a spiral-shaped buffalo stone.

I swore out loud and nearly dropped the card when the character on it started to speak. I heard a *tisk-tisk* noise, and then Chambers waved a finger at me.

Hello, Grayburn, he said. *I've been wanting to talk to you for some time, but it's damnably hard to catch your ear. You must have been a busy man, this past month.*

"How–?" I gasped. "Where–?"

I turned the card over and looked at it, like a child searching for a person behind a mirror. The back was the same solid black it had always been. I turned the card face-upright again. Chambers was still staring at me.

I'm in the astral plane, of course. And do you know, it's quite a fascinating place. It seems to conform to my notions of what Heaven might be like, although it changes whenever someone new ventures along. I've developed a theory to explain that—I call it Belief Convergence. When two astral beings with different notions of what the afterlife should look like meet, the scenery shifts through a riot of surrealistic imagery. It's very much like the stuff of dreams, and so I've concluded that–

"You're dead," I said in a hoarse whisper.

Of course I am, Chambers said with an exasperated sigh.

"But how can I talk to you? When I used the song to cure my cancer, my psychic powers vanished. I shouldn't have been able to contact you at all."

Chambers put his hands on his hips and frowned at me. The gesture reminded me of a schoolmaster I'd once had. *Strikes Back lied.*

It took a moment for his utterance to penetrate my brain. When it did, my eyes widened. "You mean that I can still have precognitive dreams and contact the dead?" I asked wonderingly.

Chambers laughed. *You're doing it at this moment, are you not?*

I could only nod.

You have a great gift, Grayburn. You're a true sensitive, in every aspect of the word. You've a talent for communicating with the dead. It's no wonder the owl spirit chose you as its own—the messenger of death could find no more appropriate person to serve as a bridge between the dead and the living. That was why the owl came to you at the moment of your death, in the operating theatre, and sent you back to the land of the living.

Chambers looked around, as if trying to see beyond the edges of the card. *Have you a pen and ink—and paper?*

"I think so," I replied.

Good. Then take them in hand, and get ready to write.

He waited while I reached for pen and ink. When I was ready, he gave me a twinkling grin. *I'll wager this will be the most renowned pamphlet the Society for Psychical Research has ever seen. Just make sure you get the title right—"Observations From the Other Side"—and spell my name correctly.*

I had to smile. "Have no fear, Albert. I will."

Chambers dictated the first lines of text to me, and I began to write.

We spent no more than an hour or two on the text that first evening, but in the weeks that followed I used the card to speak to Chambers on several more occasions and, eventually, the manuscript was completed.

By that time, I was back in Medicine Hat, waiting for Steele to assign my next case. Q Division was out in the open now—since the Day of Changes, there was no profit in concealing our existence. Indeed, the reverse was true. Knowing that a special division of policemen had been formed, each man of which was handpicked for his psychic powers or magical abilities, was a comfort to the settlers of the North-West.

Much later, I set pen to paper a second time. This time, the words were not Chambers's, but my own.

I awoke with a start, my heart pounding, certain that I'd heard someone shout my name, I wrote. *Yet all was silent in the darkened barracks....*

☀—☀

Afterword

Marmaduke Graburn was the first North-West Mounted Police constable killed in the line of duty. He was shot in the back on November 17, 1879, near the NWMP horse camp at Fort Walsh after he rode back up a trail to retrieve an axe. While an Indian named Star Child was arrested for the murder, he was later acquitted. The identity of Graburn's killer remains unknown.

While most of the characters and some of the events in *The Apparition Trail* are drawn from history, the story as a whole is fictional. *The Apparition Trail* is alternative history: an attempt to answer the question of what might have happened had magic awakened in the world—enabling Native rituals to produce concrete effects and European attempts to create perpetual motion devices. With magic, the history of the Canadian west would have been greatly changed.

In 1884, the year in which *The Apparition Trail* is set, the Indians who ranged over the North-West Territories (the current provinces of Alberta and Saskatchewan) were in desperate straits. The buffalo on which they relied for food, shelter and clothing—herds that had numbered several million animals just a few short years before—were on the edge of extinction. The preceding few winters had been the coldest and most difficult in living memory, and all game animals were scarce. After consuming their horses and dogs, the Indians were reduced to eating gophers and grass in an attempt to survive. Several thousand people starved to death. Adding to this tragedy were the ravages of smallpox and other European diseases, which killed thousands more.

In 1876, the Cree signed Treaty Six, which (at the Indians' insistence) included the provision of food in times of famine. Rather than living up to this promise, the Canadian government issued the Indians rations that were inadequate (the per-person ration for Indians was only half that issued to a North-West Mounted Policeman). The government further stipulated that food would only be given to those Indians who worked in exchange for it—this at a time when some were too weak from hunger to hunt. Indian agents like Tom Quinn took a hard-line approach: the Cree nicknamed Quinn "the bully," and the "man who always says no."

Some bands made an attempt to switch to farming, but the equipment the government provided was inadequate, and many of the farming instructors who were sent to teach the Indians had no knowledge of Prairie farming requirements. Crops failed, and again the Indians went hungry.

Some Indians did fight back, staging acts of political protest. In 1880, Chief Beardy erected a toll-gate across the Carlton Trail. In 1883, Chief Piapot set up camp in the path of the Canadian Pacific Railway in an attempt to stop construction of Canada's first coast-to-coast railway line. It was Chief Big Bear, however, who worked the hardest to advance the Indian cause by way of his attempts to unite the scattered tribes of the North-West Territories and to present a unified voice to the Canadian government.

Sadly, Big Bear is recorded in the history books as a traitor and instigator of murder, rather than as the spokesman he tried to be. On April 2, 1885, warriors from his band, led by Wandering Spirit, shot and killed nine settlers at Frog Lake—including two priests. The shooting started when Quinn refused Wandering Spirit's order to join settlers that the Indians had taken hostage. After two warnings, Wandering Spirit shot him; Quinn had said no for the last time. The Indians looted the settlement, then fled, taking their hostages with them.

Wandering Spirit led the band to Fort Pitt, a NWMP fort commanded by Francis Dickens, son of the famous novelist. There, a gunfight with three NWMP scouts who blundered into the Indian camp left one Mountie dead, and another wounded. Dickens decided to abandon the indefensible fort; the Indians let the police retreat, but took more settlers hostage.

The Frog Lake murders and the forced surrender of Fort Pitt came at a time when the Metis (settlers who were half Indian, half French) were staging an uprising. Just a few days earlier, the Metis had traded shots with the North-West Mounted Police at Duck Lake, killing three Mounties. The actions of Big Bear's band were seen as part of a general uprising and the Canadian government responded proportionally.

As chief of his band, Big Bear, who had tried to stop the killing at Frog Lake, was held personally responsible for the murders there. A column of several hundred militia and NWMP pursued the band relentlessly for the next two months, attacking them twice. The "spring of blood" that Big Bear had seen in a prophetic dream several years earlier had come to pass.

Around the same time, Chief Poundmaker traveled north to Battleford to profess his loyalty to the Queen and the Canadian government. He found the town empty, the settlers having fled to the safety of the nearby NWMP fort in the belief that the Indians were coming to attack. Poundmaker's band looted the town, carrying away food and other supplies and burning a church and a judge's house.

Poundmaker's band was also pursued by a column of militia and NWMP, which attacked the Indians at their camp near Cutknife Creek. The Indians were outnumbered nearly two to one and were low on ammunition, but they held a strategically superior position on a hill overlooking a ravine. They also had advance warning of attack, through a man named Kohsakahtigant who was warned in a dream by a sacred *manitouassini*, Old Man Stone, that danger was approaching. After a tense battle which saw eight militia and NWMP killed and fourteen wounded—and six Indians killed and three wounded— the NWMP and militia were forced to retreat.

Big Bear and Poundmaker ultimately surrendered to the NWMP and received jail sentences. Both died shortly after their release from prison.

Wandering Spirit, and seven other Indians who had killed white settlers, were sentenced to death, and were hung en masse in Battleford in front of local Indians who were forced to watch this example of Canadian frontier justice. Some of the condemned men urged their people to capitulate to the settlers; others urged them to fight on and sang their death songs proudly.

It is reported that, in the days while Big Bear's band was fleeing with its hostages, Wandering Spirit's hair turned completely grey. Before his hanging, he unsuccessfully tried to take his own life by stabbing himself in the chest with a knife while being held captive in a prison cell.

While the majority of *The Apparition Trail* is fictional, one event is drawn from history: the story of the Manitou Stone. This large boulder, situated on a hill near the Battle River, was held sacred by the Indians. According to an ancient prophesy, if ever the stone were moved, war, disease, and famine would follow.

In 1868, Methodist Missionary John McDougall stole the Manitou Stone, removing it by wagon to his church at Victoria Mission. According to McDougall, this "raised the ire of their (Indian) conjurers." The stone was ultimately shipped to a Methodist church in eastern Canada.

McDougall and his family did not disappear, as they do in *The Apparition Trail*. McDougall lived until 1917, and during the Metis rebellion of 1885 served as a scout and translator for the Canadian militia.

The majority of the NWMP officers and men described in *The Apparition Trail* are drawn from history. Sam Steele was an exceptional officer who joined the NWMP at its inception in 1873, and he commanded "Steele's Scouts" during the Metis rebellion of 1885. He later went on to serve in the Klondike during the gold rush, and in the Boer War in South Africa.

The larger-than-life character of scout Jerry Potts is also drawn from life. It would be difficult to create a more fascinating character than this hard-bitten frontiersman: Potts really did wear the skin of a black cat as his personal protective charm, and he was as tough a fighter and skilled scout as they come.

Sergeant Brock Wilde is also a historic figure—although he met his death as a result of a bullet, rather than through Indian magic. He died in 1896 after being shot by Charcoal, an Indian accused of murder whom Wilde had been pursuing. According to NWMP lore, Wilde's body was guarded by one of his faithful hounds, which police were forced to shoot after it refused to back down from its vigil.

The American gambler Four Finger Pete is described in the memoirs of NWMP Inspector Francis Dickens, who discovered Four Finger Pete's body after the gambler had been shot by his Peigan wife. Dickens sympathized with the woman, whose name is not recorded; he had seen the results of the beatings that Four Finger Pete gave her. Dickens covered up the death, reporting to his superiors that Four Finger Pete had simply disappeared.

Arthur Chambers is entirely fictional, although the Society for Psychical Research is an actual organization, founded in 1882. The theories of magic and the ethereal plane have their root in the beliefs of Theosophy, a mystical philosophical system that arose in 1875.